P9-CDS-479

The
HAMILTON
Affair

ALSO BY ELIZABETH COBBS

American Umpire

Broken Promises, A Novel of the Civil War

Major Problems in American History: 1877 to the Present

All You Need is Love: The Peace Corps and the Spirit of the 1960s

The Rich Neighbor Policy: Rockefeller and Kaiser in Brazil

A NOVEL

ELIZABETH COBBS

Arcade Publishing · New York

10 9 8 7 6 5 4 3 2 1

Library of Congress Cataloging-in-Publication Data is available on file.

Cover design by Brian Peterson
Cover photo credit: iStock

Print ISBN: 978-1-62872-720-3
Ebook ISBN: 978-1-62872-723-4

Printed in the United States of America

PART ONE

Love and Revolution

1768–1781

CHAPTER ONE

January 1768

Christiansted, St. Croix

"The leader of runaway slaves shall be pinched three times with red-hot iron, and then hung . . . Each other runaway slave shall lose one leg."
Proclamation of the Royal Council, Danish West Indies, 1733

THE BOY FROWNED, PRESSED A FOLDED handkerchief to his nose, and scanned the crowd for the third time. The noxious tang of the Spanish slaver that had sailed into port at daybreak was overpowering. Soldiers stationed themselves every few paces to oversee the off-loading of Africans, but blacks still outnumbered whites ten to one. Women balancing baskets of green coconuts on their heads wound through the press of laborers going about their usual work alongside the sparkling sea. The dock was crowded.

Damn Ajax, Alexander thought. Where had he gone? It could take hours to find the servant, who was probably flirting with a girl when he ought to be rolling a barrel to the store at 34 Company Street.

Passersby may have thought Alexander Hamilton unnaturally serious for an eleven-year-old, but he had much on his mind and a leaky enterprise to keep afloat.

Colored stevedores loading barrels of sugar for North America appeared not to notice the repellent miasma that signaled a long voyage with a packed hold. Neither did the long chain gang of newly arrived Africans, greased for auction, who now stood naked and impassive next to the seawall. One towered above the rest: a tall man whose cheeks bore the ritual scars that marked manhood in another world. But it was the fresh bite of a switch across his temple that drew the eye. Blood had run under the rusty iron collar around his bare throat.

They would need to clean that up, Alexander thought, or jeopardize the sale price.

A man with one leg sat on a nearby barrel repairing a fishing net for his master. Crabs scuttled and clicked inside the wicker basket atop the merchant's table next to him. A towering brougham with embossed gold panels rolled into the busy square and an elegant elbow clad in yellow satin rested on its carved window frame. Young Mrs. Koenig must be headed to church. The crowd parted. Not ten yards away a stray goose flapped into the wake left by the magnificent carriage.

Alexander spotted the geese-girl, the one Ajax liked. Her small white flock clustered around her skirt while Ajax's chapped knuckles curled above hers on the herding pole. The girl's bright smile indicated she didn't notice the bird's truancy. He would get her in trouble, too.

"Ajax!" Alexander hissed. A gentleman did not raise his voice even to a servant, Mama said. He hurried across the gap and tapped the tall, good-looking boy on the shoulder. "Ajax!"

Ajax glanced down unsurprised and smiled. The boys had known each other since infancy. Both recalled when Ajax, one year older, could beat Alexander at every game except marbles. "Master Alexander. Monstrous sorry. Just coming." He looked back at the girl and slid his hand closer to hers on the shepherd's crook.

Of course, such a comely lass was hard to ignore. Alexander resisted looking directly at her, though he noticed the way the orange turban complemented her flawless dark skin. They had first spotted her in the marketplace last summer. She was pretty even then, but Ajax swore her breasts were bigger every week. At night in the dark the thought of such things had become an exquisite torment.

"Mama needs that flour today, not tomorrow," he said to Ajax. He met the slave girl's warm brown eyes for the barest instant—it was impossible not to, she was so fetching—then looked toward the bird waddling in the direction of the fort whose cannon-studded ramparts and dank prison cells protected Christiansted. "Get the goose," he told Ajax. "Then back to the store. The brig sails for Providence on the tide."

Alexander turned away to forestall backtalk. He could count on Ajax—once in motion—especially when they were in public. Mama told him he must learn to be a master and give orders, and it had gotten easier, but his old playmate still balked like a billy goat if no one else was watching.

The walk from the docks wasn't long even though Christiansted was the largest town on St. Croix—an emerald paradise that was part of a chain Columbus named the Virgin Islands in honor of a saint who led her entourage of eleven thousand maidens into an ambush on the road to Rome. There was a lesson in that, Alexander thought, when the Jewish woman who tutored him looked out to sea after telling the tale.

He walked slowly so as not to trip in his brother's old shoes, which tended to slip at the heel. A young squire exiting a coffeehouse nearly bumped into him and Alexander doffed his cap, but the silk-tailored gentleman shot him a disdainful look and kept walking. *He must know*, Alexander thought. Christiansted was a small town. A blush crept over his cheeks and he picked his way more guardedly along the busy lane.

Company Street ran nearly a mile uphill. The slave auction of the Guinea Trading house anchored the bottom of the slope while the heavy stone cathedral of St. John's weighted the top. Stores, homes, and bordellos jostled in between. Most had upper stories of wood cantilevered over lower ones made from cut stone to withstand the hurricanes that whipped the Caribbean every fall.

Alexander crossed the lane just before the church cemetery. The slaver's ammonia fumes reached him again and he pressed the linen to his nose as he stepped over a mud puddle and opened the last door on the street to a small shop selling dry goods and notions.

The items on the shelves were pulled to the edge to give the impression of abundant supplies. They couldn't afford much inventory and Mama insisted they put their best foot forward no matter what. Bottom rows displayed cheap luxuries to tempt ill-paid sailors—tobacco, playing cards, ribbon, and small bottles of rum. Top shelves held dearer commodities for officers, such as ivory dominoes, meerschaum pipes, mother-of-pearl buttons, and hats in the current style. An archaic astrolabe that a bibulous purser once traded for drink had sat there for years.

There were even a few battered leather-bound books from London, including one Alexander sometimes read to Ajax when Mama wasn't around. The scientific descriptions of coitus in Aristotle's *Secrets of Nature* fascinated both boys. They took particular interest in the philosopher's claim that *"He who hath a long and great Nose is an admirer of the Fair Sex and well accomplished for the Wars of Venus."*

They knew this fact already, but the part about nostrils was new to them and they giggled whenever a customer with a small nose came into the store. With his head for memorization Alexander would solemnly quote Aristotle after the customer had left—unless he couldn't help himself and broke up laughing: *"When the Nostrils are close and thin, they denote a Man to have but little Testicles, and to be very desirous of the Enjoyment of Women, but modest in his*

Conversation. But he whose Nostrils are great and wide, is usually well hung and lustful."

Ajax would point triumphantly to his wide nose and Alexander would feel a twinge of envy. The expensive book never sold but it was well-read.

Barrels of rice, flour, black-eyed peas, and brined beef lined the opposite wall, where casks stood on top of one other. If a barrel was particularly heavy they waited for Alexander's older brother, James, to return from the carpenter's workshop to help them lift it.

The store was empty. "Mama?" Alexander called.

A moment later he heard sharp heels clack on the wooden stairs that led down from their living quarters.

"*Mon cher*," Rachel Lavien said. She smiled as she swished through the rear door carrying a stack of scarves. Hardly anyone called her Rachel Hamilton anymore, as the townsfolk had when they lived on Nevis, but Alexander tried not to think about that since the world could not be changed. Long ago the court in St. Croix had forbidden his mother to remarry, nullifying his parents' union. The truth caught up with them when Mama moved the family back to Christiansted.

She placed the garments on the top shelf, then turned to him. "Did you find Ajax? Captain Andresen promised to be back before noon. He'll take all we can spare."

His mother wore her favorite red skirt with an ivory blouse that showed off her full bosom. Most women wore their dresses in the low-cut fashion yet few filled them as handsomely as Mama still did at thirty-eight. Alexander sometimes wished she wasn't quite so beautiful as there would be less trouble, but one might as well wish away the glare of the sun on the waves.

She looked at Alexander with eyes that matched her black hair and made her skin seem as fine as a porcelain figurine's. Some Huguenot women were swarthy, Alexander had observed, but his mother possessed the more refined French traits, with her high cheekbones and elegant carriage. She could carry on a whole conversation with her delicately arched eyebrows, lifting one to express amusement, two to let him know he hadn't caught a double entendre as adroitly as she expected. The second daughter of a prominent physician, Rachel Lavien was cultured and quick. No one said Alexander got his brains from his mother, but most surmised it.

From James Hamilton, the fourth son of a laird in faraway Scotland, Alexander inherited a delicate constitution, tawny hair, violet-blue eyes, skin that burned too easily, and an expired affiliation with minor aristocracy. Papa always meant well, or at least that was Alexander's memory of the feckless merchant whose ambitions never amounted to much but who sang Scottish ballads in a warm baritone while he carved toys and whistles for his two sons. He had abandoned the family a few years earlier, when Alexander was eight.

Voices were raised that night as on others—Mama shrill over the rumble of his father. Alexander scooted to the bottom of his cot and cupped his hands over his ears until all he heard was a hum like a conch shell. When he awoke in the morning and ran to find Ajax, he spotted his mother sitting by herself in the courtyard, drinking tea in stony silence.

He didn't blame his father, partly because James Hamilton wasn't around to shoulder it and partly because Papa hadn't filled a room with personality as Mama did without trying. Her will governed their lives like the moon did the tide. Once Papa was gone, Mama just didn't talk about him.

Alexander's older brother, James, good with a hammer and nails, was apprenticed at the carpenter's shop by day. Nights he spent what he earned at a local tavern—distant and moody since Mama and Papa's troubled parting. Not that the Hamiltons' disaster was unusual. The wreckage of broken homes was strewn across the Caribbean, where disease, debt, and plain bad fortune afflicted even the privileged.

Alexander tried his best to be a good son. Someone needed to watch over their mother.

"Don't worry, Mama," he said. "Ajax will be here in a minute. We can give Captain Andresen four barrels. The oldest is a bit weevily, but better than anything else he'll find in town."

Alexander had checked their supplies the night before since his mother didn't have much patience for inventory and one might as well ask his brother to dance the minuet on a barrelhead as keep a ledger. If Joseph Andresen took four casks of flour they would still have three for regular customers, whom they could placate by discounting rice if necessary to keep them from running to another store. Captain Andresen would pay double, so it was worth the risk of running out of flour. A cargo out of New York ought to arrive soon. Alexander bit his thumbnail, then remembered not to and stopped.

"Did you find Ajax skylarking?"

"No, Mama. He stopped to catch a goose. Mrs. Koenig's brougham almost turned it into mincemeat."

Rachel Lavien raised an eyebrow. She looked skeptical. "Ajax belongs to me. If I wanted him to help others, I would hire him out. *Tout de suite*."

"Yes, Mama, I know."

Indeed, Alexander knew that unless their store became busier Ajax must soon be sent out for wages. Rachel Lavien's five adult slaves already labored elsewhere. Alexander couldn't picture Ajax not working alongside him, but anything was better than allowing their finances to get too close to the bone. Then slaves must be sold and he might never see his friend again.

Mama wouldn't let that happen, though. She always figured out something. And he could help her more now that he was old enough to keep books.

"We're doing better. You'll see," he said.

Rachel reached out to tousle Alexander's fair curls and he smelled her lemon-verbena soap. "My young man. Always taking care of us." She took up a duster made from tail feathers and turned her back to tidy the shelves.

His mother could be infuriating—prideful, restless, headstrong. She had fled her first husband despite the threat of imprisonment and driven his father away. Or perhaps James Hamilton left because he was embarrassed by his sons' illegitimacy. Regardless, Mama held them together and Alexander loved her fiercely.

The door swung on its creaky hinges to admit a British sailor whose long, traditional braid was clubbed tightly in half with ribbon. The man left the door ajar as he came in to examine the wares. Alexander slipped behind him to shut out the awful odor of the street.

His mother stepped to the plank counter. "Good afternoon, sir. May I assist you?"

The man ducked his head as if dodging her words. He looked past her at a point on the wall behind the counter. "Need a scarf."

Rachel gestured to the new stack on the shelf. "You've come to the right place, sir. We have bonny ones just in from New Jersey. Made from the best ewe's wool. They'll keep out any breeze the Atlantic can blow at you."

The sailor turned to the scarves without speaking. He seemed stumped by Mama's ready flow of words, as many men were. If she weren't so voluble life might be easier. Or perhaps it was her loveliness that was the problem.

The seaman selected a dull green and walked to the window to hold the scarf to the light. He pulled the weave in one direction and then the other. He returned and placed the item on the counter. "How much?"

"A guinea, please."

His head jerked up. Now he looked at her directly. "A guinea? For a blinkin' scarf?"

She stared back. "They're from New Jersey," Mama said without a shimmer of her long eyelashes.

The man grimaced.

Alexander waited. He heard the thump of a barrel rolling up the boardwalk. It must be Ajax. The boy ought to know the geese-girl wasn't worth being hired out. Alexander shifted his weight onto his right foot to take pressure off the blister that his brother's shoe had raised on his heel.

The sailor reached into his blouse and lifted a drawstring pouch that hung from his neck. He poured a mixed collection of foreign coins onto the rough plank, counted them with his thick fingers, and pushed them over. Alexander spied a few shillings, a grimy rix-dollar, and three Spanish pieces of eight. No gold guinea. It was short of an English pound by at least four shillings. Even at a favorable exchange rate it wasn't enough to cover what they had paid for the scarf, much less make a decent profit. They needed sales—but good ones.

"There," the man said.

Rachel Lavien began picking up the coins. "That looks about right."

The man rested his heavy hand atop the green fabric on the counter.

Alexander held his breath. The amount would set them further back in their account with the Christiansted importer to whom they still owed money. The merchant was an ugly man, quick to make threats at tardy invoices.

The sailor's fingers closed around the scarf.

A shilling turned on its side and rolled. Alexander darted forward and caught it as it fell off the edge. "*Maman*," he whispered. "*Ce n'est pas assez*."

Rachel took the shilling from her son and continued picking up the money. She squinted at the last coin as if considering, then said, "Actually, this seems a trifle short."

The sailor grasped the scarf tightly in his ham-like fist and leaned closer. "That's a pound sterling and more."

His calloused hands were heavy and his hairy forearms immense. He seemed bigger than before.

Alexander felt a prick of alarm. Their store was the last one on the street, with only the deserted graveyard at their backs. But

Mama was calm. She had spine. "Alexander, would you please calculate this for me?"

"Keep the boy out! 'Tis enough."

His mother gave a rueful smile that showed off her prettiness. "My son has a better head for foreign currency than I."

"It's said you know the value of a coin," he growled. "*Fille de joie*."

Rachel Lavien's smile vanished and her skin blanched. She wasn't invulnerable after all. Some blows landed.

The air seemed to go out of the dim storefront and Alexander struggled to catch his breath. Motes of dust drifted in the light thrown down by the fan window over the door. Sometimes Alexander felt he could keep his family from disaster now that he was eleven, but other times he felt as puny and inconsequential as a speck in the breeze.

Daughter of joy. How could such an innocent phrase be so joyless?

The sailor chanced a sly grin. "Of course, I can pay a bit more, if you'll discuss it in the back."

Alexander's face grew hot. He looked toward the heavy broomstick behind the counter. The menacing crewman bulged with muscle and was a foot taller than Alexander but he no longer cared. No one dared speak to his mother like that.

Yet his feet seemed planted to the floor, as if a keg of sticky tar had spilled under his shoes, and he watched helplessly as the sailor leaned closer to Mama, who jerked away when he drew a cruel finger down her cheek. Her lips tightened and her eyes widened, and for once she was mute.

Alexander's heart hammered. He must do something, he must act, he must stop the man.

The door opened, and it wasn't Ajax after all.

Thomas Stevens hesitated at the threshold, taking in their stricken expressions. The elegant King Street merchant wore a sober frock coat of fine linen dyed gray. He and Rachel had known one another since childhood. Some said Master Stevens had been sweet on Mama when they were still young and she was a debutante—before her catastrophic marriage at sixteen to the infamous Johann Lavien. Now the gulf in respectability made him seem an ambassador from a foreign nation.

"Good morning, Mrs. Hamilton," he said. The polite salutation was a benediction, absolving their terrible dishonor.

Alexander found his limbs would move again and drew himself as tall as he could. He stepped behind the counter alongside his mother. "You'll need four shillings more. If you wish, you may return with the balance later this afternoon."

Rachel Lavien put her arm around Alexander and drew him to her. Alexander's heart ached. If Mr. Stevens hadn't chanced by, what would have happened?

The sailor stared hard, then dug out another silver piece. He slapped it on the counter. Without another word he snatched up the scarf and left.

Such an honorable greeting. *Mrs. Hamilton.*

Alexander longed with all his being that it were true. He wouldn't wake up frightened half the time.

CHAPTER TWO

June 1770

Saratoga, New York

"Nothing, I am sure, calls forth the faculties so much as the being obliged to struggle with the world."

Mary Wollstonecraft, *Thoughts on the Education of Daughters*, 1787

FROM WHERE ELIZABETH SCHUYLER LAY ON her back, gazing straight up, the sky was a shade of cobalt that reached deep into heaven and defined the color blue for all time. Life in Saratoga, perfect and complete, brimmed with infinite possibilities no matter what the troublesome Sons of Liberty said.

The pastures that stretched from the family's country manor down to the Hudson smelled of last week's scything. The grass appeared level when she first stretched out, heedless of her new white dress, but a stone now dug into her shoulder blade. Rocks hid like that, no matter how smooth a field looked when you first lay down. It was like marriage, if her sister Angelica was to be believed: you must lie in your lumpy bed once you had made it. Which made Eliza wonder why anyone bothered.

She inched sideways until the stone no longer pressed. A lone falcon drew lazy circles overhead. The bird was hunting, just like a

Mohawk in the river with his spear pointed down, waiting for the fish to rise. She had never seen an impatient Mohawk, except that once.

A petal hit her cheek. Eliza blinked.

"Wake up, sleepyhead," Angelica said.

"I am awake." Eliza propped herself on one elbow and brushed away the sticky petal that had fluttered onto her white bodice. A smear of yellow pollen bloomed on the clean linen. "Look at that. You know what Diana is going to say."

"You think she won't notice the grass stains on your back? Pray sit up. Tell me what to do."

Eliza eyed her sister's defrocked daisy. "Practice your violin. You missed your cue last night."

Angelica tugged at another petal. She sat on a blanket she had spread to protect her taffeta gown. "He loves me." She plucked the last one and frowned. "He loves me not."

Eliza pushed up her sleeves and lay back down. "I'm glad that's settled."

She rolled onto her stomach and folded her arms under her face to take the pressure off her new breasts, which made the hard ground more uncomfortable than before. The sun felt good on her bare neck. There were no more flawless skies than the God-given beauties over Saratoga.

"You're impervious to love," Angelica said, and picked up a volume of poetry stamped with the family crest. Their father adored books. But after Parliament set new taxes, he and Mama became so upset they refused to buy anything at all from London. Not even a pamphlet. The Schuyler family's large library was stuck around the year 1765.

"'Had we but world enough, and time, this coyness, lady, were no crime,'" Angelica recited as she wound a brunette curl around her finger. "Andrew Marvell."

Angelica always thought she knew more. Always. Of course it was Marvell. Papa insisted on all the English classics.

"Coyness is your crime, Ann. No lady was ever less coy than I."

"That's why you'll never marry. I can't choose among my potential suitors, while you feign no interest. It's vexing. You ought to have a shred of curiosity about my fate."

At fourteen, Angelica Schuyler was already a belle, a state she had achieved by careful application to task. Precocious in learning and charm, she far preferred bustling Albany, a town of nearly four hundred homes, to quiet Saratoga. Gentlemen who came to see her father there invariably took discreet notice of his eldest daughter. Although not yet allowed to powder her hair, Angelica had coaxed Diana into giving her a bouffant halo that morning. Silky ringlets cascaded over her shoulders, framing her oval face. The housekeeper was normally too busy to fuss with such things, but Angelica was her favorite. She was most people's favorite.

"I've no interest in impractical things," Eliza said, and turned her head turned the other direction to cool her cheek. It was almost a summer sun. "When the troublesome creatures become a practical concern I'll think more about them."

It was an airy response and she was pleased that it sounded sophisticated. Society ranked wit highly. Angelica usually got in the first thrust, but Eliza was learning to parry.

She meant it, too. Mama believed selecting a husband was the most important choice in a girl's life. Angelica considered it the most fascinating. Not Eliza. To her, marriage was a faraway peak in the Catskills, lost in a dim haze. Eliza would study the route when required to make the journey.

Until then the boring subject of suitors could be ignored in favor of more lively ones. Rabbits, for example, were far more intelligent than commonly assumed. Raccoons were, too, though they could be stinky and their razor claws were a hazard even as newborns. Popinjay, the bluebird she had snatched from the house cat, still visited Eliza's windowsill for bread crumbs every morning. Tame or wild, all the animals she knew on the farm were far from dumb, though that's what ignorant, unimaginative people called them.

The only boy who had ever caught her attention—and kept it more than a minute—was the Mohawk she met the day that Father yielded to her pleas to accompany him to the meeting of the Six Nations after she vowed to be quiet the entire visit and promised never to bring snakes into the house again. It thrilled Eliza to persuade Papa and reinforced her feeling that if there was one thing she knew about herself, it was that she was convincing.

What she didn't understand was why she couldn't forget the impetuous, reckless boy with the strong hands and fierce eyes.

The other Schuyler children were still asleep when she and Papa left that morning—except little Cornelia, who chewed on her braid and told Eliza that she would go, too, when she was grown-up. Outside, the slaves had already stoked the fire at the smithy, and the gristmill and sawmills were humming. The doorway was dim, so Eliza couldn't see the disapproving expression on Diana's African face. She knew the housekeeper didn't think she should go, but no one questioned Colonel Philip Schuyler, so Diana only said, "Mind your p's and q's, Miz Betsey," when Eliza climbed into the calash. Despite the glimmering frost on the driveway, she tingled with excitement and didn't feel the chill.

Prince, the eldest son of the other housekeeper, Maria, wore a livery of green and yellow that contrasted with his dark skin. He started the calash down the driveway of crushed white oyster shells that led away from the Schuyler estate, past the wheat fields and toward the sugar orchard where maples had just started to leaf.

Diana and Maria managed every detail of the household between them. The preternatural efficiency of the Janus-faced housekeepers allowed Mistress Kitty—Eliza's mother, Catherine—to concentrate on the family's social responsibilities and the seemingly endless task of producing new Schuylers. Mama had borne eleven children thus far, six still living.

The sky lightened as they sped along the forested river road in the spring dawn. Wrapped in his thoughts, Philip Schuyler hardly spoke, though he patted Eliza's knee from time to time. "Do you see that post, Betsey?" her father asked when they had driven an hour. "That's the new parcel."

Eliza recognized the marker but nodded as if the information was new. She had never taken such a long and important trip with her father. He could count on her to pay attention, even better than Angelica, whose head was filled with folderol.

The deep forest gave way to farmland again as they neared the Mohawk Castle. Eliza had heard her father and other Albany men talk about Indian castles many times. She knew they couldn't possibly look like the European palaces pictured in books, yet the phrase conjured grand and magical edifices and she was terribly curious to see one. She understood little about the purpose of the conclave, except that her father was worried that the conflict with Parliament might disrupt their peace with the Iroquois. Papa had inherited their Saratoga estate as a boy, when Indians burned the house and murdered his uncle. Good will must never be taken for granted.

The fields on either side of the carriage weren't very different from theirs. Rows of corn and oats looked well tended, and neat paths divided what might have been family parcels. Only the absence of fences was distinctive. The Six Nations didn't believe in owning cattle since deer were so plentiful, Papa once told her, so had no need to guard against wandering bovines.

Eliza at last spied the village on a gentle hill overlooking the river. Stout tree trunks sharpened into spikes walled the large village. A warrior on a watchtower gazed over a spiky rampart at their carriage and beckoned them through the tall gateway. The calash finally wheeled to a stop in front of a brown-bark longhouse that was not much of a castle, to Eliza's disappointment, though it was larger than the biggest church in Albany. A double row of smaller longhouses stretched along either side.

Her left foot had grown numb during the ride, and Eliza shook it under the heavy blankets to dispel the tingling. She didn't want to stumble in front of the Indian children now gathering with bright-eyed attention under the watchful eye of a young, copper-skinned girl about her own age.

"Don't fidget, Betsey," her father said, and Eliza gingerly wiggled the toes inside her boot. She never understood why it hurt so much to rouse a sleeping limb when it wasn't painful to wake the rest of her.

Prince jumped down and held the lead horse by the bridle while Master Schuyler helped his daughter out of the high vehicle. She put her surer foot onto the running board and did her best to jump down without showing her ankles.

An imposing man pushed aside the blanket that cloaked the doorway of the meeting hall and walked out to greet them. He wore buckskin breeches and a red and black mantle draped over one bare shoulder. He gave her little more than a sideways glance. No one noticed a girl-child.

A younger Indian in European garments followed him. The chief gave a short speech in one of the languages of the Six Nations, though Eliza could hardly tell which. She felt fairly certain that one of the man's words was *Schuyler*, though it sounded like "Skicker" in his unintelligible tongue.

"Welcome to the home of the people," the younger man translated in the dignified cadence she associated with Indians, whose formal delegations often visited Saratoga. "The Onondaga are not yet present. The Iroquois League will gather when they arrive. But first, Schuyler must take meat with us this morning."

Philip Schuyler stood with military bearing in his red colonel's uniform. Like the chief, he had high cheekbones and a large, aristocratic nose. His light brown hair was gathered in a queue at the back of his neck and the high neckline of his silk cravat set off a pointed chin. A firm mouth and calm expression gave him an aura of decisiveness. Eliza felt a surge of pride. Her brave Papa had fought alongside the Mohawk before she was born. Together, they defeated the treacherous French at Lake George.

"Schuyler is honored to share food and a pipe with our ancient friends." Papa spoke more slowly than usual and took a large package tied with bright red ribbon from Prince. "I hope you will accept this unworthy gift from my fields. It is last summer's tobacco, dried and cured by my servants."

The Indian leader, whose face was lined and grave, accepted the gift with a nod and another polite speech.

Eliza wondered why her father spoke so diffidently. Silk ribbon came all the way from Manhattan and they never had enough of it, not with four daughters in the house. And tobacco was currency—as valuable as British pounds, which were rarer than roosters' eggs ever since trade between the colonies and Britain had stopped.

Philip Schuyler gave his daughter his arm. They proceeded into the longhouse. Eliza burned to examine the castle but knew better than to stare like a simpleton, so she looked around as if taking care not to stumble. The shadowy interior smelled of wood smoke and roasting meat. Shelves burdened with gourds and lidded baskets lined the walls, and ears of drying maize tied by their silks hung from the rafters. Groups of men lounged on rugs, some made from bearskin, others from cloth. The translator showed them to a bench facing a low table made from a single plank. *Thank goodness*, Eliza thought, since she hadn't the faintest idea how to sit on a bearskin with the dignity she knew her father expected.

The appetizing smells of corn and venison reminded Eliza that she had skipped breakfast. She had never seen her father eat with his hands, but copied his gestures as he took the meat served on a pancake of purple maize. He ate as delicately as if dining on silver plate at the head of the table in Albany, enjoying a terrine of smoked grouse. Eliza munched through three delicious cakes before she struck grit in the ground corn.

She winced, and pushed the crumbled stone to the side of her mouth. How could she take it out politely? The men were engrossed in food and conversation, and her father was trying to explain the recent deaths in Boston where British troops had fired upon a threatening crowd. Eliza contemplated keeping the grit in her cheek for the next few hours.

She felt eyes on her. Across the room, an Indian youth of medium build sat cross-legged. Unlike many of the others, his sleek hair was tied back instead of shaved. He wore the feathers of a Mohawk and gazed at her forthrightly. Eliza knew she ought to drop her eyes, but returned the stare.

His dark, almond-shaped eyes were neither friendly nor hostile, just intent and observant. Eliza wondered if they looked like her own. Her mother had praised her eyes more than once for being "as black as an Iroquois beauty's."

The young man took a small piece of bone from his mouth. Still holding her gaze, he sucked on the bone to remove the fat and then, reaching very deliberately, placed the refuse on the serving board in front of him. Eliza felt for the stone inside her own mouth, removed it with her fingers, and laid the grit on an empty platter. She glanced up and smiled but the young man no longer met her eyes.

When the food was cleared away, the council began. Iroquois of all ages came in, until Eliza began to wonder how many more could possibly fit in the double rows that encircled the meeting space. The proceedings were measured, sedate, and long. No man interrupted and each spoke his whole piece with great calm. Her father gave an oration that seemed wordier than the Indians'. Only the chief spoke at greater length, and with such solemnity that Eliza feared she might fall asleep and hit her head as she went down.

Then the young man with the long hair stood. Others had remained seated while speaking, and Eliza sensed that the assembly listened to him with special interest. His voice was urgent. It rose and fell with more passion than she heard in the others. Something was wrong and he was trying to set it right. His eyes searched out every face in the longhouse, though they did not land on her again. At last the chief intervened sharply and the young man said one last phrase with great conviction before he folded his legs and sat back down.

When the meeting ended, and the assembly dissolved in a bustle of activity, Eliza asked her father's permission to take some air. She was stiff and yearned to get out of the packed and stuffy longhouse. In the commotion, she lost sight of the interesting boy who had helped her. She wished she could thank him, though she wouldn't know how.

The spring twilight had just started to gather, turning the rushing current of the wide river the color of dark plums. The fresh breeze felt clean. The Iroquois were dispersing, some swinging onto horses with bows strapped to their backs, others walking toward canoes outside the main gate. Eliza saw that Prince had pulled the calash beyond the castle walls and she thought she might have time to stroll to the water.

A tumult at the river's edge drew her attention as she approached. A group of young braves was gathered round one of the canoes. Voices were raised and the tone was heated. One man started to untie his boat and appeared ready to cast off when another stepped forward and shoved him full on the chest, causing the canoeist to stumble backward and wet his moccasins. He regained his balance, but the other man pushed again and this time the canoeist fell into the water, landing on his hands. It was the young Mohawk brave who had stared at her.

He leaped to his feet, pulled his attacker forward, and flipped the man into the shallows. Now both were drenched.

The untethered canoe bobbed at the bank. A jabbering crowd milled about the pair and a small boy took to splashing them, thinking it was all a game. As Eliza watched, the canoe slanted toward the powerful stream just beyond the reeds.

She ran the last few yards to the water's edge, splashed into the shallows, and grabbed the dangling bowline with both hands, which caused the stern to angle closer to the fast current. The rope was thick and wet. The boat was covered in sewn bark and heavier than it appeared. The water was faster. She felt her grip weakening. The canoe was getting away.

A pair of hands clasped the line in front of hers and a bare shoulder brushed against her. Suddenly the craft was coming to shore. The longhaired Mohawk pulled with his strong brown arms. He gave her a smile and said something she didn't understand. The onlookers were laughing now, amused at her mad dash.

Eliza concentrated on pulling the canoe, though she found herself mesmerized by the young man's sinewy brown hands, so sure and capable, until her heel struck a stone under the water, slick with moss. The current caught at her skirts and whipped the heavy fabric between her legs. She fell back into the young brave, who faltered, and they went down together in the shallow water, Eliza on his lap. He grasped her reflexively around the waist to break their fall and the canoe shot past them to the shore. Eliza looked up into his face, so close to hers, and noticed the start of a new beard on his upper lip. She caught her breath sharply, mortified yet oddly pleased to see him so close up.

"Miz Betsey! What have you got yourself into?" Prince said, wading into the water and pulling her up by the arm. Her sopping skirts were as heavy as a horse blanket. "Here you told Mama you was gonna act like a lady. Lord a mercy!"

Her father and the chief approached from behind.

Philip Schuyler's face was a study in horror, embarrassment, and anger. "Elizabeth! Come here this minute."

Eliza soon had a wool shawl draped round her shoulders, back in the longhouse. She hung her head, not daring to meet her father's disappointment. She had let him down utterly and would never hear the end of it. The whole family, even the servants, would tease. Everyone thought Angelica was more clever and sophisticated—and she was. Eliza's eyes burned but she refused to cry in front of the men. What had she been thinking? Would Papa ever forgive her? And what must that boy think? Overcome, she pinned her attention to the hem of the shawl until the chief rose to his feet.

With a stern but kind expression, he gave a short speech that the translator put into English for them. Now the chief looked straight at her, then at her father, then back at Eliza.

"Schuyler daughter is brave and quick. She saved a canoe that took two warriors a week to build. She is not afraid men will laugh. I adopt her into this longhouse. Her name will be One-of-Us."

The young brave watched from across the room—and grinned. Now his eyes were warm.

Lying on her arms in the field, the memory of that remarkable day felt as good as the sun on Eliza's back. She was the only Indian among the Schuyler children. That was a fitting retort when her brother John, younger than she but oldest of the boys, told her girls couldn't climb. Or ride a horse after dark. Or go into town alone.

She was an Iroquois and that meant doing things.

"Betsey. Are you paying any heed at all?" Angelica said.

Eliza was not, but her older sister's tone caught her attention. She realized that Angelica was still stuck on the subject of beaus and had been talking nonstop.

"You may not care about marriage now, Betsey, but you'll change your mind someday. Someday you will. And if you've given no thought to how to choose a man you can live with, you're going to end up with someone ugly and poor. Or worse, dull."

The sun had grown fierce. Gnats rose out of the hot, damp grass and puffy white clouds ambled in the sky. It was time to go inside. She thought again of the impatient Mohawk whose words had stirred the Iroquois assembly and gotten him a dunking. He had courage. He had something to say.

And she had saved his canoe.

Eliza lifted her head and picked a blade of blond chaff from the tangled hair around her face. As smart as Angelica was, she didn't know everything. "If I ever marry, I don't want a husband I can live with. I want one I cannot live without."

Not that Eliza would worry about it. A New Yorker like that didn't exist. If he did, he'd be as unpredictable and dangerous as a wild Indian.

CHAPTER THREE

February 1768

Christiansted

"At this court of assistants one James Britton, a man ill affected both to our church discipline and civil government, and one Mary Latham, a proper young woman about 18 years of age . . . were condemned to die for adultery . . . They both died very penitently."

John Winthrop, Governor, *The History of New England, 1630–1649*

ALEXANDER WASN'T READY TO OPEN HIS eyes. He felt much better and his mind dashed to all that needed doing, yet his legs still felt like sacks of maize and an unnamed mystery tugged uneasily at his consciousness, just out of range. Something seemed different. Not right. What was that smell?

The breeze brushed his face lightly in contrast to the hot winds that had blasted Mama and him the day before. Or was it the day before that? She now slept with her back to him, heavy in the bed.

The dawn air swelled more strongly and palm fronds outside the window clattered against one another. The draught felt like Ajax wiping his face. Ajax had been there with a cool towel the first night, as his faithful friend always was whenever swamp sickness seized Alexander's limbs.

This time was different, though. The ague overwhelmed him more quickly and brought unusual boils.

Mama had sent him outside that afternoon to amuse himself in the lane. A gentleman did not labor on Sunday after church. Ajax could go, too, she said, which should have alerted Alexander that something was out of joint. Mama didn't encourage them to play together anymore. But she was feeling poorly and wanted to lie down. A nap and a glass of mobee made from ginger ought to restore her. She gave him a piece of molasses candy as he went out the door and pressed one into Ajax's hand, too. Though she pretended otherwise, Alexander knew she was fond of the slave boy born under her roof.

They hadn't been outdoors more than an hour when Ajax looked at him queerly. He gripped the iron barrel hoop that Alexander intended to snatch on the next roll. Ajax usually won at that game, but Alexander's hands had hardened.

"What's that?"

"What's what?"

The day was warm despite the West Indian trade winds. Alexander wiped sweat from his brow and plucked at the damp cotton fabric of his blouse. Ajax must be plotting a feint and trying to distract him.

"That thing on your face."

"What thing?"

"*That* thing," Ajax said, pointing.

Alexander hardly remembered what came next. His knees went weak, as if Ajax's words had reminded his brain of an overwhelming problem, and within the hour he was lying in the bed above the store with his fever climbing and falling in the gathering dark. At some point Alexander realized Mama was lying beside him. She was talking but he couldn't understand her words. Once, she threw her arm across his face as if he wasn't there and he pushed it away without waking her.

Ajax stayed up all night, covering the hot pustules on Alexander's face and chest with cool towels that he dipped in fresh water when they grew warm. A slave woman Alexander didn't recognize helped Mama. Then Mrs. McDonnell took over, and finally Dr. Heering, with his collection of purgatives and emetics. Mama spit in the basin until her face was shiny and she fell back on the pillow. But she held his hand tightly when Dr. Herring said Alexander must be bled and told him not to be afraid. He couldn't recall who bandaged his arm afterward. He heard his brother James knock vainly on the door.

Even in his delirium, Alexander knew the ague must be bad if the adults banned James from the sickroom and Anna Lindstrom McDonnell lifted a finger to help Rachel Lavien and her illegitimate child.

"She should put a red lamp in that window," Mrs. McDonnell had said to Mrs. Helmutson one Sunday when the family walked into church. St. John's welcomed sinners like Rachel Lavien, though it would not baptize or school her bastards. Mama led them to their regular pew, head high, but when they sat down, she leaned in Alexander's direction. The curl on her forehead fell sideways and Alexander noticed again, as he had before, the white scar left by Johann Lavien. "Never look back," she whispered, the only allusion she ever made to her decision to abandon her first husband and their infant—for which the court had jailed Mama and forbidden her to remarry. "You'll trip over what's next."

Alexander pulled the bedclothes higher. He reached behind his back to touch her, his brave mother. "Mama?"

Rachel Lavien didn't stir. The air was sweet-sour. Alexander withdrew his hand and closed his eyes more tightly. "Mama?" he whispered.

Alexander hadn't realized anyone else was in the room, but he heard Mrs. McDonnell get up from the chair and walk around the bed, her clogs tapping like a sleepy woodpecker. "Mrs. Lavien?" she asked in her harsh, Danish-inflected English. "Mrs. Lavien?"

The bed shook. Alexander's lids were too heavy to open, but he felt the mattress rock on its ropes. Something was amiss. *Sleep tight,*

Mama said when she winched the cords snug at night. If he didn't open his eyes, nothing bad could happen. He and Mama would be well soon.

"Poor lass," Mrs. McDonnell said in a soft voice he didn't know she had.

A chill raced up Alexander's torso. He knew he must lie still so as not to rouse Mama, but his legs and arms trembled violently. The breeze turned icy. Alexander felt his mind slipping.

Although his eyes were shut, he spied his mother's hairbrush on the bureau across the room. It stood on end, followed by her tortoiseshell comb and a frilly teacup. They turned at the corner in infantry formation, marching closer and closer to the edge. Fear clawed at him though he didn't know why. Would Mama's pretty comb fall? Would the bone china break? Alexander felt a mortal dread, then realized he must be dreaming. The palm fronds outside now beat against the window, as if trying to get in.

"She's over there," Mrs. McDonnell said awhile later. She didn't say *poor lass* this time. Mama was sleeping very quietly.

"We'll have to seal the chamber," a man said. "Best get the boy out."

"Where can he go?" Mrs. McDonnell said.

I'm not going without Mama, Alexander wanted to say, though his mouth stayed shut against his will.

"She had a nephew in town, didn't she? Wasn't her sister married to James Lytton?" the man said.

"Can't you let the lad stay the night? He still has the fever."

"There's the best reason to get him out of this plaguey room. The court says to inventory her belongings, and I can't seal him in here. 'Tisn't right, p'raps, but there 'tis."

An Irishman, Alexander thought before he fell back into a dreamless sleep.

A few days later, Alexander stared down at the road through the mourning veil donated by the probate judge. Dirt sifted into the creases between his toes as he walked behind the casket. The black netting cast spotty shadows that drifted like clouds over his bare feet. The hot road was blistering, but Mama needed him and the town committee had collected funds to purchase just one pair of shoes. Someone decided that only the oldest child needed to be shod. Alexander's brother James, excused from the carpenter's shop for the day, led the procession in his newly cobbled footwear.

The small group made its way down Company Street, turned the corner at the Guinea Trading house, and came uphill on King. Carriages on the way to market impeded their progress once or twice, but pedestrians gave the group a wide berth once they saw the black cloth and the parish clerk with his Bible. Merchants stilled their voices before shouting out their wares again after the group passed. "Rest in peace, love," Alexander heard someone call from an open window, and he glanced sideways through the veil, touched that a respectable townswoman remembered Mama kindly until he saw the painted, sad-faced whore wave her white handkerchief. He didn't lift his eyes again.

Alexander's left shoe had gone missing in the inventory made when he was still delirious and he couldn't wear just one. The store and its goods, the slaves, the furniture, the crockery, Mama's skirts and blouses, even the milk goat in the courtyard—all had been seized. Ajax was gone without a good-bye. The officers of the probate court pounced on Rachel Lavien's goods as if her sons were thieves who might steal them, given a chance. James and Alexander Hamilton were spared their clothes, but the rest of their life had vanished as abruptly as if a hurricane swept their home out to sea.

Where would he get another pair? What kind of work could he get without shoes? How would he eat?

If Alexander had been wearing his old pair in bed or tucked one under each arm, they would not have been lost. It was a foolish thought—and the hand-me-downs hadn't fit well—but he wished he had them now. Mama would never have sent him out barefoot in public, shamed in front of the town. Only a few days earlier, he'd planned to stuff cotton in the toes to make them fit more snugly, but kept forgetting.

The creases between his toes were deep brown now and his feet as grimy and ugly as those of any slave laboring in the nearby cane fields.

The tinkling of a cowbell broke Alexander's reverie. The dirt road out of Christiansted angled upward as their procession reached the first cane field, and became grassier and softer. He realized that the ground under his feet had mercifully cooled. The stout parish clerk labored to catch his breath. The wagon with its heavy load groaned as their destination came in sight.

Alexander knew that his beautiful Mama lay in the coffin on the bed of the wagon much as he knew about zebras in Africa and rings around Saturn. It was information, yet unreal. But the overturned soil and gaping hole on the hillside overlooking the iridescent bay were very real. Every day after this, Rachel Lavien would lie under the mahogany tree in the family plot next to his uncle's old house, out of view of the jail that once imprisoned her and the cemetery that now barred her.

He would never see her again—or Ajax. His childhood friend had been led away in chains. And where would he and James go? They were alone and penniless in a world that despised them.

Some people were born bastards, others slaves. That's the way it was.

Alexander's throat swelled. Mama was better than those who scorned her. She didn't need their churchyard to be close to God. On the gentle hillside she would hear the boom of the surf on the island's clean sand and no one could ever again insult her honor in ways that sent a dagger through his heart. He wanted to do more for her, but all he could do was follow her coffin.

Tears came at last and Alexander was glad for the veil that covered his face so no one could see.

He had failed her. If he had been a better son, they would have had more money and the doctor might have come sooner. Now poor Mama was gone. Who would love him again?

CHAPTER FOUR

November 1769

Christiansted

"Each player must accept the cards life deals him or her: but once they are in hand, he or she alone must decide how to play the cards in order to win the game."

Voltaire, 1694–1778

ON A FALL MORNING, ALEXANDER FASTENED the last button on his frock coat and examined himself in the mirror. The old coat was rumpled but clean. He pulled down on the hem until it was straight and smooth. There. He would never be tall like Neddy, but he thought he looked presentable enough to make an impression on the niece of Master Kortright, expected any day from New York with her maiden aunt.

He set aside the volume on anatomy that Neddy had given him and quickly put the bed to rights in the room under the south gables. Alexander was determined that no one would ever think him a sponger. He kept the borrowed room scrupulously clean and tidy, grateful for the roof over his head.

He had also developed the habit of an early start to avoid seeing Neddy's empty place at breakfast. Thomas Stevens had taken him in after Mama's death a year ago, and the family's oldest boy, who was now Alexander's best friend, had recently left for New York to complete his studies.

When Alexander stepped into the lane moments later, the trade wind nearly snatched his hat, but he clasped it firmly and proceeded toward the offices of Kortright & Cruger down King Street. He'd promised to look for the company's vessel every morning, though, so he walked right past the lead-paned windows of the counting house when he reached the corner.

Alexander carried a cargo list and a blank ledger sheet folded into fourths. His first task—after securing Miss Kortright and her aunt a respectable carriage—was to inspect the shipment before dock thieves could pilfer it. Fortunately, the anticipated vessel would not be carrying slaves, who depressed Alexander. The preceding week, he and another clerk worked until dusk pricing more than three hundred of the wretches, whose nakedness and bruises they'd had to ignore. When he saw a tall boy with a ring around the neck, nausea seized him—and he nearly ran from the auction house.

Did Ajax wear a yoke now? The image burned like salt in a fresh cut.

Sunshine glittered on Gallows Bay, where the Royal Navy hanged buccaneers. Alexander spied the white sails of two ships clearing the coral reefs. One appeared to be the *Sally Lucia*.

He turned his mind to the encounter ahead and mentally rehearsed clever expressions as the vessels tacked into the small harbor, pushed by the sprightly breeze. Miss Kortright might be hideous, but he wanted to be prepared in case she wasn't.

He'd recently overheard a planter's son ask a young lady, "Is that the moon in my eyes, or does Artemis grace our presence?" The courtly phrase sounded ridiculous to Alexander, but the pretty girl gave the man a saucy smile and inquired if he might be Adonis. When she tossed a glance over her shoulder, the rosewater silk at her waist twisted in a way that made Alexander want to feel its slippery folds. He decided then that he best pay closer attention to the art of wooing.

The bark-rigged *Sally Lucia*, its sails reefed, glided slowly into the company dock. A man in the crosstrees took in the last bit of canvas while a boy edged out on the cathead. Someone threw a thick line onto the dock. Within moments, the ship was fast and a gangplank thrown down.

Alexander spied gray-bearded Captain Codwise on the fo'c'sle. "Permission to board, sir?" he called. The captain beckoned and Alexander walked straight up the weaving, bobbing plank, pleased by how sure-footed he'd become since his apprenticeship to the firm.

"Good morning, Captain Codwise."

"Same to you, Master Hamilton. Sorry to report, but the fair damsels are not aboard. I got this just before sailing." He withdrew a battered envelope from his faded coat. "Mayhap the old lady changed her mind about hurricane season. Not that I minded."

Alexander took the letter addressed to Master Kortright. He tried not to show his disappointment. "The fairer sex doesn't make for a fairer voyage, I've heard."

"Bad luck. I like 'em better on land."

"You must enjoy Christiansted."

An amused expression lit the captain's weather-beaten face. "Yes. 'Tis famous for the dusky ladies. Though I don't let the men entertain themselves long. Whoring is their downfall and I can't afford to lose a minute."

"I mustn't either, if I'm to satisfy my master. May I go below, Captain, to check our shipment? I suppose it's at the top?"

"More bad news. I had to shift my ballast. A storm hit as we approached the Virgins. The cargo's all ahooey."

"Stormy virgins sound like trouble indeed," Alexander said with a smile, though the delay would cost him his afternoon. He needed to dun shopkeepers who owned the firm money.

"Speaking of trouble," the captain said. He lowered his voice and nodded in the direction of a departing passenger just stepping off the gangplank. "Picked him up in the Carolinas." Codwise coughed into his fist, glanced furtively at Alexander, and then looked away. "His name is Lavien. Peter Lavien."

Alexander watched the man disappear into the crowd. The half-brother he had never seen. Come to collect.

"I'd best inspect the cargo," Alexander said, and made his way below.

The cargo deck was dark after the brilliant sunshine, though the hatches admitted enough light to reveal oaken barrels wedged wall to wall. The bilge water smelled of dead fish and spoiled salt pork. The atmosphere was stifling—like his life. Alexander knew he should call for assistance with the cargo but couldn't face anyone, so he slipped behind a closely packed row and leaned against the clammy bulwark.

He would never wipe away the image of Johann Lavien shouting his base accusations in front of the probate judge while Alexander and his brother James awaited the court's ruling. It was the last time the two brothers sat side by side after Alexander had gone to live with the Stevenses, and James took a cot with the carpenter's family. The brothers had always squabbled over small things—they were as unalike as water and stone—but they avoided one another altogether now. For reasons Alexander didn't understand, Mama's death had pushed them further apart. Perhaps they reminded one another of their mutual shame. Separately they could pretend they were something else. Strange to think, it was Ajax whom Alexander yearned to see, though he would never have admitted it. James worked in the carpenter's shed at the far edge of town. Ajax was gone forever.

Johann Lavien had traveled from the other side of the island for the hearing that morning. His mother's ex-husband was not as Alexander pictured. Although he knew the Danish fortune hunter was considerably older than Mama, his stringy gray locks and stooped back were a shock. Lavien's gnarled hands, which clasped the young heiress with passion before he spent all her money, were as curled as dried leaves. His hoarse voice betrayed a long association with tobacco or drink or both.

Yet it was not a weak voice. Despite the judge's hints that he would rule in Lavien's favor, the man bellowed like a bull until it seemed every ear in Christiansted must hear his vulgar allegations through the open windows.

"Born in whoredom they were. Says so right here." Lavien waved the divorce decree from a decade earlier. "The bitch slept with any man who'd have her."

"Mr. Lavien. The terms of the divorce are not under consideration. Please restrain yourself."

"She wasn't supposed to remarry. Her whoresons aren't entitled to a damn thing. It says so."

"I know what the documents say, Mr. Lavien." Disapproval crept into the judge's voice. "I'm compelled, despite your comportment, to agree with the plea."

"I know my rights!"

Lavien's attorney tugged at his client's elbow.

"Your rights are not at issue," the judge said, "but the rights of the deceased's three children—the son born in wedlock to you and Mrs. Lavien, and the obscene children born after the divorce. The Hamilton boys . . . Lavien boys."

James Jr. hung his head but Alexander looked straight at the judge, refusing to blink. He needed to understand why the court wanted to destroy their lives and how the judge could face the actual obscene children before him.

But the bewigged magistrate seemed little concerned with the orphans in his courtroom. He banged his gavel. "By the decrees of the King of Denmark, I hereby award the estate of Rachel Faucette Lavien to Peter Lavien, the natural born and only legitimate child of the deceased."

Thomas Stevens placed a hand on their shoulders. "Your poor mother. It's not right."

Alexander didn't know what Mr. Stevens meant, but felt too disgraced to ask. What wasn't right? Had Mama been falsely accused? Or was it simply not fair that, due to her sins, James and he had been robbed of any patrimony? And what was justice anyway? Their father was born fourth in a world that gave everything to the first son.

Even Thomas Stevens's pity felt unendurable, and for a moment Alexander longed to shake off his benefactor's hand, though he didn't. More than once Alexander had caught neighbors' salacious smirks, as if Stevens's generosity to the young orphan was repayment for some special *favor* pretty Rachel once bestowed. At that moment in the courtroom, the whole world seemed rotten and squalid to Alexander.

And now, from the decks of the *Sally Lucia*, Peter Lavien had arrived to collect his blood money. The half-brother whom fortune had favored would enjoy every penny Mama had left. Cousin Peter Lytton had bought Rachel's books at the probate auction last summer—the works of Plutarch and Pope that she loved—and gave them to Alexander before he himself died a month later. The shillings from that purchase would go to Peter Lavien, as would money from the sale of Ajax.

Would the younger Lavien even search for his half brothers—Rachel's *whoresons*? Should Alexander seek him out?

Never. Peter Lavien would have to come to him. If the man didn't, he wasn't a real brother.

Alexander pressed his palms hard against his eyes. He wished he could blot out the past. From the ship's captain down to the town crier, everyone would always know his sordid story: every respectable merchant, every pretty girl, every town drunk. He was irrevocably tainted.

"Master Hamilton? What ho? Are ye down there now?" Footsteps on the ship's ladder accompanied the high voice of a crewmember.

Alexander took a deep breath and stepped into the light. "Yes, I am," he said with all the dignity he could muster.

It was the lad Alexander had noticed on the cathead when the ship docked. A rash of pimples on his lean face suggested he was around Alexander's age, twelve or thirteen. The boy was barefoot. A piece of coarse hemp served as drawstring for his dirty, collarless blouse.

"I need assistance with the cargo, if you would be so good," Alexander said, conscious of the contrast between them. For Alexander, careful dress and formal language were shields against the world's disrespect. He wondered what misfortune had sent the ragged boy to sea, and reminded himself he wasn't the only orphan in Christiansted.

"Yes, sir. Captain sent me for the purpose. Shall I call the lads for 'elp?"

Alexander laid his brown frock coat across the top of a cask. "Pray do," he said. "We'll need it."

Alexander didn't know how he would ever erase his agonizing shame, and wrote as much to Neddy that evening. Barely sixteen yet compassionate beyond his years, Ned had learned to read Alexander's heart in the months they lived together before he left for New York to study medicine.

"*I despise the groveling and conditions of a clerk or the like to which my fortune, etc., condemns me,*" Alexander scribbled in the dim glow of the candle.

Neddy well knew what "etc." stood for. The whole world did.

"*And I would willingly risk my life though not my character, to exalt my station.*"

Alexander could hardly imagine what deeds might exalt his station on St. Croix and allow him to meet other men's eyes with pride. But Plutarch's *Lives*, which he and Neddy had read together, showed they were possible. In ancient Rome, even bastards sometimes earned fame and respect through oratory or daring. Chroniclers praised their triumph over long odds.

Alexander studied the yellow candle flame. He imagined himself in an officer's trim uniform, a bright sword fastened to his waist, marching at the head of a victory parade—no, mounted on a horse, one arm in a sling—admired by cheering throngs who threw flowers in the returning heroes' path. When the governor of Christiansted gave a speech praising Alexander's gallant service, Alexander would reply that all credit was due the brave men who had followed him into battle. Girls in the crowd might weep. The prettiest would flirt with him later at the victory ball.

He smiled at the fanciful thought, then frowned. Mama wouldn't be there to see. Who knew where Ajax would be.

Alexander clenched his quill more tightly. He must go on alone; he must find his opportunity. At least there was Neddy.

Alexander groped for a way to end the letter. He didn't want Ned to think him conceited or uppity, yet a keen determination to change his fate had fevered his brain ever since he spotted Peter Lavien that morning—and he longed to tell someone.

"*I'm no philosopher and it may be justly said that I build castles in the air*," Alexander wrote in a final flourish. "*My folly makes me ashamed and beg you'll conceal it. Yet, Neddy, we have seen such schemes successful when the projector is constant. I shall conclude by saying I wish there was a war!*"

Alexander sprinkled sand on the page to dry the ink. Perhaps he was a deluded fool. But what choice did he have? Even fools must try.

CHAPTER FIVE

July 1770

Albany, New York

"All might be free if they valued freedom, and defended it as they should."
Samuel Adams, 1722–1803

Angelica was simply showing off, Eliza thought, irritated at her sister's eagerness to volunteer for more spinning.

The mother cat reclined with her green eyes half shut while Eliza counted the nuzzling kittens. Had the dog snatched one of them? Many Toes purred softly when Eliza lifted her plump hindquarters, careful not to detach the nursing infants. A ball with gray, white, and orange patches curled under the long, fluffy tail.

She shifted the runt and felt the mother cat's furry belly for a wet nipple. "There you go, baby," Eliza whispered, and latched the black-nosed kitten to its mother. The runt had gotten noticeably bigger.

"Is it going to live?" Cornelia's cornflower eyes were wide.

"He should. Of course he will," she said. Her little sister had been horrified when Eliza explained that runts usually died. Cornelia had been up at dawn every morning since to inspect the basket under Eliza's bed.

Angelica appeared in the doorway of the girls' bedroom on the second floor of the family's Albany mansion. "Feeling better?"

"Yes," Eliza said. "The chamomile helped."

Angelica folded her arms. "Why aren't you downstairs, then? I've spun a whole skein already."

Eliza frowned. "Miracles never cease."

She doubted that Angelica had ever spun a skein straight through in her whole life before being converted to the cause of liberty by young Mr. Livingston. Angelica usually sat at her sewing with the face of a prisoner serving a very long sentence. Now her sister acted as if she'd invented the spinning wheel.

"Peggy and I have carded a sack apiece. Mama says you need to come right down."

Eliza thought the Sons of Liberty could wait while she made sure the runt didn't starve, but she knew Mama wouldn't. "Watch him, Cornelia. Put him back on if he falls off," she said.

Cornelia bobbed her thick braids and Eliza realized she might as well let her youngest sister take over anyway. Cornelia seemed determined to become a nursemaid to stray wildlife, like her big sister, which led Eliza to reflect that she ought to mention Papa's feelings about garter snakes. They had shown a propensity to offend Mama in her boudoir.

Angelica smiled as Eliza passed in the doorway. "We really do need you. You're so fast."

Eliza recognized the attempt to jolly her. Everyone knew Angelica could charm bears out of hibernation. Yet she felt mollified despite herself and was smiling by the time they entered the downstairs parlor arm in arm, Angelica regaling her with the latest tale of Mr. Livingston's inept gallantry.

Dark-haired Kitty Schuyler glanced up without slowing her wheel. Their mother was expecting any day, but this had not diminished her productivity. She and Eliza's younger sister Peggy sat with large bags of carded wool near the picture windows that overlooked the gentle slope rolling down to the Hudson. In the back corner of the room, Diana and two other servants spun linen thread that hissed through their fingertips. The yellow wallpaper that Papa had bought in London heightened the parlor's sunniness, and a Brussels carpet patterned with garlands of pink roses softened the clicking of the women's treadles.

"Good morning, *mijn lief*," Kitty Schuyler said.

Eliza kissed her mother's cheek and took a place at one of the spinning wheels that had sprouted like mushrooms across Albany. The women of the family had always worked, but now it seemed they hardly did anything else.

Mama was determined not to buy another bolt of fabric from London. To increase their yield of wool she had told the kitchen to stop serving mutton. Papa commissioned a flax mill at Saratoga to make the town self-sufficient in linen, for which the Sons of Liberty awarded him a medal. The family rarely drank real tea anymore, only sassafras, which, as far as Eliza was concerned, tasted exactly like fresh manure smelled.

She sighed and readied her spindle. A small tax on imports hardly seemed worth the extraordinary fuss everyone was making. Angelica had even taken to calling herself a Daughter of Liberty, as absurd a thing as Eliza had ever heard, short of little Cornelia pretending she was a boy and demanding everyone call her Sam.

Eliza felt herself becoming annoyed again. It was one thing for Mama to make them spin away yet another afternoon and quite another for Angelica to act as if she was delighted to pour the entire summer into such a tiresome task for the good of the country when all she wanted was to impress one of the many gentlemen already besotted with her.

"Will Papa take us when he goes to New York for the Assembly?" her older sister now asked their mother. Angelica's hands moved with unaccustomed nimbleness. Eliza supposed even a mule could be taught to spin if it was sufficiently motivated.

"He wouldn't think of going without us. He's already made arrangements with Lady Moore at Government House."

"Oh, I adore her parties!" Angelica said. "Her last dancing master showed us all the new steps from Paris."

"You mustn't expect as many entertainments this time. I'm afraid the consequences of Parliament's stubbornness have fallen hardest on bystanders like poor Lady Moore."

"How so, Mama?" said Peggy. She was a year younger than Eliza and blue-eyed like their father. The sunlight lit her blond hair as she squinted against the rays that slanted through the windows.

"Even patriots can be misguided. Ruffians assaulted the governor's carriage with eggs when the tax went on stamps. New York's ladies were quite rude to his wife. Sir Henry's common sense calmed the public, but his position isn't easy."

Mama and Papa didn't approve of those who took out their anger toward Parliament on the governor personally.

"Do you think Lady Moore will mind that we're resisting taxation without representation?" Angelica now used such phrases as if she had minted them.

"For the sake of friendship, I won't wear homespun to her dancing assemblies," their mother said.

"Shall Eliza and I take our London frocks to New York, then? To spare Lady Moore's feelings?"

Eliza brought her wheel to an abrupt stop. "To spare Lady Moore's feelings? You wouldn't wear homespun at the governor's mansion for all the tea in China, Angelica."

"I'll wear homespun at my wedding if I must. Parliament wants to reduce us to slaves and we won't have it."

"This whole tax nuisance is silly," Eliza said. "I'm sick and tired of it."

"Elizabeth!" Mama said.

Diana and the other servants raised their heads. Kitty Schuyler looked over at them and nodded. Diana led the trio out of the parlor. "You've been as mournful as a basset hound since you entered the room. What's upsetting you?"

Eliza looked down. She didn't quite know. This time of the month made her queasy and irritable—but that was embarrassing to admit. And it didn't help that Angelica was always pressing her to act the part of debutante when all Eliza wanted was to run outdoors and check on the animals or stroll down to the stream to look for fish caught in the weir. And now their normal chores had doubled with the patriots' non-importation nonsense.

"I don't understand why we can't just pay the taxes, Mama," Eliza said, aware that such a view was near to blasphemy. "It's only money."

"You aren't thinking of those for whom every shilling takes bread from the mouths of their babes. And it's not just money. I lost a child while your father was gone during the war. We nursed the wounded in our own barn. Papa defended the king, and now Parliament tells him he's not deserving of an Englishman's rights because we reside on this side of the Atlantic instead of the other. It's wrong. Your father will not be their servant, nor will we."

Mama didn't usually lecture. She paused for a breath. "Do you understand, Betsey?"

Eliza knew the stories of the French and Indian War: the men killed, women tomahawked, children torn from their families by the Algonquin. When it was over, their Mohawk allies had arranged a hostage exchange that took place in the driveway of Aunt Schuyler's Albany estate. For the stolen children it meant being orphaned twice. Mama told them about one boy who cried inconsolably at being separated from his adopted Indian mother and hid under a wagon from his strange, pale-faced parents.

Eliza felt ashamed. She didn't want Mama to think she didn't care. Yet it was hard to see what all that had to do with the price of tea.

"But we *are* the king's servants, Mama. You've always said that. We—"

"We serve the king, but he serves us, too," Angelica said. "And when he doesn't prevent Parliament from treating us as inferiors, then he ceases to be our king!"

"Girls, please. One goes too far, the other not far enough. What you need to understand, Betsey, is that we will do everything within our power to bring England to reason."

Their mother pushed away the spinning wheel, stood, and placed a palm on her lower spine. Her distended abdomen strained against her dress. She crossed the room to place an arm around Eliza's shoulders.

"Don't fret, *mijn lief*. It's only a bit of spinning."

Eliza leaned into her mother, comforted and saddened at the same time. The baby made Mama's belly hard. She hoped they would both be all right. Newborns sometimes died. Mothers, too. Wasn't life dangerous and complicated enough without picking fights over small, faraway problems?

"Yes, *mijn moeder*," she said softly.

Eliza didn't mind working hard. She never had. But their perfect world was unraveling and she didn't know where it would end.

CHAPTER SIX

February 1771

Saratoga

"I heard bullets whistle and, believe me, there was something charming in the sound."

George Washington, 1754

"FACTS ARE STUBBORN THINGS," ANGELICA READ aloud.

Eliza looked up from her needlework, eyes innocent. "Is that what you call yourself?"

Philip Schuyler laughed and removed his clay pipe from his mouth. "I believe she has you, Ann."

"But Papa," Angelica said, "I'm quoting Mr. Adams."

The kitten on the table next to Eliza's sister reached out its paw and swatted at the page. Angelica rustled the journal to shoo the animal but it stayed put.

Colonel Schuyler sobered. "Are you reading from the trial?"

"Yes. The jury must respect the facts, Adams says."

Eliza tied the last knot in the bootie she was knitting for Mrs. Cavan's baby. Mama was making a basket for the expectant parents, who were Papa's tenants. It was a dark February evening and snow edged the windowpanes of the snug upstairs parlor in which the two girls sat companionably by the fire with their father.

"I admire Adams's willingness to defend them," he said. "He's very brave."

Angelica read from the *Albany Gazette*. "Barrister John Adams blamed the patriots for their hooliganism."

Philip Schuyler set his pipe in a tray and leaned forward. "What did Mr. Adams say about the soldiers?"

Eliza started a second bootie. Papa always thought about the rank and file. Although he disagreed with the Crown, he'd once commanded Redcoats himself.

"Adams said that the Boston crowd was throwing sticks and rocks when the first Redcoat fired. The soldier acted in self-defense." Angelica lifted the journal closer to the whale-oil lamp and the cat hit the page again, but she ignored it. "Adams said, 'Do you expect the man should act like a stoic philosopher, lost in apathy?'"

"Well put," Philip Schuyler said. "A soldier has a right to defend his life."

"Do you think John Adams might have to defend his?" Angelica asked.

The ball of yarn rolled out of Eliza's lap. The cat pounced and Eliza leaned over to retrieve the yarn from its claws. "Whatever for?" she said as she straightened.

Angelica and Papa exchanged looks.

"They call it the Boston *massacre*," her fifteen-year-old sister said.

"I know that. I do read."

Occasionally, Eliza admitted to herself, as she'd rather make something than simply sit with a paper. A bootie would keep a child's foot warm long after the maid threw out the *Albany Gazette*. But public events had increasingly intruded into their private lives during the past six months and she picked up the newspaper more frequently now.

"Then you ought to know that John Adams has been pilloried left, right, and center," Angelica said.

"But he won his case last December, didn't he? I thought the Boston jury acquitted the soldiers."

"Nine men of property agreed with Adams that the Redcoats were merely defending their posts," their father said. "But the mob doesn't care."

"It was a mob that started the ruckus," Angelica said. "They might throw rocks at Adams next."

Eliza still didn't understand. "If Adams speaks the truth, won't other patriots defend him?"

Angelica sighed. "Surely you recall the battle between the Livingstons and DeLanceys, when they branded their opponents poachers and prostitutes? Some factions think Adams insufficiently rebellious. They call him a Tory."

"Oh." That Eliza understood. Politics in New York City were notoriously vicious. But she hadn't realized the patriots had factions, too.

Angelica's eyes sought out their father's. "Do you think the Boston verdict will hurt the cause of liberty, Papa?"

"I think it will help. Or it should. I'd never wish to be part of a country that tolerates mob rule. There's no greater threat to liberty than a crowd with torches."

"Shall we have a separate country, then?"

"I hope not. We have a sensible monarch in King George and it's disloyal to suggest otherwise."

Eliza remembered something. "But that's what Patrick Henry said. The Virginian. 'If this be treason, make the most of it.'"

"And he later apologized," her father said.

Pompey, Diana's youngest son, appeared at the door of the salon. "Master. Missy needs you in the drawing room. The commissioners from Albany are here."

Papa left to greet the delegates they'd anticipated all evening.

Eliza looked over at her sister, lost again in the newspaper. The cat was hiding under Angelica's chair.

Her sister seemed to share a special bond with their father. "Angelica has a masculine mind," their uncle once said. Eliza hadn't known if he was pleased or shocked. Some considered curiosity the worst of the female vices, and Reverend Hoidal frequently criticized Eve's unseemly plucking of the apple of knowledge. But Papa seemed to enjoy Angelica's inquisitive turn of mind. Perhaps other men admired that in a woman, despite what they said.

"What do you think, Angelica? Shall we separate from England?" It was the first time a word of outright rebellion had crossed Eliza's lips and she felt an unexpected thrill of adventure—about politics for once. She supposed she was starting to care about the world outside Saratoga.

Angelica paused. "I don't know the answer. What I do know is, the Sons of Liberty are serious—and England has defeated every enemy since the Spanish Armada. They'll crush the insurrection if it turns violent." Her expression grew pensive. "I fear for our men. I hope they won't be pushed into it."

"Papa wouldn't have to go to war, would he?"

"He might wish to."

"Surely not," Eliza said, though she knew Papa would never shirk his duty, which gave her a hollow feeling as it might take him away from them. Unpredictable dangers crouched in the world outside Saratoga. "We must pray that doesn't happen."

"The patriots pray to George the Third," Angelica said as she placed her paper on the table and stood up, "but if you can sway God the Father, I'm sure they'd be grateful." Her sister smoothed the front of her green paduasoy gown and left the room.

Eliza looked down at the bootie she had started. It seemed less of an accomplishment than before. Why didn't she grasp intrigue as readily as Angelica? She would never be as smart.

Eliza put aside her knitting, took up the ball of yarn, and got down on her knees. She held out a wooly strand until the cat snuck from under the chair, whereupon she picked it up and sat the calico in her lap to stroke.

Something else troubled Eliza. Now that she was alone, the night seemed darker and the freeze outside more menacing. Angelica said Papa might fight, but not which side he would take. Philip Schuyler loved his red uniform. Could he really turn his back on King George? Wouldn't that be treason?

They hanged men for treason.

CHAPTER SEVEN

June 1773

New York City

"I begin with writing the first sentence—and trusting to Almighty God for the second."

Laurence Sterne, *The Life and Opinions of Tristram Shandy*, 1759

ALEXANDER GRIPPED THE SHIP'S RAIL UNTIL his knuckles turned white. He caught his breath and squinted against the fierce sun that caused his eyes to water.

It was hard to pinpoint the exact cause of the miracle on the horizon. Was it the September hurricane that had ripped Alexander from Christiansted or the Reverend Hugh Knox? Or was it the two-headed specter of tragedy and opportunity that had always haunted him—and came a few months earlier in the form of poor cousin Ann?

"I *will* go to New York," Ann Venton said when she called upon Alexander in the parlor of Neddy Stevens's home on King Street. "My father, rest his soul, saw through the brute faster than I."

Cousin Ann was the only surviving child of Mama's sister, who had married better but died younger. Ann's inheritance had brought renewed attention from her estranged husband.

"Will it be enough to start over?" Alexander said.

"Yes. I don't have the funds yet, but I will once the probate court meets. That's why John wants me back—to get his hands on my money. One bankruptcy wasn't enough. But I will not stay with him!"

Cousin Ann was plainer than Mama, yet Alexander caught glimpses of the family resemblance at moments like this, when she blazed with determination.

He touched her arm. "Show me the notice."

Ann held out the crumpled journal. Bruises lingered on her wrist from the last time John used physical force. Now Ann's husband intended to use the law, which was crueler.

Alexander smoothed the paper. He wondered if Johann Lavien had posted similar warnings when Mama fled to British Nevis, where he was born.

JOHN KIRWAN VENTON forbids all masters of vessels from carrying Ann Venton or her daughter off this island.

Alexander wished he could save Ann, but his earnings were so meager that he wasn't sure when he could pay off his new waistcoat. "Do you have enough right now to buy passage to New York?"

"Yes. But what if someone stops me at the wharf?" Ann's lower lip trembled, tears spilled from her eyes, and her resemblance to Rachel Lavien vanished. Mama had been fearless.

That's when Alexander urged Ann to grant him power of attorney. Though he was only sixteen, the court wasn't likely to object since he'd run his employer's business when illness took Nicholas Cruger away to America. Alexander would purchase Ann's passage, and once the probate court released the remainder of her inheritance, he would send it on.

His cousin sailed the very next day, but not before handing Alexander an unexpected document. In instructions to her executor, Ann left funds for a scholarship that a town committee had started on Alexander's behalf. His friendship with Reverend Knox—and the reverend's publication of Alexander's eloquent account of a hurricane that flattened Christiansted and shook their souls a few months earlier—had impressed a group of philanthropists with the young clerk's precociousness. Hard work and painstaking politeness had finally brought him good fortune. Then Ann pledged a substantial sum of rix-dollars, backed by fifteen hogsheads of West Indian sugar, to turn the inadequate purse into a viable one.

That was the event responsible for the vision ahead.

He had been searching the shoreline since dawn. A distant smudge eventually became a town. He now spied tall buildings and imposing churches behind a row of black wharfs that stretched farther upriver than he could see. The city was immense, bigger than anything his imagination had devised.

Without knowing why, Alexander felt certain this was where he would live his life. The metropolis in the distance spoke to every longing he'd ever had for a world where no one knew his past or ever would.

His spirits had risen with every minute of longitude. They now soared. He wanted someone to hug. He wanted to shout and sing and dance a jig. In New York he would become a doctor like his grandfather had been. Like Neddy was going to be. They would save lives together.

The ship floated restlessly in the tidal flux of the Hudson River. A cock's crow drifted over the slack water. The captain brought the vessel around. The massive dock approached so rapidly that Alexander feared a collision, but the crew berthed the vessel and a Negro stevedore immediately made fast to the heavy cleats. "Slick as a whistle," Alexander said to himself.

He glanced down at his trunk, which seemed to have shrunk since Christiansted. It contained the sum of his possessions: clean linen, two suits, his best shoes, and a handful of books. He wondered if he could get it to the dock without looking like a clod or if he should part with a shilling for a porter.

"Is it help that you're needing there, sir?"

An Irishman appeared at his elbow. The fellow's trousers were frayed, but his shiny hobnailed boots appeared new. Newer than Alexander's own shoes, which he had polished the night before.

Alexander had never seen a white porter, he realized. In Manhattan, whites could as easily be servants as masters. If he wanted to become the latter he must act the part of gentleman from the start. Shillings be damned.

"Yes. Thank you. I wish to go to Water Street. I'm looking for the shop of Hercules Mulligan."

"I know him. The governor's tailor. This way, then, sir." The porter lifted the trunk onto his shoulder.

Alexander followed the man down the gangplank into a sea of humanity. Stevedores rubbed elbows with merchants. Bejeweled women with towering coiffures hung on the arms of men in satin waistcoats. Alexander peered into shop windows as they passed. Shelves were crammed with goods. This was the British Empire he'd read about. Mama's old store seemed shabbier than ever in his memory.

They walked at least ten blocks before the porter finally stopped in front of an old Dutch building with stepped gables. "Here 'tis."

Alexander looked at the wide door decorated with a pair of wooden scissors. He wished he had more time to collect his wits. What if he made a fool of himself? The porter knew all about Mr. Mulligan. Such a prominent merchant might look down on a boy from a seedy, provincial backwater.

He drew a deep breath, gathered his shaky courage, and lifted the knocker. He was here and must go through with it.

A barrel-chested man with a red, round face opened the door a few moments later. The tailor wasn't exceptionally tall, but he still seemed large next to Alexander's slender five-foot-seven frame. He frowned as if he'd been interrupted.

"Mr. Mulligan, sir—" Alexander began.

The man broke into a smile. "My boy! You've arrived at last. We heard the ghastly reports. Ship almost caught fire before you made Boston, eh? I trust this leg was less eventful. Come in, come in." Hercules Mulligan handed the porter a few coins. He put up his hands when Alexander reached for his purse. "Absolutely not. My brother would tar and feather me."

"Thank you, sir," Alexander said as he stepped inside, almost breathless with relief at the kind reception. He hadn't even produced his letter of introduction. Mulligan's brother, a junior partner of Master Kortright, must have described him well. Or perhaps his West Indian accent had given him away.

Bolts of fine fabric reached the ceiling of the gentlemen's shop. One wall featured sober browns and blacks while the opposite held riotous weaves of turquoise, green, purple, crimson, and yellow. A board displayed buttons of gold gilt, conch shell, and embroidered velvet. A pearl and silver stickpin caught Alexander's eye.

"We'll get some tea into you before church," Mulligan said as he led the way upstairs. "Best to make the assault well-fortified. Our preacher does prattle on."

"He would starve you on the road to heaven?"

"Exactly. Fortunately, my wife takes proper measures. We were just sitting down."

The breakfast room above the shop bore out the tailor's assertion. Mrs. Mulligan presided over one end of a table loaded with fresh trout, smoked ham, and warm bread rolls, her husband the other. Their young son sat next to Alexander, while Mrs. Mulligan reached out occasionally to rock a bassinet at her side.

"Tea, Mr. Hamilton?" Mrs. Mulligan filled his cup without waiting for an answer. Her face was as round as her husband's. "Shhhh," she said to the baby when it whimpered.

"We're enjoying it while we can," Mulligan said.

"You're committed to non-importation, then?" Alexander said. He placed his napkin in his lap and cut into a bit of ham, careful to hold the knife and fork properly.

Mulligan nodded. "Absolutely. Parliament's a bunch of petty tyrants. Though I admit it's a grand comfort to have two chests from Cathay in the basement. Mrs. Mulligan hates a shortage."

His wife placed a serving of ham and fish in front of the four-year-old next to Alexander. The little boy glanced up at their guest, then stared at his plate.

"If this goes on much longer, we'll be reduced to sassafras. A nasty brew," Mulligan said.

"Rabble-rousers will surely yield at some moment," Alexander offered in a neutral tone, unsure which Mulligan prized more—the high ideal of liberty or basement stash of tea.

He had read in the Christiansted *Gazette* about the protests against Parliament. Alexander had processed enough import taxes to understand they could be burdensome, but found the complaint puzzling. From what he'd seen of Manhattan, British stewardship was worth a few guineas. New York was a world away from Danish incompetence on St. Croix, with its muddy streets and ramshackle port.

"Don't count on it. Gentlemen can't be seen buying British cloth if they value their lives. Imported fabric just sits there." Mulligan grimaced as he filleted his trout. "The patriots are ruining me."

Alexander understood the war between profit and principle. He would never again work as a merchant if he could help it. There was no honor in it.

Now was his chance. He clutched his fist under the table, impatient to begin. He'd conjugated Greek grammar every morning on the ship's deck, babbling aloud like a madman, but was still far from competent to translate the *Iliad*, as he must do to win admission to college.

"Mama!" the little boy wailed. He had knocked his milk glass sideways and Alexander's plate was drenched along with the tablecloth.

"Jonathan!" Mulligan said sternly. "Again?"

Short Mrs. Mulligan flushed with embarrassment and tried to reach across the table with a napkin, though her heavy bosom impeded her progress.

Alexander took the linen from his lap and mopped the table. He was glad the boy had done it and not him.

"I spilled my milk so often when I was little that my mama purchased her own nanny goat." He pointed to his soupy plate. "Look. You made the trout swim again."

The little boy's eyes widened and the family burst into laughter.

A serving girl gave Alexander another plate of fish and ham.

"Reverend Knox suggested I apply to Elizabethtown Academy across the river," Alexander said. "May I ask your opinion, sir?"

"There's a fine man. I heard Reverend Knox give a sermon after he was ordained by Aaron Burr, head of the College of New Jersey before he died."

"Reverend Knox's sermons on St. Croix lifted me from despair many a time," Alexander said, "especially after our last hurricane."

"Your famous hurricane letter! My brother sent it." The tailor turned to his wife. "We read it in the Christiansted *Gazette*. Remember, Mary?"

Mrs. Mulligan gave her full attention to the conversation for the first time. "*The roaring of the sea was sufficient to strike astonishment into Angels*," she recited. "How ever do you find such beautiful phrases? You're just a sprout."

Alexander felt a swell of pride and then a blush, one of the curses of a Scottish complexion. Did she mean he was young—or was that a comment on his height?

Mulligan took another bread roll. "Elizabethtown is a fine grammar school," he said.

"Reverend Knox thinks it would ensure acceptance at King's, or even the College of New Jersey."

"You'd be moving in high society, that's certain. Lord Stirling's a patron, I believe."

"Lord Stirling?"

"Owner of the grandest estate in all New Jersey. Fancies himself a Scottish earl. Whatever he is, Stirling has the finest manor on the far side of the Hudson. Gardens, stables, even a deer park. Drives about in a coach-and-four with a coat of arms."

Alexander looked down. The buttons on the waistcoat didn't match the ones on the breeches. Shame swept over him. A less exalted school might be better.

"Mrs. Venton sent a sum for a new suit, by the by," Mulligan said, perhaps with a tailor's intuition. "You're to be properly kitted out. I'll let you have any fabric that tickles your imagination. Can't sell it anyway."

"Cousin Ann? She's been so good to me. Thank you for your kindness, too, Mr. Mulligan."

"Tell me. Which college are you aiming for?"

"I have a friend at King's, so I prefer it to New Jersey, but I'll enroll wherever I can graduate soonest."

Mrs. Mulligan signaled a servant to take the baby from the bassinet. "'Tis time for church, Mr. Mulligan."

The tailor laid his hand on the lid of the teapot. "It would be a cryin' shame to waste what's left, Molly my pet. What with tea so dear."

His wife folded her arms.

"Oh, well. Off to church with us, then," the tailor told Alexander. "And when the best part of the day is gone, we can take your measurements."

"Yes, sir." Alexander came around the table to pull out Mrs. Mulligan's chair. "I'll look forward to it."

To gaze up into one of the great steeples of Manhattan would be exhilarating. But it would be even better to have a gentleman's suit from Hercules Mulligan, Alexander thought. Then only manners could give away low birth, and he had polished his to a high sheen. No one need ever know the truth.

CHAPTER EIGHT

April 1773

Saratoga

"In sorrow thou shalt bring forth children."

Genesis 3:16, King James Bible

ELIZA HEARD THE SOUND OF SCURRYING in the hall but ignored it.

Angelica opened the door and came to sit on the bed. She held a book. Eliza glimpsed the title. *The Gypsy Countess*. Another romance novel.

"It's turned wrong," Angelica said.

Eliza slipped a finger into the Bible to save her place. It had been more than two years since a jury acquitted the perpetrators of the Boston Massacre, but those shocking events had changed the Good Book for her. Ancient stories of tyrants and martyrs seemed more real—and frightening. Her family remained on tenterhooks. "What's turned wrong?"

"The baby. I guess the baby has to be turned a particular way."

Eliza jerked up. The Bible tumbled to the floor and she leaned to retrieve it. They daren't offend Providence now. "Mama's baby is turned wrong?"

"That's what Diana says. What does that mean?"

Over supper their mother had complained that the baby left her no room to eat and excused herself to lie down. Eliza thought she was just overdue for peace and quiet. Philip Jeremiah—a bright, sunny boy who was a constant nuisance—had accidentally shattered a porcelain pitcher of milk cooling on the porch. Mama threw away his slingshot.

Eliza hadn't witnessed childbirth, but had seen Prince deliver colts. One time, the groom reached his arm up the mare's backside to turn the baby. His arm came out slick with blood. The colt must descend head first, he explained.

Angelica disliked the barn—she considered it dirty—and hadn't been there. For someone who daydreamed so much about courtship, Angelica understood less than her sixteen-year-old sister about its mortal hazards.

"Labor hasn't started, has it?" Eliza said. It upset her that Diana hadn't told them anything. They weren't children anymore and Papa was away in Albany.

"I don't think so. I overheard Diana talking to Maria a few minutes ago. They were whispering outside Mama's room, all quiet. But then Maria ran downstairs to get something, I guess. What did Diana mean?"

"The baby has to come out headfirst or it can get stuck."

Angelica looked shocked. "Is that what happened with Mama's first son?"

No one had ever explained about the baby brother who died when they were toddlers. Mama appeared upset if an aunt or cousin mentioned him, and neither Angelica nor Eliza felt they should ask.

"No," Eliza said. "It couldn't be."

"Why?"

"Because if the baby can't come out, the mother perishes, too."

Angelica said quickly, "They won't let Mama die, right?"

Eliza put an arm around Angelica's narrow shoulders and hugged her close. "No, of course not." Yet she felt a wave of vertigo and placed a hand on the nightstand. This was exactly how mothers died. "Diana and Maria always get Mama through."

Angelica shook off Eliza's arm and stood. "We've got to send to Albany for Papa. Now."

Eliza rose, too. "We must stay calm for Mama's sake." She thought of how Prince approached the mares, as if he had all the time in the world. They stopped rolling their eyes when he touched them. His quiet presence helped them ease out their foals. "Could you go downstairs and make sure Philip Jeremiah doesn't get into any more trouble? And ask Peggy to fetch Mrs. Cavan?"

"What about you?"

"I'll find Diana. Maybe Mama's time hasn't come. Babies usually turn on their own before labor starts."

"They do?"

"Of course." Eliza didn't know if this was right, but thought it must be.

When Angelica left, Eliza crossed the wide hall to their mother's room. The door was closed. She put her ear to it, but heard nothing.

Maria came around the corner with a basin of hot water and a white towel draped on one shoulder. She stopped short, startled. Water sloshed over the side. "Land sakes. What you doin', Missy?"

Married women wouldn't talk about childbirth. It was an unmentionable mystery. But Eliza wasn't going to stand for it any longer. She'd been to the barn. This was her mother. "Is Mama all right?"

"Don't you worry now. We're just getting ready. It's always good to be ready." The distracted housekeeper nodded in the direction of the empty parlor opposite. She forced a smile. "Why don't you finish up that embroidery you started yesterday?"

A scream broke out, making both women jump. Eliza turned the knob to her parents' bedroom.

Kitty Schuyler was propped against the headboard. Her long nightgown covered her knees, but the quilt had been pushed aside. Eyes closed, braids loose, her face knotted and glistening, she gripped Diana, who leaned awkwardly over the bed. The housekeeper appeared to be falling and Kitty Schuyler was trying to catch her by the shoulders. Then Eliza realized that her mother was actually clinging to Diana, whose ropy hands cradled the swollen belly. Neither noticed Eliza. Tears streaked Kitty Schuyler's face.

Eliza turned to Maria. "Have you sent for Master Schuyler?"

"Yes, Missy. We sent a messenger an hour ago."

Diana glanced over from the far side of the bed, her dark face grim and set. She shook her head at Eliza, then turned back to Kitty Schuyler.

"Just rest a minute, Miss Kitty," Diana purred, low and buttery. "That baby's gettin' ready. I can feel it. I want you to think about the day we took that picnic. You know. That picnic by the falls you liked so much."

Mama was breathing hard. She didn't seem to be thinking about any picnic. Her face slackened, then contorted into a tight mask.

"There now, Missy, there now," Diana said. Her pitch went up a notch.

Was that fear in the housekeeper's voice? Eliza took the chair next to the bed and wiped her mother's tears with a handkerchief. She kissed her brow, in which a purple vein throbbed. "Mama. I'm here."

After another tense minute, Kitty relaxed. "*Mijn lief*," she murmured. A moment later she dozed off.

"How long has she been like this?" Eliza whispered to Diana.

"A little more than an hour. We sent for Master Schuyler and the doctor." The housekeeper looked over her shoulder at the window behind, as if the men might materialize in it, then back at Eliza. "But she's coming on fast and that baby ain't turned yet. We gotta get it turned. Before it gets too far down."

The door opened. Hannah Cavan shut it behind her. The tenant farmer's wife walked briskly around the bed and placed her hand on Diana's shoulder. Heads together, they consulted too quietly for Eliza to catch their words. Mrs. Cavan turned to Eliza. "You need to wait downstairs."

Eliza took her mother's limp hand. "My place is here."

Mrs. Cavan shook her head. "No. 'Tisn't seemly. She wouldn't want you here."

"She knows I'm here."

Kitty Schuyler grimaced again and a cry escaped her lips. Her shoulders heaved and she curled as far forward as her belly allowed. A pillow dropped to the floor. Eliza picked it up and tucked it behind her mother.

After a tortured pause, Kitty Schuyler slumped back. She took a deep breath and opened her eyes. "Eliza," she said with a faint smile, then jerked her hand away. Her wild eyes darted to Diana and Mrs. Cavan. "Please . . . she shouldn't see this."

"Miss Schuyler!" There wasn't a hair was out of place in Hannah Cavan's severe bun. "We need you to watch the other children."

"My older sister is downstairs, Mrs. Cavan, and I am not one of the children. I'm sixteen." Eliza laid her hand lightly on her mother's shoulder and leaned closer. "*Moeder*, I'm not leaving you."

Kitty Schuyler closed her eyes, too tired to argue.

"Here, Miss Kitty," Diana said. "Let's make you more comfortable. Let's lie a little more flat." She took an elbow and nodded at Eliza, who took away the pillows. Kitty Schuyler inched downward.

Maria set the basin of hot water on a nightstand. Diana lifted a steaming cloth and wrung it out. She pulled Kitty's nightgown up, revealing the high, pink dome. A charcoal-colored line ran down the taut skin, pointing toward the place from which the baby must emerge. Eliza had never seen her mother's naked belly nor imagined such a line.

"This towel is nice and warm, Missy. Just like the day we took that picnic. Remember how nice that was?" Diana draped the cloth across the taut abdomen.

Eliza stroked her mother's brow, willing her to relax. *Don't be afraid, don't be afraid*, she prayed—not knowing if she was talking to herself or her mother.

Maria dunked another cloth in the basin. She wrung it into a corkscrew and held it out to Diana to trade. Kitty appeared to be asleep.

After a few more towels, the heat-mottled dome softened. Then it rippled. What could only be a foot or elbow glided under the surface.

The huddled women gasped. Side by side, Diana and Mrs. Cavan leaned forward as if on cue and began kneading Kitty's right side, pushing upward on the abdomen with the heels of their hands.

The belly hardened and darkened. Kitty opened her eyes and twisted away. She moaned and tried to sit. Unable to bend upward, pinned by her burden, she curled sideways into the pain.

Maria put another towel into the basin, which sent up fresh steam. She must have gone out for more hot water, though Eliza hadn't noticed her leaving or returning. The image of Philip Jeremiah breaking a pitcher earlier that day came to mind. It seemed a lifetime ago.

"That's right, Missy. Just lie down," Diana said when the contraction subsided and the laboring woman fell back again. Diana placed another warm towel on the stomach. Why was the baby motionless? The skin seemed ready to split.

Eliza looked to Mrs. Cavan and Diana, but neither met her eyes. Maria stared into the basin.

Perhaps Prince could help, Eliza thought. He'd gotten the calf out. In the same desperate instant, she realized Mama would rather die than have him see her like this.

Diana and Mrs. Cavan began kneading again. They didn't replace the towel. Time must be growing short. The midwives' strong hands worked steadily. In slow, coordinated waves, the heels of their palms traced a path up Mama's side to a spot just below the crown of her stomach. They repeated the procedure. Then again. Then again. Nothing moved. The trapped baby was still.

Kitty Schuyler was dying.

Eliza drew her mother's sweaty tangles aside and massaged her temples. Eliza's heart pounded so fiercely that she felt it in her throat, heard it in her ears, but she spoke in the calmest voice she possessed. "Remember the picnic, Mama. We were all there. Papa, too. Papa was there. It was such—such a peaceful day."

Kitty Schuyler sucked in a deep breath. Her belly rose high and the towel slid to the floor. A series of appearing and disappearing lumps moved across her stomach and the child inside rotated, Diana's broad hand guiding it into position. Tears started down Eliza's cheeks.

Hannah Cavan moved to the foot of the bed. Diana lifted Kitty Schuyler by one armpit and nodded to Eliza, who took the other. They pulled her upright. Mrs. Cavan shoved Kitty Schuyler's trembling legs until they bent, and knelt between her knees. "It's time, Mrs. Schuyler," she said.

Eliza's mother opened her eyes. Pain etched deep lines in her face, but she was alert now and looked as focused as if threading a needle.

Would the baby live?

Eliza didn't know. She just needed her mother to.

CHAPTER NINE

May 1775

New York City

"I must study Politicks and War that my sons may have liberty to study Mathematicks and Philosophy."

John Adams, 1780

ALEXANDER PEEKED AT HIS NOTES AND began the verse again. Pacing with long strides, he finished the stanza from Cicero without a single slip. His Latin tutor at King's would be pleased—if the stubborn man wasn't hanged first. Alexander bit his thumbnail in consternation. Brilliant Myles Cooper couldn't see the mob headed his way.

Purple lilacs sweetened the air of sunrise, though Alexander barely saw them as he walked along the Hudson two years after his first breakfast in New York. His confidence had grown enormously since then, once it became clear he wasn't inferior to his richer, better prepared schoolmates. King's College, housed in a three-story building on Park Place, no longer intimidated him, though he could hardly believe the magnificent campus stood atop an Indian trail that once ran the length of the island. Everything about New York seemed sophisticated and eternal—the Rome of the New World.

The river trail was deserted at dawn and there was no one to resent Alexander's reciting aloud, a practice that provoked his roommate, Robert Troup. Robert and he had learned on their first night at King's that both were without family—dependent on scholarships and quick wits—and it had united them. They laughed at the same jokes and admired the same flirty debutantes. But they felt differently about sleep. When bell rang for morning chapel, Alexander purloined the sheets lest Robert find his way into the headmaster's book for truancy. If Alexander even muttered to himself before dawn, Robert became unaccountably irate. Otherwise, they complemented one another like pen and paper.

Volatile events had deepened their friendship. Not long after Alexander arrived, rebels attacked ships in Boston and New York and threw valuable tea overboard. They sank an amount that would have kept St. Croix cozy for a year. Parliament was incensed. King George closed the bustling port of Boston until the patriots made restitution. Redcoats followed.

In their cramped quarters, Alexander and Robert started a debating society that included Neddy Stevens from Christiansted, finishing up his medical studies at King's. At first, Alexander had been reluctant to condone protesters bent on destroying other people's property. He knew how hard it was to sustain a business. He'd never forget what Mama had said. "*If a thief steals one ribbon, we must sell twenty to make up the loss*." Yet he gradually came to see the colonies' struggle as one for justice—and justice was the breath of life.

The British Constitution was a marvel of fairness, Alexander said to the circle of young men whose heads increasingly turned in his direction, but it had little meaning if Parliament refused to apply the law in America. Robert Troup, a native New Yorker who understood local resentments in his bones, insisted not long afterward that Alexander address a mass assembly of tradesmen gathered on the commons to support the rebellious Bostonians.

"You'll say it best!" Robert shouted in Alexander's ear over the roar of the crowd as they elbowed their way forward. Robert pushed his West Indian roommate toward the crude speakers' platform. "We all know you're the genius."

Alexander hesitated, surprised again at his classmate's unshakeable confidence in him, then scrambled onto the waist-high stage when a man reached down his hand. Neddy passed the word that the orator was a student just turned eighteen.

Alexander almost lost his nerve when the sea of strange faces swung toward him. He opened his mouth and closed it. No words came. His heart skipped strangely. He felt speechless. These were grown men who had lived in America all their lives. This was their country. What did he know? Who was he, but an outsider? An ill-born islander? Dorm-room arguments clamored vainly in his head.

The crowd shouted encouragement. Someone yelled, "Quiet! Listen to the collegian."

Alexander caught the eye of a threadbare boy next to the stand. The solemn youth seemed peculiarly expectant. As if waiting for someone to speak on behalf of those like him who didn't have a chance. Boys like James Hamilton. Boys like Ajax. Girls like young Rachel Lavien.

Truth was universal, Alexander realized as he returned his gaze to the crowd hungry for hope, hungry for direction. As valid in Christiansted as all Christendom. So he began to speak, and once he did, the words poured forth.

They were born free, he told them. They were as worthy as men anywhere. They deserved respect, not abuse. Parliament acted as if it had the power of the Grand Mogul, but it didn't. If the people of New York had no voice in the law, it wasn't their law.

Alexander felt he knew every face and each was a brother. They were men of dignity despite misfortune, ready to stand up for what was right. New Yorkers must unite with Bostonians, Alexander told the rapt crowd. They must hold firm, or "*power and oppression shall triumph over right, justice, happiness, and freedom!*"

The crowd whistled and yelled and clapped until Alexander's ears rang. When he jumped down, he was so overwhelmed that he scarcely recalled a word he had said. After a childhood of illegitimacy in which law trampled the voiceless—and he had been unable to protect even his mother—he found he could defend the honor of men and women everywhere. It was transforming, redeeming.

Alexander's career as a propagandist might have ended there, though, consumed as he was with classes, had an anonymous Tory pamphleteer not denounced the patriots as a "venomous brood of scorpions" a few months later. Cutting off trade with England lined the pockets of greedy merchants who hiked prices on scarce goods, the man wrote. Farmers couldn't buy the simple things they needed from abroad. The boys of the King's College debating society waited for a rapier rejoinder by someone of property and standing, but the outrageous accusations went unanswered.

Robert and Neddy again urged Alexander to speak up. He knew what to say, they insisted. So Alexander sharpened his quill and penned a pamphlet of his own.

The Tory said reasonable men would petition, not fight. But the colonists had petitioned Parliament for eight years. "*What petitions can we offer that have not already been offered?*" And the problem was not merely taxes on tea, but Parliament's insistence that it had the right to tax Americans on anything and everything it wanted to. If New Yorkers didn't act like men, Parliament would invent taxes willy-nilly. It might tax families on knives, forks, beds, and even offspring. It might tax fathers for every kiss their daughters received from their sweethearts—"*and God knows, that would soon ruin you.*"

The witty pamphlet created a sensation. It sold out in two days. When the Tory propagandist dashed off a stinging reply that mocked his opponent as a dullard, Alexander followed his first thirty-page essay with one more biting. "*Though I am naturally of a grave and phlegmatic disposition*," the Tory's ignorant, "puerile" rejoinder had been "*the source of abundant merriment to me.*"

Robert and Neddy laughed so hard at the first draft that a student in the next room banged on the wall.

"Isn't *puerile* a bit harsh?" Neddy asked when he recovered.

"Not when it's true!" Alexander and Robert said in unison.

Alexander studded the lengthy pamphlet with data he found in the College library. But his favorite phrases required no research. *"The sacred rights of mankind are not to be rummaged for among old parchments or musty records. They are written, as with a sunbeam, in the whole volume of human nature by the hand of divinity itself and can never be erased."*

He had penned that for Mama, cold in her grave, and the heartless judge on St. Croix.

Alexander hadn't signed his name, as was customary in politics, but friends again spread word that a young King's College student had authored the pamphlet. "Poppycock!" one professor said when Robert Troup hinted that charity-student Alexander Hamilton was behind the widely admired piece.

But the literary effort had played havoc with Alexander's exams and study of medicine. Worse, he wasn't sure what unpredictable forces he'd helped unleash.

He stopped in the middle of the riverside path, distressed anew. Poor, stubborn Myles Cooper. It had been Alexander's Latin tutor—also president of King's College—who assigned Robert and Alexander as roommates, intuiting that orphans would understand one another. Now the same Myles Cooper faced threats on his life for criticizing the patriots. Why didn't the rebels understand that loyalists also had a right to their opinions? Why didn't Myles Cooper have a lick of sense?

A songbird warbled in the lilacs and alerted Alexander that he would soon be tardier to class than Robert. He bounded up the path and into the lane where prostitutes twitched at students' breeches after dark, causing many to forget promises they had made their mothers. At least one enchanting damsel had caused Alexander to feel contrite and he didn't even have a mother. The shabby cottages flashed by. He might just reach chapel before second bell.

But Alexander found a tall Negro unblocking the entrance at the top of the college steps. Some scalawag had piled a wall of dressed stone in front of the closed gates.

"May I help?" Alexander said and hauled on a stone.

"I'm happy for all the help I can get," came the cheerful reply.

Alexander looked again and realized it was the colored boy who supplied the students' coal bins and cleaned the library. Alexander had once spied him reading spines while he dusted the books. Twelve or thirteen, he appeared older from behind because of his unusual height and heft. Although he had the broad cheekbones of a West African, his open countenance revealed he wasn't a slave. Such facts were stamped in a person's expression—or Alexander hadn't been raised in the sugar islands.

Alexander shifted the heavy block. It slid into his arms and he carried it slowly down the steps, careful not to lose his balance.

The young laborer worked at the wall's other end. As Alexander began back up the stairs, the boy ran down with a stone under either arm. He moved as if he could carry three, had he cared to show off.

By the end of fifteen minutes the gates were free. Alexander's waistcoat was covered with dust and he was hopelessly late. Tardy or absent, he was in trouble. He decided to skip chapel to finish an overdue math assignment.

"Thank you, sir," the boy said. "That was mighty helpful."

"I'd say it was my pleasure, but I hate to tell a lie. You refill our coal hoppers, if I'm not mistaken."

"Yes, sir, Mr. Hamilton. I serve everyone who quarters at King's."

"I'm sorry. You know my name, but I don't know yours."

The boy brushed his palms on his trousers and shook Alexander's hand. "Ajax Manly. Pleased to meet you, sir."

The name was an unpleasant jolt.

"Ajax?"

"Yessir. My parents named me for the strong man in Greek times. I 'spose they guessed right cause I'm stronger than anybody I know."

The boast added to Alexander's consternation. The colored boy sounded just like Ajax. The other Ajax. The only Ajax that Alexander cared to know. This servant was so patently alive and well—sturdy and free—that it hurt merely to gaze upon him.

"Thank you for clearing the gate. I'd best get to chapel," Alexander said, then turned away.

He would go to morning prayers after all. There was a reason why men began each day asking God's forgiveness. He could never forgive himself.

The banging later that evening was so startling that Alexander let out an involuntary yelp. The candle had burned low as he hunched over his last geometry problems. Robert Troup was asleep.

"Open up!" The voice was panicked.

Robert bolted upright in bed, his tangled hair loose in its ribbon. "What is it?"

Alexander opened the door. Nicholas Ogden, a recent graduate, stumbled in. His tie was askew. Alexander smelled rum.

"They're on their way! You've got to help!"

"Who's on their way?"

"The crowd . . . from the village. They've got torches and tar." Ogden gasped for air. His chest heaved.

Robert swung his legs over the side of the bed and tripped over a mound of laundry. He pulled at a pair of trousers.

"Have you warned Cooper?" Alexander said.

It was the moment they had feared since they saw leaflets blaming Myles Cooper for the deaths at Lexington and Concord. As if a Tory in New York had any connection with British officers suppressing rebellion in Massachusetts. But the mob didn't care. "Fly for your life or anticipate doom," a broadside warned. The proud professor refused to leave.

"No. I ran from the tavern. I saw the torches through the window."

"Go!" Alexander said. Ogden disappeared.

Alexander glanced around for a weapon, but realized in the same instant that any such object would brand him a Tory.

"Go with Nick," Alexander told Robert, now dressed. "Get Cooper out the back. I'll hold them."

The roar of the mob grew audible. Nightmarish flickers lit the window and glowed on the walls of the room. Alexander ran down the dark hall toward the front entrance. "What's wrong?" someone called from another chamber. Alexander didn't recognize the sleep-coarsened voice. He slipped the bolt, stepped outside into the coolness, and closed the door behind him, hoping someone inside would have the presence of mind to bolt the entrance.

The oncoming crowd stretched as far as Alexander could see. Some men gripped muskets but most wielded brands that flamed with pitch. The stink of tar filled the night air. Tree trunks glimmered like ghosts. The mob was bigger than he'd expected. Fear sent his heart racing. He would never hold them.

"Stop," he shouted, though he barely heard his voice over the tumult. He threw out a hand. "Stop!"

Alexander couldn't discern individual faces. He must have surprised them because the closest ruffians halted briefly. The horde soon swarmed the yard in front of the stoop.

"Outta the way, boy!"

"Clear out—or take your last breath!" someone else shouted. A gun went off. A man near the front carried a noose.

Alexander must hold them or Myles Cooper would die. "Brothers! Stop for the sake of justice."

A protester with biceps that bulged through the weave of his laborer's jersey placed a rough boot on the bottom stair. He held a musket and appeared to be their leader. "We only want Cooper. Give us Myles Cooper."

Someone began a chant. "Give us Cooper! Give us Cooper!"

Alexander shouted back at the throng. "We must honor those killed at Lexington and Concord!" He felt the heat of the torches on his cheeks. "The blood of patriots is sacred. It must be avenged."

"Let's do it, then! Out of our way," someone called.

"We avenge the fallen by honoring their cause, not disgracing it. Don't betray those who died for self-government and trial by jury! The world will say you acted like Redcoats. Take my life but don't injure liberty."

A man who reeked of alcohol jumped up the stair to snatch at Alexander's waistcoat. "We don't want you, ya privileged bastard!"

Alexander slapped the hand aside at the insult, and the man fell backward, vanishing under the swell.

The mob roared. Alexander felt fingers grab his clothes, fists yank him downward into the melee. A hard elbow caught the back of his head and his teeth knocked together violently. Where was the man with the rope? Was this the end?

Then the protester in the common jersey clasped Alexander around the waist with one arm. He was carried backward off his feet while the crowd of protesters, now berserk, heaved and passed around them.

The burly fellow dropped Alexander in a corner. "We've not come for pampered dandies like you. It's the bloody Tories we're after. They'll not get away."

Alexander shrank against the wall and the man was gone. He hoped to God that Myles Cooper was, too. If not, the college president was doomed.

CHAPTER TEN

August 1775

Albany

"I was prepossessed in favor of this young lady the moment I saw her. A brunette with the most good-natured lively dark eyes I ever saw."

From the Journal of Lt. Colonel Tench Tilghman, 1775

"PAPA, TELL US AGAIN!" PHILIP JEREMIAH said.

"General Washington's uniform was the same color as mine. Blue and buff." Papa placed his hand on the head of his son, who sat on the floor. "But he also wore a wide purple sash and a hat with a giant plume. He was splendid."

The excitable seven-year-old couldn't hear enough stories about the Continental troops, Eliza observed with an older sister's condescension, though she, too, wished she'd seen the parade.

Eliza pictured the scene: the wharf bedecked with flowers and the dignitaries lined up to receive the dashing officers of the Continental Army arriving from Philadelphia. Papa said all of New York turned out to greet the rebels—and then prudently turned out again when a British man-of-war sailed up the Hudson that same afternoon. The family only heard about it afterward. Papa had been plain Colonel Schuyler when he left Albany three months earlier to attend the Continental Congress. Now he was a general. And a renegade, though no one said that aloud.

Philip Jeremiah's eyes were wide. "Did you ride next to him?"

"Charles Lee and I rode a few paces back. The commander-in-chief outranks a major general. We all have our station."

Eliza caught the undertone but her brother threw up his arms up triumphantly. "And yours is next to General Washington! 'Cause you're Commander of the North."

"Pride goeth before a fall, son."

Eliza again heard the unstated worry. The Continental Congress had given her father command of the northern front yet failed to provide funds to train New Englanders who, it turned out, resented orders from a New Yorker.

That morning, Eliza had heard Papa tell Mama over coffee, "They call me a Dutchman. And a Tory!"

Mama's eyes filled with sympathy. Perhaps to avoid salting Papa's wounds, she didn't bring up the money they had loaned the army to buy blankets.

"Hardly a one will keep to his station, and the New Englanders scorn drilling as tyranny. Every rebel thinks he's entitled to an opinion—and to quit if it doesn't become policy. The militia must be placated, Congress petitioned. I swear Job himself would lose his temper."

Mama started to pour more coffee, but Papa jumped to his feet.

"Officers in the Continental Army don't command. They beg," he said, and stalked out to plan the harvest he would miss. From what Eliza understood, Congress expected General Schuyler's rag-tag army to capture Canada by Christmas: a thousand Continentals against ten thousand Redcoats.

She was glad her father had come home for a couple of days, even if only to meet with their Iroquois allies.

His mood was better now as he sat telling stories to Philip Jeremiah while waiting for Mama to come down. The Van Cortlandts had invited her parents to dine.

"Ready, Kitty dear?" Papa said when Mama finally entered. She looked especially well in the burgundy-colored English velvet that Papa bought her after the baby came. The delivery had nearly taken her life, and Papa ignored non-importation for once to see his Kitty smile again.

"Yes," she said. "The little imp finally nodded off at the breast. It's the only way I can get him to stop wiggling. The minute he does, he falls asleep as if I had given him a potion."

"And you have, my love," Papa said.

After her parents left, Philip Jeremiah went outside and Eliza again took up the *Gazette*. Before Papa's commission, the turbulence seemed far away. A few daring youths rigged up a Liberty Pole in Albany, but Sheriff White promptly chopped it down. Now, all around her, men of the colony were bitterly divided. Some had crossed the line into treason while others defended the king. Eliza read compulsively.

She gleaned that the Tories hoped the British Army would invade south from Canada, through the Mohawk Valley, then down to Saratoga. If they proceeded from there to Albany, they would create a firebreak between the flammable northern colonies and the calmer south. The rebellion would be extinguished. Men who had supported it, like her father, would be hunted down.

Eliza looked out the window at the gray-blue Hudson. Water birds that normally darted in and out of the rushes had retired in the oppressive heat. At eighteen, she was old enough to know that if Redcoats took Saratoga and Albany, they would seize the Schuyler estates with their commanding positions facing the river in both towns. Britain's path to victory ran right through her life.

She tried not to be frightened. Of course her father would prevail.

The front door knocker sounded.

Peggy flew into the salon in a rustle of taffeta at the same moment and looked out the window. The tucked waist of her sister's dress flattered her new figure, and Eliza noticed she was experimenting with rouge.

"It's Mr. Livingston with the young gentleman from the Indian commission. I spied them from upstairs. I told Pompey to bring peach ices. Maybe they'll stay."

"Goodness, Peggy. Not so loud or they'll hear."

Eliza hadn't yet seen the Congressional delegation that had sailed upriver to Albany, though she knew Judge Livingston, who taught her to play checkers when she was little. The commissioners were touring the countryside to summon the Six Nations. Peggy glimpsed them when they arrived a week earlier, and reported that the youngest commissioner was extraordinarily handsome. That had been her very word. *Extraordinarily*. Peggy was half as well read as Angelica and twice as coquettish. The variables might be related, Eliza thought.

A servant ushered the two gentlemen into the blue parlor. Eliza set aside her paper and stood.

"Judge Livingston. What an honor." Eliza gave her hand to England's former admiralty officer, turned outlaw with half of America.

"Miss Betsey! I hardly recognize you, so grown up. Are you mistress of the manor today or is your father somewhere about?"

"My parents are visiting the Van Cortlandts. They'll be sorely disappointed to have missed you, sir."

"I'm not sorry at all," the elderly judge said with a courtly bow all the more touching for its stiffness. "It's not often enough that we're privileged to converse with young ladies. Please allow me to present Tench Tilghman of Maryland. Mr. Tilghman—Miss Elizabeth Schuyler and her younger sister, Margaret. The finest-tempered girls in the world."

Eliza curtseyed and smiled. "Thank you, Judge Livingston."

Tench Tilghman bowed to the girls. He had the studied poise of a military officer and a dimpled, boyish smile. His eyes were large and gray. They sparkled with interest. Eliza didn't think him *extraordinarily* handsome, though he was pleasant to look at. She wondered why she didn't feel Peggy's excitement. Perhaps she was too choosy.

"Verra pleased to meet you," Tilghman said with a Maryland drawl. "This is a rare treat, indeed, to see such beauty conjoined with kindness. I feel doubly fortunate."

Tilghman was gracious and his finely stitched suit befitted a gentleman of means.

"Please join us for refreshments," Eliza said. She gestured to a large wing chair. "Judge Livingston, you must take my father's place and regale us with your adventures. Have you convinced the Iroquois to attend your assembly?"

Livingston sat with the aid of a cane while the young people arranged themselves on damask settees that matched the blue silk wallpaper and Delft porcelain above the fireplace of the formal parlor. Like Papa, the judge suffered from gout. He immediately put his foot on a stool.

"We're making excellent progress with the savages despite all the British are doing to stir up trouble."

"Do you think the Iroquois shall remain neutral, then?" Eliza said.

Pompey entered the room with a tray of small frosted goblets filled with peach-flavored ice shavings. The underground icehouse was nearing empty, but they still had a few blocks on straw left over from winter.

"I believe so," Livingston said as he took a glass. "Your father's renown with the Mohawks should help. They certainly don't want to raise the hatchet. I think we shall see at least five hundred at our conclave. Mostly Oneidas and Tuscaroras. The good Lord providing, the League will stay out of the war." Livingston took a bite with the tiny silver spoon. "This is marvelous in the heat."

Eliza looked to the young Southerner, who appeared to be enjoying the ice, as well. "Is this your first time in Albany, Mr. Tilghman?"

"It is." He placed his empty goblet on the table. "I find the Mohawks terribly interesting. And the countryside is marvelous. What fertile bottomlands you have."

Eliza could just hear Angelica's pert retort. *Bottomlands*—in a family of five women. She noticed red patches starting at the young commissioner's collar. Perhaps he recognized the unintentional double entendre.

Peggy sat on the edge of the sofa. "Have you seen Cohoes Falls, Mr. Tilghman?"

"No, Miss Schuyler," he said. "Are they nearby?"

"Only a few miles from Albany, where the Mohawk meets the Hudson. They're even wider than Niagara." Peggy glanced at Eliza.

"We must take you, Mr. Tilghman," Eliza said. "Might you be free for a jaunt? I'm sure we could get up a party to make the trip."

"Yes. That would be delightful." Tilghman turned to his companion. "That is, if you can spare me, Judge."

Livingston placed his glass on the silver tray. "Of course, Mr. Tilghman. We await the Indians anyway, and at my age I welcome opportunities to recuperate from the road. Indeed, I'd better rest before supper." He braced his cane between his legs and stood. "Thank you for your hospitality, my dears."

Eliza rose and kissed his papery cheek. "You're most welcome, Judge. I hope you'll come again." She felt Peggy's eyes on her. "Shall we meet tomorrow morning, then, Mr. Tilghman?"

"Absolutely. The Furies themselves couldn't keep me away."

"I don't believe you need to worry, then. They aren't normally seen in Albany," Eliza said. She looked over at Peggy, who smiled down at the calling card Tilghman handed her.

It was unfortunate, therefore, that dawn found the third Schuyler daughter on her knees retching into a chamber pot. Eliza held back Peggy's long tresses.

"Are you . . ." Eliza began, but Peggy clutched her stomach and retched again.

Eliza rang the bellpull at the bedside and Maria appeared moments later.

"Oh, Miz Peggy. Is that your monthly?"

"I'm really not—" Peggy said, but then lay down on the rug and closed her eyes.

They each took an arm to help her into bed.

"You jest rest, missy. I'm gonna get you some tea," Maria said as she left the room. "Real tea. Not that sassafras."

Peggy curled onto her side under the covers. She opened one eye and looked at Eliza. "Just go," she said miserably.

Eliza knew words would only deepen the disappointment, so she tucked the blanket around her sister and closed the door.

An hour later, three open carriages, including the family's fashionable phaeton, pulled away from the Albany manor. Eliza's mother appeared happy to see at least one of her girls in the company of such an eligible bachelor, and waved from the porch as they left.

Eliza had expected Tench Tilghman to ride with her. But he brought his own chaise and before she could rethink seating arrangements, Peggy's best friend, Laurie Lynch, hurried into the chaise next to him. Mrs. Huger and Roy Cuyler, a local youth, joined Eliza in the Schuyler phaeton. Roy's mother went in yet another carriage with Laurie Lynch's mother. Eliza feared the girl would talk their guest deaf, and he might regret the cost of the picnic basket he had brought, but the wind blew back snatches of laughter.

They arrived at the thunderous cataract shortly before lunch. "Would you like my arm?" Mr. Tilghman called over the deafening water as Eliza started down the path to the base of the immense waterfall. The boulder-strewn descent was treacherous and Eliza had worn laced boots. Giant potholes sometimes trapped turtles and water snakes when the river ran low at this time of the summer. She glanced back over her shoulder and shook her head with a smile.

"Are you certain you don't need help?" Tilghman shouted.

Eliza looked at the Southerner and Laurie Lynch poking their way down. Behind them, Roy Cuyler had his mother on one arm. He clutched her parasol in his other hand.

"No, thank you. I'm well used to country trails," she called back over the roar.

Eliza smiled as she skipped down the trail. The ladies would be more sure-footed if they wore boots instead of garden slippers. Then it occurred to her that Laurie Lynch had chosen dainty footwear precisely so she could lean on Tench Tilghman.

The group explored the riverbank for the better part of an hour once everyone had descended. The spray wetted their faces and Eliza found an enormous black pothole, though she spied no lurking creatures in its inky depths. When they trudged back up the slope, Mr. Tilghman and Miss Lynch nearly took a spill when his boot slipped on loose rock. By the time the party reached the top, everyone had amply earned their supper.

Laurie Lynch told the Iroquois tale of Cohoes Falls while they ate. There, the Great Peacemaker—Deganawida, in the tongue of the Mohawks—had supposedly convinced the warring Six Nations to bury their differences in the mists of time.

"Not the mists of the cataract?" Tilghman said.

Laurie Lynch brushed a blonde lock from her pale forehead and smiled. "Both!"

"I had an Iroquois name given me when I was a girl," Eliza said. "*One-of-Us*."

"I have an Iroquois name, too," Tilghman said, "though not one I'd care to repeat."

The party immediately pressed him to do so.

Tilghman rested a tankard of ale on a muscular thigh encased in close-fitting leggings. "It's not official, but I apparently made a favorable impression on the Onondagas. The chief proposes to adopt me—and honor me with a wife and a new name."

"That's wonderful news, my fellow Iroquois," Eliza said. "We'll be cousins."

"Kissing cousins, I hope." Tilghman's eyes were playful.

"Fie, sir! You may only kiss your Indian wife," Laurie said. "Eliza and I shall stand as bridesmaids. Shan't we, Eliza?"

"With pleasure. Your nuptials will be the highlight of Albany's summer season."

"I don't see how you can object, Mr. Tilghman," Roy Cuyler said, "not that you'll want to. You've seen their young beauties, haven't you?"

Tilghman heaved a dramatic sigh. "But you haven't heard the name."

Stout Mrs. Cuyler took another biscuit. She held her parasol with her other hand. "Goodness, Mr. Tilghman. Stop toying with us. Out with it."

"I don't recall the pronunciation. Te-ho-ka-something. It means 'large horns.'" Tilghman pointed to his temples. "Don't tell me I have a set sprouting already."

The young people at the party burst out laughing. Mrs. Cuyler nearly choked on her biscuit, tears of amusement starting in her eyes, and Roy reached over to pat his mother on the back, though she waved him away and dabbed at her eyes with her old-fashioned apron.

"Oh, dear," Eliza said. "That cannot bode well for your marriage."

"Betrayed before wedded or bedded," Laurie said, sailing even closer to impropriety, though Albany society accorded wit a generous berth.

"Did you hear about the husband who despised cuckolds so greatly that he declared they should all be thrown in the river?" Roy Cuyler said. "His wife asked why he would say such a thing when he couldn't swim."

Tilghman smiled. "The Onondaga warrior assured me the name is a compliment. The deer is the coat of arms of his tribe, so to speak. But for an Englishman, it's rather troubling."

"Then I foresee no problem, Mr. Te-ho-ka-ka," Eliza said.

"And why is that, Miz Betsey?"

Tilghman leaned closer. He looked at her with a teasing smile that expressed a willingness to find whatever she said amusing. His eyes hinted there was much he found attractive.

But Eliza wasn't sure she wished to encourage him.

Laurie Lynch appeared enamored with the mild-mannered young diplomat, which gave her pause. More important, she simply felt like leaning back when he leaned forward. Perhaps Tilghman wasn't her type. That stranger, the one who sometimes visited her daydreams, would be loving and kind—but also daring and bold. He would have a harder edge. He wouldn't be ordinary. He didn't exist.

Eliza realized she had lost the thread. She smiled mysteriously until Roy Cuyler prompted her.

"Yes, why?" Roy said. "Being cuckolded is an Englishman's worst fate."

Eliza remembered. "Because Mr. Tilghman is no longer an Englishman."

"True," Laurie Lynch said. "We're all Americans now."

The Irish blonde with the turned-up nose sat straighter. She added, with a glance at Tilghman, "And what ladies *desire* most—the men who inspire fidelity—are those who cannot be shot in the back."

Eliza now knew why Peggy enjoyed Laurie Lynch. The girl had gumption. But her allusion to cowardice nonetheless reminded them all of the looming war. Most colonists considered dishonor worse than death. "You shall never blush for me," General Richard Montgomery assured his wife before marching north alongside Papa.

Mrs. Lynch and Mrs. Cuyler began packing the remains of the picnic baskets. Tench Tilghman gave Eliza a lingering look that suggested he wished she could ride with him, and on a whim—he was handsome, after all—she asked Laurie Lynch to trade coaches with her.

"Of course, Miss Schuyler," the blond said, though her shoulders slumped when the moment came to step into the phaeton.

No one mentioned the storm clouds gathering at the margins of the sunny sky.

CHAPTER ELEVEN

September 1776

Island of Manhattan

"British soldiers were landing at the foot of a road perhaps three-quarters of a mile south of Brooklyn Ferry. . . . [T]heir burnished arms which came in contact with the rays of a brilliant morning sun . . . gleamed like sheets of fire."

Samuel DeForest, 1776, *The Revolution Remembered*

THE BOOM OF ARTILLERY DROWNED OUT everything in the smoky twilight. Alexander had to shout directly into his men's ears to be heard. The shriek of cannonballs from the Royal Navy—which had pushed Washington's troops out of the burning city—obliterated the sound of their own guns, though Alexander saw his men light their fuses and witnessed the bright explosions that followed.

Retreat and retreat.

When Alexander had marched with other students on the parade ground that spring, and talked his way into captaincy of a New York artillery unit with tips from an old drill book he found in the library, he hadn't envisioned covering the retreat of General Washington's regular army, pushed relentlessly by lethal British

Regulars. Now there was nowhere else he wished to be, not even if it offered higher rank. Lord Stirling, whom Alexander had met at Elizabethtown Academy before entering King's College, was impressed by his pamphlets before the war. A colonel, Stirling had offered the college student a desk assignment with a major's enviable stripes. "I need your pen and wits," Lord Stirling told Alexander. But the flattering staff proposal held no temptation compared with action in the field, where death threatened and martial daring changed the battle. Only there could Alexander prove his mettle.

He had seen his college shuttered, his city evacuated, the army's position destroyed, Congress declare independence, the Royal Navy invade with three hundred bristling warships—and now this, straight from the Inferno.

The gun on his left was nothing more than tangled metal. Lord Stirling had ordered Alexander to hold the hill until General Washington's forces retreated to the forested safety of Harlem Heights. He was determined to do so or die young.

Earlier that afternoon, panicked militiamen had fled the city with their officers chasing rather than leading them. Indian allies in war paint melted silently into the trees. The army's regular troops stayed together but even their lines were ragged. Americans were outnumbered and outmaneuvered. General Washington had ridden behind the earthworks of Alexander's brigade roughly an hour earlier, though it was hard to gauge the passage of time, which moved with excruciating slowness when his men fumbled to reload and with horrible rapidity when they absorbed British fire.

Fixed in Alexander's mind was the sight of Washington swirling his horse around three tired militiamen who had dropped their muskets to share a jug of whiskey. Alexander couldn't hear whatever oaths the general was shouting as he brandished his whip over them, but he looked like Zeus destroying mortals who had disappointed him.

Then a massive ball cut the man next to Alexander in half, and the shock riveted his attention once more on the massive flotilla commanding Kip's Bay just two hundred yards away, on Manhattan's eastern shore.

A brief thunderstorm came up late in the afternoon, dispelling some of the heat and smoke but pouring water down Alexander's neck. The light grew dim. He glanced now at the powder kegs over which his men had pitched a tarp. Three barrels were almost empty, but a fourth was still sealed. They would have to abandon the big guns once they received the order to retreat. The heavier pieces couldn't be rolled fast enough to escape the British on their tail. The brigade's three light fieldpieces were salvageable, though, and they might manage the keg of fresh powder.

Alexander felt a tug on his sleeve. He leaned toward it, keeping his eyes trained on the warships he was trying to deter from disgorging more Royal Marines.

"Lord Stirling orders the retreat!" a messenger roared in his ear.

Alexander nodded once and ran up the line, shouting to his sergeants since his first lieutenant had been killed. When he got to the last gun crew, the British bombardment came to a halt and, strangely, he heard the sound of his own voice clearly for the first time in hours.

"Harness the fieldpieces. Abandon the big guns. Get moving! Make it orderly."

It occurred to him that the abrupt cessation signified a repositioning that would soon rain death from a different angle. They must head for Harlem immediately.

Alexander ran back to the tall soldier who had brought the orders. The man's collar was turned up and the point of his tricorn hat pulled low; he stared toward the immense British warships. Cannon smoke hung heavily over the broad Hudson.

The soldier had no regimental cockade. He wasn't a Continental, Alexander realized at that instant. Alarm bit into his vitals. Spies were everywhere. He thrust out his hand.

"Your orders?"

The man reached inside his coat, withdrew a packet wrapped in oilcloth, and offered it with an awkward salute. The light was too weak to make out the words, but Stirling's florid signature was unmistakable. Alexander had seen it numerous times since Elizabethtown, when his only cares had been passing Greek grammar and persuading Stirling's pretty daughter to part with a kiss.

The militiaman pushed up his hat to expose his dark face. He was one of the Negroes swelling the city's defense. "Lord Stirling is headed north, Captain Hamilton. He ordered me to offer my assistance."

A flash from a gun on the river brightened the dusk, revealing that the bombardment had restarted and the courier was the youth from King's College. Ajax Manly.

"Manly. Right?" Alexander spoke more coldly than he intended.

The youth blinked. "Yes sir, Captain Hamilton."

"King's College."

"Yes, sir." Manly stood rigidly to attention with another poorly angled salute. None of the militiamen were adequately trained.

Alexander looked back at the river. The nearest warship was still repositioning. "Take that cart." Alexander pointed to a heavy wooden cart loaded with officers' baggage, including his own. "Dump everything. Load the sealed barrel. Grab anyone not on a fieldpiece and pull toward Harlem. Now."

"Yes, sir," Manly said.

Alexander turned his back and strode toward the lighter guns. Two were hitched and headed north in the growing dark. His men were bloodied, but they were marching, not running. The last fieldpiece was idle. Why weren't they moving it? Sergeant Blum and Corporal Pollard crouched next to the gun. The mules stood patiently in their harnesses.

"Sergeant Blum. What's the problem?"

The former bookseller looked up with a smoke-streaked face. "It's the wheel, Captain. It appears the axle's busted."

Alexander knelt in the mud and ducked his head under the gun carriage. It was too dark to see, so he groped along the length of the rough axle. The wood was splintered in the middle. He stood, looked at the river, and estimated the distance. They would never drag the broken carriage to the water in time to ditch the gun. The thirty thousand enemy troops that had been pushing up the island all day weren't far, and the ships in the river menaced.

He must leave the mobile gun for the British—no matter how much he hated to add to their firepower.

"Abandon it, Sergeant. Take the mules and fall in."

Blum and Pollard unhitched the animals, slung their packs, and were gone.

Alexander looked back at New York City, where plumes of white smoke billowed against the night sky. The enemy had captured his home, the one he made for himself. His heavy guns sat cooling while the remnants of his brigade—the sixty men he uniformed with the last of his scholarship money to give them discipline and thrill their hearts—fled north out of harm's way. He was a vagabond once again.

Alexander's jaw jutted forward. This time he wasn't alone. His brothers were going, too. They would get their home back no matter what it took.

But his lieutenant, slumped over his gun, would not. Alexander picked the man's undamaged hat off the ground and placed it on the rigid face to keep off the rain. He would mourn later, when commanders read out the dead at taps. The British were still on the march.

Instead, he grasped the soldier's fallen bayonet, drove it into the field cannon's touch hole, pulled sideways, and stepped on the hilt. The tip snapped, spiking the gun.

With a final glance toward the burning city, Captain Alexander Hamilton pulled down his regimental hat, tugged at his inadequate collar, and followed George Washington's scattered army.

CHAPTER TWELVE

November 1776

Albany

"My dear Lord, sure you know us better than to talk of reasoning a young Woman out of her inclinations. . . . Time, my Lord, time is the only medicine to cure . . . folly."

Henry Fielding, *The History of Tom Jones, A Foundling*, 1749

"THAT WOULD BREAK MASTER'S HEART," ELIZA heard Prince say as he entered the barn and opened the stall next to the one in which she was hiding from the world.

Eliza wiped her eyes with the hem of her dress and gripped the dry bale. How did he know about Angelica?

The stall had been empty for the past year. Only a red heifer dozed in the corner, radiating animal warmth against the November morning. Most of the stalls were empty—the Schuyler herds gone to save the necks of the wretched Congressmen who insulted her father without stopping. And now her sister was obsessed with an Englishman of doubtful character. Mama would be hysterical if she knew half of what Angelica was likely plotting, and Papa's heart *would* break.

"He don' have one," someone countered.

Was that Pompey?

"Sure he do. Bleeds just like the rest of us," Prince said.

"You see how he treat that white man yesterday? Cut him low."

Yes, it was Pompey. How could he call Papa heartless when Papa was the soul of kindness with everyone, despite sternness toward junior officers who rewrote orders to suit themselves? And why was the houseboy in the barn?

"That's just his way of gettin' respect. The soldiers need to know who's boss."

Eliza heard the slap of a saddle.

"Well, he ain't my boss. I'm leavin'."

Eliza held her breath in the chill air. She shrank lower on the scratchy bale.

"Might not be worth it," Prince said. "Master will sell you down river—south—if he catches you."

"Freedom's always worth it. That's what he tells white folks."

Prince said something in reply that Eliza couldn't hear over the horse's jangling tack and heavy footfalls. The barn door met the iron latch with a clank. Eliza let out her breath.

Could Pompey mean it? The *Albany Gazette* had reported the effects of Lord Howe's offer of freedom to slaves who sided with the Crown. Thousands had bolted from New York and Virginia. Now Pompey appeared ready to join them.

Tears came again, and Eliza wiped them with clenched fists. The loss of Montreal was bad enough, and the treachery of General Horatio Gates sufficient to infuriate a saint, but now Papa had to contend with disloyalty in his own home as well. It seemed the only man he could trust was George Washington, under assault hundreds of miles away.

And now here was Pompey—and Angelica, whose dreadful accusation had driven Eliza to the barn.

"Were you not paying attention during arithmetic? It's simple subtraction. Their wedding anniversary from my birthday. Five months."

Eliza hardly recognized the pitiless tone. Is this what becoming an adult meant? Tearing others down so you could stand taller?

"Perhaps you were early," Eliza said.

"Four months early?"

Angelica spoke so acidly that Eliza didn't trust her tongue and she fled the house for the comfort of animals that never lied or connived.

Angelica had been trading secret notes with John Barker Church ever since he arrived in Albany on army business. The rumors about Church's financial shenanigans in Britain trailed him, but Angelica admired his expensive London wardrobe and laughed at his sophisticated schemes. She could have any suitor she wanted. Numerous gentlemen would win their parents' consent, as Church would not.

But that was the problem. They were approved. Provincial. "Albany would drive Patience off a monument," Angelica said. She wanted to see the world, and didn't give a fig for how it affected anyone else. Eliza felt like throwing all of her sister's silly novels in the fire—and forewarning their parents.

Yet how could she betray Angelica? Sister loyalty was Newton's first law. Fidelity to family and parents was the second. Eliza must simply make Angelica reconsider.

And what about Pompey? Here was yet another bit of treachery.

Eliza couldn't reverse Congress's decision to appoint nasty Horatio Gates to investigate her father for sending ill-equipped men into battle. A subordinate officer, Gates clearly hankered after Papa's job. He had likely spread the vile rumors of treason and incompetence. It drove Eliza mad to think of backstabbing officers and politicians who wrote poisonous letters while better men risked their lives.

If she'd been born a man she would defend Papa. Or stand for Congress herself. But that was impossible. Instead, she must report Pompey. She would go straight to her mother and reveal that he planned to break the law, betray them all, and run to freedom.

Eliza studied the heifer, oblivious to human troubles. Would Papa really sell a man south? The question knocked on a closed door she didn't want to open. "All men are created equal," the Declaration of Independence had stated only five months before.

There was something ominous about the way Prince said *south*. The image came to mind of Papa's favorite hound returning with the mutilated fox he'd run to ground. It felt more wrong than right to expose Pompey. She couldn't do it.

Eliza's heart sank further. Everything permanent seemed to be dissolving, from Britain's empire to the Schuyler family. Papa had two treasonous daughters, Eliza thought with self-loathing. They had both let him down.

CHAPTER THIRTEEN

December-January 1776

McConkey's Ferry, Pennsylvania

"An officer came to our camp, under a flag of truce, and informed Hamilton . . . that Captain Hale had been arrested within the British lines, condemned as a spy, and executed that morning. . . . His dying words . . . were . . . I only regret that I have but one life to lose for my country."

General William Hull, New York, 1776

"CAN YOU LIFT YOUR HEAD?"

Ajax Manly's breath came out in white puffs. The temperature inside the tent was little different from the snow-covered camp outside.

"Of course," Alexander said and shifted higher. The movement dislodged more phlegm, and he coughed into his handkerchief. Neddy Stevens advised him to sit out the winter somewhere safe, but he had dismissed his friend's solicitude. Doctors were notorious hypochondriacs.

Ajax Manly held out the spoon. He sat on an empty keg next to the cot.

"I can feed myself, damn you." Alexander knew his ill temper wasn't reasonable, yet Ajax's unvarying vigor despite infernal weather and limited rations tried his patience. He took the spoon and the bowl, then closed his eyes.

"Ready to whip your weight in wildcats, I see," Ajax said.

Alexander opened his eyes and dug stubbornly into the stew. Chunks of beef glistened among the cabbage and potatoes.

"Where did we get meat?"

"Don't know."

The beef was chewy but the hot food cheered Alexander. He felt strength return.

"There must be a reason for the meat," he said as he handed the empty bowl to Ajax, "and not just because it's Christmas."

Ajax nodded. "Of course there is."

Alexander still didn't believe the boy was sixteen, as he claimed. Ajax just wanted to qualify for duty. He was preternaturally savvy for a youngster, as his comment showed.

They had slipped into an inexplicable familiarity since the last retreat—after the army escaped New York, then New Jersey, then into Pennsylvania. It was at the Raritan River, where their unit covered Washington's rearguard once again, that Alexander reluctantly accepted the boy. They had even dropped the formalities of rank when alone. Though the practice conflicted with the military sensibility that had deepened in him over the discouraging months, something in Alexander resisted treating the youth as a subordinate. It simply made him feel right that this Ajax was not a slave, but free. Sometimes he imagined he was addressing his old friend, still eyeing pretty girls. It helped Alexander forget the unanswerable question, was Ajax even still alive?

The young Negro's strength had also become legendary in their artillery company. Their numbers had fallen by half—a terrifying percentage, though it wasn't as bad as Washington's regular army, which diminished visibly with every defeat. Ajax was one of only two blacks among his men, the other being James Taylor, a housepainter-turned-soldier with an unexpected flair for sighting cannons and blowing up Redcoats.

Ajax had won everyone's admiration at the Raritan River. Beforehand, General Washington called Alexander into his tent to emphasize the importance of the engagement. It was the second time the forbidding commander singled out the young captain of New York's gutted but still fighting artillery brigade. When the Virginian asked his opinion on how best to position field guns in case of crossfire, Alexander answered professionally, though his stomach did backflips at the implied compliment. Unfortunately, Raritan turned into another rout.

Once again, their New York unit covered men's backs and stemmed losses. But even this wouldn't have been possible had young Ajax not provided the burst of strength that saved their second gun. A mule stumbled backward on a rocky outcrop when a wheel slipped on loose gravel near the peak. The heavy gun carriage shivered. Heedless of the risk that he might be crushed if the cannon gained downhill momentum, Ajax sprang to the carriage and pushed it into place while Taylor tugged frantically on the animal's lead.

"You *are* manly," a Welshman joked.

"My pa took the name when he won his freedom for 'manly service' during the French and Indian War," Ajax said. "Just like America's gonna win its freedom now."

Ragged with exhaustion and shaken by defeat, Alexander was moved by the youngster's sunny comment. "I once had a friend named Ajax," he told the boy when their unit made camp that night on the freezing ground. That was probably where Alexander had caught the fever that landed him in a hospital tent. Ajax had hovered like a mosquito ever since.

"They don't hand out rations like this for nothing," the boy now said.

"Any scuttlebutt on what Washington is planning?"

God knew they needed a plan. Chased across three states, their bedraggled force would soon be in the wilderness consorting with Indians. The British army had expanded to forty thousand while

Washington's force shrank to three. Worse, their enlistments expired on New Year's Eve. Most men would tramp home. The British war machine would roll over the last sparks of the rebellion and mash them into the mud of Pennsylvania.

A number of summer soldiers had already abandoned the cause. From his sickbed Alexander had overheard numerous complaints about stocky, self-important General Horatio Gates, who had recently ridden into their winter camp with the air of a man saving the army from amateurs. He'd brought reinforcements lent by besieged General Philip Schuyler, yet shortly afterward Gates abandoned his men in the cold field to "consult" with Congress from the warmth of a snug mansion in Philadelphia. Some had slipped away and gone to Philadelphia themselves. Rumor had it that Gates's friends in Congress wanted him to replace George Washington as head of the army. In Alexander's opinion, Gates was a wide-hipped politician dolled up as a soldier.

"Camp is awash with rumors, but nothing unequivocal," Ajax said.

"There you go," Alexander said in a peevish tone, which made him realize he was still sick—and should take care not to reveal it. *Was that fever talking?* He hoped not. "Words like *unequivocal*. One would think you'd gone to finishing school. Hardly self-taught."

"I can't help it you have a suspicious mind." The boy looked at him with exasperating good humor. Had anyone raised the same question about Alexander's self-education on St. Croix, he would have given a slashing retort.

"As I was saying, no *unequivocal* orders have come down," Ajax said, "but the cook wagon is dishing out meat. Something's afoot."

"Then I had best be as well," Alexander said, and pushed back his blanket in dismissal.

Ajax stood, tucked the spoon into the bowl, and left.

Even before Alexander reached headquarters, he received his written orders from one of the staff officers hurrying about the camp that fanned outward from the landing where an enterprising tavern keeper had strung a chain across the Delaware River and attached a flat-bottomed barge. McConkey's ferry took travelers and goods back and forth between New Jersey and Pennsylvania.

Alexander read the orders amid a crowd that stirred like bees from an overturned hive. His artillery, horses, and mules would cross on the barge after dark. Infantry would take turns in a flotilla of high-sided cargo boats. From there, they would march south ten miles down Bear Tavern road to surprise the enemy at dawn.

The general must be hoping to catch the Redcoats deep in their Christmas wassail—and counting on the star of Bethlehem to guide them. How else would they parade in the dark across a frozen landscape?

Drifts no longer reached the eaves of the ferry house where the general was meeting with his top officers, but the snow that remained was packed. The wind was fierce and the sky's grey sheen promised fresh powder by morning. Flat shards of broken ice dipped and rocked among greenish whitecaps that slipped downriver on the Delaware.

Most of Alexander's New Yorkers still had decent boots, but the Continentals had hiked right through their inadequate soles. Hundreds had wrapped their frostbitten feet in rags. Alexander had seen bloody footprints in the snow more than once. Congress hadn't sent new boots in two months. A nighttime maneuver would finish off the weakest.

Yet it was best to go down fighting, Alexander thought. Better to march than wait to be cornered. He wondered if George Washington enjoyed games of chance. Dice must be popular in Virginia.

Billy Lee, the general's personal servant, walked by, and Alexander caught his eye. Lee held a new French musket and the reins of his master's horse. The prize stallion raised its feet elegantly with each step, nearly dancing on the icy path.

"Billy Lee. How's His Excellency this afternoon?"

The manservant looked Hamilton up and down. He wore a red headscarf for warmth underneath his leather cap. Billy Lee was the only slave Alexander had ever seen who looked and acted nothing like one. Perhaps it was the effect of being trusted with a gun.

"The general's likely wonderin' the same about you. You gonna make it?"

"I've rarely felt better."

Lee frowned. "You've surely looked better."

The stallion perked its ears at the sound of a mare's whinny from the far side of camp. He pawed the snow with a forefoot. "The general's just fine," Lee said, and continued on his way.

Alexander took out the pocket watch that cousin Ann had given him when she bade him Godspeed as they evacuated Manhattan. Troops would start crossing the Delaware at 4:00 p.m., as night fell. Six more hours to prepare.

"Mules, rope, gunpowder, boots," Alexander muttered. He would check their dwindling supplies.

The snap of cracked ice was the only sound other than the soldiers' labored breath. The cannons broke the hardpack as they rolled down the road. Alexander turned around to make sure Ajax and Private Taylor still had a firm grasp on the lead ropes.

It was nothing short of miraculous that Washington had gotten three thousand troops across the river in the maw of the wild storm that blew up after nightfall. A handful of sailors from Marblehead had rowed their overloaded dories through floating debris that constantly threatened to upend them in the dark. The laborious crossing had taken several hours longer than planned. They mustn't lose a moment now. The New Jersey shoreline already had the spectral look of dawn, and the prospect of catching the enemy by surprise was fading with the night.

General Washington had passed them awhile earlier. "For God's sake, keep by your officers," he ordered the soldiers in his deep voice, just before his mount slipped on a patch of black ice and almost went down. Washington seized the charger's mane and in a flash they were gone again.

Trudging at the head of his unit, Alexander concentrated on his footing. His sore throat hurt but his legs felt strong. Trenton should be close. He must get his cannons in place before the assault began. Colonel Henry Knox, the burly officer in command of artillery, had given Alexander the assignment of preventing the enemy's escape.

Now they would strike the critical blow, he hoped. He patted the cold cannon with a gloved hand, grateful for the stubby field-pieces that had gotten them this far.

Alexander looked over his shoulder for the hundredth time that long night. Thirty men in a double row. They were the best-drilled unit in the whole army—or so two generals had told him—a fact in which his men took inordinate but excusable pride since it kept them alive. Heads down, they marched with hunched shoulders against the sleety snow that collected on their greatcoats and cocked hats.

Except one. Alexander caught Private Beasley looking up in the dim light, and they both grinned, intuiting one another. The plan was so absurd it might work. If it didn't, they would go out in a blaze of glory. They had nothing left to lose.

Muffled hoofbeats in the snow caught Alexander's attention and he turned around to see a horseman canter out of the fog. The cavalry officer delivered his order in a low but distinct voice. Alexander nodded and passed word to set up the guns on a knoll just beyond a stand of trees whose dark outlines were now visible.

James Taylor and Ajax Manly guided the mules to the rise, and the two crews rapidly set up what was left of their arsenal. By the time the artillerymen had sighted the cannons, the last regiments of the Continental Army were passing under their unit's watchful gaze.

Swirling snowfall tapered to occasional flakes in a vapor that thickened as dawn brightened. Alexander caught glimpses of set, determined faces as soldiers passed double-time under their lookout until they were gone from view again. He smelled wood smoke on the breeze and heard a dog's isolated bark. The town below must be waking.

The army's tramp sounded different in the increasingly dense fog, as if coming from another direction now. Alexander wished he could see better. He scraped the crusted ice from the wheel of the nearest gun carriage with a knife from his belt. Placing his foot on a spoke, he swung onto the iron rim for a better viewpoint, taking care not to slip.

The mist wasn't any less thick higher up. Alexander held his breath and listened. A clanging noise came at a new angle. He squinted into the fog.

The metal spikes on a row of Hessian helmets glinted in the gloom. Mercenaries with their German-grade muskets and bayonets appeared to be on routine maneuver, headed for the sleeping town. They would soon discover the Continentals' exposed flank.

Alexander leaped to the snow-covered ground. "Ready the guns."

Just then, muskets boomed from the direction of the village. A warning bell pealed, joined by the shriek of horses and cries of men. A cannon went off.

The artillery's two fieldpieces pointed at the Hessians now pelting toward Trenton's main square. Alexander watched a man swab the nearer gun with quick jabs to prepare for firing, and suppressed the urgent impulse to load it himself.

Powder and ball followed. James Taylor saluted to indicate readiness. Alexander counted to ten. German curses grew closer and joined the crescendo of musketry from the village.

"Now, boys." Alexander shouted at last into the frosty air. "Fire away!"

* * *

The hospital tent at McConkey's Ferry hadn't any door. A five-inch gap between the door frame and the blanket across it revealed glimpses of the camp. A piercing draft came in with the light, but Alexander preferred it to lying in the dark, which felt too much like death.

Outside, he could see a team of able-bodied men hammering together another temporary shelter for the wounded. The smashing victory at Trenton three weeks earlier, followed by a quick triumph at Princeton, had saved their army one more time. Under Alexander's command, the New York Provincial Company of Artillery had acquitted itself with distinction. At least, that seemed to be the import of the message from George Washington that lay under his hand on the woolen blanket. Alexander didn't feel like rereading it.

Some would jump at a promotion from line captain to staff colonel, but not Alexander. The kind of officer Alexander admired would hold himself cheap if he didn't share his men's dangers in the field. Valor was earned under fire, not at a desk. Especially, Alexander told himself, if he was a twenty-year-old bastard from a Caribbean flyspeck.

Washington's offer meant merging his state regiment with the regular army. Not an attractive prospect. When his men learned that their barrage at Princeton had destroyed the portrait of King George in the college library, they shouted huzzahs until their throats were hoarse. "You'll be the last heroes fighting," he told them. "The pride of New York, you are."

Alexander's exposed arm was cold and he pulled Washington's letter under the blanket. His limbs still felt weak from fever, but his thoughts assembled like a well-trained battalion.

Perhaps New York had pride enough. State legislatures treated George Washington like a redheaded stepchild whom they begrudged a hot cross bun. They hogged money and men for their own militias while Continentals fought for the whole country—that amorphous United States that had no real treasury of its own.

Perhaps his men ought to become Continentals. Maybe all their armed forces should.

Alexander rolled onto his side. He couldn't influence what the states did with their resources. Maryland hadn't even signed the Articles of Confederation for which men were dying when they weren't freezing or starving. Its legislators wanted better borders from Virginia to sweeten the deal.

Yet he could control what happened to his own men. If he accepted Washington's offer, and New York's artillery brigade joined the continental forces of George Washington, they would come under a single, coordinated command.

Alexander wasn't sure he wanted to serve in it. George Washington was rumored to have a bad temper. Of course, only a bloodless angel looked upon ineptitude with forbearance, and angels didn't win wars. Yet what if the Virginian expected personal, not just military deference from his youngest, newest aide—a West Indian of dubious parentage and obvious poverty? Alexander had observed more than once that the right hand of a great man usually wiped his ass.

"I will not be anyone's servant," he told the crook of his arm. The very words made his head hurt. "I will not grovel."

As captain of New York's artillery brigade he was independent. He had earned a respect he'd never known and could never win on St. Croix. Why should he give that up? Why him? Let someone else do it.

Alexander stared out onto the dirty snow of Pennsylvania.

Their army had won two battles but lost nearly a dozen. They simply had to win more. Regardless of what it cost, he needed to be sure the army was straining every last nerve to prevail. At Washington's side, he might make a bigger difference. And the general might reward him later with command of a larger force in the field. Alexander would make his name permanently.

He shoved the missive under his pillow and closed his lids at last. New York's artillery company would merge with the Continentals. He would accept Washington's invitation to wield a pen for the army. For now. Unless the general demanded more deference than he was due, or tried to tie him to a desk.

CHAPTER FOURTEEN

August 1777

Albany

"The fair nymphs of this isle are in wonderful tribulation as the fresh meat our men have got here has made them as riotous as satyrs. A girl cannot step into the bushes to pluck a rose without running the most imminent risk of being ravished, and they are so little accustomed to these vigorous methods that they don't bear them with proper resignation."

Lord Rawdon, First Marquess of Hastings, on Staten Island, 1776

"YOU'RE IN CHARGE," MAMA SAID. SHE squeezed Eliza's hands to impart strength. The pastoral quiet of the long-awaited summer was deceptive. Eliza knew the monster was almost upon them.

She squeezed in return, sending strength back. "Yes, Mama."

"I don't think it's going to happen—or I wouldn't go—but if they come, take your brothers and sisters across to Fort Crailo. Peggy can carry the baby. Go fast. They won't harm the others."

Kitty Schuyler wasn't explicit, since the possibilities were too horrendous to put into words, but they both knew that Indians didn't take slaves as hostages. They took whites.

Jane McCrea's mutilated body flashed through Eliza's mind but she fended away the image. The dead girl had been found naked only weeks before on the same river road that Mama must take to Saratoga.

"Do you have to go?" Eliza said. She had always thought Papa could protect them from anything. It wasn't true.

"Yes." Mama's tone brooked no argument. "The army needs us. The fields must be destroyed. The harvest, too. What's in our barns would feed Burgoyne's Hessians for another month."

"Can't someone else deliver the message?"

Mama wore an expression Eliza had never seen. Tense. Angry. Wild almost. "We can't think of ourselves, Eliza! The farmhands will balk if I'm not there. I'll torch the wheat myself, if I must. A general's wife can't know fear."

She pulled Eliza to her and hugged hard. "You're strong. You always have been. Safeguard the others."

Eliza silently cursed Angelica's selfishness. Was love really blind? Not that Angelica could have foreseen Burgoyne's victory when she slipped out of the house after dark and eloped with John Church a month earlier. Now the British were poised to capture Saratoga and Eliza needed her sister sorely, but she alone must help their parents, who might give their lives to slow the assault.

Eliza stood taller. "Go," she said.

Kitty Schuyler strode from the room with a knife in the belt of her riding skirt. She didn't look back.

Eliza walked to the window and placed her hands on the walnut side table under it. She watched her mother climbed into a calash with only Prince to protect her. The servant helped his mistress into the vehicle, climbed in after her, and gave the reins a determined shake. Eliza appreciated him more at that moment than at any other in her twenty years.

Mama was married to the American general in charge of stopping "Gentleman Johnny" Burgoyne, who had captured every fortress from Lake George down to Ticonderoga. Burgoyne was now on the verge of snatching Saratoga, then Albany. Her mother might as well paint a bull's-eye on her back.

Eliza watched the carriage start up the road that young Jane McCrea had taken only two weeks earlier to join her Tory fiancé, camped with Burgoyne in the hills above Saratoga. McCrea and her companion must have chatted about Jane's upcoming wedding. The weather was sultry in July, but elms shaded the road and it would have been a pleasant ride until the painted braves stepped noiselessly from the dark woods. Although the Seneca people had partnered with the British, they showed no respect for the Tory women they grabbed. General Burgoyne couldn't protect even his sympathizers from his allies. He'd bargained with the devil, who had stripped Jane McCrea of her scalp along with her clothes.

Eliza again fended away the thought, and curled her fingers under the edge of the table. Black walnut was heavy but, as her mother said, Eliza was strong. She pulled the piece across the hall and shoved it under the handle of the front door. Next she would check the window locks, speak with Diana about what to do if Redcoats came, and ask the cook to pack food that wouldn't spoil should they have to flee across the Hudson. Then she would pray. And get a knife.

CHAPTER FIFTEEN

October 1777

Whitpain Township, Pennsylvania

"All is mystery and dark beyond conjecture. But we must not be discouraged at a misfortune; we must rather exert ourselves the more vigorously."
Alexander Hamilton to John Jay, 1777

ALEXANDER TRIED TO SLEEP DESPITE THE slope in the floor that threatened to roll him into the next man. He needed to be on the road to Albany before daybreak.

Against daunting odds, the northern portion of their army had escaped destruction. Horatio Gates had wrested command from Philip Schuyler at Saratoga and smashed the overextended British with the help of Benedict Arnold, a Connecticut merchant who had emerged as one of their best officers. The British no longer threatened New England and upstate New York. As a consequence, General Washington had entrusted Alexander with the tricky task of prying reinforcements out of Horatio Gates—puffed up in his glory—who no longer needed all his men. Washington had instructed Alexander to consult the deposed Philip Schuyler as well. Increasingly, the general turned to Alexander first when handing out the hardest assignments.

Night had fallen hours earlier. Alexander needed every bit of rest he could get for the two-hundred-mile ride.

"Surely you could do better than this, Ham," Robert Harrison said over the pulse of the crickets. The Virginia neighbor of General Washington rustled in his bedroll. "I keep sliding downhill."

"*Mon dieu.* It is like this always?" said a hushed voice with a French accent.

The men spoke quietly. General Washington occupied the small chamber next to his aides, and no one wished to disturb him.

"Why is it my fault?" Alexander said.

Tench Tilghman spoke over his shoulder. "Because you're the only one who can talk a farmer out of his bed."

"Or his pretty wife into it?" the Marquis de Lafayette said.

The Frenchman's command of English was increasingly sure and he rarely needed a translator anymore. Eight months younger than Alexander, the amiable marquis was now aide-de-camp, though Congress had given him the rank of major general to curry French favor. Nursing a recent bullet wound, the young aristocrat lay with his knee elevated on a trunk that made a square shadow against the bright moonlight.

Tench Tilghman heaved with laughter and Alexander elbowed him though the blanket. "Shut up! You'll wake the general." Then Alexander laughed, too.

"I have heard two names for *notre petit colonel*," Lafayette said, "the Little Lion and the Tomcat. What is this?"

Robert Harrison sat up in his blanket. In silhouette, his tousled hair looked like feathers on a startled hen. A trained attorney more than a decade older than the others, Harrison had a dignified manner. "A tomcat, monsieur, is one of those large, ginger felines that is first in line for any female in heat."

"Which is why General Washington's wife named her new tomcat Hamilton," Tilghman said. "It was Harrison who dubbed him the Little Lion. After the Battle of Princeton."

"That's right," Harrison said, "when Ham's brigade blew the king's head off. But tomcat fits better I don't know how or why, but Ham attracts females like a pig draws flies."

Alexander smiled in the dark. "You mean like kings excite crowds. And isn't envy one of the seven deadly sins?"

"It's damned unfair that you get all the women," Tilghman said.

The last soiree Martha Washington had arranged to keep their spirits up, right before Congress evacuated Philadelphia, now seemed years earlier. Yet it was only a few months ago that Alexander had danced away the night with pretty Kitty Livingston and half a dozen other young women. Willowy Martha Bland, with her dashing repartee and revealing décolletage, had kissed his cheek when she tucked a posy in his buttonhole. The belles who attended dances to sustain officers' morale appeared besotted with Alexander's West Indian charms. He did his best to win them over and usually succeeded. Becoming Washington's aide-de-camp had vaulted him into the social stratosphere, though staying aloft was contingent upon discretion about his past.

"Strategy, my dear Tilghman," Alexander said. "A little care, a little preparation, is essential for victory. To a damsel, every soldier's a potential hero."

Tilghman turned onto his back and addressed the night air. "I do take care, Ham. I even button my trousers and pick the tobacco from my beard. So why do I feel defeated if you're there first? Being tall, dark, and handsome ought to count for something against a Caribbean runt."

"Ah, but a woman must be wooed step by step. Miss one and she thinks twice," Alexander said. "Her hair, her smile, her wit—if she has any—must all be given full due. To Venus, praise is more alluring than gold, more intoxicating than brandy."

"The Americans are, *mon frère*," Lafayette asked in Alexander's direction, "*gauche*? They are too slow. A man must let a woman know *tout de suite* that she is a goddess. That her skin is like buttercream, her hair like silk, her breasts like *bonbons*. In France, we do this. And on St. Croix, no?"

"*Oui. Bien sûr.* I think of every woman as my mistress or lover when I speak with her," Alexander said.

"Well, you'd better keep your mitts off at least one young lady when you get to Albany," Tench Tilghman said. "I have first claim to General Schuyler's daughter—the one I met during the Iroquois conclave. So don't go making eyes, Ham. The rest of us need wives, too, if we're going to populate the hinterlands."

"Schuyler has daughters?"

Alexander had never met the New York general relieved of duty by Congress. The situation had been dreadful, of course. General Schuyler's loss of Fort Ticonderoga—which everyone criticized—turned out not to be his fault. Right after that, even though Schuyler had stopped the Indians and cornered Burgoyne, General Gates got the promotion for which he'd been campaigning. Sam Adams of Massachusetts wrote the petition that persuaded Congress to replace the so-called Dutchman at the last moment.

Horatio Gates took the army Schuyler had built, captured nearly six thousand Redcoats, and collected the laurels due his predecessor. Alexander had heard that Schuyler's own wife torched her fields to foil the British and Burgoyne retaliated by burning the family estate to the ground. Now Congress was agog at Gates's genius. It had been a sweet victory, though, and America's biggest win.

Sometimes it seemed New Englanders cared more about showing up New York than defeating Great Britain. It was but another example of the infuriating pettiness that exemplified the civilian approach to war. New England's favorite son was now in charge and Schuyler was out.

Alexander wondered if General Washington had made the best choice by entrusting him—the youngest aide barring Lafayette—with the job of wheedling reinforcements from Horatio Gates. Alexander didn't expect the fame-hungry general to be cooperative even though the Canadian threat had vanished. Alexander must convince America's worst prima donna to share resources with his last rival: George Washington. In theory, Gates must comply with his commanding officer. But Philip Schuyler of New York had also been Gates's commanding officer once upon a time. The damn fools in Congress might soon do to General Washington what they had done to Schuyler and turn him out for not winning big enough, soon enough.

"Schuyler has an endless supply of daughters," Tilghman said. "Plenty to keep you busy."

Lafayette shifted restlessly and draped his leg over the trunk at a different angle. Alexander wondered if it still hurt. The bullet at Brandywine had made a wound slow to heal. He had befriended the young Frenchman, a newcomer to America like himself.

Alexander took the burlap roll from under his head and sat up. "My dear *monsieur*, isn't that trunk terribly uncomfortable? Surely you need something softer."

Alexander crawled to Lafayette's side in the dark. He lifted the leg and propped the roll under the knee. "Is that better?"

"*Oui, mon frère*," Lafayette said with a sigh. "I'm so glad you are not dead after all."

Robert Harrison laughed. "Me, too. Colonel Lee had us worried when he announced your demise at the Schuylkill, Hammie. We wouldn't have fretted if we'd known you'd just gone for a swim."

"I wouldn't have worried either if a Hessian hadn't relieved me of my horse."

Although Alexander spoke lightly, the dying mare's scream still echoed in his nightmares. The dream was always the same: he torched the flour mill, which roared up in flames just as Redcoats pounded down the hill. When Alexander dragged his horse onto the waiting barge, the animal reared and a bullet struck its face, which exploded in blood. He and another soldier tried to steer the raft across the rain-swollen Schuylkill, but the current kept pushing them back toward the shore. The other man was killed.

In the dream, bullets made spitting sounds around Alexander while, paralyzed, he drifted toward the Redcoats. In reality, he dove into the stream at the last minute, swam to the other side under fire, and dashed off a note to Congress that the British were at the gates of Philadelphia. A boy from a nearby farm rushed his message to the capital twenty miles away.

When Alexander straggled into camp hours later, the rest of Washington's aides poured out of the farmhouse. Having seen Alexander's horse and companion perish, Colonel Harry Lee had reported him dead. Lafayette, Tilghman, and Harrison were half laughing, half crying, as they embraced him. When the general himself clasped Alexander around the shoulders, he knew they really were his family, as Washington called his young staff.

"When do you think to return from Albany?" Lafayette said.

"I don't know, *monsieur*. Within a few weeks, I expect. Before the snow gets deep. By Christmas—*Noël*—at the latest."

"Let's hope next Christmas isn't as cold as the last," Tilghman said sleepily. His voice had drifted to a low register.

"Let's hope the general doesn't cross the Delaware again. I froze last time," Harrison said. "If I have to do that again, my prick is going to break off."

The men erupted in laughter, except Lafayette who said, "What is this?" Then he caught the meaning. "The *général* is a great man, but a man. He will not allow that."

George Washington was everyone's hero. Despite the army's terrible losses, there was something about the Virginian—the powerful undercurrent of his conviction—that swept them along. He was larger than life.

"I'm afraid our dear leader doesn't appreciate the risks endured by other men, *monsieur*," Alexander said. "You see, his is just too big to freeze."

Robert Harrison laughed as hard as anyone else, but apparently thought better of it after a moment. "Hush," the oldest aide said. "A little respect, boys. Honestly, Ham."

Alexander grinned though his eyes were shut tight, and rolled onto his other side. He really must get some sleep. Horatio Gates was a wily opponent. If Alexander couldn't best him, their campaign would be doomed. And Britain would hunt his best friends, his only family, one by one.

CHAPTER SIXTEEN

November 1777

Albany

"We arrived at Albany . . . not, as we supposed we should, as victors! We were, nonetheless, received in the most friendly manner by the good General Schuyler, and by his wife and daughters. . . . They treated us as people who knew how to forget their own losses in the misfortunes of others."

Baroness Frederika von Riedesel, 1777, wife of a Hessian prisoner

ELIZA SHOOK SNOW FROM HER RIDING cape before hanging it on the hook in the hall. Diana and Maria had their hands full enough without pulling up damp carpets, too. The family had dispatched its latest prisoners only a few days earlier.

Papa insisted upon treating the enemy officers courteously even though General Burgoyne had burned Saratoga just before the British defeat. "It was a military decision," Papa said. "I might have done the same had I been in his shoes."

When the battle was over, the high-ranking soldiers needed somewhere to stay until General Horatio Gates could arrange the customary prisoner exchange. Papa had offered their home at Albany. The one the British hadn't razed.

Eliza rubbed her numb hands together. She was chilled and melancholy and needed a hot cup of tea after visiting Jonathan Cavan, who had lost an arm and a leg below the knee at Saratoga. When Eliza arrived at the tenant farmhouse that morning, she found that Hannah Cavan had leashed her twin toddlers to the table in order to cook, clean, milk the cow, split logs, and care for the bloodstained linen on her husband's stumps. Their six-year-old fed the animals, but he was thin and hollow-eyed and couldn't manage the two-year-olds. Jon Cavan's sandy freckles were nearly white. His hair, brown last summer, showed gray against the pillow. Hannah Cavan was wrung out.

Eliza ironed laundry and played with the toddlers, wondering if it might have been better if Cavan simply hadn't returned. He'd never again support his family. But Mrs. Cavan stopped to touch the man's face whenever chores took her near his cot, as if to reassure herself that he had been spared.

"That confirms my suspicion. He's giving us the weakest brigade."

The door of Philip Schuyler's office was cracked and a stranger's vibrant baritone carried into the hall. His voice had the caramel resonance of a singer.

"Nor does it surprise me, sir," the man continued, "coming from an officer content to steal valor rather than earn it. The battle of Saratoga was yours to wage, General Schuyler. Not his."

Eliza didn't recognize the speaker but shared his feelings. She despised Horatio Gates—loathed Horatio Gates—though she knew she ought not to.

"Gates held the men together at the critical moment," Papa said. "We needed the victory."

"That's generous, sir, but it's my conviction, and I'm sure it's shared by others not blinded by regional loyalties, that you're far more deserving of our country's gratitude. You built the army against all odds—overwhelming odds—and lured Burgoyne into the trap."

Eliza stood still in order to better hear. Who was this man? Their visitor was articulating precisely what she'd spent weeks yearning that someone, *anyone*, would say aloud. After all Papa had done, Congress had cast him aside like an apple core at the crowning moment.

Papa ignored the compliment. "What matters now is that General Washington receives reinforcements," he said. "The brigade that Gates proposes demonstrated a terrible lack of discipline at Saratoga. It cost them more casualties than the others. They've been decimated."

Eliza heard the thump of a glass on the table. Papa must have poured brandy to take off the afternoon chill.

"Gates said he couldn't spare even them, but I told him 'no' wasn't acceptable. Washington must have at least one brigade, preferably two."

Someone gave orders to imperious Horatio Gates, hero of the hour? Eliza would like to have seen that.

"I should like to have seen that."

Eliza nearly smiled to hear her father repeat her thoughts. Papa never admitted his disappointment, even though Congress stripped him of authority in front of the whole country. Instead, he sent reinforcements to Gates as fast as he could, then hosted Gates's prisoners at the expense of the Schuyler family. The Schuylers had crammed into two bedrooms to allow the enemy officers a place to lay their heads.

That was Papa. Always the high road. But it must have hurt. Eliza was grateful to the visitor for recognizing her father's contributions. Papa's humiliation stung her spirit.

"Gates eventually agreed to the one division, but I found him as stingy with General Washington as he was jealous of you, sir. Such behavior is contemptible when men's freedom is at stake."

Eliza drew back. *Contemptible*? Had she heard right? That was how she thought of Gates, but no one dared say it after Saratoga.

The speaker was confident and commanding, and she agreed with him, but he was foolishly bold.

"General Gates may be thinking more about his own freedom of action than freedom in general," her father said.

"I fear you are right, sir. I see that he nearly had me hoodwinked. Thank you for alerting me to the brigade's weaknesses, General Schuyler. It appears I must go back to the well, whether or not Gates is willing to share his water. I'll demand a second brigade at the very least."

Pompey entered the hall with a kindling box from the front parlor. He darted a curious look at Eliza, then slipped out the front door. She turned to rearrange her heavy cape on the hook.

There was something unusual about the officer. His voice had a West Indian lilt, but that wasn't it. Perhaps it was his rich tone, or bold denunciation of Horatio Gates. Eliza found herself inexplicably fascinated.

She gave the coat a last tug to straighten its folds and crossed the hall to the door of her father's office. She lifted her hand to knock, then dropped it. She felt shy.

"At least General Gates didn't begrudge me the good reverend, Dr. Mendy. I served with Mendy during our retreat from Harlem Heights. The men will need an energetic parson this winter. A third have no shoes. They're dangerously discouraged. Many are close to desertion."

"I don't recall Reverend Mendy," her father said. "He's good? Not the type to bolt at the boom of a cannon?"

Eliza knotted her fingers. Papa's guest said things everyone else was too timid to put into words. She must meet him. Eliza checked the pins in her chignon and pushed open the door.

The officer sat with his back to the door. "He's just what I prefer in a military parson except that he doesn't whore or drink. But Mendy will fight and—most important—he'll not insist on your going to heaven whether you want to or not."

Papa sat with his sore foot propped on a brocade stool. He smiled up at her. "Eliza, my dear. I didn't realize you were home."

The stranger jumped to his feet and turned around. Eliza stopped breathing. Although the officer stood only a few inches taller than her, his snug uniform revealed a strong, athletic form. His eyes were a striking color—nearly violet—and he held his chin at a tilt, as if expecting a challenge. The officer was young and remarkably handsome. He looked ready to take on the Iroquois. His audacity reminded her of one Indian in particular.

Realizing his gaffe, the man blushed to the roots of russet hair that he wore long, tied at the nape of his neck. He must be embarrassed.

As well he should be, Eliza thought, her nerves rattled. She wasn't a plaster saint but she didn't applaud sin. A parson who whored and drank. The thought of it!

"Please, pardon me, *mademoiselle*. I had no idea a lady was present," the young man said and gave a military bow.

"Eliza, allow me to introduce Lieutenant Colonel Alexander Hamilton," Papa said without getting up. "He's on a mission for General Washington. I've asked him to join us for supper."

"I'm pleased to welcome you, Colonel Hamilton. I hope you'll not object if we say grace before breaking bread. Some of us intend to go to heaven—though we shan't force you to come along."

Eliza spoke more tartly than intended, yet gave him her hand.

"Only an angel could forgive me," he said with a smile. "You must be destined to get there."

He kissed her hand with a practiced elegance. Of course she would forgive him. She could probably forgive him anything.

Papa laughed. "An excellent recovery, Colonel Hamilton."

Diana appeared in the doorway. "Master Schuyler," the matron said in her best company-come-to-tea manner, "supper is served."

"Thank you, Diana. Colonel Hamilton, this way please."

Limping with gout, Papa led them across the central hallway. Hamilton followed with a light step that gave an impression of grace and energy artfully controlled. Eliza darted a look at the gilded hall mirror as they passed and pushed back a strand of hair.

The fire's glow on the red-flocked wallpaper gave a rosy hue to the polished silver and porcelain. There were only three plates.

"I thought Mama would be home in time for dinner, Papa," Eliza said.

"No. I'm sorry to say that she'll be unable to join us." Her father turned to their guest as they sat. "My wife has taken our younger children to visit my aunt, who's feeling poorly."

Hamilton's eyes showed concern. "I hope it's nothing serious. Is your aunt elderly?"

"Ancient but robust. It's only a cold. Though at her age we're naturally watchful."

"Is she the last of her generation?"

"On my father's side. On my wife's we have too many to count. Between the Van Cortlandts, Van Rensselaers, and Livingstons, we're related to half of New York."

"Then you're blessed, sir. I've always felt that a thriving family is paradise come early."

Papa passed a basket of fresh bread. Hamilton took a slice and buttered it efficiently. Eliza noted that his motions were precise and quick. Every gesture seemed self-assured, and she felt her shyness well up again.

"What about you, Colonel Hamilton?" Papa said. "Do you have family in New York? Or are they all in the West Indies?"

Eliza shook her head as Pompey offered rice. Despite the rigors of her morning, she found she wasn't hungry.

"I'm fortunate to have one cousin in New York, but my father and brother are in the Caribbean."

"Has the war made correspondence difficult?"

Pompey placed a large portion of rice on Hamilton's plate. Eliza observed that the colonel looked up with a friendly glance, as if to meet the slave boy's eyes, though Pompey kept his lowered.

"The war has made communication more challenging," Hamilton said, "but I confess we aren't close as I'd like. My mother died when I was a boy. The trade winds seem to have scattered us."

Hamilton turned to Eliza. His gaze felt as intimate as a hand upon her shoulder. She reached for her wine goblet. The spacious room seemed smaller than usual.

"Miss Schuyler, your father tells me that your family recently hosted the British officer corps. That was noble of you."

Eliza made herself look at him. Although Hamilton's coat was cut from an excellent fabric, it was faded, as if washed too many times. Officers purchased their own uniforms and many dressed resplendently. Eliza wondered if he was redirecting the conversation on purpose. Perhaps he came from modest circumstances.

"I would like to think the British might do the same for us, if tables were turned," she said. "But their needless destruction of Saratoga makes that difficult."

Eliza again heard a stridency she didn't intend to convey. What was wrong with her? Although she felt like crying about Burgoyne's destruction of her childhood home, she shouldn't betray it to a stranger, especially such an attractive one.

Only Papa had confronted the disaster with fortitude. Eliza still couldn't bear the sight of the naked chimneys in the charred fields, but he was already putting up a smaller house and cutting trees to replace the outbuildings destroyed by the Redcoats. Eliza didn't see how the family's fortunes would ever recover.

Papa set down his fork and gave a rueful look over his wire-rimmed glasses. "Betsey, dear, such things happen in war. General Burgoyne was simply doing his duty."

"I've heard you say so before, Papa, but I cannot imagine *your* defining the destruction of homes and farms as a duty. Burgoyne is a brute!"

Eliza flushed. She wished she'd held her tongue.

Hamilton smiled. "Only a fool marches into a family dispute, General Schuyler. But if forced to make an alliance, I must side with your daughter. I also can't imagine you turning innocent civilians out of their home."

"I hope you're right, Colonel Hamilton," Papa said, "but war takes men down roads they never imagined."

Hamilton nodded and returned his attention to his plate with the dispatch of a soldier under orders to proceed to the next assignment.

Eliza took a sip of wine. Her throat had gone dry. She ought to have paid closer attention to Angelica's lectures about conversation. Her sister would have an amusing story to tell.

"I'm afraid we weren't quite the perfect hosts to our British guests," she said. "Though we did try."

Colonel Hamilton looked up at the suggestion of a tale. "That's hard to believe, coming from a family so renowned for its generosity."

"My younger brother couldn't resist needling the gentlemen about their misfortune. Papa and Mama gave their own bed to General Burgoyne, and we placed cots around it for his adjutants. When Philip Jeremiah, who's only nine, heard there were real Redcoats across the hall, he was very excited—and put his head in the room to catch a glimpse. 'Now you're my prisoners,' he told them, and slammed the door."

Hamilton's eyes crinkled. "Your brother will make a fine soldier."

"Or jailer."

"Mrs. Schuyler was horrified," Papa said, "after all she'd done to alleviate the sting of surrender. I believe my wife nearly emptied our wine cellar."

"General Burgoyne was happy to assist," Eliza said.

"It's well known that Gentleman Johnny doesn't enjoy being cut off from his claret, which must have played into your father's strategy." Hamilton turned to his host. "Seriously, sir, hadn't they used most of their supplies by the time of battle? We heard you felled half the forest between Ticonderoga and Saratoga to slow their advance down the road."

Papa recounted at length the events with which Eliza was familiar, having lived through the terrifying months when the Redcoats crept closer day by day. The young colonel asked detailed questions about the equipping of the Continental troops, and both men expressed their aggravation with obtaining food and ammunition from the thirteen states.

"How can we prevail with no treasury, General Schuyler? Our pockets are empty. King George merely sends to Parliament for whatever he needs."

Papa shook his head. "I'm not sure which is worse—lack of money or lack of discipline. Every infantryman fancies himself a general."

The two men spoke freely and, to Eliza's surprise, as if there was no difference in age, rank, or pedigree. Hamilton asked a question whenever her father's story slowed. By the end of supper, it was clear the colonel and her father had taken a firm liking to one another.

Alexander Hamilton nevertheless offered his apologies when Pompey placed the silver epergne of jellies and sweetmeats in the center of the table.

"I hope you'll forgive my rudeness, *mademoiselle*," he said, turning at last to Eliza. "I've utterly monopolized your father and now compound my *faux pas* by leaving before dessert. If I come this way again, I hope you'll tell me your own views on all that's happened."

"Of course," Eliza said, both flattered and dismayed. "It's unfortunate you have to leave so soon. Can't you at least stay for a cup of tea?"

"Your father will attest that my business is urgent. And even if I didn't need to pry another brigade from Horatio Gates, my companions would have my head if they knew I had lollygagged an entire afternoon in such enchanting company. They'd never believe I was here merely in the line of duty, Miss Schuyler."

"We wouldn't wish you to neglect your orders, Colonel Hamilton," Eliza said as the young man pushed back his chair.

Her father rose to show their guest to the door, where the two men spoke for such a long time that an icy blast followed Papa back into the room when he returned to the table.

"I read Hamilton's pamphlets at the start of the war, and heard of his coolness under fire," he said, "but I had no idea what a thoroughly fine officer he is. His grasp of military matters is remarkable in one so young. And he's got strength of character. I see why Washington sent him. Gates will hold on to his troops like a boa constrictor—but Hamilton will fight like a tiger." Papa reached for the wine and refilled his glass. A smile played on his lips.

Eliza was happy to see her father enjoy himself. Hamilton's warm defense of Papa's achievements soothed the hurt they had all felt since the bleak day when Papa announced that Congress had relieved him of command. The young colonel's company had restored her father's glow.

Yet Eliza wasn't sure about her own feelings. The West Indian said she was enchanting, but the war consumed all of his conversation. He had thoroughly ignored her. She might as well have been a portrait on the wall.

Eliza took a deep breath. And that was simply awful because, for the first time, she might have met a man who—for no good reason beyond his daring words and devastating eyes—she simply couldn't live without.

CHAPTER SEVENTEEN

June 1778

Monmouth County, Pennsylvania

"Challenges for undivulged causes may be reconciled on the [dueling] ground after one shot . . . But no apology can be received in any case, after the parties have actually taken their ground, without exchange of fire."

Irish Code Duello, 1777

THE DISTANT POPPING SOUNDS WERE NOT what they expected.

Alexander looked over at the general sitting astride his trembling white charger in the oppressive New Jersey heat. It was approaching noon. Washington's broad, patrician face was completely still, listening. General Charles Lee should have sent a messenger by now.

The general turned to him. "Colonel Hamilton. Ride on. I'll bring up the main body and the artillery. Damn it! Find out what the hell is happening up ahead."

The profanity, mild as it was, surprised Alexander. The general strictly forbade swearing. Yet he shared his commander's anxiety. Would Charles Lee really fight? If the man didn't, would their army finally collapse?

The two brigades that Hamilton had wrested from Horatio Gates, combined with the army's constant drilling, meant they were as ready as they would ever be. Yet arrogant Charles Lee, second in command, had advised Washington's war council that it would be futile to attack the Redcoats until French reinforcements arrived. A former British general, Charles Lee wasn't shy about doling out his superior wisdom. Men born in the colonies generally listened with their mouths agape. Washington's junior officers responded to Lee's dismissive predictions about their army with the martial pluck of a gaggle of dairymaids.

"It's no use pursuing the Redcoats after the losses at Valley Forge," Lee had said two days earlier. He waved the hand from which he'd lost two fingers in a duel years earlier. "You'll have to wait for the French. They're much better soldiers."

To his credit, Washington overruled both Lee and his own timid war council. The British were evacuating Philadelphia for New York. It was the perfect opportunity to pounce on the Redcoats' exposed flanks. Although the bleak winter at Valley Forge had killed nearly a third of the army, the survivors were better disciplined than ever. When a German volunteer, the Baron von Steuben, offered to drill them in European warfare, the troops had responded with the grit of men who knew it was their last chance. The news that France had finally sided with America rekindled Washington's determination to take the offensive.

Alexander agreed. George Washington must show Congress that he could battle the enemy without waiting for foreign rescue. He otherwise risked losing command to General Gates, whose ambition hadn't abated despite his recent embarrassment when a letter from a subordinate who said America needed more men like the heroic Gates and fewer like Washington—a weakling who would ruin the country—had found its way into public view.

Gates deflected attention from his failure to put down such mutinous talk by accusing Alexander Hamilton of stealing the private letter during their meetings in Albany. Washington rejected the preposterous claim, revealed as a lie when Gates's junior officer was caught leaking yet other information.

Alexander fumed whenever he thought of Horatio Gates: an inferior leader who had stolen Philip Schuyler's glory, threatened George Washington's command, and impugned Alexander's honor into the bargain. What a wretch.

And now there was no word from Major General Lee, yet another diva.

Lee had not reacted well when Washington rejected his advice, though Lee was offered the privilege of leading the charge against the retreating British. Alexander would have traded life itself for such an opportunity, but the Englishman sourly declined what he called a fool's errand. General Lee changed his mind only after Washington proffered the glory spot to the Marquis de Lafayette. Once the youthful Marquis accepted, Lee changed his mind and demanded the honor for himself—which Washington felt compelled to give him as the more senior officer.

Alexander himself had transcribed Lee's orders, sent in the middle of the night and again before dawn. Washington ordered him to be aggressive. When "fair opportunity offered," General Lee was to attack with his advance guard.

What fairer opportunity could there be? Washington had given Lee five thousand troops to strike slow-moving columns encumbered with wagons of food and gunpowder. The Redcoats would wheel around to protect their supplies, whereupon Washington's main body would descend upon the disorganized enemy. Or such was the plan.

Alexander saluted. "Yes, sir," he said, and spurred his horse in the direction of the sporadic gunfire. The temperature had already soared past one hundred in the steamy countryside. He would find Lee.

Alexander galloped full speed over the meadow grasses and milkweed that Lee's men had flattened in their advance. He took the road where he could and jumped hedgerows where he couldn't. A dogwood snatched his hat as he dashed under its branches, but he pelted forward, unwilling to waste a second. The sound of gunfire became more distinct as his horse took the rise just before Monmouth Courthouse, but he still couldn't hear the drumbeat to which advance brigades marched.

Alexander reined his horse on the crest. Below, thousands of uniformed men with muskets slung over their shoulders were marching toward him. Some ran. A few had taken cover behind trees and were still firing—which accounted for the popping sounds—but the army was in rout. The Continental Army was retreating back toward Valley Forge.

Beyond the wide valley, on another rise, British officers were organizing a line of cannons and howitzers in the blazing sun. Cavalry units with gleaming swords formed along one side of the meadow. British infantry clothed in scarlet crowded the ridge beyond. The Redcoats stood with their muskets pointed at the Americans, awaiting the order to charge en masse.

Charles Lee had ordered a full retreat and not bothered to tell them. If the British took advantage, their men would be slaughtered.

Alexander spied the American general a few hundred yards below amid a knot of officers. Lafayette was with him. Alexander urged his mount downward and nimbly jumped a low fence. He must turn the sea of men.

The horse snorted as Alexander reined to a stop. Lee's features hardened at the sight of Washington's chief aide.

"General! I beg of you, sir. Make a stand."

"Good day, Colonel Hamilton," Lee said. "I cannot fight with the men I've been given in the circumstances we face. Move—or there'll be a bloodbath."

"My dear general," said Alexander, "Let me stay with you. We must hold the line."

Lee looked beyond him. "'Tis over, Colonel. We'll fight another day."

"Washington is coming up, General Lee. Surely you read his orders."

"Enough of your insolence, Hamilton." Lee flicked his reins.

Men streamed around them. A tall militiaman with a coonskin cap and long rifle glared as he passed.

The Marquis de Lafayette nudged his horse forward at an angle to the general's mount.

"*Oui, mon général.* We must fight." The Frenchman's face shone with perspiration and his cravat was limp with sweat, but his eyes were eager. "The Redcoats, they are still assembling. Allow me to head them off—or they will trap us."

Lee looked at the French aristocrat to whom Washington had originally entrusted the battle. His lips pursed as if tasting vinegar, but he shrugged. "Take your men and engage the cavalry while we retreat, General Lafayette. Keep them off our flanks."

"Yes, sir." Lafayette unsheathed his sword, turned his horse, and dashed back to his lines.

Alexander knew he shouldn't admonish Lee. But he also knew what the general wanted. To him, there was only one real general, whose voice Alexander copied in every letter he wrote. Sometimes, all Washington had to say was "Ham," and Alexander knew what he needed. Alexander didn't presume a friendship of equals. But the two men had something far more important: a joint and instinctive understanding of what must be done, and complete confidence that the other could be counted upon to do it.

"The main army isn't far behind," Alexander repeated.

Lee accepted a flask of water from his aide. The general's face did not show the effects of the extreme heat though he drank for a long moment before returning the bottle. "We're falling back, Colonel Hamilton. I suggest you come with us."

Alexander turned his mount toward the ridge over which he had just flown. "The artillery requires barely half an hour to catch up, sir. A short delay—a brave stand—it's all we need."

Lee kept riding.

"Please, sir. Pray reconsider," Alexander said. The army was disbanding before his eyes.

A group of horses pounded over the hill. Washington was upon them in seconds. He must have broken away from the artillery columns.

"General Lee. What is the meaning, sir?" Washington's eyebrows were like drawn daggers. His blue eyes blazed. He nearly stood in his stirrups. "Why are our men in retreat?"

Lee stiffened. "Sir, the American troops would not withstand the British bayonets."

"You damned poltroon!" Washington shouted. "You never even tried them. Son of a bitch!"

"But, sir. The Redcoats have taken the field."

"Because you gave it to them, you pompous, silly ass!"

Lee started to protest, but Washington cut him off. "General Lee, you're relieved of command. Retire to the rear."

Washington advanced into the field and reared his white charger. Every soldier within a hundred yards stopped to look up at the familiar hand raised over their enterprise, over their very lives.

"Stand fast, my boys, stand fast!" General Washington shouted. "Turn and meet your enemy. Our artillery will support you. Today, we will win. Today is our day!"

Alexander looked around and knew every man felt precisely the same. Washington offered all they needed. *Resolve*.

The troops cheered loudly and turned—no one faltered an instant—and swept across the meadow toward the advancing British. Live or die, they would fight. It was all Alexander wanted. He would cover himself in glory or blood, or both.

The rest of the day was a blur of heat and dust and gunfire. Alexander found himself at nearly every point on the line, urging others onward, cutting off those who took fright, delivering orders to outlying generals, striking a Queen's Light Dragoon with his hanger sword when the man tried to intercept him. Nothing mattered but each precise second and what he did with it.

The general's white stallion collapsed from the heat and the Virginian sprang to a second horse. A cannonball fell at their feet, throwing dirt in their faces, but Washington took no notice. Alexander saw Ajax, unmistakable with his height, reorganizing an artillery brigade that had bolted. Camp wives in their dusty skirts worked at the margins. They brought water for men and horses. One took her fallen husband's place on a gun crew and swabbed out the hot barrel.

Every soul on the battlefield—man, woman, beast—gave its all. Even Charles Lee stayed in the end, defending their rear. The long day ended in a draw, but it was the fight for which Alexander had been longing since he gave up his brigade.

Casualties were heavy. More than one hundred soldiers died, forty from sunstroke in the brutal heat. Alexander later heard that a Hessian Jäger shot the horse out from under John Laurens, an aristocratic South Carolina officer who had befriended Alexander. Aaron Burr of New York and several other well-known officers lost their mounts as well. But the Continentals inflicted a harsh blow on the Redcoats, who lost twice as many as they did. Washington's troops had proven they could fight.

Alexander heard the casualty figures from the pillow of yet another hospital cot. His horse had spooked when a British infantryman jumped from behind a hedgerow and fired straight at him. The animal fell with a bullet to the heart. Fortunately, someone else cut down the enemy soldier. Alexander had been pinned under the dying horse, conscious only of the peril of being crushed under its sweating torso and the earthy smell as it lost bowel control amid the smoke of the battlefield. Alexander rolled away when the horse writhed one last time. He couldn't place weight on his right foot for days afterward.

He had limped with a crutch into Charles Lee's court-martial. The major general demanded the chance to clear his name, as was customary in matters of honor, and conducted the cross-examination himself. Lee told the court that Alexander had endorsed his actions while on the battlefield.

"That's not so, sir," Alexander said. "I did my utmost to remind you of General Washington's orders, which were to stand firm. Indeed, to me, you appeared anxious to retreat."

The court upheld Alexander's assessment and those of other officers in the field, including Lafayette. The military tribunal found Charles Lee guilty on all counts and suspended him for a year. Lee's friends in Congress tried to overturn the decision, but failed. For George Washington, the Battle of Monmouth Court House was a military and political victory.

Yet Philip Schuyler was right. War took one down unexpected roads and they were usually dark.

Ajax Manly was wrapped to his chin against the freeze when he handed Alexander the ivory-handled dueling pistols in the wan light of December. The young soldier's hands shook. Alexander couldn't tell if it was from nerves or the extreme cold, but it reminded him that the New Yorker was still a boy despite his remarkable strength.

Ajax's youth had been on display that morning as well, when he babbled on about the serving girl whose unusual green eyes had captured his heart. An officer from Georgia had brought the young woman as part of his entourage. In Alexander's experience, most Southerners expected to be coddled by slaves when they weren't fighting for America's freedom.

"I'm gonna marry her when we win," Ajax said. The boy who had never seemed particularly interested in girls now insisted upon the worst choice. For weeks, Ajax had dogged the canteen where the servant baked bread for her master and his battalion.

The situation made Alexander almost ill. How could he tell the boy what he must hear? Why did Alexander have to be the one to say the obvious? That milk spoiled and life was cruel? Yet a duty of friendship was to tell painful truths. You couldn't make a woman yours when she was literally the property of someone else.

"Her owner's not going to give her up," he said.

"I'm saving my pay. I'll buy her."

"Find another."

Ajax shook his head. "You don't understand how one woman can be special. That's the sad fact, Ham."

Alexander hated it when Ajax acted as if he knew more about life, but didn't yield to the annoyance. "Say what you will, Ajax. I know plantation owners. I grew up around them. You didn't. They don't need the money and they hang on to slaves they like. Don't get attached."

Ajax ignored Alexander's warning. And now the boy's hands trembled as he handed Alexander the elegant weapons. Both of them liked John Laurens. In fact, Alexander had come to adore the witty, highborn South Carolinian. Laurens had taken an equal interest in the unknown West Indian who had risen so quickly in the ranks, encouraging him to marry one of the appealing heiresses who attended Martha Washington's dances. Alexander doubted that any father would consent, but John Laurens had tempted him to hope. Now his friend might not live to see another morning.

Alexander accepted the dueling pistols. "Thank you, Ajax. Would you please wait behind the trees?"

The identical flintlocks weren't as heavy as Alexander expected. They seemed too light to take a man's life. He measured the powder and selected two balls.

John Laurens leaned against a birch tree, his blond hair tied at the nape with blue velvet, while General Lee studied the bleak sky a short distance away in the company of his second, Major Evan Edwards of the Eleventh Pennsylvania. Snowstorms had pummeled the countryside since the start of December and the dueling ground four miles outside Philadelphia was white. Another storm threatened. No one spoke while Alexander loaded. The bare limbs of a nearby tree sawed against one another in the wind.

"Major Edwards," Alexander said when he finished. "Would you examine the pistols, please?"

Edwards stepped forward to scrutinize the weapons. He nodded.

Alexander turned. "Shall we begin, my dear Laurens?"

John studied Alexander. They both knew he was ready. John had been poised a month at least, his outrage mounting with each fresh rumor that Charles Lee had insulted General Washington.

The Iroquois called Charles Lee "Boiling Water" because of his hot temper. Given the vitriol that Lee had spouted at nearly every opportunity since his court-martial, the name appeared apt. The disgraced officer had narrowly avoided a duel with Baron von Steuben only a few weeks earlier after disparaging the drillmaster's bravery. But Lee would not leave off his malicious comments about George Washington. Resolved to defend the General's honor, John Laurens issued the challenge that Lee haughtily accepted.

Alexander understood that John couldn't live with himself if he wasn't prepared to defend his fellow Southerner against accusations that undermined the general's authority. What sort of officer would he be?

And John was brave to a fault. After Brandywine, the Marquis de Lafayette observed, "It wasn't John's fault he wasn't killed or wounded. He did everything necessary."

Laurens, Lafayette, and Hamilton—all roughly the same age—had become inseparable when they discovered they shared the conviction that all men should be free, including blacks. It made them conscious of sailing beyond the pale together. They agreed that nothing justified the contempt whites felt toward Negroes, whose natural abilities ranked with those of Europeans. Alexander supported John's striking proposal that Congress grant slaves their freedom in exchange for joining the revolutionary army. Laurens's social stature—his wealthy father was president of the Continental Congress—made it a real proposition.

John also had much to lose. He was heir to the country's largest slave-trading house. If bondsmen were allowed to fight for their liberty, John Laurens courted bankruptcy. His integrity healed Alexander's heart. Slavery need not be eternal.

"How do you wish to proceed, Major Edwards?" Alexander asked.

Evan Edwards turned to Charles Lee.

General Lee looked down his beaky nose and casually took his pistol. "Let's advance and fire when it seems proper."

Alexander avoided staring at the hand from which Lee had previously lost two fingers. Twenty years older than Laurens, Lee had decades of experience on John. Affairs of honor were supposed to be impersonal, but for a terrible moment Alexander simply hated Lee.

"Is that agreeable, Colonel Laurens?" Edwards said.

"Certainly." John handed his gloves to Alexander, took his gun, and walked to the edge of the clearing.

Alexander stepped to the sidelines. They had seen so many men cut down. It felt like a lifetime of blood and suffering and waste. But he hated duels especially. They seemed like little more than private executions.

Yet soldiers clung to the tradition. The code duello allowed men to defend their dignity when it was all they had left. And a man without honor was finished. To Alexander, it was one more mark against Horatio Gates that he had broken down in tears before a recent duel, which was called off in consequence. Unpaid, unshod, unwashed, military men viewed heroism as their best and sometimes only compensation. The Declaration of Independence ended with the words, "we mutually pledge to each other our Lives, our Fortunes and our sacred *Honor*."

To a soldier, it made sense. Honor was currency. No real man relinquished his without a fight.

Yet the thought of John Laurens dying that day made Alexander's knees weak. He clenched his fists lest he be unmanned.

Charles Lee walked forward. Laurens advanced toward him. The opponents raised their pistols, turned sideways, and drew a bead.

Alexander prayed the shots would go wide or that John would find his mark before Lee killed him.

Two reports rang out. The pungent smell of gunpowder invaded Alexander's nostrils. He started forward to catch John, then realized that neither man had fallen.

Laurens looked at Alexander. "Another round, please." He handed his pistol over for reloading.

"Wait," Charles Lee said. He placed a hand against his right side.

Major Edwards stepped forward. "Sir! Are you wounded?"

Laurens caught Lee under the elbow. "General. Are you all right?"

Charles Lee looked down at his hand. Blood covered the stumps of his fingers. He pressed tentatively again on his waist, and winced. "The injury is not as severe as I feared upon first feeling the ball. It's but a flesh wound. We can begin again."

"Surely honor has been satisfied, sir," Edwards said.

"Let the matter end here," Alexander said. "You've both acquitted yourselves bravely."

John Laurens released Lee's elbow and the general held out his gun for reloading.

"If the general wishes to resume the duel," Laurens said, "I can make no objection." He spoke with dignity, but his face was taut.

"General Lee, there's no personal matter between you and Colonel Laurens of which I'm aware," Alexander said. "Lacking that, surely each of you has defended his honor sufficiently."

Lee took a handkerchief from his breast pocket and wiped the blood from his mutilated hand. A wet spot had appeared on his waistcoat. The proud Englishman didn't answer.

"If you insist upon continuing, sir, I'm too protective of my friend's honor to oppose it," Alexander said, "but I wish you'd reconsider."

"I do so, as well, General Lee." Major Edwards held the reloaded gun in abeyance. "A shot apiece seems adequate."

Charles Lee scooped up a handful of snow and held it against his waistcoat. He looked at Laurens. "I trust the judgment of our seconds, sir. If they decide we should end the duel, I'll abide by their decision." He turned to Edwards. "I have no personal enmity toward Colonel Laurens. But only he can answer whether the same is true for him."

The question hung in the frosty air. It was the nub of every duel. Was there some personal hatred that death alone could satisfy, or was honor the only itch that needed scratching?

Alexander looked at John. The light was dim on Laurens's refined features.

John brushed aside a lock of blond hair. "I was informed on good authority that General Lee had slandered General Washington personally. I found myself bound to resent this on account of my relation to General Washington. This was my sole motive."

"I gave my opinion of General Washington's military conduct. I might do so again," Charles Lee said. His expression was steely and he offered little ground. "Every officer is entitled to his views, and I do not hold myself accountable to you, sir, in that respect. But allow me to clarify that I never criticized General Washington personally. It would be incompatible with my own character as an officer."

Alexander and Edwards exchanged quick glances.

"It seems you've both satisfied your honor," Major Edwards said.

"Indeed," Alexander said. "Your civility does justice to you both, as does your bravery."

Everything now rested on Laurens—proud, rash, stubborn, and committed. Alexander held his breath. The sentimental Marquis de Lafayette wouldn't be the only one devastated. Alexander couldn't bear to lose another brother. John Laurens might end the duel with a word, but he was extraordinarily partial to Washington.

Laurens gave his opponent an appraising look. A duel was as formal as a Chinese wedding.

"I accept your explanation, General Lee. Thank you for the opportunity to clear General Washington's name." He smiled. "Perhaps you'll join me for a cup of rum at Indian King Tavern. We can toast Congress's safe return to Philadelphia."

Alexander sighed with relief. Honor had been gratified. There would be no more deaths, at least that day.

He hoped never to see another duel. He couldn't imagine taking a man's life that way.

CHAPTER EIGHTEEN

February 1780

Morristown, New Jersey

"When I saw the liberty poles and the people all engaged for the support of freedom, I could not but like and be pleased with such thing. . . . And living on the borders of Rhode Island, where whole companies of colored people enlisted . . . [I escaped] into the American army, where I served faithful about ten months, when my master found and took me home . . . notwithstanding the songs of liberty that . . . thrilled through my heart."

Jehu Grant, 1777, *The Revolution Remembered*

Aunt Gertrude leaned forward to tuck a fur-trimmed blanket around Eliza and her companion, Kitty Livingston. The sled tilted under the bulk of Papa's sister. Wind caught the tassels of her fur-trimmed bonnet and blew them back toward the brightly lit farmhouse as the group sped down the lane to General Washington's headquarters. Moonlight cast diamonds on the crystalized snowdrifts.

"There," Gertrude said, resuming her seat. "We want pink cheeks for the dance but not at the risk of frostbite. Beauty before comfort, within reason."

"Thank you," Eliza said with a smile.

Papa's sister was well-matched with her husband, John Cochran, a doctor who had worked unceasingly to inoculate their troops against smallpox. Uncle John was General Washington's personal physician, and he and his wife had taken a home near the army's winter headquarters at Morristown. Eliza looked forward to meeting the famous Virginian at the dance to which she and Kitty were invited that evening.

"You're in the nick of time," her aunt told them when they first arrived. "General Washington is holding one of his dancing assemblies tomorrow night. You'll be the belles of the ball."

The rest of that day and the next had been a whirlwind of preparation for what her aunt assured them would be a memorable evening despite winter's austerity. American officers sporting gold braid, French officers bedecked with medals and lace, and George Washington resplendent in his Virginia finery would all vie for a dance. When Aunt Gertrude described General von Steuben as the most gallant soldier in the army and insisted—with starry eyes—that his dashing Prussian etiquette defined courtliness, Eliza and young Kitty laughed at the married woman's girlish enthusiasm.

"Mrs. Cochran, I do believe you're in love," Kitty said.

"Married not buried," Aunt Gertrude said as she twirled a lock of Eliza's chestnut hair around a curling rod. "I assure you my dancing instincts remain very lively."

Watching her aunt in the mirror, and catching Kitty's reflection while she powdered her ringlets, Eliza admired their carefree attitude. Neither appeared nervous about the coming dance. Of course, Aunt Gertrude would claim Uncle John's arm after she took another officer's arm for a dance or two. And Kitty Livingston would attract the attention of most gentlemen, since anyone blessed with eyes or brains was drawn to the vivacious heiress.

But Eliza was anxious. She had brought the dress made from grandmother Van Rensselaer's embroidered silk that showed her figure to best advantage, and loved dancing for the sheer physical pleasure of executing patterns with flair, but this occasion was special. Eliza worried she might misstep.

When Aunt Gertrude invited her to visit, Eliza knew it would bring her into the constellation of bachelors orbiting George Washington. The rebellion had attracted adventurers from every European monarchy eager to see action. Numerous debutantes had already visited the army's winter quarters, like village girls reaching for ribbons on a maypole. If Angelica had not eloped with John Church, whom the family now accepted warmly since they had no choice, her sister would have finagled an invitation long before it occurred to Eliza.

"What an excellent idea, *mijn lief*," Mama said when Eliza mentioned visiting her aunt and uncle, whose home was always open to the Schuyler children. She smiled meaningfully. "Colonel Tilghman is still with the general, I believe."

But Tench Tilghman was not why Eliza had taken her future in her hands. Mama and Papa had encouraged several gentlemen to court after Eliza turned the advanced age of twenty-two, yet she found herself comparing each to the colonel who had blown through Albany two Decembers earlier. Some were handsomer, most were taller, all were richer. But none spoke as Alexander Hamilton did in a voice that penetrated her indifference. No one roused her as he did.

Yet Eliza also resented the honeyed timbre that had cast a spell over her and then gone silent for such a long time. She wanted to get the echo out of her head, and finally decided that she must hear his voice again to prove that Alexander Hamilton was not really as compelling as he appeared that cold, overwrought afternoon when the war got under her skin.

She also half-hoped for the opposite conclusion—reluctant to abandon the excited, spellbound feeling his memory gave her. She wasn't sure whether it would be worse to find he wasn't special, or that he was and she hadn't the power to captivate him.

Aunt Gertrude confirmed that all of General Washington's aides were in residence. Harsh snowstorms had trapped both the British and Americans in their fortifications. The business of fighting was at a halt. Officers on both sides filled their evenings with soirees and parties attended by local debutantes. Papa's friends in occupied New York City complained that royal officers had made as many conquests in American drawing rooms as on the battlefield.

"Will there be other ladies at the dance tonight?" Kitty asked over the jingle of sleigh bells and muffled footfalls of the horses.

"I'm not sure," Aunt Gertrude said. "Polly DeVos and Cornelia Lott left just last week. They were in Morristown nearly a month over the Christmas holiday."

"Those two left behind a trail of broken hearts," Uncle John said. "'Tis a pity I've nothing in my medical bag to stanch the wounds."

"Polly was incorrigible. A pretty flibbertigibbet without a hint of conscience," Aunt Gertrude said. "Those poor men hadn't a chance against that chatterbox." She straightened the blanket protectively over her husband's knees.

"I don't think the American officer corps is as defenseless as you might imagine, Gertie dear," Uncle John said.

"Oh, I know some are rakes. That Colonel Hamilton is quite the ladies' man. But I heard even he was a goner over Polly. Mark my words, there'll be wedding bells yet in Morristown."

Eliza's heart sank.

Uncle John leaned into his point. "I'm sure someone will chase that Polly until she catches him. But Hamilton is a rank amateur compared with the Marquis de Lafayette. I declare women faint clean away when he kisses their hands. His Parisian accent is deadlier than a thirty-two-pounder."

"You underestimate our Little Lion," Kitty said. "I've known Colonel Hamilton since he attended Elizabethtown Academy, before the war. He's quite versed in the ways of Cupid. I doubt Monsieur Lafayette can best him."

Kitty's rosebud lips closed with a knowing smile. Eliza wondered just how familiar Kitty and Alexander Hamilton were. She felt a stab of unreasonable jealousy.

"I didn't realize you were acquainted previously," Eliza said.

Kitty raised an eyebrow. "Hammie? Oh, yes," she said as the sleigh drew up to Washington's headquarters at the Ford mansion. A string quartet sounded through glowing windows.

Sentinels helped the party from their carriage. Eliza gave her cloak to a Negro serving girl as they stepped through the beautiful portal. The dance was in full swing. Although men far outnumbered women, five or six couples had taken the floor. Officers of all ages congregated around a banquet table upon which platters of roasted chicken, sugar beets, and plain bread were arrayed around a pepper pot tureen. The warm, earthy scent of the soup reminded Eliza that she had skipped dinner. She was famished.

A plump, short woman sat near the hearth in what appeared a place of honor. Her elegant dewdrop earrings twinkled in the firelight and a matching garnet necklace graced her white neck. Her gown was made of brown homespun, though, and time alone frosted her unpowdered hair. She rose and came forward with hands outstretched in welcome.

"Mrs. Cochran, Doctor Cochran. I declare! What a delightful sight. Thank you for coming on such an inclement evening."

"It would take more than snowdrifts to keep us away, Mrs. Washington," Uncle John said with a bow.

"Don't tempt fate, Dr. Cochran. One more storm like our last and the soldiers will have to burrow like rabbits. As it is, I can hardly keep my head above the drifts on my way to the hospital."

"My orderlies shall carry you piggybacked, if necessary. The patients rally when they see you. Your presence is my best medicine."

"I visit whenever I can, Dr. Cochran, but I doubt my husband will grant me leave to go by piggyback." Martha Washington glanced affectionately at a tall, robust man in the prime of life who stood near the punch bowl, dressed in a suit of black velvet with cut-glass buttons. He appeared at the end of a joke, because three or four officers with expressions of merry anticipation burst into laughter a second later. The general laughed, too, though Eliza noticed that he kept his lips closed and shook with silent mirth.

Washington must have sensed his wife's attention because he glanced over, and a look of such intimate understanding passed between them that Eliza felt she had seen into a faultless marriage.

Mrs. Washington turned back to her guests. "Whom have you brought us, Dr. Cochran? I know Kitty, of course," she said, and gave the New Jersey maiden a kiss on both cheeks.

"Mrs. Washington, please allow me to present my niece Elizabeth Schuyler, the daughter of Major General Philip Schuyler."

Martha Washington must have heard about Philip Schuyler's disgrace, but only good will showed on her face. "What a fine and generous man your father is, Miss Schuyler. There are few officers my husband esteems so highly. Welcome to Morristown."

"Thank you, Mrs. Washington. My father sends his greetings. My mother begs you to remember her also. She asked me to give you this." Eliza handed Mrs. Washington the packet she had carried from Albany.

Their hostess unwrapped the gift and took out the pair of Irish lace cuffs. "My goodness. What lovely needlework."

"May I help you fasten them?" Eliza asked, reassured by the grand lady's unaffected manner and obvious pleasure.

"Yes, please."

Eliza buttoned the lace cuffs around Mrs. Washington's wrists.

"Thank you, Miss Schuyler. Our wartime homespun never looked so fashionable." The older woman held the cuffs out for general admiration, and the Cochrans and Kitty Livingston expressed their approval.

"To me, you are the height of fashion, Mrs. Washington," Eliza said.

Indeed, here was Eliza's ideal, she realized in that moment: a woman who remained at her husband's side regardless of danger, made herself useful to others in need, and had a kind word for the least important person present. "I hope you'll allow me to accompany you to the hospital sometime."

Mrs. Washington expressed her willingness to include Eliza in the future and encouraged her to dance with every soldier present, then returned to her throne at the fireplace accompanied by Aunt Gertrude, for whom a young officer courteously set out a seat. It wasn't until he turned around and caught Kitty Livingston's eye that Eliza realized it was Alexander Hamilton.

"Kitty!" Hamilton came forward and took the debutante's hand to kiss. "You're as radiant as spring. I feel winter's chill subsiding already."

It was the same melodic, irresistible voice. Drat. Eliza reminded herself to breathe.

"Hammie. Or should I say, Colonel Hamilton?" Kitty said with a smile. "I hear one must stand behind a screen to withstand the brilliance of your military career."

"Your Ladyship behind a screen? I more easily imagine Venus as a wallflower. But you needn't worry about glare. I stand in the shade of our valorous general."

Hamilton spoke cheerfully, but Eliza wondered if his words had a double meaning. Most men didn't relish being overshadowed.

He turned to Eliza. "And who is this enchanting creature you've brought?"

Kitty touched Eliza's bare elbow. "Allow me to present my dear friend, Elizabeth Schuyler. You must know her father, General Philip Schuyler."

"He does," Eliza said. She had resolved to be herself, rather than a coquette. "It's a pleasure to see you again, Colonel Hamilton. You may recall visiting our home in Albany."

Hamilton clapped his hand to his brow, then bowed. "Miss Schuyler. Of course! Please forgive me. I was distracted by Horatio Gates on that occasion and am confounded by Mrs. Washington's excellent rum punch on this one." He took her hand and kissed it. "Can you forgive a repentant sinner?"

The band paused. Eliza heard the opening strains of a new tune. "If he knows how to dance."

Hamilton and Kitty Livingston laughed.

"Then please allow me to prove I can," the colonel replied and, still holding her hand, drew her away from Kitty and onto the dance floor. Another officer claimed the young heiress, and the couples joined the lines of women and men facing one another.

Eliza was glad they couldn't talk during the fast contra dance. Her heart thumped as ridiculously as the heroine of one of Angelica's novels and she feared that if Hamilton spoke she would trip over her own feet. When the dance concluded, he offered to collect plates for them, and Eliza accepted a chair that he produced. She wondered if he would cajole Kitty to join them. She hoped not.

"Please tell me about your father," Hamilton said when he returned with small portions of meat and bread. The serving table was now nearly bare. "How is General Schuyler?"

Eliza looked down at the slice of roasted chicken and had the odd sensation of not knowing what to do with it. She poked at the food. Would Philip Schuyler take center stage again? Had she really braved winter's fury to meet a man who had forgotten her face? Was she really that pathetic?

She glanced up. "My father is well, thank you. He's almost completely rebuilt Saratoga, and Congress appointed him to the Board of Indian Affairs. He's working to keep the Tuscaroras on our side."

"I'm sure he'll manage that feat quite ably, as he has all others," Hamilton said. He took a healthy bite of his supper.

Eliza hadn't noticed his lips the first time they met. Now she found herself conscious of their fullness, and the way they curved in deeply at the corners.

"I was utterly disenchanted by Congress's decision to replace him with Gates, whose only talent is scheming," Hamilton continued. "We could use your father here. General Schuyler must miss the front."

"No, I don't believe he does. He says he'd rather ride his hobbyhorse than a warhorse. Papa loves improving the countryside."

Hamilton's eyebrows rose. "Then your father is even more uncommon than I thought—and must suffer from vanity less than other men. It's a rare officer who can accept a place behind the lines. Most detest violence, but if it comes, feel compelled to serve."

"Do you feel that way also, Colonel Hamilton?" Eliza found it hard to imagine him fighting for his own life—or worse, taking another's.

"Absolutely. There's no place I'd rather be than in front of a brigade."

"Is that where you'll be this spring, when the weather thaws?"

Hamilton gave a rueful laugh. "No. I shall be in front of a column of numbers. Adding and subtracting and writing letters to Congress. I'd like to join my friend John Laurens, who's been given a southern command, but General Washington needs me here."

"They say the pen is mightier than the sword."

"In peacetime, yes."

Hamilton set his empty plate on a table behind him. His expression changed to anxious concern as he spied hers. "My dear Miss Schuyler, you've hardly touched your supper. You're such a tiny thing already. We've precious little female companionship. What shall we do if we lose you?"

"I dined earlier," Eliza lied. "And I've heard that . . . that our officers suffer from a surfeit rather than a shortage of womanly admirers."

Hamilton's eyes showed amusement. "Your candor is refreshing, Miss Schuyler. We've been fortunate in the last week or two. You have me at a disadvantage, though. I'm fortified only against the usual feminine wiles. Your directness disarms me."

Eliza searched for an appropriate quip. A tall black man approached them before she could respond.

"Please excuse me, Colonel Hamilton. May I please speak with you, sir?"

The young man wore an expression of rigid self-control that seemed out of place at a dancing assembly.

"Of course, Ajax. I'll be along in a moment."

The man nodded and withdrew.

"I'm terribly sorry, Miss Schuyler," Hamilton said, "but Ajax never interrupts without good reason. Will you please excuse me?"

"Of course. No apology is necessary. Servants are a responsibility."

The warmth left Hamilton's eyes. "You misunderstand. Private Manly is my friend, not my property."

Eliza's face flushed. She looked down at her plate, recalling John Laurens's scandalous proposal, reported in the *Albany Gazette*. If the men were intimates, as he said, Hamilton might endorse Laurens's motion. Eliza didn't think the plan wise—and the South Carolina assembly had swiftly squelched it—but she might have guessed Hamilton wouldn't possess a slave. Angelica would have surmised it, quick as she was.

"I'm in an unpopular minority," he said more gently. "Your assumption was natural. In fact, I . . . I did once own a slave by that very name. Ajax. You see, I'm no angel."

Eliza looked up. Hamilton's eyes were searching. For some reason, the subject didn't seem easy. "I swore to myself that I would never do so again. Can you understand?"

Eliza wasn't sure what exactly he wanted her to fathom, but when he looked so earnest, as if reaching for her soul, she felt she could comprehend anything. "I don't completely," she said, "but perhaps you'll explain another time."

"Yes, another time."

Hamilton looked over at his grim friend, who hovered at the edge of the room. He stood, obviously focused on Ajax Manly. "Good evening, Miss Schuyler. It gives me a pang to leave so abruptly, but it was a pleasure meeting you. Again."

Eliza set her untouched plate on the table as Colonel Hamilton took his leave. He had forgotten the encounter in Albany that troubled her more than a year and had no compunction about abandoning her now. And she had offended him by mistaking a free man for a slave. Once again she appeared unable to say the right thing. Would he really explain his views at some point, or was he just being polite? She had no idea.

But Eliza did know one thing. Her inexplicable, immediate infatuation with Alexander Hamilton had not been a passing fancy. His presence was just as disturbing as she'd remembered.

Damn his eyes, Angelica would say. Now what was Eliza to do, and where was her maddening sister when she needed her?

Alexander had seen men weep after battles, but never this kind of heartbreak.

"She's gone," Ajax said. He choked down a sob, his shoulder against the frozen wall of the dark outbuilding. "Just gone." His voice was bereft of hope.

Alexander felt like putting his arm round the boy, but didn't. Ajax was fiercely proud. "When did she leave?"

"I don't know. She just suddenly wasn't there."

Alexander kept his gloved hands in his coat. The temperature had plummeted and it was shockingly frigid. He could hear the music from the mansion, but knew better than to suggest they go inside. The throng of white officers, many from plantation states, would hardly sympathize. "Did you inquire?"

"Of course. I . . . I hadn't seen her all day, but I was helping the artillery boys build a hut so I thought we just hadn't crossed paths."

"What did the kitchen staff say?"

Ajax was silent a long moment. The night grew colder.

"They said her master's headed south. Posted home to Georgia. She went with him. She could have stayed, but she didn't, and now she's gone." He turned away. His shoulders shook.

Alexander cursed life. He would never evade slavery's stink. He didn't transcribe every order, but he could have followed the Georgian's career more closely. Not that it would have changed the outcome. These things were always the same. Alexander placed his hand on Ajax's arm. "She had no choice."

Ajax turned. His cheeks glistened in the moonlight and he brushed them roughly. "Yes, she did. I would have fought for Letta. I would have taken her to Manhattan. We could have gone over to the British."

"Did you tell her that?"

"Again and again."

"What did she say?"

"She just laughed. Told me I was a boy. That I didn't know what I was talking about."

Alexander wasn't surprised. Letta was two or three years older than Ajax. She understood slavery in ways the New Yorker couldn't.

"I told her my parents are still in New York—British territory—and that they would take us in, but she said she couldn't. Her mama and brother are down south."

"It's hard to leave what you know," Alexander said.

"Hard to leave slavery? For someone you love?"

"Are you sure she really loved you? Women are fickle. You know that."

Ajax screwed up his mouth. "It's men who are fickle. Loving one woman one day, another the next. Remember when Malcolm Shaw was two days overdue? Everyone fretted he'd been killed, or taken prisoner, or, worse, gotten married. Men blame women for their own shallowness." His eyes narrowed. "*You* know that."

"So why didn't she run away with you?"

Ajax turned back to the wall. His voice was rough. "She said you just have to accept some things."

Alexander didn't respond. He felt for Letta. Flight into the unknown was frightening. Even if all went well, she would never see her family again. And she'd be turning around to look for bounty hunters the rest of her life. Few wanted to pay freedom's price—unless they had no other choice.

"I will never, ever, love a slave again," Ajax said. He passed a sleeve over his eyes. "Shit, it's cold out here."

"It is. Why don't we see what the gunnery boys are up to? I bet they've squirreled away some applejack. Let's drink."

"Sure." Ajax walked up the path toward the rude huts at the edge of the deep, unbroken wilderness.

Alexander pondered Ajax's words as he followed him up the snowy hill. Men were fickle. He was fickle. Even randy John Laurens had told him he must think more seriously about marriage.

"The lack of connections holds you back," Laurens had said. Congress gave promotions to men blessed with family and property. When Alexander was turned down for yet another appointment, though he was the best-qualified man, Laurens said flatly, "You need to marry someone who can establish you."

Alexander knew John was right. He'd even sent his friend a list of requirements in case he tripped over a South Carolina beauty seeking a poor man with a murky past.

She mustn't cherish money since his pockets contained only lint and he didn't want to be scolded for poverty. She must be affectionate, loyal, and shapely. (He had eyes in his head, after all.) Her political views wouldn't matter—Alexander could convert any woman to his—and she needn't possess more than an average supply of religion. He prized piety, but couldn't abide a woman who set such store on heaven that she despised earthly delights. Alexander wanted a lusty partner, not a prude.

Should John find no ready takers for such a dubious prize, and be compelled to advertise, he must paint his obscure friend in bright colors: Alexander's high achievements, amazing expectations, physical perfection. "*Mind you do justice to the length of my nose*," he wrote. Alexander smiled, remembering the book in Mama's store. Perhaps he should have added something about his nostrils. He hoped John had laughed.

The knee-deep snow crunched and squeaked under their boots. Alexander matched his steps to Ajax's footprints. To be honest, he wasn't sure he really wanted to marry.

Sometimes he longed for a woman to hold and the kind of family he had never had. Other times he rejected the idea. Whom could he trust? People let one another down routinely. Happy families were cruel fables told to children. And if he wanted to marry, even if only for practical purposes, what kind of father would grant his permission? Alexander wouldn't lie outright about his past.

Yet what was the alternative? Watching life through the windows? Accepting the crippled fate of a bastard? Allowing Johann Lavien to win?

The music in the distance swelled faintly. The door to the mansion must have admitted more revelers. Alexander thought of the woman he had just met—for the second time.

Elizabeth Schuyler had a slim waist and her powdered curls contrasted strikingly with her intelligent black eyes. Her hand trembled when they walked onto the dance floor. He was sure of it. She wasn't as polished as Kitty Livingston, but there was something attractive in that, and she had a sense of humor. He now recalled their first meeting. She had been more reserved in Albany. Tonight she seemed freer and softer.

Alexander also couldn't help noticing the swell of her soft breasts when he gave her the supper plate. Well, he admitted to himself with a smile, he could have averted his eyes.

Despite the cold weather, Alexander felt the familiar surge of warm, thwarted desire that bedeviled every unmarried man whenever he wasn't starving, freezing, fighting, or all three. His chest grew tight at the thought of finding the velvety tips of those full curves.

He would inquire where Miss Schuyler was staying. John Laurens would certainly approve. Betsey, as Tench Tilghman called her, had a lovely face and her family owned most of Albany. Philip Schuyler was at least fair-minded, and Tilghman had had two years to make good on his dibs.

There was also something about her. Not coquettish—but magnetic and determined. He sensed passion in her makeup, and desire swept him again.

Ajax Manly stopped when they reached the rude hut from which smoke poured through a makeshift hole in the roof.

"Wait." The boy stepped back, pulled his cocked hat lower over his eyes, and wiped his cheeks again with the back of his mittens. "Now."

Alexander opened the door for them both and they went in out of the winter night.

CHAPTER NINETEEN

February 1780

Morristown

"About two hundred of our wounded men . . . were brought from the field of battle in wagons, and for want of tents, sheds, or any kind of buildings to receive and cover them, were placed in a circular row on the naked ground. It was a clear, but cold and frosty, night."

Samuel Woodruff, Connecticut militiaman, 1777

BUNDLED AGAINST THE COLD, WITH BRITTLE light glinting off his white whiskers, the aged manservant scraped at the crusted frost of the windowsill until Eliza finally saw the road. Two soldiers on horseback rode past through the new drifts, headed east, just as an empty supply sled passed in the other direction. Business at the army camp had resumed after three snowy days.

Eliza decided not to think about Alexander Hamilton ever again. She was tired of her own foolishness. She had always been the levelheaded sister, with her practical shoes and prudent advice. What was she doing, gussied up in satin and fussing with powder? She had wasted seventy-two hours wondering if Colonel Hamilton would call. If he wanted to, he would have.

Uncle John entered the front parlor. "Are you ready, my dear?"

"Yes, Uncle John." Eliza picked up her fur muff and followed him out the front door. "Do you think Mrs. Washington will come today?" she said as they settled into the sleigh.

"I expect so. She usually visits for at least a short while, unless she's too busy with her knitting. She repairs mittens—for those who have them. I do hope you get to see her again."

Eliza trained her eyes on the road ahead. "Me, too."

"Are you definitely returning to Albany, then?"

"Yes. I don't know what I was thinking, traveling so far during winter. I belong at home."

"Your Aunt and I shall miss your company. Though I doubt Kitty Livingston will." He placed his gloved hand over hers, and wiggled his brushy gray eyebrows for comical effect. "Competition, you know."

Eliza laughed. "A racehorse doesn't worry about a workhorse."

"She should if it's a quarter horse. You're a fine sprinter, Eliza." He patted her hand. "You underestimate yourself."

Her uncle's kindness lifted her spirits. Any lingering self-pity vanished when they reached the hospital and went inside.

The smell hit her first. Vinegar doused on the ground to stem the spread of disease barely masked the profusion of odors. The stench of unwashed bodies, excrement, and rotting flesh mingled with the aroma of boiled coffee. Acrid smoke from green logs caused her eyes to water. Eliza tried not to retch.

At least a hundred patients lay in a circle on damp, dirty straw, their feet pointed toward a campfire in the center of the barn. Some had skimpy blankets, others huddled under their greatcoats. A few slept. Others stared at the rafters or talked quietly. Eliza spotted an orderly covering a man in the corner with a sheet.

Dr. Cochran set his surgical bag down to look for something inside. He told her the night before that he had applied maggots to clean the dead flesh on his patient's wound, but the gash left by a wood axe resisted healing. He needed to remove the man's leg to stop gangrene.

"I can't show you around right now," he said as he withdrew a saw from the bag, "but please start by washing faces and hands. The orderly, Corporal Wiese, will let you know what to do. I'll be next door."

It was too cold to remove her cape so Eliza folded her thick sleeves and hung her muff on a nail on the barn wall. Corporal Wiese gave her a bucket of warm water. Taking up the washcloth he flung in it, Eliza knelt in the straw at the side of a thin boy who seemed about fourteen. He stared at her without speaking.

"Good . . . good morning, private." The words stuck in Eliza's throat.

"Good morning, Miss," he said in a high, immature voice. His eyes seemed the only thing in his face.

"May I wash your face and hands? Dr. Cochran thinks it will do you good."

"Yes, ma'am."

The lad closed his eyes, which made it easier to look at him, and Eliza wiped his bony cheeks. She ran her hand over his hair to remove bits of straw from his blond cowlick. He reminded her of Philip Jeremiah.

Eliza worked her way around the circle of men. The water in her bucket grew cold and black. She finally caught up with Corporal Wiese washing the stubbly chin of an unconscious soldier.

"Soup's on the trestle," he said. "Start where ya did before, miss, and we'll meet in the middle. Careful not to spill. We don't have much." He looked doubtful. "Can you lift the pot, now? 'Tis heavy, miss."

"Of course," Eliza said.

She brought the soup pot back to the boy soldier, who had fallen asleep though it was barely midday. The blood-soaked bandage covering his right shoulder was unraveling. Eliza tucked a loose corner and roused him gently. The boy opened his eyes.

"Here you go." She held her voice steady, but could not control the tear that started down her cheek. Eliza brushed her face with a sleeve. "My, it's smoky in here."

"We call it fire-cake, Miss. That's what we call the smoke when we don't have nothing else to eat."

She held up her spoon. "Well, today there's good warm soup. Open your mouth, please."

Eliza fed him the thin broth of potatoes and parsnips, pushing aside the bits of dirt and ash floating on top. There was no meat. The boy soldier fell back asleep after a few spoonfuls. Eliza continued around the circle until Corporal Wiese caught up with her again. When he took the pots back to the camp kitchen, Eliza looked around for more to do.

Two men now stood over the covered body in the far corner. Eliza recognized one of them as Ajax Manly, Alexander Hamilton's friend. He said something to the other soldier, then glanced around as if seeking something.

Eliza approached the sad bundle on the floor. It might be mistaken for a pile of laundry if the pink palm of a Negro didn't loll on the straw. "May I help? Is there anything you need?"

Ajax Manly looked hostile. "Are you jesting? We need everything."

"I mean, is there something I can bring you?"

"We need a stretcher. Someone seems to have taken the one that used to be here."

"Probably stole it for firewood," said the other man, a white orderly who looked very haggard. He shrugged. "You take his hands. I'll get the feet."

"I will not see this soldier dragged through the snow," Manly said. "He gave his life for this damned country. The least we can do is carry him decently to his grave. We need a stretcher."

"Don't have one, and we have to move him," the other man said. "Doc wants the bodies out of the barn as soon as possible."

"Don't touch him. I'll be back," Manly said, and strode from the barn.

The orderly looked rueful. "What ya gonna do?"

Doctor Cochran's voice rang out. "Help, please!" Eliza turned to see her uncle poke his head into the barn.

"Yes, doctor," the orderly said. He looked at Eliza. "You stay here, Miss. Doc must need help holding that fella. Mind whatever Wiese says, all right? And make sure the fire doesn't go out."

Eliza approached Corporal Wiese, stooped over the spigot of a hogshead, filling a stoneware pitcher with vinegar.

"Should I spread fresh straw?" she said. "I saw a rake outside."

"I bet you didn't see any straw. Farmers around here ain't in a sharing mood. Why don't you fetch some firewood?" Wiese pointed to a bent-willow basket.

Eliza pulled her muff off the nail, unrolled her sleeves, and stepped into the raw morning with the basket over her arm. Alexander Hamilton and Ajax Manly tramped toward her, each carrying one end of an empty stretcher.

The young colonel looked surprised. "Miss Schuyler."

Now he recognized her. She would have been transported three days earlier, but after all the anxious waiting and the events of the morning, she was past caring. "Good day, Colonel Hamilton."

Eliza turned to find the woodpile behind the barn. The wind had blown aside an oilcloth tarp that someone had placed over the logs. Eliza dug for the driest pieces, which she loaded in the basket. She untangled the tarp and re-covered the snow-dusted wood. Her mittens were wet and filthy.

When she reentered the smoky barn, Corporal Wiese was talking softly to an agitated, delirious soldier while rewrapping the man's bandages. The body in the corner was gone. Ajax Manly was nowhere in sight.

Alexander Hamilton stepped from the shadows. "There you are, Miss Schuyler. I wondered where you went. Please allow me to take that for you."

The colonel slipped the basket from her arm and stacked the wood next to the fire to dry, squatting on his haunches.

"Where did Mr. Manly find the stretcher?" Eliza said. "It seems the army has nothing it needs."

He looked up with a smile. "General Washington's servant, Billy Lee, located it for us."

"Did you know the dead man, Colonel Hamilton?"

"No, Miss Schuyler, but Private Manly did." He stood. "There, the fire looks well supplied now. Might you join me for a cup of coffee? You must be frozen."

Eliza looked about the barn. Her uncle was still occupied and her chores were finished. It appeared Martha Washington wasn't coming. "Yes, thank you, Colonel. I may as well."

As they stepped into the daylight, Alexander took Eliza's arm to guide her on the icy path. She found his nearness unsettling. When he leaned close to open the door, she smelled the soap on his skin and the pleasant trace of his breath.

The large farmhouse kitchen was empty. Hamilton insisted on draping her wet gloves over the fireplace screen. He poured two cups of coffee that he placed on the table before sitting down.

"I hope Private Manly wasn't rude," he said. "He's normally the soul of kindness, but it's been a difficult week. He's not himself. I hope you'll forgive him if he was abrupt."

"What happened?"

"What hasn't happened?" Hamilton took a sip from his cup and set it back down. "I'm sorry. Now I'm being abrupt, and you've been kind. There aren't many civilians willing to attend the hospital. We're just terribly out of humor at the lack of provisions. Congress hasn't two shillings to rub together, and the states won't refill its purse. The army is broke. Our soldiers go days without meat."

His countenance darkened. "I shouldn't say it, but we begin to hate the country for neglecting us."

"Are the Negroes particularly affected?"

If Hamilton hated Congress's indifference, what might colored volunteers feel, Eliza wondered?

"Thank you for asking. Most people don't. Some don't even want blacks in the army. They think it sets a bad example. We've had to argue repeatedly to let them stay."

"Why do they fight for us?"

"They don't. They fight for freedom. Of course, some go to the British for it. But some come here as well. General Washington pretends not to know they're runaways. We assume they're all free men." Hamilton looked out the window. He appeared melancholy. "Our nation is riddled with contradictions, Miss Schuyler."

Eliza said nothing, and for a few moments there was silence between them.

He turned his gaze back. "The man who died this morning gave his life for a country that treats him like an animal. But if we win, we'll make it a better one. I tell myself he knew that."

"Private Manly wanted the body carried out properly," Eliza said.

"I did, too. A decent burial is the least we can provide."

Eliza thought of Pompey, who hadn't followed through on his threat to leave. Like all their slaves, he had defended her family from Indians and Redcoats, and worked to feed and clothe them. Papa took good care of his servants, but if Hamilton was correct, they deserved more. It hurt Eliza to think her family was in the wrong. Hamilton must believe them as wicked as the Southerners.

Eliza's coffee had grown tepid. No point in tarrying, she thought as she downed the last bitter dregs. She would leave Morristown on the morrow with her pride intact.

"Thank you for your kindness, Colonel." She placed her hand on the table to stand.

Surprisingly, Hamilton's mood shifted yet again. A smile lit his handsome face.

"Miss Schuyler," he said, and put his hand over hers. "I hope I'm not being unpardonably forward considering the circumstances. But ladies of beauty and character are terribly rare in these parts.

I wonder if I might call on you some evening when the general doesn't need me."

Hamilton's strong hand was protective. Eliza's heart pounded as if a stranger had unexpectedly rapped at the window. She willed herself to be calm. Why should she still consider him, when he had so neglected her? She should leave Morristown, as she had wisely planned. She was the sensible child, everyone said.

"Yes," Eliza said. "I would like that."

CHAPTER TWENTY

February 1780

Morristown

"Marriage is . . . the most natural state of man, and therefore the state in which you are most likely to find solid happiness. . . . A single man has not nearly the value he would have in that state of union. . . . He resembles the odd half of a pair of scissors."

Benjamin Franklin, "Advice to a Young Man," 1745

TENCH TILGHMAN HAD ONLY RECENTLY RECUPERATED from a fever, but the hardy Marylander buckled the straps on his Dutch skates and glided across the pond before Alexander could attach his clumsy blades. He didn't see how anyone balanced on them, but officers of all ages and half a dozen young women were already cutting circles on the farmer's white pond. Top-heavy Mrs. Cochran, married to Washington's personal physician, skated past as sedately as if carrying a pie to a neighbor. It clearly wasn't difficult.

Alexander had attended an ice-skating party at King's College before the war, but spent the entire time warming the twisted ankle of a rosy New Jersey debutante who had contributed to his reputation as a flirt. He hadn't ventured onto the ice even once. Yet

Betsey Schuyler had proposed today's outing and Alexander was determined not to let Tench Tilghman or any other man upstage or outskate him.

Eliza held hands with Kitty Livingston on the ice, who wasn't very sure on her feet. Kitty went wide-eyed as her blade hit a rough patch, but Eliza kept a firm grip and the two girls laughed as they picked up speed again and darted around a crooked branch that stuck out of the pond like a swimmer's frozen arm. Moments later the pair doubled back and sailed past Alexander. Eliza waved a mitten and smiled impishly.

All the skaters glowed from exercise in the frosty air, but Eliza seemed more alive than anyone else. Her black eyes gleamed as she glided confidently in the brisk breeze, steadying her awkward friend. When her bonnet blew back, held on only by the string tied around her slim neck, she ignored her streaming hair and kept skating.

Alexander wiggled his boot through the toe strap and secured the balky fastener around his ankle. Tilghman had said there was a trick to tightening the device, but dashed away without explaining.

"Try not to fall," Tilghman called as he sped toward Betsey Schuyler, then turned neatly to skate backward when he crossed in front of her. Eliza smiled at the challenge and, switching hands with Kitty, turned to skate in reverse. When the girls came to a brief rest so Eliza could retie her bonnet, Tilghman inscribed a wide circle around them and came to a precise stop in front of the apple-cheeked maidens.

"Damn show-off," Alexander muttered. He stood up cautiously but was reassured when the skates stuck upright in the crumbled snow at the pond's edge. The contraptions were actually quite stable. Alexander found he had little difficulty balancing. He stood taller and straighter, pleased to observe that he was as poised as any other officer of the Continental Army.

Kitty Livingston beckoned him over. "Hammie," she called out across the milky ice. "Join us!"

Eliza smiled from afar, too, and Alexander felt his heart beat more forcefully under her keen gaze.

He leaned forward, as he had seen the others do, shuffling one leg, then the other. It was even easier than anticipated. Before he knew it, he was coasting across the ice at a respectable speed.

Tench Tilghman's smile dimmed as Alexander neared. Eliza Schuyler looked more admiring.

Alexander had brought a packet of fancy chocolates to share with the girls. He reached for them in his greatcoat just as his skates developed an inexplicable aversion to one another. Alexander willed his feet together as hard as he dared, but the distance between his skates stubbornly widened.

Kitty Livingston's small mouth formed a pink "O." Tilghman glided out of the way. Eliza Schuyler put out her hands to catch Alexander.

He leaned back to avoid hitting her and the skates slipped at the same instant. He skidded onto his rear, taking General Schuyler's daughter with him onto the ice.

"Dear me! Oh, my!" she said.

Eliza's full skirts flew above her knees, exposing her stocking-covered legs and lace petticoats.

Mortified, Alexander instinctively pulled Eliza's hem over her knees. The poor girl! Who knew where Tilghman's eyes were. "Forgive me! I'm so sorry. Are you all right?" His face reddened. He would always be the gauche newcomer.

Kitty Livingston put out a hand. Eliza struggled to her feet with her friend's help. She brushed her skirts and extended a hand to Alexander in turn, smiling down without a trace of the scorn he had earned. "One expects a spill now and then on the ice—or one isn't really flying. I suppose you didn't skate every day in the Caribbean."

Alexander gratefully took her hand. "Only ahead of the law, Miss Schuyler—when my employer was trying to evade taxes." He stood up, taking care to dig his skates into the ice. "Are you sure you're all right? Nothing broken?" He looked at her wrist and felt an absurd sense of alarm. "What's this mark?"

She looked down. "Just a scrape."

Tilghman swooped closer. "Miz Betsey. Allow me to take your arm. Doctor Cochran should have a look at that."

Alexander held on tight and pulled a clean handkerchief from his pocket, glad that he had remembered one. "May I, Miss Schuyler?" He wrapped the makeshift bandage around her wrist and tied it with the surgeon's knot Neddy had taught him.

Eliza examined it closely. "That's a work of art, Colonel Hamilton. Thank you."

Alexander felt a swell of pride immediately deflated by the realization that he had no dignified way to get off the ice. The trees at the shoreline looked as close as Paris.

"If you're ready to try again, I'm happy to teach you," Eliza said. She looked at Tilghman. "Would you mind helping Kitty?"

"Pining for the opportunity," Tilghman said to his credit, and Kitty gave him her arm.

Alexander thanked his lucky stars for having made a fool of himself. The young woman had an unusual combination of strength and femininity. And she was kind—so much kinder than he expected of an heiress.

"God bless you, Miss Schuyler. I've always wanted to learn to skate legally."

CHAPTER TWENTY-ONE

March 1780

Morristown

"Having been poor is no shame, but being ashamed of it, is."
Benjamin Franklin, *Poor Richard's Almanack*

ALEXANDER LOOKED OVER AT ELIZA. THE candlelight cast ribbons in her shiny chestnut hair, and the skin of her cheek looked velvety. She was knitting a glove for a wounded drummer boy she had befriended at the hospital. Eliza collected strays—homesick soldiers, orphaned kittens, one-legged veterans, shy spinsters, and so on. When he tried to kill a spider for her, she insisted on delivering it unharmed to the barn on a twig.

"What do you mean that our currency problem is an illusion, Colonel Hamilton? If that's so, why does a bushel of corn now cost six times what it did two months ago?" Eliza Schuyler's uncle was nearly apoplectic. Doctor Cochran held his pipe away from his teeth. It had gone out. "And those reprobates in New York! Give them more money? Are you mad?"

Doctor Cochran couldn't grasp the fact that lack of confidence in the money supply drove down the currency's value. America needed a national bank to put its house in order. It took a fistful of Continentals to purchase what one dollar bought a year earlier.

Alexander had tried to explain the concepts he learned in Malachy Postlethwayt's *Universal Dictionary of Commerce*. But as often happened, stubborn assumptions impeded comprehension. In Alexander's experience, prejudice and ignorance were the brick and mortar of men's prisons. Say "bank," and otherwise sane gentlemen foamed at the mouth and started barking. He knew with scientific certainty what would save their revolution from economic collapse, but he might as well teach Greek to the Cochrans' Scottish terrier.

Alexander had been courting Eliza Schuyler for nearly a month. He had visited the Cochrans' home almost every evening since the skating party. Each time he came away more bewitched by the pretty young woman whose goodness was a balm on all his scars and whose lack of guile he found fascinating. If she tried harder to ensnare him, she would be easier to resist.

"She doesn't have an ounce of vanity," he told James McHenry, the stout Irishman who had joined Washington's military family. Alexander refrained from discussing Eliza with Tench Tilghman. The suave Southerner menaced all his plans. "I don't believe she has any idea how pretty she is."

"Then you'd better decide how you feel before the lass finds out," McHenry said, "or she'll take aim for bigger game."

Alexander found her family endearing—especially the witty, mischievous Angelica, who had arrived in Morristown with her English husband—but after a time, he wished he could drown all of them. He wanted Eliza alone. On this particular evening, Doctor Cochran might have retreated into his study had Alexander not foolishly started spouting his economic theories. He could kick himself.

"Uncle John," Eliza said without flagging in her knitting, "tell us about your research on smallpox inoculation. Have you submitted your notes to Mr. Franklin's Philosophical Society?"

His niece's query brought a wrinkle to Doctor Cochran's brow. "No, it seems there's never enough time."

Eliza wore a simple burgundy gown that showed her slender but voluptuous figure to superb effect in Alexander's eyes: white neck revealed, bosom suggested, waist and hips a swirl of delicious, satiny curves.

"How fortunate that you were able to leave the hospital early today," she said.

"That's an excellent reminder, my dear." He set down his cold pipe and turned to Alexander. "Would you indulge me, Colonel? I have a bit more time than usual to rummage in my papers. I ought to use it to advantage."

"Of course, sir."

Once the doctor had left, Alexander crossed the quiet parlor to examine Eliza's handiwork, or so he pretended. He took the seat next to her and picked up a glove she had just finished. Perhaps the next pair would be for him. If he was lucky. If she didn't turn away aghast.

"How do you know how large to make the gloves?"

Eliza smiled up at him. Alexander felt he could swim in her dark eyes.

She held up her right hand. "I just placed my palm against Private Brady's. I saw how much bigger his was than mine, and knitted accordingly."

"Don't tell me you're holding hands with our drummer boy." Alexander felt a stab of jealousy. "Your charms might induce heart seizure, and we can't afford any more casualties."

Eliza smiled as she resumed knitting. "I believe you're jealous, my dear colonel. That's exactly how I size mittens for my younger brothers."

"I'll not be jealous if that is how you treat your brothers." Alexander reached over, took Eliza's needles, and set them in the basket at her side. "But your kindness induces me to hope for a different place in your affections. I want to know your heart—everything you feel, shady or bright."

Eliza made no protest when Alexander raised her hands to his lips. He kissed the backs first, then her delicate palms. They smelled of flowers. She caught her breath. He felt his own deepen.

Eliza withdrew her hands. He looked at her inquiringly. He couldn't bear for her to pull away now.

"Alexander," she said, for they had entered into a first name basis a few weeks earlier, "I've no qualifications as a coquette. You mustn't make love to me as you do girls in town. I'm a country mouse."

"Then the cities should be leveled. I've never met anyone as captivating as you."

A pink blush suffused Eliza's face and Alexander felt emboldened to take her hands again. They were so small. He was overwhelmed by the sense that she was defenseless. She had erected no barriers. Only a dress and petticoat shielded her, yet she didn't draw away.

The desire to possess and protect overwhelmed him. Alexander took a deep breath. He wanted to tell her she would always be safe with him. But first he must know if he was safe with her.

"Please don't mistake me for a man who woos a different damsel every day," he said. "I'll admit I'm ardent, but the Almighty gave me a good heart along with a good head. Before we met, I preferred to die a hero. You make me want to live."

Alexander swallowed—and then went hollow inside. He hated what he had to say next. The words, the thoughts, the reality were repugnant. He felt as naked as a slave on the block in Christiansted. It took more courage than anything the war had yet required, but he wanted none of the sordid shadows that had ruined his parents. No matter the cost, he must tell her.

"There's something you should know—and if it causes you to send me away, I promise to bear no grudge. You deserve someone worthy. I'm earnest, but I'm poor. I can't offer you what men of better birth can."

Eliza squeezed his hands tightly. Alexander fought the compulsion to crush her in his arms.

"I know all that," she whispered. "Love is wealth enough."

Alexander took a deep breath. "My family isn't like yours."

She smiled. "I have family enough for two."

"No. It's . . . I'm not what I appear."

Rancid shame rose in his throat, but he went on. He must tell her the worst. "My parents weren't legally married. I was born in disgrace."

Then, as plainly as he could, his eyes fixed on the floor, Alexander told her the terrible tale he had never told anyone else, either because they knew it or because they didn't. Mama's dishonor and death, his father's disappearance, his own illegitimacy.

Eliza didn't move during the excruciating speech.

"I'm an outsider, Betsey. Always waiting for the moment people find out and despise me as a pretender. My mother was good, but they called her a whore." He stopped. The word was bitter. "Every man dreams of a son. Under Danish law, I don't own the name I would give him." Alexander stared now at the hands she hadn't yet stolen back. "Forgive me, Eliza."

The room sounded empty. Only the wind in the pine branches disturbed the silence. Alexander looked up.

Tears rolled down her beautiful cheeks. Alexander couldn't tell if she wept for his misfortune or because their courtship had ended.

He let go of her hands. There was stern comfort in doing what must be done. He would rather destroy his own future than hers. He'd always known happiness wasn't his lot in life.

Eliza took her knitting basket off the couch and placed it at her feet. She turned to him and slid her arms around his chest.

Alexander inhaled the intoxicating scent of her thick, glossy hair. Every bit of her smelled wonderful.

Unaware until that instant of the unbearable tension that gripped him, Alexander softened. A lump rose in his throat. He pulled away. It took his last reserve of self-restraint. He met her eyes.

"Are you sure? If people find out, they'll never let you forget what I am. And what I'm not."

Eliza placed a finger to his lips, then pressed. "Alexander. I know *who* you are." She looked toward the open doorway. "And yes, I'm sure. Why do you think I tricked Uncle John into leaving?"

Alexander stared, then burst into laughter. "You scheming vixen!" He gazed into her eyes. So she wasn't entirely without guile. "You're beautiful. You're perfect."

He wrapped his fingers around her wrist and pulled her to him. He never wanted to stop kissing her.

CHAPTER TWENTY-TWO

December 1780

Albany

"More than kisses, letters mingle souls."

John Donne, 1572–1631

ELIZA HELD THE LETTER IN HER lap. She sat nervously on the edge of the double bed in the small guest room of their Albany mansion, across the hall from her brothers and sisters. Her parents' room was two doors away. Family surrounded Eliza while she waited for her new husband to knock. She was glad they were near, yet wished they were leagues away.

"Are you certain, *mijn lief*?" Mama said the day before, as she sat heavily on the bed's feather comforter to stroke Eliza's hair. Well into her twelfth pregnancy, she rested her other hand atop her swollen abdomen.

Eliza's parents had given their approval without hesitation, and come to view Alexander as a son in the eight months since their engagement. Eliza knew Alexander had revealed all when he asked for her hand because Papa later told her that he consented because he felt he had read Alexander's soul. Papa recognized the blind injustice of birthright. When young, he had divided his inheritance with his younger brother and sister, not entitled to a penny under the laws of primogeniture.

Eliza knew Mama was asking something different. Was her daughter ready for the hardships as well as joys of marriage? The stranger who rested under Mama's palm—who might die stillborn, or kill her—bore witness. The bed made it real. Eliza would lie in it with a man. Her husband.

Eliza reassured her mother she was ready, though of course she wasn't.

The celebration had gone forward at the appointed hour in the blue parlor. Schuyler, Van Rensselaer, and Van Cortlandt cousins crowded together, jabbering in Dutch and English. Relatives flocked from both sides of the river despite the dusting of snow before dawn, and sleighs filled the avenue in front of Albany's stateliest manor. Everyone was too polite to notice that the groom had no family—other than his military family of John Laurens and the Marquis de Lafayette.

Papa welcomed guests at the front door despite his bad toe, and Eliza heard the pleasure in his gruff voice all the way up the stairs, where Diana pinned pearls in her hair. Maria raided the larder for the first wedding of a Schuyler child in the Albany mansion, and tables creaked under roast turkey, glazed ham, root vegetables, sugar cake, cranberry preserves, and Mama's traditional *spake en applejees*, made from pork, apples, and onions. When the Dutch Reformed pastor asked Alexander if he would love Eliza until death parted them, her fiancé looked at her with eyes that saw no one else.

"*Ja,*" he said in the language of Old Albany.

Eliza went upstairs before the last guests left. She washed in the bath a servant had placed behind a screen, and changed into the silk negligee adorned with Belgian lace that Mama had taken from a trunk of family heirlooms. She was prepared. But not.

Eliza took up the letter in her lap. Alexander had sent dozens from the front during the long summer and fall, after they said good-bye at Morristown following a courtship of barely a month. "*I meet you in every dream,*" he wrote. She unfolded the page.

"*I love you more and more every hour. The sweet softness and delicacy of your mind and manners, the elevation of your sentiments, the real goodness of your heart, its tenderness to me, the beauties of your face and person, your unpretending good sense and that innocent simplicity and frankness which pervade your actions; all these appear to me with increasing amiableness and place you in my estimation above all the rest of your sex.*"

Someone played the piano downstairs. Eliza read his ornate prose one more time. Alexander loved her more "every hour." But was she really "above all the rest"? Would he always think so? Would he still feel that way after tonight? She had little idea what she must do to please him.

During the reception, Alexander had caught her round the waist more than once to plant a kiss on her cheek. Late in the evening, he fed her a marzipan cookie and brushed a crumb from the corner of her mouth. Yet none of that felt as intimate as his glance across the salon when she turned to leave the party.

In that instant, while the last revelers were still drinking, smoking, or talking, and either didn't notice her exit or pretended not to, Alexander's look made her feel naked in front of the room. She climbed the grand staircase so quickly that she nearly missed a step at the top and ducked into the guest room at the back of the house with a racing pulse.

Eliza had grown up in the country. She had seen horses, pigs, and sheep copulate. She'd seen birds in the trees do it. The repetitive motion was recognizable at any distance regardless of the shape or size of the animals. Faces impassive, they worked at reproducing their species without shyness or discomfort.

Yet humans were anything but inexpressive. Men made jokes and women giggled behind their aprons. "How far to Maidenhead down this road?" a man on horseback asked a serving girl whom Eliza had seen polishing silver outside a tavern. When the travel-stained rider gave the lass a leering wink, the quick-tongued girl said, "You'll never get there in those clothes."

Whenever Eliza saw the bare skin of Alexander's exposed neck, she yearned to touch it. But she didn't know where else the sensation might lead, and had only a vague idea how the act that animals performed would feel. She knew men wanted sex more than women. And she was prepared to do her duty to the fullest possible extent. Her great fear was that Alexander would be disappointed. She didn't think she could bear that.

Eliza shivered even though the room was warm from a fire laid in the hearth hours before. She refolded the letter, tucked it under the mattress for luck, said her prayers, and slipped beneath the feather comforter. A single candle cast its yellow nimbus over the room, softening the corners.

Alexander knocked a few minutes later, waited a heartbeat, and came in. He locked the door behind him. The bolt sounded like a clock striking midnight.

Eliza held the covers to her chin and peered at her new husband in his blue and buff officer's uniform.

Alexander laughed. "Are you playing hide and seek, my little charmer? Ready or not, then. I'm going to find you."

She pulled the comforter over her head. Candlelight filtered though the white fabric, but she couldn't see him removing his clothes. Eliza listened for the thud of his boots, like her brothers made when they kicked off theirs, but heard only a soft shuffle of fabric, buttons, and ties. He must be tidier than the Schuyler boys.

The mattress dipped, and she felt a quick draft as he got under the covers. Eliza held her breath. She froze, waiting for Alexander to place his hands on her and mount.

His warm feet touched hers.

"I found you, ladybug." His voice was low and soft. "Oh! Your toes are so cold."

Eliza closed her eyes and sighed quietly as Alexander stroked her feet with his. She sensed him scoot under the quilt. He grasped one foot with his hands. His bare body was low in the bed and he brought her clean foot to what she thought was his chest, hard under the smooth skin.

Alexander massaged each toe with his nimble fingers, heating and flexing the foot. Eliza relaxed. And then, to her surprise, she felt his tongue slide in and out between her toes. His mouth and hands seemed subtly everywhere. Slowly, tantalizingly, his smooth palm inched up her inner thigh until it rested a fingertip away from her soft opening. He moved up next to her and gave her a long kiss.

The anxiety that had stolen upon her during the celebration, and the worry about where her guests were, or whether they had gone home, disappeared. She kissed Alexander again and again, until her chin was chafed from the sandpaper shadow of his beard. The noises of the house vanished, and all she heard was her own breath and Alexander's tender words. She was enraptured. Her husband made her feel she could do no wrong.

They fell asleep tangled in one another's arms and legs. When Eliza awoke to dawn seeping through the shutters, she knew she would never get out of bed willingly. Someone would have to drag her by the ankles so long as Alexander lay naked next to her under the covers. Her body felt as tender as if she had tumbled down a hill, but she understood at last why her mother had risked a twelfth pregnancy.

Bliss wasn't a word. It was a scent, a touch, a taste, a sound.

Eliza had thought sex was what women did to please men. With gentleness and passion, Alexander showed her that it was what men did to please women. She wanted more.

CHAPTER TWENTY-THREE

October 1781

Yorktown, Virginia

"A ball came from the enemy, struck a man, and cut off his leg at the thigh, and then struck a stack of arms. . . . General Clinton, coming up just at that moment, put things to rights, and I remarked to the men in his hearing, 'Come, my brave fellows, stick to your posts and the day will soon be ours,' and for this remark I was very soon rewarded with a good breakfast from the general, which was very acceptable as I had not had a meal for twenty-four hours."

Edward Elley, 1781, Yorktown, *The Revolution Remembered*

THE MONTHS SINCE ALEXANDER'S MARRIAGE HAD been happy and harrowing. The wedding in Albany was his first leave in five years, and the break from the military, bathed in Eliza's affection, made him realize he couldn't go another minute without a command. He'd rather quit the army. He almost had.

Ironically, only his pen could win him a sword. Now, in a brief letter that might be ignored, he must marshal words to persuade the one individual who stood between him and the battlefield. It might be his last chance to win honor for the name he would soon give a child. Otherwise, all the men whose success was assured from birth would speed past to snatch the laurels they took as their due.

Alexander shrugged his shoulders to unknot them as he sat at his portable desk in the field tent at Yorktown. He placed the letter to Eliza aside. It contained all the joy he felt whenever he imagined her swelling belly and expressed none of his fears.

His new wife had sent only three letters to his twenty, and he had lectured her not to imagine "this neglect will go unpunished!" She must repent by loving him twice as much as before, and by presenting him with a boy rather than a girl, who—if she inherited her mother's beauty and father's rascality—would otherwise torture the men of New York.

Alexander hoped Betsey would smile when she read that. It was a game they played, pretending not to agonize over one another's welfare. The last thing he wanted was his wife to endanger herself and their baby by worrying about his survival.

In return, Alexander tried not to picture the scene of last summer, when loyalists and Indians attacked the Albany mansion in an attempt to kill or kidnap General Schuyler, though the master of the house had unexpectedly gone to Saratoga for the day. The marauders threw a razor-sharp tomahawk that narrowly missed Alexander's sister-in-law Peggy, who rushed downstairs to save Kitty Schuyler's newborn baby, wailing in its bassinet in the parlor. Eliza, pregnant with her first child, and Angelica, pregnant with a third, hid upstairs behind a wardrobe while the family's servants desperately held off the kidnappers until the town garrison arrived.

The thought of his wife and unborn child under assault put a fishhook in Alexander's soul that yanked him north. If they were in danger, he must save them. But Alexander also knew, as did Eliza, that real safety lay only in Britain's defeat. The war that had brought them together might separate them forever.

The conflict had worked its way south, from Canada down to Virginia. Benedict Arnold, whose heroism at Saratoga turned into treason when he became so disgusted with Congress that he defected to the British, burned Richmond to the ground the month after Alexander's marriage. Virginia governor Thomas Jefferson called out the state militia, who answered with their usual delay and incompetence. A philosopher, not a fighter, Jefferson rode out of Richmond barely ahead of the Redcoats. Virginia was now the apex of their fight. General Washington had decided to make his stand at Yorktown, the oldest settlement in the colonies, where the British had amassed their biggest force. Another British army still occupied New York City, but Washington gambled that a defeat at Yorktown might convince George III to capitulate altogether.

Alexander flinched at an explosion outside the tent. He brushed the dust off his lap desk and took out another piece of paper.

The Marquis de Lafayette exercised field command of the American army. The Comte de Rochambeau commanded the French army. Washington was commander-in-chief over both. The Europeans were better fed and better equipped than the American forces, and their uniforms put threadbare Continentals to shame. Louis XVI had placed more infantry in Virginia than the US Congress and sent twenty-nine warships to back them up. The combined might of the two allies was finally aimed at England's southernmost stronghold. Counting state militias, they had almost twenty thousand troops arrayed against Lord Cornwallis's tough nine-thousand-man army. After six tormenting years, the Redcoats finally had their backs to the wall, pinned down in their makeshift fort on the York River.

French engineers had coached Washington's troops as they wormed their lines toward the besieged encampment. Now they needed to dig a second trench in order to position their big guns close enough to force Lord Cornwallis's surrender.

Washington had given Alexander a small battalion of his own. When engineers completed the first trench, the Marquis de Lafayette granted Hamilton—out of friendship—the honor of marching his troops into the new ditch in front of the beleaguered fort.

Alexander's men had proceeded with flying flags and beating drums while British cannon loosed punishing fire on them. His men marched stoically under the screaming shells down into the first trench. One soldier not hardened to the risk, or weakened by malnutrition, fell to his knees in the dirt and retched. Alexander saw doubt pass over the face of the men behind him.

Bravery meant risking everything. It meant cowing the enemy with sheer ferocity. No one must falter. Fear mustn't gain purchase. "To the top, boys!" Alexander yelled to his line. "Show them what Americans are made of!"

He pulled the sick man up by the collar. The fellow stumbled and Alexander pulled harder. "Climb!" he ordered, and scrambled out of the protective trench onto the explosion-pocked field facing the British fort.

The men followed with a roar, and for ten exhilarating and terrifying minutes they executed their best parade maneuvers while cannonballs blasted fresh craters around them. Not a single soldier faltered. When Alexander finally gave the signal, the battalion jumped back into the trench nearly mad with joy that no one had been killed by their commander's insane bravado and that the whole battlefield had witnessed their daring.

Yet Washington's army still needed that second, closer trench. The fort remained out of range of their biggest guns.

British snipers in two redoubts—satellite forts outside the main wall of the encampment—kept picking off American sappers charged with digging the final trench. General Washington had decided someone must capture and disable the redoubts after dark. The French army would appoint one team, the American army another. Since the Marquis de Lafayette commanded the Continentals, he would decide which American brigade received the supreme honor—and the Marquis had given the job to one led by a Frenchman whom he'd known for years.

There was only one person with the power to reverse Lafayette.

Alexander cupped his chin in his hand. He stared through the tent flap at a tree snapped sideways by a cannonball. The quaking leaves on its lower branches remained green, but those on the crown that sagged in the dirt had wilted and browned.

Virtually anything he said to George Washington would be useless. He certainly could not call upon any affection the general once felt. Not after Alexander had practically told him to go to hell.

Washington deserved it. Alexander had served through scorching summers and blinding winters. He had endured the tongue-lashings Washington reserved for intimates when the rest of the world let him down. The general couldn't afford to alienate Congress or the foot soldiers that threatened to bolt every other day, so the men Washington called his family took the brunt. Like children did in most families, Alexander supposed.

He wouldn't have minded shabby treatment had the general eventually rewarded him with a field command. Instead, until the day Alexander walked out, Washington spurned every request with a terse, "I need you here."

Alexander grew to hate those four words blighting his destiny. Lafayette and Laurens had both served in multiple capacities. The well-born patricians had been field commanders and foreign emissaries, not just aides-de-camp. Only Alexander could not be spared. He'd come to feel like a dog on a leash.

The month after his wedding, something broke. When the general upbraided him on the stairs for not moving fast enough, in full view of everyone at headquarters, Alexander couldn't take it anymore. He'd come to the end of a path without knowing it.

"You've kept me waiting ten full minutes," Washington said, peering down his aristocratic nose. "I tell you, sir, you treat me with disrespect!"

He spoke in the stern, self-righteous tone he took when working up to a full boil. Washington looked down from the second-floor landing as Alexander ascended, which put him at eye level with the Virginian's well-polished boots. Alexander had long recognized the ways Washington used height to overawe others.

The general's tone was as contemptuous as if Alexander had left every powder keg open in the rain and picked his nose before Congress.

It wasn't what he said. It was how he said it. Alexander wished Philip Schuyler had been there so his father-in-law could understand why Alexander had replied, "I'm not conscious of any disrespect, sir. But since you tell me so, I'll leave today."

As always, Zeus's temper cooled as quickly as it heated. Within the hour Washington dispatched Tench Tilghman to express his apology and talk Alexander into staying. The Marquis de Lafayette made a second plea on Washington's behalf the next day.

But Alexander had had enough. If he stayed, he would never, ever, have his own battalion. He hadn't left St. Croix to sit out the American Revolution at a desk. He hadn't endured countless privations to watch others hog the glory. A soldier let himself be used with the promise of fair opportunity for advancement. Yet men to whom everything had always been given still received preference. The situation was so maddening that Alexander felt like slamming a door. Instead, he left the camp at Morristown for good and returned to Albany.

Washington proceeded to ignore him for five months, refusing to give his former aide a command of any type, but he eventually relented. Hamilton was simply too good to waste. And so Alexander marched his new battalion from New York to Southern Virginia across four hundred miles of mountains, ravines, and bogs in the hope of becoming the man he yearned to be.

The question now was how to convince Washington that Lafayette should give the final charge of their war to an American officer, not the French one he had already designated. Preferably Alexander Hamilton.

He bent and dipped his quill in the inkpot he had placed between his boots to keep it from tipping whenever a cannonball shook the earth. *That was it.*

His pen raced across the paper. When George Washington had been a young officer in the British Army, his superiors resisted giving him a decent command because he was only a colonial. Of all men, the Virginian should understand why an American must lead their men up the last redoubt.

If Alexander had but one night to live, this was the one he wanted. Every ambition, anger, hurt, and hope was concentrated in this moment. He didn't want to die, but death was always the price of life, and he would be happy to pay it sooner rather than later if it meant immortal glory.

John Laurens and Nicholas Fish, an old friend from King's College, paced down the two columns in the flickering torchlight, repeating the code word Alexander had given them and making sure the men unloaded their guns. General Washington insisted on complete silence. There would be no accidental gunfire when someone tripped on the spikes the Redcoats had planted in front of their redoubts.

Colonel Laurens, tall and slim, stopped to cinch the strap on a man's musket. John must have just shaved, thought Alexander, because the firelight gleamed on his smooth cheeks.

Doubts hadn't troubled Alexander when he selected the officers to serve under him. To have Laurens at his side was joy itself. His friend from South Carolina would command the group that circled around and attacked the rear of the fort. There was no one Alexander trusted more, or alongside whom he would rather draw a last breath.

Colonel Jean-Joseph de Gimat, Lafayette's comrade who had yielded command to Alexander at General Washington's insistence, would lead the right column and attack the redoubt from the front. Alexander would advance at the head of the left column, followed by Nicholas Fish, whom Alexander had known since debating club days. With his hound-dog jowls and bright blue eyes, Fish had kept them laughing with his droll humor. Playing with words, it was Fish who suggested the code word "Rochambeau" just that morning because it sounded like "Rush on, boys!" Fish's pliable face was now seamed with worry.

Alexander glanced up at the night sky, awaiting the signal corps rockets that would create a diversion and indicate the attack. Stars winked behind gauzy clouds. They were the same ones that looked down upon the grave of his mother. He wondered whether his brother was still in Christiansted. Alexander had written several times over the years, but James never wrote back. Was he dead, too?

Looking at the stars, Alexander felt the immensity of the universe. Some men would join that vast mystery within the hour. Was there a God up there, as Eliza believed? Would the Almighty watch over Alexander's wife and child better than He had protected Rachel Lavien?

Alexander pushed aside the fear for his young family. Corporal David Slayton, a father of three, told him that a man forgot his wife and children during battle as if they'd never existed. Such thoughts were luxuries, like hunger, fatigue, and pain. The struggle to survive blotted out anything that might trip a man.

A shriek split the calm night. Two bright red arcs careened through the sky toward the dark fort.

John Laurens, Nicholas Fish, and Jean-Joseph de Gimat tensed. Alexander fixed them with his eyes. "Now," he said, and pointed his bayonet skyward. "Follow me."

Alexander ran silently toward the silhouette of Yorktown's walls. His men and officers ran behind him. Ahead, incurious lightning bugs flitted in the tall, dark grass. Somewhere in the distance he heard the quiet handsaw of a resolute sapper dismantling the British fortifications. Unsung field engineers laid down their lives constantly.

Alexander hoped they would cut away the sharpened tree branches before his men reached the walls, but he had given the order not to not wait for the abatis to fall. Speed was their best weapon. Delay meant deaths. He would lead his troops over the top regardless of what stood in front of them.

An empty shell crater appeared out of nowhere. Just in time, he leaped wide-legged over it and ran on. He hoped others saw it, too. He heard ragged breathing and realized it was his.

The redoubt loomed up in the dark. A sapper sawed at the thicket. One of the defenses was down. Alexander spied an opening where a bottom spike had fallen sideways, waist high. Troops rushed up around him.

"Boost me," he ordered a soldier who kneeled immediately. Alexander stepped onto the man's shoulders, launched himself onto the wooden barrier, and leaped atop the parapet, where he nearly fell down on the other side. He heard other Continental soldiers scrambling up, each man struggling against the abatis.

Alexander caught his balance. He jabbed the sky with his bayonet. "Rochambeau, boys! Rochambeau!"

Alexander jumped down into the fort. A British soldier wearing only trousers emerged from the night, his sword raised. The man swung viciously. Alexander jumped aside and stabbed the Englishman's ribs. Blood hit his cheek.

Continental troops rained down, yelling and fighting. John Laurens jumped over the back wall. A Hessian bugler sounded an alarm until a Continental knocked the instrument from his mouth. Alexander turned at the loud report of a musket and saw Colonel Gimat stumble and fall headlong. A colored volunteer in a Continental uniform struck the musketeer with a blow to the head.

It was over in fifteen minutes. The bloodstained British major who offered his sword said simply, "We surrender." There was little else the man could do, chin set, eyes burning with humiliation, with only sixty soldiers against the two hundred Continentals who had overrun his position.

Alexander ordered his troops to regroup, except those he assigned the task of guarding prisoners. Two supported Colonel Gimat, who had taken a musket ball in the foot. John Laurens lined up the forward columns. The troops were back in formation when Alexander heard a scuffle and saw Fish hasten toward a handful of men near a flagpole. The glitter of firelight on a bayonet caught Alexander's eye. He followed.

"Damn you to hell! You killed the best soldier I ever knew," a Continental soldier in a captain's uniform yelled at an Englishman whom two others held fast. Their faces were stained with gunpowder and one had a bloody slash across his brow. "Now you'll pay!"

"You'll slay an unarmed man?" the British officer said. Despite the bayonet against his chest, he spat in the face of his captor.

Alexander caught the American's arm. "Captain. Step back in formation. Now. We'll not sully our honor in this fashion."

The soldier looked at Alexander, his face livid with rage. He tried to pull away.

Alexander tightened his grasp. "Any Redcoat who doesn't resist will be spared."

The captain shook his head, then muttered, "Yes, sir."

"You," Alexander told the men holding the prisoner. "Put him with the others. Make sure he gets there or you'll answer to a court-martial. You can be sure I will check."

He looked again at the Englishman to fix the face in his mind.

Yet Alexander did not see the defeated officer again until two days later, when General Charles O'Hara marched the entire British army out the gates of Yorktown. Lord Cornwallis ordered the surrender, but refused to face Washington himself and kept to his quarters in a sulk. O'Hara, Cornwallis's subordinate, was handed the mortifying task.

The day dawned bright and clear. The starved and beaten Redcoats filed out of the fort in two parallel rows that stretched nearly a mile. Smartly outfitted French soldiers lined the road on the left. Ragged American troops stood on the right. Alexander sat his horse next to John Laurens, who was talking to Tench Tilghman. Neither Laurens nor Tilghman heard the insult that Alexander caught when the British officer whose life he had defended in the redoubt marched past unexpectedly.

Alexander and the Englishman recognized each another on the spot. They could have been cousins—blue-eyed and tawny-haired. But the Englishman gave Alexander a look of disgust. "Bastard," he snarled before turning back to the gauntlet leading to the pile of surrendered weapons.

Alexander felt calmer than he had in years. Where was his instinct to dismount and slug the man over the common insult that held such special meaning for him?

Victory had drained his fury and the time for violence was over. Triumph was too sweet to spoil. Alexander would never again have to fight for his honor and his life. Or so he thought.

PART TWO

Betrayal and Redemption

1790–1854

CHAPTER TWENTY-FOUR

June 1790

New York City

"It is the man and woman united that make the complete human being. Separate, she wants his force of body and strength of reason; he, her softness, sensibility and acute discernment. Together they are more likely to succeed in the world."

Benjamin Franklin, "Advice to a Young Man," 1745

"MAY I HAVE TOO MANY?" THE four-year-old said. He held up his bowl with sticky fingers. His lips and chin were stained pink.

Eliza smiled. Little Alex was like his father in so many ways, always ready for pleasure. Eight-year-old Philip, born just after the Battle of Yorktown, had inherited his father's fire.

She picked a leaf from Alex's reddish curls. He and his older brother had wrestled outside before breakfast. If the laundrywoman hadn't just left with a full basket, Eliza would have added the boys' grass-stained blouses.

"Please?" Alex's blue eyes widened. "Please, *Moeder*!"

It was a blatant attempt to wheedle more cherries. Eliza's mother kept teaching the boy Dutch, though Eliza repeatedly told her that they wanted the little ones to learn French first. Kitty Schuyler gave the children whatever they wanted so long as they said please, thank you, and grandma in Dutch. Grandpa Schuyler was worse. A month earlier, Eliza had found a sharp Indian arrowhead at the bottom of the bag of sweets her sons brought home from their last trip to Albany.

"You may have five. Can you count them?"

Alex nodded. "Yes!" he shouted.

"Let's see," Eliza said in a hushed voice to demonstrate how he should speak indoors.

Alex counted from one to five, but placed two cherries in his bowl on the last number. He looked up. Eliza stared back. Alex took the extra cherry out of his bowl and held it to her mouth. "It's for you, Mama."

A crash filled the room. Eliza spun around to see three-year-old Fanny Antil splayed on the floor. The little girl burst into tears. Behind her, Philip struggled to right a heavy chair and little Angelica sprang from her seat to help him. Eliza's immediate thought was that they would wake Baby Jamie, taking his first nap of the day. She just couldn't stand that. Not after the night she'd had.

"Philip!" Eliza said. She placed the cherries on the sideboard next to the bread she had cut for breakfast and hurried to Fanny. "There you go, Fanny. It's all right. That was loud, wasn't it?"

Eliza hoisted the three-year-old onto her hip while Philip ducked under the table to fetch the cushion that had fallen onto the floor. "I'm sorry, Mama," he said. He put the cushion on the chair with a pat.

"You need to apologize to Fanny, Philip. She's little. And I've told you before not to hang on the furniture."

Eliza had told Philip not to swing from chairs, climb on tables, pull the cat's tail, play with balls in the house, put his finger in the butter churn, yell down the stairs, or do any number of things. But his misbehavior upset her most when someone got hurt, especially

Fanny. The orphan couldn't remember the mother who died when she was only one, and had already begun to forget the father who gave her to the Hamiltons.

Alexander admired Colonel Edward Antil, a one-armed veteran who graduated King's College just before the war broke out. Four years after Yorktown, Antil found himself widowed and caring for six children. When Alexander told Eliza, she agreed they should take the youngest until the colonel remarried. Then Antil died, and Fanny was theirs.

Eliza looked sternly at Philip. Angelica danced on her toes behind her brother, but Eliza ignored the girl's supplicating hand gestures. Eliza had been up twice the night before. Once when Alex needed the chamber pot, and again when Fanny had a bad dream. She never fell back to sleep.

"He didn't mean to, Mummy," Angelica said. The girl's eyes were luminous like her aunt's and the same dark ringlets spilled down her back.

Eliza jiggled Fanny higher on her hip. She wiped the toddler's wet cheeks with her apron. "Philip?" she said. An expression of Dutch severity crossed her face.

The high-strung boy looked down. Eliza just didn't know what to do with him. He'd become so contrary.

"What's that racket?" Alexander said as he walked through the open door into the dining room. "What are these jackanapes up to, this fine morning?"

Eliza's husband wore black silk breeches and a white waistcoat that flattered his lithe, muscular figure. He'd risen before dawn to work at his desk, but must have just washed—she could smell his fragrant skin over the aroma of warm bread. The atmosphere instantly felt less charged. Help had arrived.

Eliza felt like setting Fanny down, locking the children in a closet, and going back to bed with her husband. She would much rather snuggle than chase five willful urchins. But he needed to go to the government's new Treasury Department. President

Washington had appointed him chief, impressed by her husband's understanding of economics and insight into their new scheme for the government. The impulse to escape into his arms had also produced a baby every two years.

When Eliza developed milk fever with Jamie, they had easily met the cost of a wet nurse. Now that Alexander had quit his law practice to take a government salary—and refused Papa's offers of help—such an expense would upend their budget. Angelica sent pretty trinkets from London, where she and her wealthy husband rubbed shoulders with the Prince of Wales himself, but a fleur-de-lis flowerpot wouldn't still an infant's cries.

Alexander was a wizard with the country's finances, but a naïf with theirs. Eliza didn't know how they would meet the rent on their pew at Trinity Church.

Her ardor cooled. "Your son overturned the chair," she said.

Alexander assumed a grave expression but the corners of his mouth twitched. Her husband had sung the boy's praises from the instant he was born. Their eldest could do no wrong.

"Philip. You know I count on you to help Mama when I need to work. You must do your best to make us proud. What if something happened to Fanny—or Alex?"

Eliza wondered if her husband mentioned Alex to forestall the troublemaker from suggesting they give Fanny Antil to a street peddler. Philip might consider the orphan an unnecessary nuisance.

"When you wrong someone—even if by accident—you must apologize immediately." Alexander draped his arm around Philip's shoulders, man to man. "It's a matter of honor."

Philip had Eliza's dark curls and eyes, but his jutting chin was cut exactly like Alexander's. Looking up at his father, he clenched his jaw with the resolve Eliza had seen in her husband countless times. The boy turned to the toddler on Eliza's hip.

"Fanny." Philip took her foot and gave it a gentle shake, as if she were a pretty rag doll. "I'm sorry I tipped your chair. I didn't mean to. Do you want to go outside and play with me?"

Fanny's face lit up and she wriggled down. "Yes!" she said, and tugged Philip by the hand toward the rear door. Angelica followed. The square of grass in the back, edged with jacks-in-the-pulpit and bachelor buttons, was the children's refuge from the swift carriages, crying vendors, and busy horsemen outside 58 Wall Street. Philip looked over his shoulder, following the adoring females who commandeered him. Alexander smiled at his son.

Eliza started to tell Alex to sit when he slid off his chair to tag along, but caught herself. Her husband left home so early every morning that they rarely had a patch of daylight to themselves. The little boy could finish his cherries later.

Alexander sat down and applied butter to a slice of bread. His lips moved silently, as if rehearsing a speech. Eliza picked up her embroidery and took the chair next to him. His handsome face had grown puffy in recent weeks and, in the strong light of morning, bluish shadows lurked under his eyes.

Alexander normally spared Eliza the details of his work, and to their children invariably presented a blithe spirit. She wished he reacted as philosophically to temper tantrums outside the home. Past months had been filled with bruising public debates that shook her calm and made her wonder if Alexander had been wise to accept President Washington's request.

When the general took the oath of office half a block away a year earlier, Eliza little suspected so much difficulty would accompany their attempts to set up a government. She assumed that defeating Britain would be the hardest thing they would ever have to do in their lives.

She had been wrong. Alexander's tired face showed it. Implementing the new Constitution turned out to be unexpectedly controversial. One critic of Alexander's Treasury Department called him a liar and nearly provoked a duel. Governor Clinton became a sworn enemy when Alexander observed that Clinton's proud war record didn't include being shot at. Her husband's military comrades still loved him, but political opponents faulted him for almost everything he proposed. Alexander's frank retorts made things worse.

The incandescence of Washington's inaugural had blinded her to difficulties she should have anticipated, given the factionalism they saw during the Battle of Saratoga. But in 1789, everything seemed rosy. The colonies had won the war and, just as miraculously, created a unified country instead of collapsing into a heap of feuding neighbors. She and Alexander had danced until the wee hours at the ball following the inauguration.

Everyone was excited that night. No one could stop smiling. A benefactor gave every lady a Parisian fan ribbed with carved ivory and painted with a portrait of the new president. Eliza fanned herself madly until the breeze off the Hudson finally cooled the night air of the jammed Assembly Ballroom.

General Washington invited her to dance and Eliza couldn't recall ever feeling prouder than when the nation's greatest hero offered her his arm. Washington didn't seem as gay as he had during their parties at Morristown, but he appeared more relaxed with her than with other ladies he was obliged to ask.

"Tell me about young Philip, Mrs. Hamilton. I suppose he's exited the crawling phase."

Washington had visited them in Albany years before, when Eliza and Alexander were still marveling at the infant they produced so quickly.

"He has, indeed, Mr. President. Except when he's on his hands and knees searching for bugs under our porch." Eliza executed a turn under the president's raised arm. At fifty-seven, Washington was still magnificent—straight and strong, with all his own hair.

"Boys and bugs do go together. I myself enjoy few things more than combing my garden for insects. A day outdoors is well spent."

Washington spoke lightly, yet Eliza wondered if he missed Virginia, and how he felt about being in New York without Martha, who had yet to arrive. His wife had spent more than half the war at his side. Everyone wished to be close to the general, but perhaps he felt alone.

"We have specimens to spare, Mr. President. You must come for a glass of cider on our porch. I assure you New York has its own panoply of pests."

He laughed. "Your husband has told me the same on numerous occasions."

"Philip used to say, when he was little, that the bugs were happy to see him. My husband has yet to make that claim."

Washington's gray eyes were penetrating. "That's because he towers over them, Mrs. Hamilton. It frightens them."

The president bowed as the music came to a diminuendo, and gave his arm to another lady.

It was Eliza's first inkling of what was to come and the last event at which they'd had no enemies. Not one, that she knew.

Now the Republic frightened her almost more than the Revolution, when she understood the dangers better.

Shortly after the inaugural, Washington asked Alexander to take one of the three posts in his cabinet. He recruited General Henry Knox and Thomas Jefferson for the other two. Alexander's job was the most prominent and pressing.

Jefferson was in command of their minimal foreign relations, General Knox in charge of wars that didn't threaten. Alexander's task was to rebuild the nation's damaged economy, rescue its bankrupt government from an avalanche of debt, and prove to a doubting world that a country could prosper without an aristocracy. America would otherwise disintegrate. Wolfish foreigners would pounce. The president had faith that Alexander, who had fought as effectively for the controversial Constitution as he had battled Redcoats at Trenton and Yorktown, would manufacture solutions. Few men had such diverse talents. Few had the same history with General Washington in the worst and best of times.

Eliza glanced at her pale husband over her embroidery. Alexander jotted numbers on a pad while he finished his tea.

Her husband had used wit, charm, and intelligence to convince Congress to pass his proposals and reject those of the man who was now his principal opponent.

Eliza had never fully trusted James Madison. The spare, bookish Virginian possessed the income of a prince but dressed like a parson. He had served in Congress during the war—and never risked life and limb. Even when he was still her husband's friend, Madison seemed remote and calculating to her. But Alexander had enjoyed the dry little man immensely, and even gotten him to laugh, such as when Alexander borrowed a neighbor's pet monkey and they sat on the garden porch tossing it grapes.

Back then, Hamilton and Madison collaborated with John Jay on a collection of essays that people now called *The Federalist*. Jay was a New York lawyer who helped negotiate the peace treaty at the end of the Revolutionary War. He and Alexander had been friends for years. *The Federalist* convinced New York's skeptical legislature—by three heart-stopping votes—to ratify the US Constitution.

Afterward, Alexander accepted the Treasury job despite friends' objections that his growing family would sink into poverty. Alexander had a new and thriving law practice. Why not enjoy it? His war record was impeccable, his heroism esteemed, his reputation secure. Why court the censure sure to attend so much responsibility for the new government? Robert Troup, Alexander's old college roommate, and Gouverneur Morris, a fellow opponent of slavery, advised him to turn it down.

Eliza didn't know what to wish for. She was proud that General Washington wanted Alexander, but the warnings stuck in her mind.

Her husband didn't ask her permission. He accepted Washington's offer on the assumption that Congressman Madison, whom Alexander called Jemmy, would stand behind him. With Jemmy in the Legislature and Ham in the Executive, they would create the government they had dreamed up on paper.

"There will be justice, Eliza," Alexander told her, his eyes shining. "Justice and prosperity."

When Alexander said the word *justice*, Eliza saw twenty-foot angels with golden swords. She wondered if the country would thrive at her family's expense. Yet Alexander's confidence was infectious.

The months had reversed his expectations. Jemmy now acted as if Alexander's proposals to strengthen the nation were all a great and disturbing surprise. Madison opposed every measure drawn up by the Treasury: plans for raising taxes, paying down the war debt, building a capitol, and so on. Her husband had prevailed with Congress despite Madison's opposition. They still spoke when necessary, but the atmosphere was chilly.

"Jemmy's incorruptible," Alexander once told Eliza. "He just doesn't know how the world works. On his plantation, pheasants fly to the table roasted. Wheat grows in bales. Jemmy wouldn't know how to saddle a horse or load a gun without a servant's help. I bet he's never dug a grave. But he has a brilliant mind and he loves our country."

Eliza tried not to see fat Horatio Gates in skinny James Madison, yet too much had happened since 1776 not to worry.

Alexander finished the last piece of bread. He took a peach from the bowl in the center of the table and bit into it. "Hmm, these are succulent." He smiled as the rosy juice ran down his chin. "Are they from Saratoga, darling?"

"Yes." Eliza took up her napkin and dabbed at his chin. "Papa sent them downriver just yesterday. Two bushels of peaches, along with cherries."

"We'll never starve, my love."

"We're more likely to be crushed. Papa and Mama don't appreciate that there aren't storage barns here on Wall Street."

Alexander placed his arm around Eliza's shoulders and drew her close. "Someday, my angel, I'm going to build you a real house.

We'll put a barn right behind it. You'll have to tell me what goes in it. Hay, right?"

Eliza leaned into him and sniffed his neck. He smelled so good. She felt desire return. "Yes, hay. And you'll have to purchase a lot because I'm going to roll in it with you."

Alexander glanced at the door. The children were still outside.

"Is that a challenge, my little charmer?" he said as he tipped her chin. Her husband kissed her neck, and Eliza sensed the spot where the sharp hint of his beard met his silky lip line. She shivered.

"Be careful," he said softly. "You know I love a challenge."

CHAPTER TWENTY-FIVE

June 1790

New York City

"After we were disbanded, I returned to my old master at Woodbury, with whom I lived one year, my services in the American war having emancipated me from further slavery and from being bartered or sold. . . . I enjoyed the pleasures of a freeman; my food was sweet, my labor pleasure: . . . life seemed to shine upon me."

Memoirs of Boyrereau Brinch, 1810

ALEXANDER SLID THE SHEAF OF TREASURY stationery into his valise. The printer to whom Ajax Manly was apprenticed gave the government a good price and Alexander an excuse to visit his old friend.

Ajax wiped his hands on a rag stained with black ink. "I'm going to take the longer payout."

"Are you sure? It'll be awhile before you get your money."

Like most veterans, Ajax still hadn't collected his earnings from the war that ended seven years earlier. He was one of thousands to whom America was literally indebted. Alexander himself wasn't in that category since he had renounced years of back pay to show Congress he would gain nothing personally if his proposals were accepted. The Treasury Department had devised a plan to compensate veterans with land or long-term bonds. On land, Ajax could build a home or farm. If he chose the bonds, he would get new bonds in exchange for the old, delinquent ones. They wouldn't mature for several more years.

Ajax passed the rag over the counter, pausing at a greasy smudge that he cleaned with a few hard strokes. The print shop, in which summer's heat had been building since daybreak, was closed for the night.

"I don't want Western land. Who knows what it's like?"

"Land will go up in value. People are moving west."

"My old bonds have already accreted in value," Ajax said.

Ajax was volunteering at the African Free School started by the New York Manumission Society, and Alexander assumed he was borrowing books while teaching others to read. That would be like him. Someone must have donated a book on finance for the school library.

"I'm glad you didn't sell early," Alexander said.

"You might have warned me not to."

"I did."

"Back when. After Yorktown. You could've warned me again when I had stockjobbers coming in off the streets to sweet-talk me out of them."

Ajax didn't sound angry, but Alexander knew his friend expected more from his old artillery captain. Alexander spent the better part of most days fielding grievances from old acquaintances and new ones. But he didn't have time for complaints right now. Not if he wanted to be on time for the showdown with Jefferson and Madison.

Alexander shook off a feeling of weariness. "I'd be rightly accused of corruption if I tipped you off. I couldn't even tell my father-in-law what we were planning. General Schuyler was so frightened about losing his investments that his hair stood on end. Eliza was worried sick."

Ajax shrugged and swiped at another grease spot. "If you say so."

The Treasury's unexpected proposal that Congress repay its old war debts at face value had flushed speculators from every crevice. Hard-up veterans who had sold their promissory notes at a discount were angry to see prices shoot back up. They felt fooled. It was unfortunate, but no one had forced them to sell their bonds early. To Alexander's way of thinking, veterans should have placed more faith in the country. Some had. Ajax had.

Civilians complained, too. Those who bought bonds after 1776, and sold them before the maturity date, felt entitled to the appreciation. The average man wanted as much profit as possible and someone to blame if he didn't get it.

"Didn't you tell me years ago that you wouldn't settle for less than face value? Why should I think otherwise?"

Ajax stopped moving his rag. "I did say that. The bonds looked so fine with their fancy seals. Still. I'm relieved Congress approved your plan."

"Me, too." Alexander took the stool in front of the counter. He could rest at least a moment. "It was a near thing. Madison wanted us to track down every original bearer, no matter how many times the bond had exchanged hands, and hand over any appreciation. It was madness."

"How'd you even do that?"

"I don't know. I don't think Madison knew. He assumes I possess a magic wand."

Ajax flashed a smile. "I've heard you called a sorcerer."

"I get enough insults from my critics. Must you repeat them?"

Ajax sauntered to the open window. He pushed down the sash, locking it for the day, and cocked his head toward Wall Street. "You don't relish being called king of 'Hamiltonopolis'?"

A white woman carrying a basket of folded laundry passed the closed window. She smiled through the glass. Ajax lifted his hand in greeting. The woman was attractive despite a large birthmark that spilled across one cheek. Alexander wondered if she was the war widow Ajax had mentioned. Alexander hadn't realized she was white but it didn't surprise him. He sometimes thought Ajax harbored a prejudice against colored women—or had just given up on marriage. He could never wed a white woman and might like her for that very reason.

"I don't have time for this nonsense," Alexander said. Irritated at the political gossip, he closed his valise and stood. The oily ink of the printing press was nauseating with the window closed. "You'll finally get your back wages. Be grateful."

Ajax turned back around. There was a grin on his face. Alexander's old friend wasn't upset about the lack of warning after all.

"I am grateful. You know what I'm going to do with them? I'm going to buy my own shop. I'm not working for anybody else ever again."

Alexander grinned back, his spirits restored. It was a miracle: a colored man who not only was free, but would own his own business. It was the sort of thing that made every sling and arrow worthwhile. In Massachusetts, a slave had recently sued for emancipation under the state constitution and won his case. In New York, a petition to the legislature that Alexander signed five years earlier was on the brink of success. If passed, it would end forever the export of men, women, and children from New York to the West Indies like cattle.

Alexander felt fresher despite the heat and odor of the shop. Ajax had revived him. He was ready for Madison and Jefferson. He might even give them what they wanted in exchange for what the country needed.

"Bravo!" he said. "Treasury will buy its stationery from your fine establishment."

Ajax put out his hand to seal the deal.

Alexander shook it. "Your shop and others, of course."

He had to be careful. Opponents would accuse him of corruption no matter what, but he mustn't give them grounds. The Treasury's reputation—and survival of the new government—rested on his own personal integrity.

"Bonsoir, monsieur."

The elegantly liveried black man at the door of Jefferson's small but well-proportioned house on Maiden Lane greeted him in flawless Parisian. This was Alexander's first visit to the residence of the enigmatic widower and former envoy to Louis XVI. Thomas Jefferson had delayed accepting Washington's cabinet appointment for months—three and a half months—as if unsure a federal system merited his time.

"*Bonsoir*," Alexander said. "Is your master at home?" He wondered at the butler's identity. Slavery had long been illegal in the French capital. When revolution pulled down the Bastille the year before, abolition became total. A Parisian accent in a slave was odd.

The man smiled and said, "Yessuh, Mr. Hamilton. The secretary is expectin' you, suh."

Ah. Virginia through and through.

The servant showed Alexander into the front parlor. Across the open hall, Alexander spied a dining table laid with expensive Limoges. Silver candlesticks towered over the delicate place settings.

Alexander took his seat. Oak bookshelves edged with cedar were going up in one corner of the parlor and crates of books sat on the floor. The scent of fresh varnish mingled with a delicious aroma of garlic, herbs, and caramelized onions emanating from a kitchen somewhere.

Moments later, Jefferson shuffled in wearing slippers. The secretary of state's long auburn hair was tied with black ribbon and he wore breeches of a deep blue silk that contrasted with a red waistcoat and brilliant white shirt. Alexander wondered if the man's garb honored America's flag or the banner of revolutionary France. His arms were folded casually. James Madison followed. Madison was nearly a foot shorter, but Jefferson stooped as if too modest to lord his height over others.

Jefferson was remarkably handsome compared with the congressman—alert gray eyes, firm chin, generous mouth, high forehead. Madison's hawkish eyebrows, long nose, and thin lips made his intelligent face look pinched. Both wore their hair unpowdered in the new republican fashion.

Alexander rose.

"Mr. Hamilton. Welcome." Jefferson shook hands, then refolded his arms. "I'm delighted you could join us."

"I'm grateful for the invitation, Mr. Jefferson."

Alexander wasn't merely being polite. Only the day before, Alexander had run into Jefferson outside Washington's private residence, where the patient secretary of state allowed himself to be buttonholed for nearly an hour. Curious passersby must have wondered why they didn't go in out of the heat. Alexander was beside himself—it showed in his hastily tied cravat and the raw edge of the one thumbnail he allowed himself to gnaw—but he must get through to the Virginians.

Jefferson and Madison were intimates. Their massive plantations weren't far apart and they half lived in one another's homes. Alexander hoped Jefferson might prevail over the unwarranted suspicions that had turned Madison from a gifted facilitator into an irrational obstructionist. Alexander simply couldn't fathom why his friend had become a foe.

"It's my pleasure," Jefferson said. "I've not yet dined with the two great architects of the US constitution." He turned to Madison. "And you know my passion for architecture, Jemmy."

"At least it's an innocent one, Tom," Madison said.

Alexander bowed. "It's good to see you somewhere other than the assembly, Jemmy."

"Alexander," Madison replied with a bow.

Thomas Jefferson looked from one man to the other. "Since the two of you are on a first name basis, Mr. Hamilton, you must call me Tom. We've been strangers too long. Your exquisite sister-in-law Angelica Church was my only consolation during the miserable months I was marooned in England. So we're practically family. Did you know she gave me your *Federalist*? Please. Make yourself comfortable. Do sit."

Alexander took his chair while Madison sat opposite. The secretary of state perched on the arm of a divan next to the construction project, arms still crossed. Was Jefferson was naturally reserved, Alexander wondered, or closed to compromise? His posture was curious. Was the man pretentious, devious, or merely shy?

"Thank you. Please call me by my Christian name, as well. During the war I even answered to 'Ham,'" Alexander said, then cursed himself silently. He must avoid such references. War stories were inapt considering the oft-repeated tale of Jefferson's flight from Richmond while governor. He grasped for a change of subject. "Are you settling in? It appears you still have some boxes."

"Tom is famous, or I should say infamous," Madison said with a smile, "for remodeling any residence where he lays his head more than a night."

The congressman appeared less taciturn than before. Perhaps Jefferson's magic was working.

"I confess it's true. I'm incorrigible. My crates just sit there. I want to get the room right first." Jefferson leaned backward, one shoulder higher than the other, to appraise the new bookcases. "I'm still not infatuated with the look of those shelves."

"Did you meet Gouverneur Morris before you left Paris?" Alexander said, feeling for the olive branch of friendship.

Jefferson refocused. "Yes. I even presented him a business proposition, though it came to naught. He's a charming man. Made quite an impression among the ladies. Even with the wooden leg."

Alexander smiled. "I suppose you know how he got it?"

"The leg?" Jefferson said. "In the war, I assumed."

"During the war, but not in it."

"I heard he jumped from the window of a two-story house when the lord of the manor arrived at an inconvenient hour for his wife," Madison said. "Is that true?"

"Let's just say Gouverneur's friends wished he had lost a different body part in the fall, given how much trouble it gets him into."

Madison and Jefferson laughed. The secretary of state gestured to a tray of small cordials on a low table.

"By the way," Jefferson said as they picked up their glasses, "thank you for answering my request for funds so efficiently. I now have enough to pay my office staff. I wish the bankers of Holland were as prompt as the US Treasury."

Alexander took a sip of the fine Spanish sherry. "Yes, a penny loses its luster in the grip of a Dutchman. What leads you to the forbidding portals of a Dutch bank?"

Jefferson's rolled his eyes. "Do you believe I'm still awaiting my salary from when I was emissary to France? The Continental Congress put the funds in a Dutch account. They might as well have thrown them down a well."

"Perhaps I could write the bank on your behalf. I know something about dunning debtors." The memory of banging on merchants' doors in Christiansted came to mind, but Alexander chose not to mention it.

"Would you? That would be very kind. They owe me at least 350 pounds sterling. God knows what that is in Dutch currency—and that I can use it."

Alexander made a mental calculation. "Roughly four thousand guilders, I believe. Forward me the precise details. I'm sure they'll respond to the US Treasury."

Alexander sensed Madison stiffen. The congressman probably considered Hamilton's offer further proof of his unholy connections with European bankers. The Virginian was simply ignorant of the ways of the world.

"The only thing worse than not being repaid for a debt is having someone foist his debts on you," Madison said.

The congressman's tone was pleasant, as always. His understated approach had earned him the nickname "Big Knife." Madison excelled at cutting deals because he made people feel he was conciliating them even when his position was unchanged. Yet Alexander must find a way to strike a genuine compromise or they would have no country. Their entire future was at stake. Why didn't Jemmy see that? How could someone so brilliant become so stupid?

Yet Madison had alighted deftly on the crux of their disagreement. The Virginians did not want to pay other states' bills. They opposed the Treasury's attempt to roll all the debts of the Revolution into the budget of the new federal government.

"Isn't that what makes a family?" Alexander said. He tried to sound as casual as Madison, from whom he had much to learn about politics. "My father's obligations are mine? Everyone works to retire the family debt so they can prosper together?"

The best argument was sometimes a question.

"Yes, but I'm hardly responsible for my second and third cousins," Madison said. "Their spendthrift ways harm me only if I share my purse with them."

"King George is no longer America's father in any case," Thomas Jefferson said with a smile. "We're under no obligation to pay his old accounts—or the loans other states took out during the rebellion. America was born free. Government debt enslaves the next generation."

"Virginia has fulfilled its duty," Madison said. "Other states should do theirs."

They had him cornered. Jefferson's personal plight ought to be instructive.

"The bankers of Holland tarry in returning our deposits because they fear we'll go bankrupt," Alexander said. "They see the money they possess as collateral against what they lent us. They won't grant new loans, either. Virginia may have repaid her debts, but how long will her credit be good if Massachusetts and Connecticut default? Men are judged by the company they keep. So Virginia will be judged. Which depositors will be short-changed if Americans don't speak with one voice?"

Alexander restrained himself from saying more. If he appeared zealous, he would never convince them. The wealthy of Virginia, who lived off tobacco and cotton, had little sympathy for the indigent of New Hampshire, who farmed rocks. And Jefferson was fourteen years older. He might resent a lecture from a younger man whose star was rising.

The secretary of state gazed loftily at a painting of Galileo above Alexander's head. "Virginia has met her obligations. If the federal government assumes the revolutionary debts of the individual states, Virginia will pay twice."

The butler reappeared wearing a stiff apron. The smell of roasted poultry followed him. Alexander found he was hungry despite his anxiety. He hadn't eaten since breakfast with Eliza and the children.

"Master Jefferson. Please pardon me for interruptin', suh. Supper is served."

"Thank you, James. You may light the chafing dishes."

Jefferson smiled at Madison and Hamilton. "We're in for a treat. James attended cooking school while we were in Paris. He's trying something new in honor of our gathering. I've instructed him to chill one of my choicest wines to accompany the experiment." The secretary of state leaned forward to stand.

Alexander put up a hand. "There's been much conversation recently about the location of America's future capital."

Jefferson settled back on the divan.

"I believe that our revolution was one fight. That we were in the war together." Alexander allowed no irony to creep into his statement to the men who had watched the bloodshed from a safe distance.

"The state militias, for which we paid—"

"Proved inadequate, Tom. When we build our capital city, we'll want it to reflect our combined strength. It should symbolize that we're one family, with a common future. That our obligations are mutual, and will be mutually met."

Madison did not bend, but he inclined slightly. Jefferson shifted on the arm of the divan.

"I agree that if the federal government assumes the debts of the states, Virginia will pay more than her share." He looked down and brushed a piece of imaginary lint from his waistcoat. "For that reason, perhaps the family home ought to be located on the Potomac, as some have suggested. Build our capital city there—giving Virginia pride of place at the hearth." Alexander glanced up in time to see Jefferson and Madison exchange a look.

"Would New York continue as the temporary capital until then?" Madison spoke in his usual neutral tone, as if inquiring whether Alexander preferred white wine or red. But they all knew it was the critical question.

The middle states had to be placated, too. Inland Philadelphia was terribly jealous of both New York and Virginia. Wrestling the privilege from New York would gratify Pennsylvanians' pride, and they might gamble that an expensive new complex in Virginia would never materialize. Temporary expedients had a way of becoming permanent. If Madison held out such a carrot in Congress, Pennsylvania might sign on. Then Virginia would grab the prize.

"Why not?" Alexander said. "If the federal government absorbs the states' debts, its credit will improve. European banks will be happy to finance construction. It's smart business for them. What do you think? Would ten years be adequate for constructing our new capitol on the Potomac? Pennsylvania could have the capital till then."

Thomas Jefferson stood. "Gentlemen, this has been enormously productive. Shall we continue the conversation over supper? I wouldn't wish to see James's talents wasted."

Alexander locked eyes with Jemmy. The congressman said nothing, but nodded.

Hamilton and Madison followed their host to the dining room where a bronzed goose adorned with pearl onions gleamed in the center of the table.

Alexander didn't share Eliza's supreme confidence in prayer, but he said one anyway as he took his napkin. Philip Schuyler might never forgive him for trading away New York's glory. He prayed his father-in-law would understand.

They had ensured the continued existence of the nation. Financial obligations knit a family. And whether Jefferson and Madison realized it or not, he had just put a powerful government with a mighty purse at the head of it.

They might not be pleased when they figured that out, but considering their arrogance, he wasn't sure he minded.

CHAPTER TWENTY-SIX

February 1791

Philadelphia, Pennsylvania

"When I accepted the Office, I now hold, it was under a full persuasion, that from similarity of thinking, conspiring with personal goodwill, I should have the firm support of Mr. Madison. . . . *I do not believe I should have accepted under a different supposition."*

Alexander Hamilton to Edward Carrington, 1792

ALEXANDER LEANED OVER HIS DESK, SCRIBBLED a line, screwed up his face, and resumed pacing.

"If they served a single month in my department, they'd know it's essential," he muttered. "They aren't the ones answering creditors day in and day out. What are our choices?"

Eliza didn't answer. Her husband often talked to himself while he worked.

The flame in the grate blazed up at a dry stick, but Alexander appeared not to notice. Eliza took another sock from her basket. It was dim in the winter darkness and the beeswax didn't give off as much light as the oil lamp in the main parlor. But she couldn't desert her husband, so she had brought her sewing into his office after putting the children to bed.

Alexander had rented a house within half a block of the Treasury's new quarters on South Third Street in Philadelphia. Eliza wasn't happy about the small bedrooms and dark kitchen, but she appreciated the nearness to Alexander's work. He walked the boys to school.

"They hate banks, so where do we put the government's money? In private banks. And when the government needs loans, where do we go? To foreign banks. Jefferson says he wants a common currency, but who's to issue it? We need a public institution, damn it all." Alexander turned to Eliza. Candlelight winked off his gold wedding band.

Pounds and shillings were still the currency of the government. Other currencies flooded the marketplace as well. Whenever the servant girl went to market, she invariably came back with a mess of foreign coins. Eliza had explained to the maid more than once why a rix-dollar wasn't as valuable as a Spanish one.

After Congress assumed the revolutionary debts of the states, they had taken up her husband's next plan: a national bank. But the vote was sectional. Nearly everyone north of the Potomac voted for the bank, and everyone south voted against it. Madison led the opposition, of course.

Alexander no longer called him Jemmy. Much as Eliza hadn't warmed to Madison, she wished they could go back to the days when her husband opened the door eagerly at the Virginian's knock and kept her up nights yakking about their dreams. Then the two had made plans like flint and steel made sparks.

Now, Madison and Jefferson both claimed the government was exceeding its authority.

Alexander's eyes drifted to the fire as he chewed his thumbnail. Eliza repressed the desire to stop him and concentrated on her darning. She wished she could coat his thumb with the nasty ointment she used on Angelica, but she'd sworn off her reform campaign. Alexander rarely drank and was kind toward the children. A man needed a vice.

Eliza had scanned the newspaper that morning while listening to Angelica's lessons. "Didn't Patrick Henry say the bank is a plot?" she asked.

"More or less. He called it another example of the North's plan to enslave the South."

Eliza picked up her scissors to trim a knot. "I find it ironic that the Virginians complain about our attempts to make them into slaves when they each keep at least a dozen."

"I don't think that's it," he said. "At least not entirely. I've heard Madison is worried that the bank will cement Philadelphia as the capital. I've said again and again that it won't stop our move to the Potomac, but the Virginians just don't trust us. They hate anything that strengthens the North."

Her husband resumed pacing, murmuring softly and nibbling at his thumbnail.

Eliza set her basket down and folded her hands. "Alexander. What are you going to do about it?"

Alexander looked up. His expression was half-helpless, half-resolute. "Do? I'll do whatever I have to do. The president has asked me to make my case and Jefferson to make his. Washington wants to know why he should sign the bill—or veto it."

Eliza felt a tremor of alarm. Alexander had worked so hard to get his legislation through both houses. Surely the president wouldn't kill it. Washington had never cancelled a law passed by the people. If he did, they'd say he was acting like a king. "Surely he won't use the veto?"

Alexander shrugged. "He might. Don't forget. Mount Vernon overlooks the Potomac."

Eliza couldn't believe her ears. "Alexander Hamilton. Don't tell me you doubt him for one minute. No man is more incorruptible than George Washington."

He ground his fists against his eyes, then blinked tiredly. "It's just that the Southerners are so maddening. Do you know what Madison now says? He says we don't have the authority to do whatever is necessary and proper to operate the government." Alexander picked up an open book on the desk, jabbed at the page, and read aloud. "But it says right here, *wherever the end is required, the means are authorized.* Do you know who wrote that? Madison! Two years ago." Alexander slammed the book shut.

Eliza contemplated the principle, which sounded like motherhood. One had children without knowing all that would be required to raise them, but a woman did whatever was necessary to make them behave and meet their needs. Then she prayed.

"Why does Madison think differently now?" she said.

"Why do men contradict themselves? Why are we dissolving into factions when we swore we never would—when we created a central government to prevent just that? Do you know what will happen if this government doesn't work?"

Alexander placed *The Federalist* back on his desk. "We'll break into a heap of feuding states, that's what. Jealousies will divide us. The English, Spanish, and French will look on with amusement, then do with us what they will. That's what happens to the weak, Eliza. That's what has happened throughout all history."

She wished she had read the morning paper more closely. Angelica wouldn't ask such basic questions. Sometimes Eliza wondered if she were clever enough for her husband, and feared he might grow bored. She couldn't bear the thought.

Perhaps her face revealed self-doubt because Alexander walked over to stroke her hair. She leaned against his waistcoat.

"Madison contradicts himself because he's in the opposition now," Alexander said. "It must not have occurred to him that everything wouldn't always go his way. Jemmy is a good man, but he knows little about real compromise."

"What will you do?" she repeated.

Alexander walked back to his desk. "I had one of our allies read Madison's own words aloud in the Congress. That's why the bank bill passed. But now I must make sure it isn't vetoed. Jefferson has given Washington his reasons. Tonight I'll finish mine."

Eliza glanced up at the ornate timepiece that Angelica and her husband John had sent from London. Its brass wand pointed toward twelve. "It's nearly midnight. Can't it wait till morning?"

"No, I'm almost there." Alexander picked up the papers on which he had been working. They were messy with ink and jammed with his script. "I just need a few more hours."

Eliza didn't understand precisely why the legislation should be so controversial, but she didn't have to. Alexander cared about the bank with every fiber and she couldn't watch his heart break.

"Let me help. You write, I'll recopy."

"The baby will be up before dawn. You should get to bed, Eliza. You have the house to take care of."

"Angelica will give me a hand."

It was a lie. The little daydreamer was practically useless.

Alexander smiled. "You mean like the time she put corn into boil without removing the husks?"

Eliza laughed. "You forget our agreement, Mr. Hamilton. You run the government, I run our home." She picked up the lap desk she kept by her chair. "Stop being difficult. Give me those papers to recopy."

Alexander handed her two pages. "You start on those, darling. I'll work on these."

CHAPTER TWENTY-SEVEN

June 1791

Philadelphia

"Theseus seemed to me to resemble Romulus in many particulars. Both of them, born out of wedlock and of uncertain parentage, had the repute of being sprung from the gods. . . . Of the two most famous cities in the world, the one built Rome, and the other made Athens . . . both of them [are] said to have incurred great odium with their countrymen."

Plutarch's Lives, c. 100 BCE

ALEXANDER REREAD THE CONTRACT. THE RENTAL on Market Street was large and the garden had an apple tree sturdy enough for the three boys to climb in. Angelica would probably beat them to the top. His seven-year-old daughter had the agility of a cat. Eliza complained that the girl wouldn't sit at a spinning wheel more than ten minutes and worried that Angelica would never develop a practical side, but Alexander loved her free spirit. She'd be up the tree before the movers got the piano through the front door.

He studied the figure again. The house cost £250 sterling per year. In dollars, that meant roughly $1,100, which was a substantial bite out of his $3,000 salary. But the house was nearer to the president's mansion and they could have it in six weeks if it was still available. The offer was already a week old.

Alexander sometimes wondered if he should return to his former law practice. The six years between the end of the war and the start of the new government had been prosperous ones. Putting food on his family's table ought to be his top priority. Let those who had vast estates to go with their impractical philosophies solve the country's problems.

He sat at the window and looked out at the hotel across from their lodgings. The building threw a shadow that cut Third Street in two: one half gloomy even at noon, the other hot and bright. A carriage rolled by. A black driver clothed in scarlet livery tugged on the reins of his matched steeds and turned the corner in the direction of City Tavern. On the other side of the street, two vendors stood behind their tables in the shade, taking shelter against sunstroke. Philadelphia was a furnace in late June. One man had cakes of soap on his table, the other baskets of hardware.

Alexander thought of Philip Schuyler's letter from a month earlier. *When will you send Eliza and the children?*

Alexander should have dispatched the family to Albany by now, but he dreaded being without them. The last time Eliza visited her sister Cornelia in New York, she had at least left the boys behind. Four-year-old Alex had been first to draw back the curtains around his parents' bed and climb in with his father. Philip followed. The younger boy walked up and down Alexander's spine in his sleep the whole night, but the children's companionship was worth the price of being tired.

Perhaps Philip could stay in Philadelphia this summer. Alexander himself had been almost ten when Mama moved them from quiet Nevis to bustling Christiansted.

Where she caught fever and died.

Alexander sighed. Teeming Philadelphia was even dirtier than St. Croix.

The vendors outside the window were now arguing. The tall, spindly man on the right shook a long finger at his stumpy neighbor's nose. The shorter man tugged his table into the sunshine, apparently bullied into conceding the shade.

Philip Schuyler was right to encourage Alexander to send the family to Albany. July and August were dangerously pestilent. Yellow fever was epidemic in Philadelphia. The weather could go from gorgeous to horrendous in one afternoon and it was unconscionable to delay the children's departure. He had work to keep him busy. And enemies to keep him company.

Outside the window, a handsome couple stopped at the table of the soap-seller. The husband was tall, with a strong chin. When he spoke to the woman on his arm, she looked downward. After a few moments she lifted a hand to interject, but steadied herself on the vendor's table when the man tugged her closer. She turned her head toward Alexander.

The woman had a perfect heart-shaped face. She was young, at an age that suggested all the allure of womanhood but none of its complications.

The man turned the woman by the shoulders and slapped her hard, causing her head to jerk back. Alexander rose to his feet. The man threw some coins on the vendor's table and picked up two cakes of soap. His wife opened her drawstring bag and the man shoved his purchase inside.

The girl glanced around as if to make sure no one had seen her shame, landing on Alexander's building for the barest of seconds, and the couple continued down the street.

Alexander dropped back into his chair. His pulse raced. The man acted like a Christiansted planter with his mulatto concubine. Such abuse always took him back to St. Croix. The bruise under a prostitute's eye in New York, the tears of a serving girl in Philadelphia, the look of fear in the face of an intimidated wife invariably filled him with rage. Alexander had never seen his mother with Johann Lavien, but he knew she had cowered under the man's hand.

Alexander reached for the pewter tankard Eliza had brought him earlier that morning and drank deeply. The mild ale settled his nerves. It was his family that kept him sane amid the political fevers that burned through Philadelphia. They reassured him every day how much his life had changed.

He reached for the quill and signed the rental contract. The house on Market Street, where the fresh breeze between the Schuylkill and Delaware was stronger, was safer than their present home. It would keep the family well for another few weeks and allow him to delay the moment he must banish them to Albany. Then he would endure purgatory alone.

CHAPTER TWENTY-EIGHT

June 1791

Philadelphia

"Nations, like men, have their infancy."
Henry Bolingbroke, English philosopher, 1678–1751

ELIZA SURVEYED THE DANCING COUPLES FROM a chair next to the window overlooking the corner of Spruce and Third. Servants had lit the evening lamps in the imposing Bingham mansion, but the night hadn't yet cooled and the dance floor reeked of perspiration and perfume. Eliza found her eyes drawn to socialites whose dresses reflected the newest fashion of high waistlines and low necklines that left a convenient shelf for the bosom. Quite a few women had chosen a square décolletage that gave their breasts the appearance of rolls rising from a pan.

Someone ought to open a bakery, Eliza thought, amused at the idea. She wondered if men had an impulse to poke their fingers at the doughy goods. The Revolution seemed to have loosened all the stays, including those on bodices.

A bead of sweat trickled down her spine underneath the velvet gown, chased by another. She adjusted the lace fichu that kept prying eyes from her own bosom, and cooled her face with a fan of watered silk that her sister had sent from Paris. Where had Alexander wandered? Eliza hadn't seen him in a while, though she caught his baritone when a group in a nearby parlor undertook a rendition of "The Drum," a wartime drinking song that her husband often whistled to Philip and little Alex.

Eliza stretched her feet until they arched in her satin slippers. She luxuriated in the pleasure of not chasing small children yet knowing they were well cared for. The widow recommended by Ajax Manly had proven a competent ringmaster whenever the treasury secretary and his wife attended a social function. It also felt good to simply sit. The soft chair cushioned the dull ache that signaled the approach of her monthly courses. Yet the discomfort wasn't unwelcome. It meant she had avoided pregnancy again.

They hoped to make it through another year. It had been three—her longest break yet—and she and Alexander agreed that a respite would save their finances. Eliza also didn't want her mother's record of fifteen children living and dead. More than once she and Alexander had turned their backs in bed to forestall feelings that otherwise roared up in both of them. There were only a few days every month that were completely safe—and she got pregnant easily. It was hard to stop in the middle. Little Alex came along one night when Big Alex came along too quickly.

Eliza smiled behind her fan. Just the week before, the rogue had insisted on rubbing her ankles when he saw they had swelled in the summer heat. But when he slid his fingers between her toes and whispered "Betsey" with those luminous eyes, she withdrew her foot. He patted her knee to show he understood, though he then slipped a finger into the warm crook of her calf. Naughty boy.

"I think one has an obligation to teach one's slaves reading and writing," a gentleman said to a lady as they took chairs along the wall. A towering display of roses and irises on the table next to Eliza obscured their faces. "They're human, you know. My boy Carlos plays the violin beautifully."

The man leaned toward his dancing partner, who wore a peach-colored confection of gauze and lace that elegantly displayed her ample endowments. Eliza recognized the elegant profile of Aaron Burr. His dark widow's peak pointed toward his long, well-shaped nose and his eyes feasted on his comely companion.

"Teach slaves to read? Isn't that toying with fire, Senator Burr?" the lady said with a Tidewater accent.

Eliza didn't recognize the voice and couldn't see the woman's face, but she knew it wasn't the senator's wife, a much older woman. Theodosia Burr had left Philadelphia for the countryside. Any woman with good sense wouldn't return to the bilious city before fall.

"If I were afraid of fire, I wouldn't be talking with you, dear lady."

Burr's companion gave a laugh. She tapped his thigh with a silk fan, and shook it open. "Goodness, senator. You do make a hot evening hotter."

Burr leaned toward his partner's cleavage and whispered something that Eliza didn't hear, but the woman gasped and squirmed in her seat.

Flirtation was routine in Philadelphia high society. Wit paraded alongside women's full bosoms and men's trim calves. A triple entendre was considered superior to a double no matter how inane. Eliza didn't indulge in such innuendo but considered it mostly harmless. Her own coy sisters—Angelica and Peggy—mercilessly teased Alexander, who never failed to answer with a playful sally to show he considered them, apart from his wife, the most desirable females on the planet. Had he rebuffed their carefree teasing, Eliza might have been as wounded as her beloved sisters.

As a consequence, she found Burr's statement about slaves more remarkable than his amorous allusions. Burr had been a rake even before he married Theodosia, whose cuckolded husband conveniently died of yellow fever. That was old news. But why would the senator bother to educate his servants?

Aaron Burr was a peculiar man. Like Alexander, he was a founder of the New York Manumission Society. Yet he kept slaves. Eliza first took note of this moral inconsistency when he replaced her father as senator from New York.

Papa's luck in politics was as poor as ever. America's first senators had drawn straws to decide who would have two-, four-, and six-year terms to initiate a rotating order. Papa naturally drew the shortest and served only two years in the Senate. He expected immediate re-election, but New York Governor George Clinton—an enemy—made sure the state legislature chose Aaron Burr. The young war hero, a lawyer like her husband, had wined and dined half the New York Assembly with Theodosia's money.

Eliza waved her fan more vigorously. The slurry of humid air through the open window had the consistency of warm molasses. Between her father and husband, she encountered enemies wherever she went. She often felt she was in one of those blind mazes cut into cornfields to entertain children, surprised at every turn and unable to escape. Alexander considered Papa's senatorial defeat yet another veiled attempt to hurt the treasury secretary, whom Governor Clinton despised even more than he did Philip Schuyler.

Jefferson and Madison had prevailed upon acquaintances in New York to support Burr, who would vote very differently from Philip Schuyler on motions proposed by the incorrigibly inventive treasury secretary. Thank goodness Alexander's bank had cleared Congress before Philip Schuyler was robbed of his laurels once again—and that President Washington hadn't vetoed the bill.

Layer upon layer of intrigue . . . Eliza found it hard to fall back asleep when she awoke in the night. She had stopped counting the meager hours of slumber since the figure made her feel more tired if she thought about it. She had come to believe that exaggerating men's evil was the worst possible evil—though politicians did it to one another every day.

Her husband was as guilty as the next man. He pursued every fight to the finish. And each peak spurred him to climb another.

Once the bank passed, he turned to currency and manufacturing reform. He seemed compelled to create a national government or die in the attempt, although half the American people weren't sure they even wanted one.

Eliza thought again about Senator Burr. There was someone who didn't wage war over every ideal. The clash between personal interest and political principle apparently didn't keep him awake nights. Many New Yorkers had slaves, including Eliza's parents, but the Schuylers didn't make a point of joining the anti-slavery society. Burr enjoyed the posture of an abolitionist along with the perquisites of an owner. Better-educated slaves must make good servants. Eliza didn't admire hypocrisy, yet she envied his ease. Aaron Burr had more friends than enemies. Something Alexander couldn't say.

"But he's an Angloman. An Angloman!" The woman's drawl dripped scorn and she sat taller. The peacock feathers adorning her hair poked above the floral arrangement. "An Annngloman," she said again, drawing out the syllable.

It was a new term of opprobrium that had surfaced recently in the papers, but Eliza understood it like she did a kick in the stomach.

"Everyone knows he wanted a king," Burr said.

"The general wouldn't hear of it," the woman said. "Thank goodness, we can rely upon Virginia common sense. George Washington may have served George III as a youth, but he could never be accused of being an Angloman. Unlike that dreadful Hamilton."

"I respect President Washington, but I believe we have Mr. Madison to thank for restraining our treasury secretary. Without him, we'd have a monarchy by now."

"Indeed—what with that West Indian Iago beside our great Othello," the lady said.

Eliza glimpsed Burr's profile through the screen of flowers. An eyebrow went up. Perhaps he recognized his companion's misstep in comparing slaveholder George Washington to a black prince but was too polite to point it out.

"His bank will enslave the South," she said. "That's its intent. It truly is. Hamilton will hog-tie the planters to keep them at his mercy. My husband says Virginia would be better off independent, or joined with Maryland. He says anyone who bows to the federal government—now that it's in the hands of those wicked New York moneymen—ought to be hung."

"I'm a New Yorker, Mrs. Salisbury. I hope my neck isn't in danger of being stretched."

Georgiana Salisbury, for that's whom it was, Eliza now realized, tapped Burr's thigh with her fan. "You mustn't concern yourself, senator. Every soul on my plantation will fend off the posse that comes for you."

"I'm relieved, Madame, though your beauty alone would stun them."

Georgiana wore ivory pearl bracelets and an armband of smaller pink pearls. She fanned herself. "No Southerner could possibly mistake you for a Yankee stockjobber, senator. Not the grandson of Jonathan Edwards. I shall be the envy of my neighbors."

"If they lower their nooses fast enough to see me."

"Your pedigree is a bright lamp, sir. Besides, Virginians never hang a man without getting a good look first."

Senator Burr laughed and crossed his slim legs. "In that case, I shall come south. My wife and I have been intending to make a tour of Yorktown. To my eternal regret, I missed that battle."

Eliza considered how to slip away without being noticed. But Georgiana Salisbury's next comment was so ugly that Eliza shrank lower and gripped her fan until it broke.

"Yorktown! To think that was where the bastard brat made his name. If not for Yorktown, we might never have had to contend with that man. My husband's people hail from St. Croix. The stories they tell! The war turned our social order upside down, Senator

Burr. Upside down. Or flotsam such as Alexander Hamilton could never have risen to the top."

"He has courage, Mrs. Salisbury," Burr said, and Eliza's heart swelled toward the senator despite his competition with Papa. "The man was magnificent at Yorktown."

"Courage he has, doubtless, but no breeding. Except what he conveniently acquired through marriage. I fear we have democracy run amuck. Is it too much to ask the little people to stay in their place?"

Eliza drew in her breath. Georgiana's slurs against Alexander were outrageous, but her attitude toward those not born to wealth was more monstrous yet. The world had changed. She stood.

The couple on the other side of the floral centerpiece looked up in surprise. A pimple had started alongside Georgiana Salisbury's nose under her heavy face powder.

"The little people have spoken, Mrs. Salisbury. They elected General Washington, who considers my husband his finest public servant. He placed Mr. Hamilton in charge of our nation's purse—a position of sacred trust. He didn't select one of the spendthrift planters of the Chesapeake. I've no doubts as to why."

Georgiana Salisbury's lips parted as if to retort, but Eliza refused to give her the satisfaction. "Good evening, Mrs. Salisbury. Senator Burr. Excuse me. I wish to join my husband, the hero of Yorktown, as you say."

A quadrille ended as Eliza crossed the dance floor. Her mouth was dry and hands shaking. She hoped it wouldn't be difficult to find Alexander. All she wanted was to be at his side—and find a receptacle for her broken fan.

She and the children would depart for Albany the next day. Guilt at leaving her husband behind preyed on Eliza's conscience, but Alexander insisted she go. He would be well, he said.

She hoped he was right. Their enemies knew no bounds.

CHAPTER TWENTY-NINE

July 1791

Philadelphia

"I could not but think I had been artfully dealt with; that he had . . . taken what he might suppose the just measure of my weakness, founded on my youth and inexperience. . . . Vow what he would, I saw something low and selfish in his love."

Samuel Richardson, *Clarissa, The History of a Young Lady*, 1748

"THE LADY ASKED TO SEE YOU privately, Colonel Hamilton. I showed her into the study."

The freckled maid rested the box she was carrying on the parlor table, pulled her cap down more tightly over her disheveled curls, and took her burden out the back door.

The family had been packing all morning. Eliza was at the apothecary and the children were upstairs selecting items for the trunk each was allotted for their trip. Alexander had already told Angelica twice—who dissolved in unreasoning tears—that under no circumstances could she take her piano. The harpsichord in Albany would suffice.

Alexander made a loop in the knot on the bundle of scholarly pamphlets requested by his father-in-law and pulled hurriedly, nicking his raw cuticle on the scratchy hemp. He wiped the blood with a cloth and cursed the stranger waiting in his office.

It was hard enough saying good-bye to Eliza and the children without being interrupted. He usually didn't mind the foot traffic that found him at home nights and weekends, but today was different. He was exhausted and out of sorts.

The past month had been brutally busy. The Treasury Department released the stock of the Bank of the United States to economic applause and political scorn. Alexander set up a national coast guard to catch smugglers and collect taxes. He engaged a lighthouse keeper for faraway Portsmouth, wrote Mercy Otis Warren to praise her poetry, negotiated a loan for the nation from a group of Dutch bankers, and interceded with North Carolina to ensure pensions for disabled veterans. Petitions from businessmen and pleas from war widows littered his desk. His department had helped rich and poor. Some thanked him. Others pilloried him. Such was life for the keeper of the purse.

Now Eliza was leaving. They had put off the pilgrimage as long as possible, but the time had come. Eliza would take their five youngsters north for the summer while he babysat the one hundred and twenty children in Congress.

Alexander wasn't merely overworked. He was depressed. He didn't want the family to go, but they had already stayed longer than wise.

Life had drained out of the parlor. The piano was stripped of its sheet music and a small wooden block was all that was left of the ones Jamie and Alex liked to hide in the sofa. Philip's schoolbooks were gone from the shelf and Fanny's sewing basket no longer sat on the window seat. The home was emptying.

Except for the unwelcome visitor whom he suddenly recalled. Taking care with his nicked thumb, he tightened the ribbon holding his hair and strode from the parlor.

The servant had seated the lady on a sofa in front of the window. Her back to the glare, Alexander saw only a silhouette at first. "Good afternoon, madam. How may I help you?"

The woman rose and dropped into a deep curtsy. "Colonel Hamilton . . . I mean, Mr. Treasury Secretary . . . I . . . I mean—"

To Alexander's dismay, she unexpectedly burst into tears. He handed her a handkerchief from his breast pocket. "Please, madam . . ."

As the lady dabbed her eyes, Alexander examined her more closely. She appeared in her early twenties. Black hair was swept into a French pompadour from which long curls fell over one shoulder. She had vivid blue eyes, wide cheekbones, and a petite nose turned up at the tip. A small chin gave her face the shape of a heart. She seemed familiar. He noticed a split in her lower lip. It came to him—the woman across the street a few weeks earlier.

That explained the tears.

"How may I help, madam? I'm sure everything can be put right."

The young woman resumed her seat on the divan and Alexander took a chair beside her. She smelled of rosewater.

"Tell me what you need."

"Please forgive me for coming to your home, Colonel Hamilton. I was too ashamed to come to your office."

Her thick eyelashes were clumped like a weepy child's. She pressed her hands into her lap to still them, inadvertently pushing her full bosom higher in her fashionable dress.

"Well, you're here now. Please tell me your name."

"I'm Maria Reynolds," she said in a voice so breathy Alexander had to lean close to catch her tentative words. She pronounced her name with a long "i." *Mariah*. "You must know my brother-in-law, George Livingston. I'm related through him to the Livingstons of New York—a poor relation, I admit. That's why I need help. My husband James is . . . well . . . he's left me. And he uses me cruelly. But that's over. You see, I'm . . . alone now."

At the word *alone*, Mrs. Reynolds's eyes welled up again.

"I'm very sorry. Have you filed for divorce, Mrs. Reynolds? Pennsylvania grants them now. You'd even be entitled to remarry."

Maria closed her eyes as if such measures were unendurable. "I've heard that. But for now, I just need to get away."

"Might your brother-in-law take you in?"

Maria Reynolds wiped her tears again with Alexander's handkerchief. When she appeared to trust her voice, she continued. "He would, if I had the fare to reach New York. James never gives me money. My room and board are paid for the month, but I have nothing else beside my clothes. I may be able to sell some of them, but I doubt it will . . . will be enough."

The woman's bruised lip quivered and she caught it between her teeth. Alexander winced.

Maria Reynolds raised her chin determinedly and continued. "I hope you'll forgive me for taking the liberty, sir, but I thought that as a fellow New Yorker, or treasury secretary, you might be able to help. It's said you'll help anybody."

Alexander patted his waistcoat pocket, thinking he could manage the fare to New York, but then recalled that he hadn't yet been to the bank for the family's trip to Albany. "Allow me to lend you the fare, Mrs. Reynolds. I don't have the cash right now, but I can get it later this evening."

"Would you? Oh, Colonel Hamilton, I'd be so grateful." Mrs. Reynolds's eyes showed new hope. The tears were gone. When she smiled, she was a striking young woman. "I'll be safe in New York. James sometimes comes back drunk, but he won't follow where I have family."

She leaned closer, hands clenched. Her soft décolletage strained further and the edge of a tender brown crescent peeked above the satin bodice of her dress. "Thank you! You're as kind as they say," she gushed. Her expression was admiring.

Alexander's heart hammered. He stood up. "Of course, Mrs. Reynolds. It would be my pleasure, I mean, honor to help." He sat down behind his desk and took pen and ink from the drawer. "Would you kindly write your address? I can't show you the door, but I'll bring an adequate sum later today."

Maria Reynolds wrote her address in large script. With a bright smile and two more apologies, she took her leave.

Alexander stayed seated. After a long moment, when the latch met the front door, he picked up the slip of paper.

He tried not to think about her smooth nipple, revealed so innocently. He had forgotten how puffy and ripe was the breast of a woman who had not nursed children. Her handwriting betrayed a rudimentary education. The letters leaned against one another at awkward angles and she had misspelled the name of her own street. Maria Reynolds lived in a boarding house on "Forth" Street—Fourth Street—only a few blocks away.

Alexander sighed and adjusted the cloth of his trousers. God knew that thirty-four-year-old treasury secretaries were only human. He wondered if he should pay a messenger to deliver the loan considering the temptations of the flesh, then told himself not to be ridiculous.

Alexander had been married ten years, during which he had comfortably withstood the multiple enticements of what randy Gouverneur Morris once called "fleshy Philly" over a glass of ale at City Tavern. It was absurd to think he faced any danger. Maria Reynolds was a respectable woman who had appealed to Alexander's humanity. His duty was simple—and she lived right around the corner.

A muffled bang sounded overhead. Philip must be getting the better of Alex in a pillow fight. It was nearly two o'clock, Alexander realized with a flash of guilt. He and the children were supposed to be done by now, yet he still needed to arrange some materials and get to the bank. He had no idea if the children had finished their packing.

"Sir? Missus is home," the maid said through the half-open door as she walked by with another box.

"Alexander?" Eliza's inquiry came from the back of the house. She must have come through the rear. "Alexander?!"

He hustled toward the harassed voice, which sounded exactly like a mother undertaking a two-hundred-mile journey with five children under the age of ten.

"Let me get those." Eliza's purchases stuck out at all angles from the overburdened baskets that he took from her and set on a table that was already loaded with packages of every description, all serving some purpose in his wife's complicated calculations.

"Trunks packed?" She spoke rather breathlessly. "I got most of what we needed, but I believe the apothecary's scales are weighted. One would think he would know enough not to cheat the wife of the treasury secretary."

"One would think," he agreed. "Sorry, I lost track of time. A petitioner stopped by."

Eliza stopped moving for a second. "But the children are ready," she stated. "They've packed everything they need, right?" The question was edged with impatience.

"I'm not sure. They were under way a while ago, but let me check."

"Check? Alexander, I needed you to get them organized. The porters will be here any moment for the trunks. I can't do everything."

"Eliza, you don't do everything," he snapped.

"Well, I seem to have done so this afternoon!"

Alexander held his tongue as he did a thousand times a day and turned to go upstairs. His reasonable wife was being unreasonable. He couldn't help it that government business tugged at him day and night. He would like to go to Albany, too, where his in-laws and their servants danced around the grandchildren and made a fuss over visitors. Eliza was abandoning him to Philadelphia and upset because he wasn't helping her get out of town fast enough. Like he had nothing else to do.

"Let them go," he mumbled under his breath as he took the stairs two at a time. Even his family's departure felt like one more chore to accomplish.

The landlady who answered the door of the boarding house clutched at the empty air around her feet. "Bleedin' cat! Prithee catch her, sir."

Alexander snatched the tortoiseshell kitten by the scruff of the neck.

"Thank you," the woman said. "I need 'er for the rats."

"Certainly, madam. Is Maria Reynolds at home?"

"I ain't got any notion, sir. But you're welcome to see for yourself. She's up the stairs. Room looks over the street behind." The landlady held the door wide, the cat tucked under her arm.

The wooden banister was grimy from long use. Alexander refrained from touching the rail as he ascended the steep stairs. He walked to the end of the long hallway, where he found a door with Maria Reynolds's name printed on the room card. A wall sconce held the butt of a dusty candle that looked as if it hadn't been lit in a decade.

He knocked. There was no answer. He knocked again softly, hoping she was out or asleep so he could slide the envelope through the mail slot.

A chair scraped against the floor. The door opened.

"You came!" Maria Reynolds said. Her dark curls were unpinned and loose about her shoulders. A damp strand clung to her neck.

He withdrew a billfold from his pocket. "Of course, Mrs. Reynolds. As promised."

"No. Not in the hallway. Please, come in," Maria Reynolds said rapidly. She ducked behind the door and he had little choice but to follow.

Alexander entered the shadowy apartment. It was a simple room with a large unmade bed under the curtained window. Two trunks stood beside a chest. One was open, revealing a tangled heap of silken garments. When he caught sight of a beribboned lavender corset, Alexander knew he mustn't stay. He turned.

"Mrs. Reynolds—"

She locked the door and before Alexander could say anything else, grasped his hand.

"Thank you, Colonel Hamilton. Thank you! If you only knew. You're as wonderful as they say."

"It's a simple loan, Mrs. Reynolds. I'm happy to help. Please take it. I must go."

"I wish I could repay you somehow."

"There's no hurry. When you get to New York." He tried to let go of the hand without offending her, but certainly couldn't kiss it in farewell. That was too intimate, given the setting.

Alexander backed up slightly to gain some distance, but Maria came closer, then threw herself against him. Was she crying? No, just trembling. He patted her back and finally embraced her when it seemed she could not otherwise be soothed.

The young woman clung to him as if to a mast in a storm. She was shorter than Eliza. Her slender frame eventually quieted and she turned her head sideways on his chest.

"He says I'm useless. That he'd been a fool to marry me. That anyone would be. When I didn't please him enough, when I didn't do everything he asked, he hit me."

Alexander couldn't bear to think what requests she'd found so objectionable, but from what he'd spied across the street, James Reynolds was vulgar and cruel. He held Maria tighter, wishing he could change the world.

But he also felt a growing disquiet. Though he tried to ignore them, her full breasts stirred him. He recalled the crest of her brown nipple and hoped she couldn't feel his response. He struggled for control.

Alexander dropped his arms and pulled away again. "Really, Miss . . . Mrs. Reynolds. I must go now."

She looked up at him, eyes filled with trust. "I didn't think you'd bring the loan. I really didn't."

She paused, then took his lapels, laid her head on his coat, and said something too muffled to hear. Her voice vibrated against his chest.

He felt like he was in a dream from which he knew he needed to shake himself awake. Yet there was his hand lifting Maria's chin, his fingertips just touching the soft underside. She had a tiny beauty mark on her cheek that he hadn't noticed before. It was the same delicate color as her nipple. "What did you say?"

Her face expressed longing and desire. Alexander felt her thighs through the petticoat.

Maria Reynolds's voice was hardly above a murmur but now quite distinct. "I need you. Please. Let me thank you for your kindness." Then she rose to her toes, placed her lips on his, and kissed him with the probing tip of her sweet tongue.

Alexander closed his eyes. He resisted no longer. Waves of pleasure as magnificent as the surf on St. Croix washed over his head. He bent her to him and dove under.

CHAPTER THIRTY

August 1791

Albany

"For some days past, the Anglo Monarchical Tory party have appeared at the Theatre in full triumph—and the President's March and other aristocratical tunes have been . . . vehemently applauded."

The Aurora, Philadelphia, 1798

THE SUN HIGHLIGHTED PHILIP SCHUYLER'S SILVER hair as he demonstrated the proper method for hitching a horse. Eliza couldn't hear what her child was saying to his grandfather, but the boy's gamin face through the picture window and obvious pride at being at the center of attention made her smile.

Philip Schuyler handed the reins of the stallion to his dark-haired namesake. The nine-year-old looped them through the iron ring, shrugged his bony shoulders, and said something that made her father laugh. Below them, the grassy bank sloped gently down to the dappled Hudson, flowing forever past the Schuyler home.

Eliza placed another cross-stitch in the sunbonnet she was making for Fanny. She finally had time to finish it. Three-year-old James had recovered from the fever that overtook him when they arrived in Albany. Her husband, who had studied medicine before deciding that law was a better sword against injustice, had sent her a long list of anxious suggestions.

Eliza followed his advice carefully. She dosed Jamie with barley tea and boiled all their son's drinking water in a cast-iron pot even though Diana laughed at Alexander's fussiness. "Take good care of my lamb," he had written. Alexander sent a second letter asking her not to neglect her own health, and get plenty of fresh air and exercise. *"Dear Betsey—beloved Betsey—Be attentive to yourself!"*

He advised her to stay in the countryside as long as possible. Philadelphia remained unhealthy.

The door to the mansion opened. Eliza heard her son's boots in the hall. "May I please ride Excalibur again tomorrow, Grandpa?"

Her father replied in a gravelly buzz and the boy clattered up the staircase to the second-floor bedroom he shared with his brothers.

Philip Schuyler entered the parlor.

"The little mother. There you are." Her father limped to his wing chair and poured himself a cup of tea from the pot on the table. "Your son had me gallivanting up and down the towpath this morning. I'm afraid he's covered in mud from the fish weir. He's full of notions, that one. Worse than Philip Jeremiah used to be."

"No child can be worse than Philip Jeremiah," Eliza said.

"Speaking as a mother or sister?"

"I speak for all women. Remember when he took apart your Swiss watch?"

Her father removed the timepiece from his waistcoat pocket and looked at its worn face. "It took the jeweler three weeks to reassemble. Still loses fifteen minutes a day."

"I admit my own Philip can be a handful. He has his father's high spirits."

"Not the spirits of the girl who used to bring snakes in the house?"

Eliza laughed. "I couldn't help it that my patients refused to stay put."

"Hmmm." Her father leaned his head back and closed his eyes. His breathing grew even as he dozed.

Eliza used the remainder of her satin thread to embroider a white rose on Fanny's bonnet. She found herself taking extra care with Fanny's clothing to disguise a preference for Angelica. The orphan didn't need to know. Eliza wondered how much of her husband's ceaseless tinkering with the government reflected his own youth, when he was so often an outsider looking in. "I wish we could fix things for her—life shouldn't be such a game of chance," he once told Eliza as they watched Fanny play by herself.

The teacup rattled in its saucer.

Eliza looked up, her needle poised over the bonnet. "Papa, why is Alexander so resented? They call him an Angloman."

Her father held the cup to his lips. He sighed and shook his head.

"Is your tea cold? Shall I ring for more?" Eliza said.

Her father took a sip, then downed the brew. "No, sweet pea. It's fine. I was just thinking about your question."

Her father set down his cup. "When we wrote the Constitution, no one knew if a country could function without a king. Alexander raised the question openly in the convention at Philadelphia. James Madison privately had the same worry. So did I. So did many people. But now people remember that only Alexander had the nerve to say it openly. So opponents claim he wants to be king or is trying to establish one."

"Is that it?"

"Well, some are pigheaded, too. And jealous. They think him an upstart."

"But how can they claim he's trying to destroy the Republic? After all he's done? Hasn't he worked harder than anyone to make the country succeed?"

"Remember what rivals said before Saratoga? That I wanted Britain to win? Some people have no other way to explain why they aren't in front or on top. Someone else must be at fault. Or a traitor."

Papa gazed out the window as if seeing the past. "An Angloman means you're a British puppet. Not a real revolutionary. Saying it is how you hurt a man." He looked at Eliza. "But you mustn't worry. Ham has his supporters. George Washington for one. That counts for everything. John Jay, Gouverneur Morris, Robert Troup—all his old comrades are behind him."

Eliza wished they weren't mostly New Yorkers. Robert Troup visited them in Philadelphia occasionally, but his law practice in Manhattan kept him busy. If only Tench Tilghman were still alive. He was such a good friend. He had died a few years after Yorktown from the consumption he caught during one of the Morristown winters when illness dogged the troops. She thought of his searching expression at Cohoes Falls, so long ago.

"We could use Tench Tilghman now," Eliza said.

Her father smiled. "Yes, Tilghman was a Southerner we could count on. He would have spoken to the need for stronger government."

"And John Laurens. Don't forget John Laurens," Eliza said. Alexander had been heartbroken when John was shot from his saddle in a skirmish in South Carolina in 1782, at the tail end of the war. He'd been just twenty-seven.

"Forget Laurens? I may as well forget the first time I ever saw an Indian hatchet a Frenchman. I never knew a Southerner with a stronger dose of dash. Such a shame."

A child cried out and a thump sounded directly above their heads. Eliza stood quickly. Her father grabbed for a cane and winced at his gouty toe. Eliza reached the hall first. Three girls stormed down the stairs to the midway landing.

"Philip put a frog in our teapot! It jumped out at us," Fanny said.

Angelica's lips were sealed, but she nodded. The girls' visitor, ten-year-old Dolly, daughter of Laurie Van Cortlandt, née Lynch, bobbed her blond braids. Dolly had her mother's blue eyes and small nose but hadn't inherited the coquettish manner Laurie flaunted years before at Cohoes Falls.

"The frog startled me so much that I dropped the teapot," Dolly said. "The handle broke. I'm sorry, Mrs. Hamilton."

"Philip is so mean!" Fanny said.

"There wasn't any tea in the pot," Angelica said. "Nothing spilled."

Eliza rested her hand near the old tomahawk scar on the banister. The Tory attack when Eliza was pregnant with her first son—now terrorizing innocent girls—still gave her nightmares. She wished her parents would sand the gouge but Mama considered it better than a medal. "Where's Philip?"

"Here, Mother." Her son started down the stairs.

The three girls parted for their tormentor, who wore a face that reminded Eliza again of young Philip Jeremiah. "Angelica and Fanny," she said, "pick up the pieces and take them to Diana. Perhaps she can glue the teapot."

Angelica's fingertips grazed her older brother's as she passed him on the stairs.

"You come right down, young man," Eliza said. "Here General Schuyler spent all morning with you, and you can think of nothing better when you get home than to be rude to your sisters and their guest."

Philip reached the bottom of the staircase. "Yes, ma'am." He didn't look up.

"I'm surprised at you, Philip," his grandfather said, leaning on his cane. "You come from a long line of gentlemen. I'm sure your father would never place a frog in a lady's teapot. I know I wouldn't."

Something in his voice made Eliza want to laugh but she suppressed it.

The boy stared at his boots, which were caked with river mud. "It was just a little frog."

"And what in the world are you doing traipsing around Grandma's clean house with dirty shoes?" Eliza said. "You weren't raised by Indians."

"Yes, ma'am." He lifted one foot off the carpet and balanced on the other. "I'm sorry."

"Take yourself out back. Clean your shoes. Then I want you to apologize to Dolly. You are never, ever, to do that again."

"Never, ever," her father said.

The boy made his way out the back door, which let in the sound of a servant chopping wood.

"A frog in the teapot. Oh, dear. He must have found it at the weir," Papa said when the back door closed. He laughed so heartily as he stumped back to the parlor that Eliza smiled.

"Why in the world would he plague poor Dolly?" she said when they were seated once again. "She's been nothing but nice. I'll bet she jumped a foot."

"It's the girl's own fault." Her father reached for a handkerchief to dry his eyes. "She ought not to tease like that."

"Tease? Why, she was the soul of courtesy when she arrived yesterday morning. The innocent child even asked Philip about his riding lessons."

Philip Schuyler returned his foot to the hammock and nodded at the teapot. He smiled broadly. For a moment he looked like a boy despite his parchment skin.

She handed him a fresh cup. "Well?"

"Don't you see? Philip is sweet on Dolly. That's how boys act around pretty girls. They torment them. That little minx may or may not be aware of her effect, but I assure you she's having one. Dolly is lucky Philip found a frog instead of an eel."

Eliza laughed—Dolly must be her mother's daughter, after all—then reflected that she ought to have noticed Philip's infatuation. Her son had been skulking near the girls all day. Alexander would have known better and spoken to the boy before he got into mischief.

The soft knock on Eliza's door late that night startled her, and her hand jumped, leaving an ink smear on the letter she was writing. "Yes?" she said.

"Mother?" The floorboard squeaked. Philip put his head round the door.

"What is it, Philip?"

"I can't sleep."

Eliza sighed. She replaced her quill in the inkstand and set aside the ruined paper. "Come in, Philip."

Philip's dark curls were tousled and the collar of his nightshirt was rolled under. He sat on the floor at her feet and laid his head in her lap. Eliza placed a hand on her son's hair. His face was turned away.

"It's not fair. I'm always in trouble."

"You're not always in trouble, Philip. Grandpa said you helped him quite a bit this morning."

"That was Grandpa. I'm always in trouble with you." He spoke softly.

Eliza smoothed his tumbled locks. "That's hardly so."

Philip lifted his head and looked up at her. "What about when Mr. Mulligan visited?"

Hercules Mulligan, a war veteran who was her husband's oldest friend in New York, had stayed with them recently when visiting Philadelphia. His youngest child, a boy Philip's age, came along. The scalawags dared one another to walk the roofline of the carriage house. When the Mulligan boy slipped and broke his arm, Eliza was livid. They might have snapped their necks. She sent Philip to his room without dinner and forbade him from going outdoors the next two days.

"Philip, surely you understand that God wants us to be good, and atone for our sins. It's my responsibility to teach you that."

"Angelica and Fanny are never in trouble."

"They aren't as willful."

Philip laid his head back down. "It's not fair."

His gravity surprised her. "Why is that, darling?"

He spoke without looking at her. "You like them more."

Eliza could hardly believe her ears. Could he be serious? She and Alexander had worried they could never love their other children as much as they did Philip. When their firstborn was a baby, they placed him between them in bed to watch him sleep. His faint breath was like music to them. When he began sitting up, waving his hands at passing butterflies and gnats, Alexander pronounced the boy an orator. The next Demosthenes! The baby's bubbly giggles brought them endless joy. Eliza and Alexander felt their souls joined in that tender breast. They wondered how any other child could be as special.

Yet Eliza also remembered what it felt like to come after Angelica. She knew they must try to love all equally. And they had. Each child was a different treasure.

Eliza lifted Philip's chin. "Don't you recall the story? How Papa rode his horse day and night all the way from Yorktown to be here when you were born?"

"Papa was so tired he became ill."

"That's right. Prince had to help him out of the saddle. Papa slept for nearly a month."

Eliza let go of the boy's chin. She wondered if she should tell him. It's not that she didn't adore all her children. She did—and yet. "The day you were born was the best day of our lives."

Philip's lips parted. "The best day ever, Mama?"

"The best day ever. That's when we met you. When we became parents."

"Papa felt that way, too?"

"Of course. You're his firstborn. That's when he decided to become a lawyer. He said he must make sure the country turned out right. For you."

Philip smiled. "I want to be just like Papa when I grow up. I'll make the world better, too."

"You will," she said.

"Then I'll never be in trouble."

Eliza laughed. "Grown-ups have problems, too. But you must pray they aren't serious."

"Yes, Mother." He stood and kissed her on the cheek. "Good night."

"Good night, Philip."

The boy turned to leave.

Eliza stood. "Philip—" She hugged him tight. He smelled of hay and soap. "I love you."

Philip wiggled away. "Me too."

When her son closed the door, Eliza crumpled the stained paper and took out a fresh sheet to finish writing Alexander about Philip's latest escapade. She wished he didn't have to stay behind in Philadelphia. Her husband missed the boy and their other children.

He missed her, too. He said so in every letter.

CHAPTER THIRTY-ONE

October 1791

Philadelphia

"Three may keep a secret, if two of them are dead."
Benjamin Franklin, *Poor Richard's Almanack*

ALEXANDER'S PORTMANTEAU WAS HEAVY WITH DOCUMENTS he had fruitlessly brought home, determined to finish his long-delayed report on manufacturing. If the country continued to buy every hat, harness, and handgun from England, it would go broke. It would end up like St. Croix, tied to cash crops and importing everything else.

America should make things. From the gewgaws people desired to the goods they needed. The country finally had strong credit and ought to do something with it. Alexander must persuade Congress to help urban factories get organized, even though Thomas Jefferson claimed they were the Devil's actual workshop, as if Southern plantations were a moral paradise. Those who clenched the Bill of Rights most tightly often had a whip in the other hand.

Yet Alexander's vow to finish the report had been worthless. He went downstairs to work after hearing the boys' prayers and ended up staring at the walls. He never opened his portmanteau. Now he had to lug it back to the office. The family's return from Albany eight weeks earlier had failed to produce the cure he longed for and dreaded. His abominable behavior felt completely out of his control.

Alexander shifted the bag to dispel a cramp in his hand and continued down Walnut Street.

Beautiful Maria Reynolds invaded his thoughts. He couldn't pick up a pencil, cross a street, lift a fork, or draw a curtain without wondering when he would see her. He hated the power she had to command every thought, to turn a column of important numbers into meaningless jumble and distract him from his responsibilities.

What was he doing? His wife was perfect, his family loving, his fame exalted—and he risked it all. He was crazy.

But Maria made him crazy. The way she touched him, looked at him, like Eliza used to do.

Her sweet scent lingered on every breeze. How would he describe it? Like honeysuckle before the green bud opened? Like fresh milk in the churn? He dreamed of pressing his palms around her waist and capturing that fragile circle above her hips with his hands.

He also lived in terror. What if Eliza found out?

Alexander shifted the portmanteau to his other hand. Few burdens were heavier than paper.

The air of Philadelphia finally had a crisp edge. The maples had not yet turned, but oaks were beginning to yellow and the breeze from the Delaware was cold and clean. Before he left for work, Alexander swore he wouldn't go near Maria's street. Then he decided he would walk down it, but not enter the building. He rationalized that he needed to inspect the new stairs at the extra offices that Treasury had rented for its growing staff. They happened to be next door to Maria Reynolds. His conniving brain told him he needed to make sure the steps were constructed properly. The government hadn't a penny to waste.

As he rounded the corner onto Maria's street, Alexander saw that morning traffic had slowed. A fruit vendor's wheelbarrow was tipped over on the cobblestones. Carriages were backed up for two blocks. A Negro teamster delivering a load of bricks was helping to retrieve the fruit that had rolled under his cartwheels. A pedestrian stopped also. The three men lobbed apples and pears into the wheelbarrow as Alexander made his way around them.

And then he was there, at the back of narrow apartment house with the small window through which he had seen sunrise more than once last summer—his arms around Maria, breathing her mesmerizing fragrance as she slept. When he woke her by licking her bare shoulder, she laughed sleepily and raised her face to be kissed.

Alexander willed his eyes to the Treasury offices next door. The new stairs were still unpainted, two weeks after the carpenters had finished. A rainstorm had already taken the shine off the fresh wood. Another downpour and the planks would swell.

He stared at the risers flecked with mud. This was what was important: the government's work. He mustn't look at Maria's window. She was soft-scented poison, sweet going down.

Alexander withdrew her letter from his pocket. Translucent from grease on the corner, the illiterate note was further proof that Maria was unworthy of him and he was unworthy of the family he was deceiving.

Alexander thought about her thin lips, her worst attribute. But it didn't help. He immediately pictured kissing them. Beginning at the corners, lightly, then persistently, until his mouth covered hers.

He had lost half a stone. He could slip his hand deep into a waistband once tight from Eliza's Dutch puddings. The night before, he had pushed a cutlet around on his plate until the gravy congealed. Taken a warm roll and returned it unbuttered to the serving dish. Only one hunger gnawed at him and it was never sated.

He looked again at Maria's letter. "*Don't leeve me*," she wrote. "*I cannot liv without you. James has left agin for Virginya.*"

The missive was dated a week earlier. Alexander wondered what business had taken James Reynolds out of town. Maria's husband had drifted in and out of her apartment that whole summer, despite his threat to leave. Once, when Alexander arrived late in the evening, Reynolds answered the door. The man was at least six foot two.

Maria hovered behind the door. "Colonel Hamilton!" she sang out before Alexander could introduce himself. She tapped her husband's arm. "Colonel Hamilton was the one who came to my aid when you . . . you went to that strumpet." Her dainty nostrils flared.

Reynolds squinted at Alexander. "I know you." His voice was coarse, as if from smoke or drink. "You're over at Treasury, right? I hear you're taking on new men. I know how to use a gun. A tax collector's gotta have a gun."

Alexander explained that his office had no vacancies, which was true, and referred Reynolds to another branch of the government. He made some excuse for dropping by and tried afterward not to think about the man's proficiency with firearms.

He had told himself he wouldn't go back after that first afternoon, when Maria's ardor caught him by surprise and he returned home too late to dine with the family before their trip. But then Eliza left for the summer and lust took over.

Alexander had taken risks all his life—fleeing Christiansted, joining the Revolution, wooing a general's daughter, fighting for the new government. But for the first time he took risks he knew were absurd. Nothing good could come of this. Before the family returned from Albany, he had even brought Maria to their home after dark.

Eliza had hardly lain with him the preceding year. He ought not to resent it—they couldn't afford more babies—but his flesh sometimes throbbed with frustration. Maria offered her body with the eagerness of a bride—and the ingenuity of an enchantress on days she considered dicey. By the end of the summer Alexander had purchased the expensive French-made condom Maria suggested, which she washed and kept for him to reuse. Such things were meant for illicit affairs, after all. No one considered them decent in the marriage bed.

Alexander was simply tired of being good. The mere thought of his lover gave him a stunning erection. Whenever he feared Eliza might suspect, he felt sick to his stomach, and formed desperate resolutions of fidelity. But then his mind rebelled and told him he deserved a more satisfying life. Other men had them.

At the beginning of October he swore not to walk down Maria's street for at least a month. To deprive the obsession of oxygen, he actually crossed off the days on his desk almanac. Each was a victory. But Maria kept writing.

He tried to talk himself out of his fixation, and found he was a poor listener. Reason had gone missing. At these moments, Maria's name became another word for affliction.

Perhaps he needed to see her one last time to understand what drew him. If he could analyze the alchemy of his addiction—as he did other knotty problems—he might extirpate his feelings. Was it the deep arch of her eyebrow or the swanlike back of her neck?

It was something in him, of course. Maria touched the nerve that had sprung to life when he peeked over the wall of the bordello on Company Street as a boy and saw the prostitute Coelia soaping herself in a washtub on the veranda. Frilly purple bougainvillea partially obscured his view, but he never forgot the slim hand pushing bubbles up her thigh and diving between her legs. The memory still aroused him. He refused to conjure such images in Eliza's presence, yet with Maria there was no reason to resist the tug of raw sensuality that took his mind off every care. It was wrong but that was the point.

Alexander sensed the tempo of the street behind him return to normal. The fruit vendors' wheelbarrow must have gotten under way. The rattle of carriages promised a hectic afternoon at the coffeehouses where stockjobbers traded bank shares.

He gazed up at Maria's blank window. A coat of dust rendered it opaque. Alexander felt he must penetrate the source of her power or be destroyed. He needed to see her one last time, for one last kiss. But only a kiss. He would not sleep with her again.

He shook his head as he mounted the stairs. "No, I will not kiss her," he corrected himself under his breath. "I will not."

CHAPTER THIRTY-TWO

December 1791

Philadelphia

"Absence diminishes small loves and increases great ones, as the wind blows out the candle and fans the bonfire."

François de La Rochefoucauld, *Maxims*, 1665

THE CARTON OF PAMPHLETS REACHED HIGHER than Ajax Manly's head. He peered around the side of the box as he brought it into the Hamiltons' front hall, past the mahogany entry table with its fragrant arrangement of evergreens and holly berries.

Eliza motioned toward a small stand. "Right there, please."

"Let me give you a hand with that," Alexander said, coming out of his office.

Ajax flicked his head to reject assistance. "You're soft, treasury secretary. I'll do the heavy lifting,"

The colored man had filled out over the years, which made him more handsome in Eliza's opinion, but she thought he ought to take greater care with his appearance now that he was a substantial proprietor in Philadelphia. He hadn't shaved the scruff on his chin for at least two days.

Eliza wondered if Alexander's friend was ever going to marry. He needed a woman to clean him up. Her husband told her Ajax wasn't interested in marriage, which was a shame in Eliza's book.

"All right, junior," Alexander said. "If you still need to prove your virility, Lord knows I won't get in your way."

Eliza spied the wooden block at that very instant, but too late to prevent Ajax from stepping on it.

The printer staggered sideways under the heavy load. Alexander sprang forward and caught the edge of the carton.

"Here I thought you couldn't dance," Alexander said.

"I just didn't care to dance with you."

"I'm so sorry, Mr. Manly," Eliza said as she swept up the toy. "That Jamie."

The printer set down the carton and opened the lid to reveal the crisp stacks of her husband's report.

Eliza couldn't wait to send the pamphlet to Angelica and read it herself. Unlike his proposal on banking, she hadn't seen the *Report on Manufactures* before it went to press.

Eliza was glad he ordered extra copies for distribution. Alexander needed all the popular support he could beg, borrow, or steal. This was the last limb of his three-legged stool, he said. With foreign credit, a domestic bank, and local industry, their children would inherit a sound nation. The revolution would endure.

"Then I can die content," he whispered one night after they blew out the candle.

That was just like him, so dramatic. "Die content?" she said. "What about just making a living once you leave government?"

Eliza asked the question with a smile in the dark, though as soon as the words left her mouth she realized he might take them as criticism of their strained budget—of which she did feel critical. She nestled closer and said, "I'm so proud of you."

Alexander handed Ajax a stack of bank bills to pay for the print run. "There's the balance."

Ajax shifted the money into the pocket of his heavy coat without counting it.

"Will you stay for tea?" Alexander said. "Eliza just pulled a pear pandowdy from the oven."

Ajax glanced sidelong at Eliza. "No thank you, Ham. I promised to deliver another job on the other side of the Delaware. I need to catch a ferry."

"Not even a few minutes? Just to shake off the chill?" Alexander said. "Surely you can rest a moment."

"Rest? Is that you using that word? Seems you never have time for anything except work. You hardly even eat." Ajax looked at him. "I think you mighta been fatter at Valley Forge."

"You haven't missed many meals," Alexander said. "Your waistline is the definition of flourishing. Who's feeding you? Has Cupid's arrow finally found its mark?"

Ajax turned up his collar. "I'd best head out. Good luck with the report, Ham. I appreciate your efforts to keep us all employed. Most do."

Behind his teasing, Ajax sounded as if he knew Alexander really was trying his best. Eliza hesitated, then tapped the man's sleeve. "Please. Wait a minute, Mr. Manly. You can take some pandowdy on the ferry. It'll keep you warm."

Eliza turned before Ajax could protest. She would wrap a slice for him and put some on a plate for Alexander. The printer was right that her husband was looking thin. The country might be thriving but it was going to kill Alexander Hamilton. He worked too hard.

The temperature plunged in the early dark. Shallow snowdrifts from a brief but violent storm muffled the sounds of the street. Winter's hush had finally settled on Philadelphia, and Eliza decided to put the children to bed earlier than usual. She was happy when Alexander said he also wouldn't mind retiring early.

When he came into their bedroom after finishing his silent deskwork, Eliza put aside the letter from Angelica that she'd been reading. Her husband must have been paying bills. When writing, he paced the floor and she sometimes caught his words.

Alexander undressed in the candlelight. He seemed concentrated on some difficult mental calculation. Nonetheless, he draped his shirt carefully over a chair and checked the window to make sure it was snug. Then he donned his nightshirt, slipped under the covers, and turned onto his side, facing away. He must be worried about the reaction to his report.

Eliza slipped her arm around her husband's warm torso. He was slimmer than he had been in a while.

"Won't President Washington support you, sweetheart?"

"Yes. I think so," Alexander said. His voice was low.

Eliza lifted her head. Had one of children cried out? But the house was quiet. Perhaps Fanny was talking in her sleep again. She settled back onto the pillow. "Are you anxious about the report?"

"Not particularly."

Alexander pulled the cover up higher on his shoulder and reached around behind his back to pull it higher over Eliza as well.

"Will there be a fight in Congress?"

"Of course. It's my idea. Madison is bound to hate it and you know Jefferson."

Eliza nodded in the dark though she didn't know the secretary of state well. Angelica had met him in Paris years earlier and thought him immensely agreeable then. But she took her husband's point. The men were opposites. They competed for the president's ear even though Washington begged them to get along, and Jefferson automatically despised anything her husband suggested. Worse, Alexander proposed new measures constantly, with which Washington usually agreed. Jefferson must resent him intensely—which was why insulting articles frequently appeared in the press. Jefferson paid a journalist to write critical stories. Her husband said the secretary of state was the only man he knew who spoke without moving his lips.

She stretched her toes until they met Alexander's warm feet. "Does his department still have only five staff members?"

"Mm-hmm." He seemed to be drifting toward sleep.

"How many does Treasury have?"

Alexander stirred. "How many what?"

Eliza snuggled closer. "Staff. How many do you have?"

Alexander looked toward the ceiling. Eliza admired his elegant silhouette—the high forehead, aquiline nose, decisive chin.

"With the revenue cutters, I think it's up to three hundred. We're hiring, though. We need help with the new whiskey tax. Why?"

"Perhaps Mr. Jefferson is jealous."

Alexander's jaw muscles bunched. "I can't see why a man in possession of ten thousand acres and five hundred slaves would be jealous of one supporting five children on a government salary. I'm the only member of the cabinet—including the president—without an independent income."

"That's not what I mean. Jefferson must be jealous of your prominence. And Washington's trust in you."

Alexander sighed. He pulled the covers to his chin and settled back onto his side. "Betsey, dear, could we talk about this in the morning?"

Eliza withdrew her arm from Alexander's waist and stared at his shoulder in the dark. It had been months since they had talked late into the night and even longer since they had made love without worrying. Jamie would be four in the spring.

She rolled onto her back. Was this the way things would be between them until her childbearing days were done? Living at arm's length? Was this the shape of her life?

Perhaps Alexander felt she was one more burden. He slept with his face turned away. She remembered the days when they slept face to face, breathing each other's breath, unwilling to be more than an inch apart.

Eliza hated Philadelphia. Alexander's work crushed them a little more every day. She wanted to go home, back to New York, where they were free and safe.

The bed creaked. Eliza felt her husband shift in the dark. He rolled toward her.

"Betsey, my love." He slipped his arm around her waist. "Go to sleep."

Eliza felt her throat swell. A tear rolled down her cheek. She didn't understand why she felt so unloved when she knew how very much he loved her. What was wrong?

Alexander lifted his head. "Are you crying?" He touched her face in the dark. "You are. My darling. What's wrong?"

"I don't know," she whispered.

"Talk to me, angel."

Eliza turned to her husband. The words stuck in her throat. Regardless of the consequences, she needed to be nearer. "Make love to me, Alexander. Kiss me like you used to." She drew him close.

Alexander returned her embrace, though she sensed restraint. His body hardened with her kisses and she heard the familiar raggedness in his breath.

He drew back. "Is this the right time?"

Eliza pressed harder against him and reached down. "I don't care if it's the right time," she whispered. "I care only about you."

CHAPTER THIRTY-THREE

December 1791 and May 1792

Philadelphia

"If I could not go to heaven but with a [political] party, I would not go there at all."

Thomas Jefferson, 1789

ALEXANDER ENTERED THE OBSCURE TAVERN WHERE James Reynolds said to meet him. The straw on the floor of the George smelled of stale beer. A single spermaceti lamp cast feeble rays onto a few scattered patrons, including a man in the shadowy far corner. Alexander recognized him at once.

The last military execution Alexander had witnessed was that of British spy John André during the Revolution. The rope stretched the officer's neck and turned his handsome face purple. Alexander hated it that Washington felt obliged to make an example of the gallant Englishman, but the revulsion he experienced then was nothing compared to the horror he felt now at his own appointment with a noose. He wondered if John André had been equally shocked at being caught.

Maria's letter was the first to arrive. She began, as always, with hysterical references to her troubles, but made plain they were now his, too. James Reynolds had uncovered their secret. He was determined to obtain satisfaction. "*If he dose not se or hear from you to day he will write* Mrs. *Hamilton*," she scribbled in the note delivered by her usual messenger—a Negro with an accomplice's unknowing eyes.

Alexander's clerk handed him the next letter an hour later. He read with mounting alarm James Reynolds's description of Alexander as his "greatest Enimy."

Alexander invited the man to call that afternoon. They sparred for nearly thirty minutes, James Reynolds hinting darkly about what would be required to salve his wounded pride. The man hadn't mentioned money but his caginess revealed what was uppermost in his mind. Reynolds said he would reflect on the problem and get back to the treasury secretary.

Alexander hardly slept the next two nights. Reynolds finally sent another note. He needed yet more time in light of Hamilton's conspicuous "station." Alexander's heart sank at the word while his brain reviewed the family's assets. Reynolds proposed meeting at the George.

Eliza was entertaining her sister Peggy, visiting from Albany with her three youngsters, while Alexander ran an "errand" before supper. The children had taken over the parlor for a puppet show that little Angelica was organizing with her cousins. His wife told him not to rush, that the Lord meant him to rest on the seventh day. Alexander tried not to think about the thunderbolts looming over her happiness.

James Reynolds watched from across the room as Alexander approached the table on which two tankards sat waiting.

The man tipped his hat with a gloved hand as Alexander took a seat. "Good evening, Colonel Hamilton, sir. I trust yer Sunday was spent in the company of family. My wife tells me you have three boys and two girls."

A chill went up Alexander's spine at the mention of his children.

Reynolds rested a forearm as long as an axe on the table. "How's yer missus? Happier than mine, no doubt."

Alexander didn't wish to speak of Eliza but reminded himself not to act aloof. "My family is well, thank you."

"Let's hope they continue so. Lord providing."

Alexander knew his family was in the hands of James Reynolds, not God above, but he nodded. His mouth was dry. When Reynolds nudged a tankard toward him, Alexander found himself sipping the ale. Then he realized he might appear weak, so he returned the mug to the table. "Mr. Reynolds, I'm happy to do whatever is in my power to satisfy your needs."

"Oh, you have the power. You've got the whole guvment in yer pocket."

"As I told you, I can do nothing for you in my own department. But I would be pleased to contribute from my personal funds to reunite you with your wife."

"I don't know," Reynolds said with a shake of his head. "My injury's considerable. I've lost the love of the best woman in Philadelphia."

"Can't I compensate you in some way?"

Alexander hoped Christmas wouldn't find them impoverished. Eliza admired Martha Washington's jewelry and he had recently discussed peridot earrings with the goldsmith on Filbert. A week earlier he thought he could afford them.

"Maria's a good, kind woman—as you've occasion to know." Reynolds rotated the tankard in his hands, staring down as if into a well of troubles. His canary gloves were dirty at the seams. "That's all gone now. You've taken away the best thing in my life, sir. I ain't been a perfect husband, but you've taken advantage of a poor, tenderhearted woman." He glanced up. "It'll take more than I can say for you to put things right."

James Reynolds had framed his case to reap maximum reward from Maria's promiscuity. Blackmail was on the table as obviously as the cheap beer.

"I understand your distress, sir," Alexander said.

Reynolds took a drink from the tankard. "I tell you what. Let me sleep on it. I'll let you know tomorrow an amount that would help us start over, somewhere outside Philly. Is that acceptable, sir?"

"What time tomorrow?" Alexander would visit the bank and put the nightmare behind him.

"How 'bout I send something by messenger, Colonel Hamilton, sir? I know a black fella who's reliable. He'll find you on your way to work. I assume you'd prefer that to a note at your home or office. Isn't that right, sir?"

Alexander heard the snap of a steel trap below the tavern's murmur.

"Yes," he said. "I would."

The boys' bickering grew louder and louder until Alex's high voice echoed down the hallway.

Alexander kept reading.

"You're a modarchist! I'm going to shoot you," six-year-old Alex said.

"You don't even know what that means," Philip said.

Alexander tried to ignore his sons. He must decide if the *National Gazette*'s latest accusations merited a response or not.

"*Bank of the U.S. Aids Anglomen*," the headline said. The editor of the opposition newspaper—a man named Philip Freneau—depicted Alexander's every move as an attempt to destroy liberty. The charges were insane, but Alexander expected them. Freneau was Jefferson's mouthpiece. The Department of State salaried Freneau to translate foreign documents even though the journalist knew no foreign languages except French, in which Jefferson himself was fluent.

The secretary was the real author of the daily abuse. Jefferson had complained to Washington more than once that Hamilton—not even born in the United States, for God's sake—meant to install a king. Alexander would have laughed if Jefferson hadn't done everything possible to turn others against him.

Madison's backstabbing was more hurtful. Alexander couldn't stop arguing with Jemmy in his mind, trying to convince the Virginian that he erred in thinking Alexander counterrevolutionary. The congressman had seemed honest when they first met. Then the planter treated him as an equal despite Alexander's modest origins. Now it appeared Madison's paranoia had no limit and that his character was as crooked as his teeth. There was no getting around the baffling fact that Jemmy hated him.

On bad days Alexander wondered if his enemies were right. The advantages of banking and manufacturing seemed self-evident to him, yet successful, well-educated men who cared about the country opposed both. Their vision of the future was entirely different from his. Who was he—a bastard from the wharfs of Christiansted—to challenge them?

Then his feelings would flip. He knew he was right. Government must be strongly organized or it would fail. Only radical efforts could correct the deepest wrongs.

Alexander looked out upon the rain that turned the brick buildings across the street the color of blood. He was a good friend but also made an excellent enemy. Life taught him early that men sometimes wanted to crush you for their own mysterious reasons and it didn't matter what they were. You must fight back.

Why did men argue? Why did they lie? Why did they cheat on their blameless wives, truth be told? Because they were men.

"Do too," Alex said. "You're a stupid modarchist and I'm going to shoot you and put you in jail."

Alexander sighed. A spring downpour kept the boys inside, and he had told Eliza he would watch them. Her nausea had subsided but she became light-headed easily. That very morning she nearly fainted when she got to her feet too quickly.

Sounds of scuffling were followed by the bang of a chair falling backward. Alexander got up and put his head in the hallway.

A tangle of small limbs and a mop of red hair on the polished floorboards showed that the younger boy had overestimated his strength.

"There's no such thing as a *modarchist*, you dummy." Philip sat astride Alex's chest. Dark bangs obscured his angular face. "You mean *monarchist*. And I'm not a monarchist."

"Are too!" the six-year-old said.

"Am not."

"Boys!" Alexander said. "Quiet. Philip, get off your brother."

The older boy rolled off and stood up. "Papa. Please tell Alex there's no such thing as a modarchist. Everybody knows it's monarchist. And he hit me." Philip brushed back his hair to reveal a red lump.

"He hit me first," Alex said, still on the floor. Mud stuck to his boots and there were fresh scuffs on the floor.

His sons usually told the truth, but their perspectives on it differed dramatically. Eliza sorted their stories with Solomon's wisdom and a pawnbroker's cynicism. Alexander considered all boys equally naughty, but his wife expected him to mete justice proportionately.

"What were you doing?" he said to Philip.

"We were playing colonists and Redcoats," Philip said in his patient-older-brother voice.

"He made me play Redcoat," Alex said. "I hate playing Redcoat. I never get to play colonist."

"And when I, well, hit him with a dirt clod—just a dirt clod, not a rock," Philip said, "he threw a stick and called me a modarchist. It hit my head."

"So you were playing outside. Your mother told you to stay inside. It's wet and I need to work at my desk."

"Yes, sir," Philip said.

"But, Papa, you always have to work," Alex said. "And we stayed on the porch."

"Is that where you found a dirt clod? On the porch?"

"Under the porch, sir," Philip said. "It's drier under there."

"Take your brother upstairs, Philip, and wash his face. And be quiet. I don't want Mama woken by your mischief. Then you will both practice your Latin for an hour."

Alexander pulled his younger son to his feet. The boy clasped his father around the leg.

"I'm sorry, Papa," Alex said.

Alexander placed his hand on his son's red curls. "And don't try to cheat me, you jackanapes. I'll be watching the clock."

Alex patted his father's bulging pocket, which crackled. He patted the trousers again. "What's that, Papa?"

"Just a letter," Alexander said and pushed his son's hand away. His voice sounded untroubled to his own ears.

"Papa, what's a modarchist?" Alex's bright blue eyes brimmed with curiosity. He seemed to have forgotten the fisticuffs. "It's a bad man, right?"

"Philip is correct. There's no such thing as a modarchist. You mean a monarchist. That's someone who wishes America had a king rather than a congress."

"That makes him bad, right?"

Alex's expression was sincere. Alexander's heart sank at the boy's innocence. He deserved a father who wasn't a liar.

"Of course," Philip said. "Monarchists are the worst."

"That's not quite right either. A monarchist just thinks differently from us," Alexander said. "A man's ideas aren't what make him bad or good. His actions show whether he's honorable. In a republic, each is entitled to his opinions."

Alexander knew such words would draw accusations of treason outside their home. Many believed monarchists deserved whatever they got. In New York, Tories had lost their property and been banned from the practice of law. Tens of thousands had moved to England and Canada.

Philip studied his shoes. He lifted one shoulder. "Papa," he said without looking up, "I saw Mr. Freneau's newspaper. *The National Gazette*. He called you a monarchist."

"I know."

"Why don't you make him stop?"

"Remember the First Amendment to our Constitution? Free speech? Of course you do. But you also mustn't forget the old rhyme. Sticks and stones may break my bones, but words can never hurt me."

Philip raised an eyebrow. For an instant, he looked exactly like his grandmother Rachel Lavien in one of her skeptical moods.

Alexander wished he could spare Philip the embarrassment of such newspaper stories. The boy must sense Philadelphia's hostility, to which his parents never referred in front of the children. The town was divided. Politicians crossed the street to avoid shaking hands with men they once embraced. The revolution in France had made it all worse. King Louis's life was in danger, yet Jefferson and his kind were in ecstasy. They wouldn't hear a word in the monarch's defense. Alexander worried about the Marquis de Lafayette, back in Paris. Who knew what would happen?

"I'd shoot Philip Freneau," the younger boy said.

Philip took his brother by the hand. "You can't just shoot people, Alex. Come. Let's wash your face."

Alexander watched his sons climb the stairs. When they reached the landing, Alexander pulled the letter out of his pocket and looked again at the alarming figure in James Reynolds's misspelled chicken scratch. Another $300.

Reynolds had first demanded $1,000, which Alexander paid from his life savings in two installments. But then the man didn't leave Philadelphia as promised. Instead, Reynolds stayed on, requesting "loans" of $50 and $100 every month or so. Alexander had paid them out of his salary and cut the family budget to the point that Eliza asked if anything was wrong. Now Reynolds wanted a larger payment, plus something Alexander couldn't deliver.

The blackmailer initially warned Alexander to stay away from Maria. But once the golden goose started laying eggs, Reynolds reversed himself and urged Alexander to comfort his wife. Maria threatened to commit suicide unless Alexander came. In her arms again, he was unable to resist the lust she stirred in him. He felt as depraved as an opium-eater, and both craved and pitied the vulnerable Maria, whom Reynolds exploited like a whore. Alexander sometimes wondered if the two had planned to entrap him all along. The sequence of events was so neat. But vanity convinced him of Maria's sincere affection.

He had spent his life taming words, making them come to order on the page. Now one alone defied him. It would not yield to his command. Why must "*or*" govern relations between men and women? Why not "*and*"? Couldn't he love Eliza and Maria?

Maria was beautiful, neglected, and attentive to his every need. When he complained of a sore kidney, she sewed bolsters to make him comfortable. When newspapers dragged his name through the mud, she said he was the most wonderful man she'd ever known. He did love her.

But when her pretty little triangle sprang to mind—so warm and inviting—he knew he was merely debauched. Then self-pity tugged at him. Perhaps he'd been seduced.

Yet the affair was more perilous every day. Exposure threatened.

Reynolds now wanted him to come through the front door of the cheap apartment house, not the back. Alexander looked at the letter again. The scoundrel had written, "*When you Call you are feareful any person should See you. Am I a person of Such a bad Carector?*"

The implications were grotesque. Did James Reynolds really expect the treasury secretary of the United States to become his bosom friend? Was Alexander supposed to act publicly as if Reynolds was anything but a man of low character? The blackmailer was probably laying a fresh trap.

But Reynolds's logic was mystifying. Why would Alexander agree to visit Maria's home openly if he was paying Reynolds to hush up their connection? Who could be feeding the man such wild ideas? Was partisanship behind Reynolds's newest request? The man hinted he knew others high in government.

Premonition swept Alexander. James Reynolds might pull down the whole federal government along with the Hamilton family. They could lose everything he had fought to create. Why in the world had he taken such horrible chances?

A door opened and closed upstairs. The murmur of a gentle voice told Alexander that the boys had awakened their mother after all. He stuffed the letter back in his pocket.

This was it. The affair with Maria was over. He wouldn't pay James Reynolds another nickel. Eliza was due to bear their fifth child in August and he mustn't threaten her health and happiness further. His family deserved better. The country needed men of honor. It needed him.

For the space of a quick breath, an unreasoning anguish at losing Maria pierced his core. He couldn't live without her. Not in the vicious atmosphere of the capital, where even his family's needs overwhelmed him. Maria allowed him to forget everything.

Then, in the next breath and with the same degree of naturalness, Alexander knew his decision was real. No pleasure compensated for such disgrace. For the first time in a year, he actually believed what his lying brain told him. Maria Reynolds was out of his life.

He looked toward the second floor where his pregnant wife was resting. What had happened with Maria was not like the betrayals that stained his Christiansted childhood. This affair didn't touch his family. He would never compromise Eliza and he cared for her as no man had ever cared for his mother. What Eliza didn't know couldn't hurt her.

Yet they used to read one another's hearts. Would the lie fester until it killed their marriage? Perhaps he ought to tell her.

Alexander's knees weakened and a dark mist came up in the room. He staggered and reached for the hall table to lean on. He closed his eyes and took a deep breath. His head cleared. No. The truth would kill her. He couldn't salve his wounded conscience at the price of Eliza's happiness.

She must never, ever find out. Indeed, she wouldn't.

CHAPTER THIRTY-FOUR

November 1792

Philadelphia

"Strengthen the female mind by enlarging it, and there will be an end to blind obedience."

Mary Wollstonecraft, *A Vindication of the Rights of Woman*, 1792

ELIZA'S CARRIAGE STOPPED IN FRONT OF the narrow house. The paint was peeling and thin curtains sagged in the frost-blind windows. When the coachman opened her door, she took his hand but lifted the heavy basket herself. She smiled, happy to be doing things again.

Eliza had given birth in August to a boy they named John in honor of John Laurens, gone ten years but still sorely missed. Once the baby settled into a routine, she resumed her visits to Madame Le Grand, one of thousands of refugees from France's violent revolution. Alexander had befriended Monsieur de Talleyrand, a diplomat who escaped the guillotine in Paris for being too conservative and the gallows in London for being too radical. In certain Philadelphia coffeehouses, hardly a patron spoke English anymore, though those who aired their troubles in public were usually male. Refugee women shivered in hovels with their children.

Madame Le Grand's husband had been a shopkeeper with the good luck of possessing a monopoly on the chamomile shampoo favored by Marie Antoinette—and the bad luck of delivering it the morning a Parisian mob stormed the Tuileries looking for Louis XVI and his despised wife. Armed with kitchen knives and knitting needles, the harridans of Paris swore to make lace of the queen's guts. Monsieur Le Grand tried to save a page in the king's colorful Swiss Guard. The angry crowd that tumbled out of the palace after bringing down the thousand-year-old monarchy left Le Grand's bloodied body alongside the boy in his striped satin uniform. Six hundred others lay butchered in the courtyard.

The shopkeeper's terrified widow bolted the doors of her store and joined the exodus of aristocrats and shopkeepers turning their backs on the increasingly volatile republican government. Even the president of the Assembly fled for his life. Taking her two sons and a small purse of Spanish dollars, Eugénie Le Grand sailed for America. Like other families without a man to support them, she and her boys were now impoverished. Eugénie took in laundry to keep a roof over their heads.

Eliza pulled her cloak tight in the frigid air and knocked on the front door. A dog inside yapped sharply. "Fifi! Shhhh," she heard someone say.

Madame Le Grand opened the door with a guarded expression, then broke into a radiant smile.

"Mrs. 'amilton! *Bonjour! Comment allez-vous?* Please to come in."

"*Bonjour*, Madame Le Grand," Eliza said. "*Je vais bien, merci. Et vous? Et vos enfants?*"

Madame Le Grand fluffed her skirts to shoo back a wire-haired terrier that seemed anxious to get out. She drew Eliza inside the small room, shifted a stack of folded clothes from a chair onto the bed, and motioned her guest to sit. The dog ran around the chair and dashed to a basket by the fireplace, where it circled twice before lying down.

Madame Le Grand's three-year-old sat in front of the small fire with his bare feet curled underneath him. He glanced up without smiling, then turned back to a set of wooden blocks. Camille had a haystack of blond hair and a cowlick that defied taming.

"*Bien, bien!*" Madame Le Grand sat down. "*Ma famille est* _________," she said, and launched into a fast, complicated explanation of which Eliza understood only "boy," "cooking," and possibly "goat."

She smiled and tried to look comprehending. Alexander employed a French tutor for the children, but Eliza had little time to join their lessons and recalled only snatches of phrases that she and Angelica had learned as girls. Whenever her husband entertained refugees, as he frequently did, Eliza found herself talking to émigrés who had brought English along with their hastily packed trunks. They were a pathetic lot whose endlessly varied stories all ended in death and destruction. Most had been part of the revolution until it started to eat its young.

Eliza noticed Madame Le Grand's surreptitious glance at her basket. She said, "*Madame. Je vous ai apparté . . . je vous apporte . . .*" The conjugation eluded Eliza. Brought? Bring? She gave up. "I brought you some things."

The Frenchwoman smiled. "Thank you, madame. I must practice my English. Is that how to say it? I think I improve much."

"Yes, madame. I wish I spoke French half as well as you speak English."

"*Mon fils*, my son Etienne, he learns new words every day. He teaches Camille and me. Monsieur Ajax allows Etienne to sweep the shop. He gives us the English paper."

"English paper?"

"*Oui, madame. Le journal.* Monsieur Ajax shows him how to read."

Eliza knew that Madame Le Grand needed whatever pennies the eight-year-old boy earned, but was surprised she had apprenticed him to a black man. "Etienne must be very bright," she said neutrally.

Eliza turned to her basket. Alexander had been very specific about which street market had the best prices. Pairs of shoes for both boys.

"My parents seem to think we have ten children, not six," she said. "They sent new boots for the grandchildren again, and we have more than I can possibly use." She held up the bigger pair. "Might these fit Etienne?"

Madame Le Grand's elegant posture became straighter. "*Merci, madame*, but Etienne has shoes already. They are fitting him very well. You have many children. Your younger boys will wear them when they get bigger."

Eliza placed the boots on the table. "It would help me very much if you accepted these. My house has shrunk with the new baby. If I don't clear away the clutter, I'll go mad."

A cough in the corner caught Eliza's attention. The little boy drew a hoarse breath and coughed again without taking his eyes from the tower of blocks he had stacked as high as his head. He was trying to place another on top. She hoped the cough didn't mean he was contagious.

Eliza had been intrepid when she was young, but becoming a mother had made her fearful in ways she hardly recognized—as ready to fret over improbable dangers as common ones. The week Philip was born she read about an exotic disease in the West Indies and was unable to sleep, thinking how to protect him in Albany.

Madame Le Grand fetched a chipped cup from the mantel. She bent to Camille. "There, there. *Bois, mon fils*."

The boy lifted his chin to sip the tea, then went back to his project. The bright-eyed terrier sat on its haunches, watching.

Madame placed the cup on the mantel and resumed her seat. "My husband he used chamomile for everything. *Tout!* He said it would keep us healthy." She smiled but her eyes filled with tears.

She took a clean shirt off the pile of laundry and dabbed her cheeks. "*Je suis désolée*. Please forgive me, Mrs. 'amilton. I miss him."

Eliza couldn't imagine herself in the same predicament, raising children alone. Alexander had been especially attentive since the birth of their fifth baby, as if cherishing her anew. He waited outside the door every minute of her labor. Keeping the family healthy was Eliza's life. The only death she didn't fear was her own. It was better for children to lose their mother than father. Widowers possessed more resources than widows.

Fortunately, Madame Le Grand had an older son—and apparently a kind friend in Ajax, to whom Alexander had introduced her. Eliza knew Parisians didn't tolerate slavery. Monsieur Le Grand must have held enlightened views of blacks despite his aristocratic connections.

Eliza held up the smaller pair of boots. "I think these will fit Camille. They seem about his size." She looked over at the little boy, who kneeled to place his last block. There was only one left.

He had stacked the others with great care. Eliza thought he might complete the structure without toppling it. Madame Le Grand must have thought so, too, because they both fell silent, not wishing to jinx him.

Camille's cowlick had escaped whatever pomade Madame Le Grand applied that morning. Eliza noticed a matching sandy tuft between the ears of the terrier, now on all four feet in his basket. His eyes were also trained on the boy. Camille's hand hovered over the column, then drew back. He lifted his hand again, but withdrew it a second time. The three-year-old's thin face was all sharp angles.

Camille looked crossly at the dog, which cocked its head sidewise. "Stop staring."

Eliza and Madame Le Grand burst out laughing.

The boy got to his feet and put his back to the dog. He placed the last block on the column, which swayed and then stopped. Camille peered over his shoulder at the dog. "*Voilá!*"

The terrier raised its shaggy eyebrows.

Eliza held up the shoes again and nodded in Camille's direction. "May I? He's so like my Jamie."

"*Oui*," Madame Le Grand said.

Eliza took socks from the hamper and left the top open so her hostess could unpack the bread, ham, and apple butter Eliza had also brought. Mothers had an unspoken pact that food for children was never an insult to pride.

Eliza wished she could do more. Or that the government would. Consumed by its interminable debates, Congress hardly noticed the starving. Women who lost husbands became invisible. Disconnected from a man, they didn't count. Some entered into compromising liaisons merely to feed their children.

Although a fresh crop of improvement societies appeared every year, Eliza wondered why there wasn't one to help such desperate souls. Alexander had started a society to promote manufactures. What about one for widows and orphans? Who might petition Congress for that? No respectable woman spoke in public, and no husband would countenance such an immodest act. There was little Eliza could do except conspire to put shoes on two boys and ease their mother's heart.

She knelt beside the three-year-old with his proud tower. "*Viens, Camille*. These will keep you warm."

As she tied the boy's shoes, Eliza said a quick prayer of thanks for her own good fortune and the husband who took care of her and their babies.

CHAPTER THIRTY-FIVE

December 1792

Philadelphia

"No persons are more frequently wrong, than those who will not admit they are wrong."

François de La Rochefoucauld, *Maxims*, 1665

THE MAIDSERVANT ENTERED THE ROOM WITH a basket of firewood. "Not now," Alexander said, then realized his tone was curt. "Thank you," he added as she backed out.

There was no more private setting than his study to receive the self-appointed posse. The children knew better than to disturb their father and Eliza would never interrupt a business meeting, especially since she expected to hear the latest gossip when they faced one another later on the pillow. They talked—and made love—more freely now. "God will decide," Eliza said when Alexander brought up the question of future pregnancies. Only one painful fact did he keep resolutely secret.

He hoped she would fall asleep that evening without him, secure she was missing nothing of importance. It was often enough that acquaintances dropped by late to discuss issues in Congress or a clerk came with something for the night coach to New York.

Alexander looked down at the bundle of letters on his desk. He had taken them from the locked drawer to make sure they were in order. Even disgrace should be suitably catalogued to make its dimensions clear. At least it wasn't the crime of which they had accused him that morning.

Senator James Monroe spoke first. "The evidence of wrongdoing is conclusive, sir," he said when he called at the Treasury with his congressional cronies around ten o'clock. The senator remained standing.

Alexander had known Monroe in the war, though not well. They were the same age. The tall Virginian served first under Washington, then went over to the state militia two years before Yorktown. A modest plantation owner, Monroe hid average intellectual powers behind excessive formality.

The senator from Virginia rejected Alexander's offer of a chair as if it were a bribe. It wasn't much of one. The office of the treasury secretary was furnished with a desk covered in green baize cloth and simple planks to hold Alexander's voluminous correspondence. The chairs were hard.

Congressman Frederick Muhlenberg of Pennsylvania, an older man and speaker of the House of Representatives—less hasty in his rush to judgment—said in a more roundabout manner, "We've discovered, well, a very *improper* connection between you and a Mr. Reynolds."

Muhlenberg glanced at his two companions. They nodded encouragement. "It appears you may have paid James Reynolds to speculate in government bonds on your behalf," he continued.

Congressman Abraham Venable of Virginia was apparently along for the ride. He tugged at his elegant blue cuffs but said little. All three members of Jefferson's Democratic-Republican faction exuded readiness. The whiff of the chase was in the air. Their party had long criticized Washington's administration for concentrating power and undermining liberty, and the trio obviously assumed they had cornered their fox.

James Monroe wore a new black suit with ankle-length trousers instead of knee breeches, perhaps to exhibit his fashionable conversion to Jacobin-style democracy. No aristocratic knickers for this slave owner. The senator must have run right to his tailor—perhaps the one on Chestnut Street whose sign promised, DIRECT FROM LONDON . . . ONLY THE BEST!

President Washington had recently appointed Jefferson's acolyte to a diplomatic post in France to keep the opposition happy. But James Monroe had mishandled nearly every instruction and was recalled in disgrace. The bungler was never right and never in doubt. Although Monroe had taken a bullet in the shoulder at Trenton in 1776, he later voted against the Constitution. The unsuccessful diplomat must delight in placing the federal government in an unflattering light. Catching Alexander Hamilton with ill-gotten gains would be the highlight of Senator Monroe's embarrassing year.

Although the delegation must think they had sufficient proof to bring him down, Alexander knew that they couldn't possibly possess evidence of financial corruption. *Cheat the nation?* Never.

Alexander's temper rose as he contemplated the men who assailed his integrity. It was one thing to read groundless accusations in political scandal sheets, where he himself baited the opposition, and another to be hunted down in person. He felt as if they had spat on him. And why bring up James Reynolds? The worthless blackmailer had just been released from prison for stealing a list of names to collect veterans' back pay.

Alexander looked at each man a long moment, letting his displeasure sink in. "Illegal speculation in securities? This is vile, spurious slander."

Congressman Muhlenberg stiffened. "We have the proof right here. Reynolds's wife gave it to us when Senator Monroe and I called. She's a young thing. Quite appealing. Reynolds has gone into hiding, but his wife confirms you sent her husband money."

Alexander felt the start of a sweat. Democratic newspapers had accused him for months of profiting from the Bank of the United States. They called him a monarchist and a traitor, and now insisted he was a thief as well. All of it was untrue. But Monroe and Muhlenberg had somehow stumbled onto Alexander's problem with James Reynolds and managed to tangle real facts with their cockamamie conspiracy theories.

Had they actually interviewed Maria?

"Reynolds's disappearance is extremely suspicious, of course," James Monroe said. "He fears reprisal from highly placed persons. The lady told us her husband knew things that would make heads tremble. Yours, particularly, sir."

Alexander gazed coldly at Monroe. Was the idiot now implying he was a thug, too? He turned to Muhlenberg. "May I see this so-called proof that I profited from office?"

Senator Monroe handed Muhlenberg a leather folio, from which the Pennsylvania congressman took several wrinkled pieces of paper. Alexander recognized them immediately. He had sent them with blackmail payments. The letters were unsigned but the handwriting had appeared on thousands of official documents since Alexander joined Washington's military family after Trenton. Innumerable people would recognize the slanted script. Why had Maria kept his letters? Had she always planned to hurt him, or only after he stopped paying her husband?

A familiar throb started up in his back. Alexander applied pressure with a hand as he read the letters. Neddy Stevens, now a doctor, had prescribed lying down whenever Alexander felt the kidney, but he refused to let his enemies see weakness. There were three missives, none indicating the purpose for which the money was sent, only the amounts. Alexander looked up.

The congressmen wore triumphant expressions that suggested, once Alexander took possession of the notes, he accepted the guilt as well. Except Congressman Muhlenberg, who looked quizzical. "Perhaps they're counterfeit?"

So Muhlenberg's mind was not completely closed. Alexander glanced at Venable. He might be another weak link. Although a Virginian, Abraham Venable didn't exhibit the same degree of hostility as James Monroe, who had studied law under Jefferson and admired him so slavishly that he purchased the plantation next to Monticello.

Alexander knew for a certainty it was Monroe who had penned five poisonous essays against him months earlier. They weren't signed, but politicians used pseudonyms like masquerades at a ball. Opponents made a game out of guessing identities, which often became quickly apparent. Monroe's had.

Jefferson preferred a front of gentility. He passed the ammunition to others. The only famous document of which Jefferson liked to claim authorship was the Declaration of Independence—so safe and noble—though it was more accurately described as a committee effort. Jefferson encouraged other men to fight his battles, and pretended to abhor partisanship. Alexander recalled a cabinet meeting at which the secretary of state sipped his tea while President Washington exploded over Philip Freneau's latest insult—delivered in triplicate since, for some perverse reason, the Philadelphia printer insisted on leaving three copies of his daily hate sheet at the Executive Mansion.

"Why is Freneau still on the State Department payroll?" the President said.

Jefferson placed his cup in its saucer. "I certainly can't fire a man for exercising free speech. That would violate the First Amendment, Mr. President."

The Secretary of State's false civility reminded Alexander of Captain Codwise's colorful saying about church deacons in Christiansted. *They couldn't say shit if they had a mouthful.*

The mantel clock behind Alexander's office desk chimed the hour. Muhlenberg, Monroe, and Venable awaited a reply.

"Do you claim, then, that these letters are counterfeit?" Monroe said. "Because if not, they show what we've long suspected. The treasury secretary—you, sir—speculated in government bonds. You passed money to Reynolds, who did your dirty work. You used your knowledge of government finance to swindle the people." The Virginian threw down his last insult. "Or so there is the appearance, sir!"

Alexander's fist tightened. Had Monroe not tacked on the word "appearance," Alexander would have challenged him to a duel right then. They attended the same drinking parties as young men, but their revolutionary fellowship had long since expired.

He handed the letters back to Muhlenberg. "These are mine, senator. I wrote them last spring. But the money that accompanied them was not for bank securities. If you'll be so good as to attend me at my home tonight, I'll show you documents that prove I sent the money to James Reynolds for an entirely different purpose. A private matter. Not a public one."

The three men were so astonished at Alexander's candid admission that he would have laughed had he seen them onstage in a Sheridan comedy. Monroe appeared ready to protest, but Muhlenberg and Venable accepted the offer promptly and politely.

Which was why he was awaiting an unpleasant encounter when he ought to be preparing for bed with Eliza. The thought of her embrace steadied his nerves, but the knowledge of his betrayal made his heart quake. He prayed to God that the forthcoming conversation would never leave the room. Among gentlemen it would not.

The door knocker sounded. Alexander heard the housekeeper ask for hats and coats. He rose when the three congressmen entered the study a moment later, followed by Oliver Wolcott Jr., the Treasury comptroller Alexander had invited as an eyewitness with their permission.

Alexander gestured to the chairs in front of the grate. There was none for him, but he was too keyed up to sit. "Thank you for coming out in this cold, gentlemen. I appreciate the courtesy."

"We're extremely curious to hear your explanation, Mr. Hamilton," Muhlenberg said as he took the padded Queen Anne chair. "Courtesy aside, I doubt any of us would have missed it."

The other congressmen sat as well, and Wolcott chose a spot on the divan under the window. Alexander noticed that James Monroe still wore his coat, from which the servant had apparently been unable to part him. A tray of crystal rummers was warming by the fire. Alexander poured his guests a cordial. He passed one to Muhlenberg, Monroe, Venable, and Wolcott, and put a glass for himself on the desk before taking up the assembled documents.

Alexander knew it was best to say difficult things promptly to avoid appearing evasive.

"Mr. Reynolds and I became acquainted a year ago through his wife, Maria. I'm not proud to admit it, but she and I had an amorous relationship. He found out." The words had been running through Alexander's head since morning. He said them in the order he had practiced.

"I don't know if Maria entered into the relationship with the sole purpose of entrapping me—certainly, pride compels me to think not—but whatever the case, once her husband found out, he insisted upon compensation. The amount ran to more than a thousand dollars, all paid from my personal account. The cost was considerable given my government salary. A third of my income. But I hoped to spare my wife. She . . . she was with child."

Speaker of the House Muhlenberg had lifted the brandy to his lips, but he sat the glass down untouched. Monroe unbuttoned his coat.

Alexander ran his hand over his forehead and turned to pace.

"I thought the blackmail would end." He paused, searching for words to explain what he himself didn't understand. "But Reynolds continued to make demands. He . . . didn't want his wife to stop."

Congressman Venable stood. "Mr. Hamilton, please, sir, you needn't say anythin' further." His Virginia accent was gruff, and his expression suggested he knew little of marital complications and was embarrassed for those who had them.

Muhlenberg held up his hand. Venable sat back down. The speaker of the House exchanged glances with Monroe. "Such private matters are of no concern to Congress."

Alexander stopped pacing and tugged at his cravat to get air. He held out the bundle from his desk. "Please, read these. They're the letters I wrote to Maria and James Reynolds, and ones they sent me. I made copies before posting. I have most of them."

"Really, Mr. Hamilton," Muhlenberg said. "We are interested only in public malfeasance."

Alexander felt he must prove his innocence conclusively. The government was at stake. He shuffled through the letters until he found the one he wanted. Where Maria had written, "*If he dose not se or hear from you to day he will write Mrs. Hamilton.*" Her scrawl turned his stomach. "Here," he said, thrusting the paper toward Muhlenberg. "At least examine this. It's from Mrs. Reynolds. It was my first inkling that blackmail was intended."

The Pennsylvanian took the note and withdrew a monocle from his waistcoat. Monroe read over his shoulder.

Alexander watched Muhlenberg's eyes travel back and forth over the page, halting to decipher misspellings and bad handwriting.

The facts were irrefutable. Alexander's worst crime was possessing another man's wife and being unfaithful to his own. Maria's hysteria was the best evidence of a romantic relationship, not a business proposition. One would have to be insane or infatuated to maintain such a correspondence with a married woman.

"The letters show that James Reynolds extorted money for nearly six months before I told him I'd pay no more. It's all right there." Alexander again held out the stack, which James Monroe now accepted.

The Virginian rifled through the letters, focusing on the dates, then returned them. "That's all? You gave James Reynolds no instructions to purchase government securities? This was only a bit of cuckoldry?"

Monroe's manner was cold yet he seemed shaken. Alexander sensed the Virginian finally saw him as a man, one with faults and desires, not just a fiend.

"Yes. As stupid, vain, and humiliating as it is, I fell under Mrs. Reynolds's spell. As you saw, she's a desirable woman. Her husband threatened to tell my wife, and I paid him until six months ago. He ceased writing when he squeezed me dry."

Alexander stopped. Too many words and they'd doubt him again. *The gentleman doth protest too much.* He reached for the brandy and drained his glass. Alcohol was bad for the kidneys but excellent for the nerves.

Monroe and Muhlenberg spoke quietly, tête-à-tête. Venable stared into the fire, hands clasped and expression stoic. Oliver Wolcott examined his boots.

"Allow me to read the letters aloud," Alexander said. He must make them understand. "I became very familiar with Mrs. Reynolds's spelling."

Venable looked up. "That isn't necessary, Mr. Hamilton. I'm quite satisfied. Indeed, I apologize for the intrusion." He stood resolutely. "You appreciate we needed to put rumors of financial impropriety to rest."

Muhlenberg pushed up from his chair as well. "Quite right. Our committee drafted a complaint to President Washington, so I'm glad we checked with you before sending it."

Monroe said nothing, but rose with his colleagues.

Oliver Wolcott's eyes communicated sympathy. It was Wolcott who had uncovered the conspiracy that led to Reynolds's imprisonment for pension fraud. If Treasury hadn't tried so hard to protect the government's money, Reynolds might not have been caught pilfering it. He and Maria might have drifted away from Philadelphia with their ill-gotten gains.

"I'm grateful you came to me, gentlemen. I would do the same, were our positions reversed." Alexander broached the matter closest to his heart. "May I ask for your word this will go no further, out of consideration for my family?"

"Certainly," Muhlenberg and Venable said in unison.

"Of course," James Monroe said. He buttoned his coat. "I'm surprised you ask. We're all gentlemen here."

"I can show myself out, Mr. Secretary," Oliver Wolcott said. He turned to Muhlenberg. "Are you going my way, congressman? I have a carriage waiting, if you'd like a ride. I believe your residence is near mine."

Alexander blessed Wolcott. Then he remembered. "One thing more. May I have Mrs. Reynolds's letters?"

"I don't see why not," Speaker Muhlenberg said. He looked at Monroe for confirmation.

The senator paused. "We may be called upon to explain our actions if Reynolds spreads more rumors," Monroe finally said. "Our colleagues may wish to see the documents we've gathered. Since the letters belonged to Mrs. Reynolds, and she gave them to us, they should probably remain with Congress."

"I don't see any harm in that," Muhlenberg said. "Seems sensible."

Monroe was wilier than Alexander had realized. He must have been a good law pupil. "You do intend to keep them confidential?" Alexander's kidney ached. He wished he could lie down. "In a safe location?"

Monroe's cheeks reddened. His cleft chin jutted forward. "I hope you're not questioning my integrity, sir. Of course I'll keep the letters in a secure location. If you like, I can make copies. That way, you'll have the very same documents we do."

Alexander wondered what James Monroe meant by a secure location. He prayed it wouldn't be the neighbor's mountaintop home. But he would simply have to trust his enemies—which defied imagination. Jefferson's so-called Democrats now had something on him. If they chose to use it, they would devastate Eliza.

"Thank you for your discretion, Senator Monroe," Alexander said with a bow.

Monroe bowed in return, as did Muhlenberg. Venable even smiled. Wolcott patted Alexander's shoulder as the committee left the room, turning at the last moment—when the other men had preceded him through the doorway—to give a reassuring nod.

Alexander listened for the front door. When he heard it close, he sat down in front of the fire and lay back with his spine against the rug like a child. He stared at the ceiling, calmed by the floor underneath.

If Eliza saw him lying thus, she would chide him for getting his clothes dirty. Alexander wished with all his soul it were the only thing of which she had cause to complain. Yet it was far too late for that.

CHAPTER THIRTY-SIX

November 1794

Philadelphia

"No distance can keep anxious lovers long asunder."

George Washington to Lafayette, 1779

ELIZA AWOKE TO THE KNOWLEDGE THAT something was terribly awry.

Silence pressed in from the four corners. The bed drapes were open and she turned her face to the window, but no light pierced the lace. Alexander had gone to western Pennsylvania with President Washington two months earlier. She was alone to the extent that a pregnant woman with six children could be considered alone. Yet the knowledge that something was amiss had prodded her awake as surely as if someone had entered the room and tapped her shoulder.

She reached past her swollen belly, lifted her nightdress, and slid her finger between her legs. She was moist but not wet, a crucial difference. Thank God, the bleeding hadn't resumed. Why, then, did she have such a strong presentiment?

The ropes under the mattress were loose and Eliza rolled onto her side to fit the curve, but it was uncomfortable and she shifted onto her back. If Alexander were home, she would feel safe. His presence made her feel all was right with the world, or he would make it so. But he hadn't been home for weeks on end. Once again, he'd left her for his mistress. America.

Eliza tried not to be upset, as happened so easily in the dark. Although she had resigned herself to producing as many children as the Lord gave her, she knew he might also take some away. Look at her mother—who had lost seven out of fifteen.

Was Alexander on a hard military cot in the forest, or a feather bed in a farmer's warm cottage? He wrote that the military campaign in western Pennsylvania had restored his youth—not a twinge of the kidney ailment that had made riding a torment in recent years. General Henry Knox, who stayed behind in Philadelphia though he was secretary of war, dropped by one afternoon to pass along the news. The old general wheezed when he laughed, and his extraordinary girth caused the sofa to creak as he leaned into the tale, but he glowed like a boy as he described Alexander's antics.

"So what did Ham do when the sentry complained it was dark and rainy? He confiscated the man's musket and took patrol himself until daybreak. I expect he put the whole army in awe."

"It may have been an excuse. You know my husband loves to pace," Eliza said.

Knox nodded. All three of his chins shook. "'Tis true. But I assure you, he was grand, Mrs. Hamilton. As ever! And he watches over the general, thanks be to God. For where would we be without him?"

Him, of course, was President Washington. It always was.

Eliza looked again at the window. A faint glimmer signaled dawn over the capital. Perhaps she had slept longer than she realized.

When Alexander and President Washington had stepped into a carriage with two Virginia bays tied to the rear, all Philadelphia fell silent. Birds went still and the rivers quieted. Everyone appeared to realize that the federal republic would stand or fall at that fateful moment. Western Pennsylvania was the test of everything. Could the government defend even itself? When the president waved good-bye, a cluster of onlookers went wild with applause. An excited citizen shot a gun in the air.

Newspapers had run stories for months about the revolt touched off by her husband's tax on whiskey. Unruly frontiersmen in western Pennsylvania, fired by liquor and lurid tales of Jacobin revenge on aristocrats in France, drew knives on tax collectors, torched homes, kidnapped a US marshal, and threatened to erect guillotines. A force of seven thousand vigilantes assembled just beyond the Alleghenies. The nation appeared ready to dissolve.

One of the leaders, a man named Bradford, encouraged Americans sick of the tyrannical federal government to emulate Robespierre. The insurgents' ardor for everything French and hatred of anything English fed a radicalism that bordered on anarchy. They swore to crush any army Congress sent to tame them.

"How are we to supposed to govern if we can't collect a simple tax?" Alexander said one night when particularly upset. "Westerners beg for federal help when Indians take to the warpath or Spain blockades the Mississippi, yet they won't part with a penny to arm the cavalry or equip a ship."

He sounded like her father during the Revolution—though events since then had created tensions Eliza never imagined possible. In Paris, the people had guillotined their king, queen, clergy, nobility, and scientists. Benjamin Franklin would have wept had he lived to see Lavoisier's brilliance extinguished like a torch in a bucket. All Europe was at war.

In America, some people simply didn't want a central government. And they had no pity for France's. "*Louis Capet Has Lost His Caput,*" Philip Freneau's newspaper gleefully announced when the shocking news arrived that the Jacobins had beheaded the king who funded America's revolution. The Capet dynasty was over.

"I cherish no illusions," Alexander said. "They'll bring us down if they can. If not by starving the government, then by force. And they call *us* tyrants."

General Washington finally decided that the rebellion must be quelled with an overwhelming show of force, lest they lose everything won since 1776. "If laws can be tramped with immunity," the president said, "then government by the people is at an end."

Few Philadelphians expected the commander-in-chief to swing up onto his own horse, but that was exactly what Washington did, alongside Eliza's husband. The president and treasury secretary rode out to counter the armed rebellion while the secretaries of war and state stayed home in bed. Eliza sometimes forgot the finer points of the constitutional distribution of responsibility, but it seemed terribly unfair.

Her husband accompanied Washington as he had twenty years earlier, though now with the rank of general. When the uprising finally subsided in late October, the president left General Hamilton near Pittsburgh in command of twelve thousand federal soldiers to tamp out the last embers. The Great Man was an old one, after all. At sixty-two, Washington surely ached at the end of each drizzly day in the saddle.

Eliza sighed, closed her eyes, and placed her hand on her abdomen to feel for the stirring of their baby. Washington had earned his rest, but when would Alexander have his? When would she have what other women did? Would it be before some crazed rival put a bullet through her husband? Alexander insisted on watch-guarding America personally, yet nobody liked a barking dog.

The political opposition accepted the president's decision to resurrect the army, but was now spreading rumors that Alexander, left in charge, would overthrow the republic and make himself king. Jefferson's followers called themselves Democratic-Republicans, as if they were the only defenders of liberty in America.

Such pretensions usually brought her husband's temper to a white heat, but the prospect of military action so restored his spirits that he merely laughed at the newspaper the morning before they left Philadelphia. When Eliza asked what was funny, Alexander glanced around to make sure none of the children were in earshot. He said that the opposition's hysteria about the army reminded him of Elbridge Gerry's quip during the Constitutional Convention, when the Massachusetts representative compared a standing army to an erection. "Excellent for domestic happiness, but a sure temptation to foreign adventure."

Once he was away, Alexander gaily wrote their boys that he expected no danger whatsoever, just "an agreeable ride" in the Pennsylvania countryside. When Eliza read the letter, only the children's presence kept her from tearing it to bits. How could he pretend the rebellion was nothing? She had lived through fratricide before. She knew what war meant.

Then she pressed the paper to her lips. *Dear God, let him live.*

Eliza felt tears well up in the dim light. She wiped them with a shaking hand and placed the other on her belly, hoping to feel an elbow or foot draw a crescent across her taut abdomen. The baby hadn't moved in hours.

The doctors who had visited the day before—one of them Neddy Stevens, visiting from St. Croix—said the danger of miscarriage was past. She was too far along. Nearly five months.

A rooster crowed somewhere in the sleeping town and Eliza heard a lonely cart clatter up Market Street. She asked herself what sins she had committed, to endure her husband's absence when she needed him most. For the first time, she felt like what preachers called "a mere woman"—a bundle of nerves and bone at the mercy of men's plans—alone with caring for her own five children, plus Fanny. How would they survive if Alexander died?

They had trouble surviving with him. Eliza hardly kept up with the grocer's bills, yet Alexander gave loans to any old army friend who couldn't make the rent. He even insisted on sending funds to the father who had abandoned him at age eight. To their surprise, James Hamilton had written for money just a few years ago, once news of his famous son trickled to the farthest corner of the West Indies. Apparently the old man was alive after all, though they learned that Alexander's brother had perished years earlier. Eliza's husband took care of the whole country, and even an undeserving old beggar on the God-forsaken island of Bequia, but who would take care of Eliza and her babies if he broke his neck falling from a horse or was killed by a renegade?

Eliza covered her face. She stopped blaming herself for feeling as she did, and just wept for herself and the children.

When her sorrow was finally spent, Eliza hoisted herself from the bed and walked to the window. The new day cast a faint pink halo. Problems always looked bleakest before dawn, she reminded herself. With the sun came the possibility of doing something.

She would call upon George Washington after breakfast and demand that he bring Alexander home. And if the president couldn't see her, she would ask Martha.

The president sent orders immediately, but a week passed and Alexander failed to come.

The laudanum didn't lessen Eliza's pain so much as prevent her from understanding it. She tried to organize her thoughts, but they flitted in and out like children playing hide-and-seek in the hall. If she could get on top of the pain, she could control it better. The laudanum made that difficult.

"Stay awake, Mrs. Hamilton. We're right here with you. Don't fall asleep."

She opened her eyes as wide as she could, but still didn't recognize the doctor—a slight, auburn-haired man with bright blue eyes who reminded her of her husband. Then she remembered. "Thank you, Neddy, I won't." Afterward she realized she should have said *Dr. Stephens*. Alexander called him Neddy.

Alexander's other friend, Ajax Manly, had caught her when she fell. The printer was a kindly man. She wished he would find a woman. He deserved one. She still didn't understand her husband's friendship with Manly. White people didn't have black friends. Even Alexander respected the distance between the races, though he thought one no better than the other in principle.

Why was everything a matter of principle to her husband? What about the principle of caring for one's family?

"We're going to sit you up, Mrs. Hamilton," the doctor said.

Was Neddy still in the room? He lived in Christiansted, but came to Philadelphia to consult with medical colleagues at the hospital Mr. Franklin had established. He and Alexander had remained close over the years and distance, and saw one another whenever Neddy visited the mainland. Alexander's oldest friends surrounded her. Where was he?

Eliza felt exhausted. She didn't want to sit up. Then the pain started again: a twirling screw of agony that absorbed all thought. If she focused, if she was very careful not to go under, she would outlast it. She knew this. She had done it before.

The room brightened. Was it daytime already? She didn't like the laudanum.

"General Hamilton would prescribe it himself," Neddy told her. "You must take it." When did people start calling her husband *General* Hamilton?

Someone lifted Eliza by the armpits. She felt a draft under the sheets. "Push gently, Mrs. Hamilton," a man said.

"Push now," a woman said with greater urgency. Had Neddy called the midwife? Or Ajax?

When the pain started, it had taken up too much space to allow room for embarrassment. Mr. Manly had been delivering something for Alexander when Eliza felt the first trickle of water, then a gush of blood. As she reached for some steadying object, he caught her by the waist. The housekeeper helped her upstairs while Ajax ran for the doctor.

"There," the midwife said. "There's the rest of it."

The rest of it? Was that her baby? The *it*? Eliza felt a cool cloth on her forehead. Perhaps they would let her sleep.

A door opened. She knew it was a door because she heard the latch. The mattress dipped next to her.

Above the laudanum and stale bedroom air, Eliza smelled Alexander. Was it a dream? It must be a dream.

"Don't go, my dearest, my treasure."

Eliza felt a hand on her hair. "Stay with me, Betsey."

Where would she go? She was always home. Her husband was the one who went away.

Alexander pressed his lips against her hand, then his cheek. It was wet. "I'm so sorry, my love."

Why was he sorry? Eliza's eyelids felt heavy, but she opened them at last. "Alexander?"

A glass met her lips. Alexander tipped water into her mouth. His brow was furrowed, cravat askew, hair uncombed. He looked a mess. "My dearest, my life. There you are. Everything's all right. I'm here."

Eliza closed her eyes. His presence tired her. The people came first. George Washington came first.

"I've written him, Betsey," Alexander said. His voice was firm. "I've written President Washington."

Had she spoken aloud? She didn't remember doing so.

"I told him we're going back to New York. I'm going to build us a home of our own. We'll be together always, my love."

Alexander's words fell like warm rain. The laudanum made them difficult to understand, but they made her feel safe. He was home—and he promised not to leave her again.

CHAPTER THIRTY-SEVEN

July 1795

New York City

"General Washington . . . was not aware . . . of the effect of Hamilton's schemes . . . Hamilton was not only a monarchist, but for a monarchy bottomed on corruption."

Thomas Jefferson, 1818

"SIT HERE, PAPA." ANGELICA'S EXPRESSION WAS as sunny as the morning rays that illuminated the front parlor of their new home. The children had adapted well to the move six months earlier, with better schools for the boys and a new governess for the girls. Eleven-year-old Angelica was particularly happy with her music teacher. She patted the piano bench. "It's time to practice," she said.

Alexander marveled at his daughter's aura of command over a general of the United States Army. Who had taught her that, the little coquette?

"Mr. Manly will be here any minute. We can practice until then, my darling." Alexander spread the tails of his coat and sat down beside her. "What piece shall we polish?"

"'When First I Knew Fair Celinda.'"

Alexander picked up the sheet music that his sister-in-law had sent from London. "Hmm. Fair Celinda wasn't very faithful. Didn't she cruelly neglect her suitor? Surely we shouldn't sing her praises."

Angelica frowned and shook the chestnut ringlets Eliza had gathered with a velvet bow. One came loose and she pushed it behind her ear. "Don't be silly, Papa. It's just a song," she said, and spread her delicate hands over the keys.

Angelica's soprano voice rose tremblingly above the notes. Alexander joined in with a baritone harmony on the line, "*Her kindness then was great, Her eyes I could with pleasure view.*"

"Bravo," he said when the last chord died away. Alexander hugged his daughter about the shoulders. "That was your best ever."

"I played it to Mama yesterday and she said the same thing." Angelica allowed her head to be kissed, then ducked under his arm. "Shall we sing it again?"

"How about something else, my love?" He leafed through the folio, stopping at what he considered a more suitable song for a girl too young to think about courtship. "Didn't your teacher work with you last week on 'My Mind to Me a Kingdom Is'?"

"Oh, Papa. That one sounds like church music. It's not gay at all." Angelica stood and took another music book off the top of the piano. When she turned to propose a tune, her fingers pinning the page, she smiled and laid a hand on his head. "Papa. Did you know your hair is thinning? You're getting old."

Alexander removed her hand. "Angelica. I'm not even forty, and my hair is not thinning. It's just combed closely. Unlike yours, which looks as if it hasn't met a brush since bedtime."

Angelica giggled and patted her father's crown. "No, really, Papa. It's very spare. Right here on top. You should show Mama."

"I'm sure Mama knows what the top of my head looks like."

Alexander heard the scrape of shoes on the stoop at 26 Broadway. It was probably Ajax Manly, come to accompany him to the meeting. Alexander had been surprised some months earlier when Ajax moved his business back to New York, but he was grateful now. One couldn't have too many supporters in a difficult crowd.

Alexander found Manhattan reinvigorating, with its salty wharfs, brisk trade, and irreverent people. The place where he started his new life two decades earlier was his real home—and blessedly far from Philadelphia's dangerous rumor mill. Yet even here ugly partisanship had taken root, prompted by England's two-year war against the killers of Louis XVI. To cut the Jacobins' supply lines, the Royal Navy was raiding the cargoes of neutral ships headed to French ports. Red-coated marines were dragooning American seamen into service. Even his old friend Hercules Mulligan, whose tailor shop was more prosperous than ever, cursed America's old enemy for hounding France's brave revolutionaries and seizing neutrals. New Yorkers would never stand for George Washington's recent calls for a truce with England, he had told Alexander the night before.

"Old John Jay may dress like a preacher," Mulligan had said, "but men here are ready to hang him for a scoundrel. His damn truce will never make it through Congress."

Tobacco smoke and the summertime heat gave crowded Tontine Coffee House the atmosphere of Hades. Mulligan lectured with a pipe in one hand. "No representative from New York will vote for Jay's Treaty, if he values his seat. And you know Senator Burr. Career first, country second."

New York senator Aaron Burr usually voted against Washington's administration. He was a charming opportunist allied with Thomas Jefferson, whose stock had soared as a result of Britain's obnoxious actions. Yet Burr's disagreement concerned Alexander little. He expected it. A lawyer of distinguished family, Burr took an expedient approach toward most things. Alexander had read in the court digest not long before that Burr was defending Maria Reynolds's petition to divorce her husband. Burr might well have heard some revealing stories from his client, but he had the good grace not to mention them to Alexander, who still sometimes awoke in a sweat at the same terrible nightmare, convinced Eliza had found out.

Of course, there was no percentage for Burr in acting unprofessionally toward a fellow member of the bar. When it came to Jay's Treaty or anything else, the senator would do what was best for himself.

Merchants like Mulligan were another matter. Jay's Treaty needed their support. It troubled Alexander that even those whose livelihoods depended on imports questioned a truce with America's main supplier. Itching for a brawl, protesters had littered the city with handbills calling for war with England.

Yet how could they entertain war against the world's most powerful army and navy? America had barely won its independence from England a few years earlier with the help of the French king now moldering in his Paris tomb, headless. The country wasn't strong enough to hazard being drawn into Europe's quarrels.

John Jay had risked an Atlantic voyage to accomplish the thankless task of buying time. The bony, sober New York attorney—married incongruously to the breathtaking Sally Livingston—came back with a treaty that kept the peace though it required both England and America to swallow bitter pills. Jay was chief justice of the US Supreme Court, yet few granted him the benefit of the doubt as to judgment. The rabble called him traitor.

"You'll be hanged properly if you come out in favor of Jay's Treaty," Mulligan said. He placed a hand on Alexander's shoulder and poured a generous dram of brandy into Alexander's cup just as a young man in an orange waistcoat with topaz buttons approached their table.

"General Hamilton, sir." The fellow had the air of one determined to speak. "I heard you at the celebration in your honor last February, when you returned to New York. The crowd was so thick there was no opportunity to shake your hand, sir. I wish to extend my welcome."

Alexander stood. "Thank you, sir. You do me honor."

"You saved us from bankruptcy, General Hamilton. You gave us government. I speak for many when I say we hope you'll run for president next fall."

"You're very kind. But our vice president is the likeliest candidate. We must wish John Adams well."

Alexander had given up on the presidency the moment James Monroe walked out with Maria Reynolds's letters a year earlier, but the praise was gratifying. His ambitions hadn't been for naught.

"Next time, then, sir," the elegant young man said with a bow.

Hercules Mulligan looked after the retreating New Yorker who hadn't glanced at him longer than at a doorknob. "There goes one of your many admirers, Ham, but he won't have much company if you defend Jay's Treaty. Remember. You've come back to New York to make money, my boy, not fresh enemies. Think of your family."

"I am. What kind of country will our children inherit if we're crushed between France and England? Americans are the ones who need to avoid making enemies.'

Mulligan shrugged. "I'll attend your meeting tomorrow, if you like, but I'm keeping my head low."

When Alexander ran into Ajax Manly on his way home from the coffeehouse, his old comrade asked if Alexander planned to rejoin the New York Manumission Society. They still needed attorneys to defend free blacks snatched off the streets for sale to the south. Slave hunters considered colored men cash in the bank.

"Not yet. I just can't afford to give away my time."

Alexander debated whether he should say more. The fact was, he owed more than five thousand pounds to John and Angelica Church. He and Eliza possessed barely five hundred dollars in assets. He had given her and the children little more than clothes to wear and furniture to sit on. Which made his rivals' continuing lies all the more infuriating. Congress had conducted its own public investigation into the Treasury Department at the Democrats' insistence, and Alexander's honesty was thoroughly proved.

Yet Commodore James Nicholson, one of Aaron Burr's friends, recently spread the rumor that Hamilton had a treasure trove of one hundred thousand pounds in a London bank.

"Eliza and I are living on a mountain of debt to our in-laws," he admitted, "and I've promised to build her a home. If I take enough cases, I think I can manage it in two or three years."

Ajax's look of disappointment vanished when Alexander revealed that he planned to speak on behalf of Jay's Treaty the next day. The opposition wanted to kill the truce partly because Jay hadn't insisted that England return the slaves it freed during the War of Independence. Virgina's plantation owners wanted their pound of real human flesh.

"I'll stand by you," Ajax said. He made Alexander promise not to leave the house without him.

A knock sounded on the door and Angelica sprang from the piano bench. "It's Mr. Manly," she sang as she skipped to the entry. A humid gust came in with the beefy printer.

"Good morning, Miss Angelica. My, aren't you getting big. Are you thirteen now?"

Angelica beamed. "No. That's my brother, Philip. But I am almost grown up. Mrs. Washington let me take dancing lessons with her grandchildren when we lived in Philadelphia. She said I'm the best pupil she's ever seen."

"Deary me. Then you may be too grown up for this ribbon I brought." Ajax reached into his waistcoat with his big hand and pulled out a slip of pink satin.

"Oh, no, Mr. Manly. When I come out in society—which won't be very long—I'm going to have a ball gown just this color. I'll wear my new ribbon with it."

Ajax winked at Alexander over his daughter's head. "I'm sure you'll be the prettiest girl in the room."

The crowd filled the square where Wall, Broad, and Nassau Streets pooled in front of Federal Hall.

Only six years before, Alexander had watched President Washington take his first oath of office on the balcony overlooking the street. Then the crowd's mood had been jovial and excited. Now the jostling felt more like pushing and shoving. Alexander spied protesters whose pockets bulged with stones. Others reeked of whiskey.

Alexander looked in vain for a stoop that wasn't taken. He glanced at Ajax. "How many, do you think?"

Ajax tugged at Alexander's sleeve. "This way," he said, and pulled his former commander through the press of bodies. Rough brown homespun stood shoulder-to-shoulder with colorful suits of linen and silk. The crowd parted grudgingly, though a few shied in recognition and Alexander heard his name. "That's him—Hamilton," one said.

Ajax looked down at Alexander. "I don't know. Maybe five thousand."

The façade of an old brownstone loomed and Alexander felt Ajax boost him onto a squat pillar flanking the entry. The printer remained eerily strong.

The demonstration was enormous. Several thousand seemed a correct estimate. Across the jammed square, perhaps a hundred yards away, a small crowd congregated on the second-floor balcony of Federal Hall, standing between the massive Greek pillars where Washington had once raised his right hand. Alexander recognized Colonel William Smith, son-in-law of Vice President John Adams, and waved. But Smith didn't see him across the throng. Hercules Mulligan stood in one of Federal Hall's tall windows, looking down upon the throng.

A pitchfork shot up, skewering a piece of burning parchment. "Damn Jay's Treaty!" a voice rang out. "Damn anyone who won't damn John Jay. Damn anyone who won't stay up all night damning John Jay!"

The crowd whooped approval but the pitchfork swayed and fell. The spot where it had been looked like an anthill doused with boiling oil. One man struggled to his feet only to have another shove him down. A frightening thump sounded like a head cracking against pavement.

Alexander took a deep breath. "Who called this meeting?" he shouted. Faces turned his way. "The businessmen of New York called this meeting so we could discuss Jay's Treaty like rational creatures! Not savages. Not like Jacobins ready to tear one another apart."

A harsh voice yelled out. "Go back where ya belong, Creole bastard!"

Alexander ignored the taunt. He had heard it before.

"Let's have a chairman," someone shouted. "Call to order!"

"Smith!" another said, and a group near Federal Hall took up the chant. Colonel William Smith leaned out over the assembly. Others started calling his name. It bounced off the brick buildings that loomed over the square. "Smith! Smith!"

Protesters held their hands skyward in an impromptu vote. Alexander's heart lifted at the instinctive gesture. Republicanism could work even when men were angry. They wouldn't collapse into anarchy, as Tories had predicted.

Colonel Smith, elegant in a burgundy dress coat, lifted his hands to calm the crowd. "Should the Senate pass this treaty or not?"

"Never!" a ragged chorus boomed.

"Let's hear the arguments, then. Let men of property and sense have their say." Smith turned to someone on the balcony.

Fair-haired Peter Livingston stepped forward. The young scion of the famous Hudson Valley clan was a leader of the Democratic faction. His lean cheeks were ruddy in the July heat. Like Smith, he was fashionably dressed in lace-trimmed sleeves and a silk cravat.

"Anglomen would sell America's honor for a few barrels of foreign goods," Livingston cried. "Do you want peace at the price of manhood?"

Alexander could hardly believe it. With Colonel Smith's help, Peter Livingston had pirated the meeting organized by Jay's supporters. The young dandy had never done a thing except marry well. Alexander wondered if his cousin Sally Livingston, Jay's wife, would ever speak to him again.

"What justice is this?" Alexander yelled over the heads in front of him. "Today's meeting was called by the businessmen of New York. Not those who slander good John Jay. We've heard their arguments. Their broadsheets clog the sewers."

"That's right. Let's hear from General Hamilton," someone called over the din.

"No. Take a vote!"

Colonel Smith pushed in front of Livingston. "Let me see a show of hands in favor of allowing the gentleman to finish his speech against the Treaty."

The crowd stretched up Wall and down Broad. Hands waved enthusiastically from all directions.

"Those in favor of allowing General Hamilton to speak first?" Hands waved again across the square, but boos and hisses sounded as well. The pitchfork shot up and was pulled down again. Glass broke somewhere.

"All right, then, Mr. Livingston," Smith said.

Peter Livingston stepped forward again. The breeze ruffled his fair hair. "Are we mice or men? Britain tramples republicanism, seizes innocent sailors, and raids American ships. What does the administration propose? What does John Jay propose?" Livingston paused for effect.

A deep voice bellowed over the crowd. "He proposes we stand behind President Washington, you infernal ingrate."

Laughter broke out and treaty supporters in the mob took up a chant. "Damn Peter Livingston! Damn Peter Livingston!"

Livingston tried to speak but catcalls drowned him out. He finally gestured toward Trinity Church and beckoned supporters to follow. Like water sluiced from one ditch to another, the crowd began pouring up Wall Street toward the church steeple.

"Wait. The treaty must be given a full hearing," Alexander shouted at the top of his voice. The rally was disintegrating.

Men who hadn't yet quit the square began turning around. A laborer in a blacksmith's dirty apron at the corner of Nassau Street held up his massive arms to wave people back toward Federal Hall.

"Let France fight her own battles," Alexander yelled. "Jay's Treaty will end this mad dash toward war. Where did the Jacobins put the hero of Yorktown? Where did they put General Lafayette? In prison. Then they executed his family."

Alexander found himself surrounded again.

A voice retorted, "John Jay's an Angloman! An abettor of Tories!"

"No truck with England!" another yelled.

"The Redcoats still hold forts on our land," said a well-dressed man near the front. "Will we finally get rid of the filthy blackguards?"

The British hadn't evacuated their old encampments in the Northwest. A dozen years after independence, Redcoats remained in America. Jay had finally convinced them to withdraw. "Yes!" Alexander called back.

"Just push the bastards off," a man in an old greatcoat said. He shook a blunt fist at Alexander. "And hang our own traitors!"

Alexander looked for Ajax, but didn't see him. The mob seemed endless. The square had filled again.

"Hang the Angloman," the man called.

Someone seconded him. "That's right, hang 'em!"

A rock appeared out of nowhere. Alexander saw it too late to duck. The stone grazed his temple. Ajax jumped up from nowhere and placed his broad back between Alexander and the crowd.

Alexander stepped around him. "If knockdown arguments are all you have, I'll come back another day! Republicanism isn't meant to be a brawl." He leaped down from the stoop, reeled, regained his balance, and placed a hand to his throbbing forehead.

Stoning fellow revolutionaries? Was this how the Reign of Terror began? With a rock, then a cudgel, then the guillotine? Had Jacobinism finally gained purchase in America?

Ajax cupped his elbow. "Let's go."

The two men pressed through the milling mob. When they were finally out of the square, Ajax reached into the pocket of his trousers and handed Alexander a handkerchief. "Here. Wipe the blood off. You don't want to scare Eliza."

They continued down Wall Street. Moments later they chanced upon another quarrel. Alexander recognized Josiah Hoffman, a leading Federalist lawyer, and Commodore James Nicholson, the very man who had embroidered lies about Alexander's supposed booty in England. The commodore shook a cane in Hoffman's face.

"Jay's a turncoat! A traitor," Nicholson said.

Splotches burned on Josiah Hoffman's pale cheeks. His fists were clenched. "Is it treason to stop America from throwing away her independence? Only a fool fights when he can have an honorable peace."

The attorney general for New York, Hoffman was normally the picture of dignity—a lawyer whose immaculate white wig seemed glued to his head. Now he looked as if ten bees had stung him.

Nicholson raised his heavy cane over Hoffman's head. "An honorable peace? Jay's another Benedict Arnold!"

Alexander stepped forward. "Gentlemen. Please. Let's take this to Tontine's. Allow tempers to cool over a glass of ale."

Nicholson spun around. His face twisted in recognition. "This isn't your quarrel, Hamilton. How dare you interpose yourself—a rogue and abettor of Tories. You'd like that, wouldn't you, to see honest men befuddled with drink? It's the coward's oldest trick."

Ajax took Alexander's elbow again. "Come on," he said.

Alexander shook off his friend's grip. "What do you mean, *coward?*" Here was another blow, worse than a rock.

"You've had your chance to defend your reputation. It's plain you're too timid. How much more gold will London's bankers pay you if Congress passes Jay's Treaty?"

"I've not dignified your lies because any halfwit sees through them," Alexander said. "But if you're suggesting I'm loath to defend my honor, allow me to convince you of your mistake."

"Excellent. Send your man to see mine. We'll settle this on the morrow."

"Done. He'll call this evening and I'll see you on the field of honor."

"I await," Nicholson said with a sneer. He turned on his heel to join the crowd streaming toward Trinity.

Josiah Hoffman turned to Alexander. "General Hamilton, sir. Please do not duel this wretch on my account."

Alexander's heart pounded as if he'd been running. "Commodore Nicholson slanders me in the court of public opinion. If I don't defend myself, the jury will pronounce me guilty."

"But Congress cleared you of wrongdoing. Your reputation is secure." Hoffman's patrician face shone with sweat.

"Apparently not or the people of New York wouldn't repeat these vicious lies."

Ajax edged closer. "General Hamilton, sir." His voice was pitched to the tone of a subordinate. "Please, sir, let's be on our way."

Ajax's public deference only fed Alexander's fury. Hypocrites who spied threats to America's freedom from Britain didn't hesitate to steal the freedom of blacks who watched their speech in front of whites. Yet men like Hoffman weren't the problem. Alexander forced himself to be calm.

"Thank you for your solicitude, sir," he said. "I must defend my honor in these perilous times. For now, though, perhaps we'd best get off the street."

The attorney general looked upset, but strode away down the crowded avenue.

"Please, Alexander," Ajax said. "For God's sake, let's get out of here."

Alexander recognized that anger had gotten the best of him. Commodore Nicholson had been ready to punch Josiah Hoffman. As much as he despised the man, Alexander sympathized with his impulse to dispense justice barehanded.

He pondered logistics as they walked home. The invitation to duel must go out first. He would ask Nicholas Fish to deliver the note. Then he would draft the apology that Commodore James Nicholson must be persuaded to give. When tempers cooled, Nicholson would recognize that words like "rogue" and "coward" must be withdrawn, lest momentary passions result in tragedy.

After all, the last time Alexander and the president hunted ducks outside Philadelphia, he had bagged more game than Washington. With a fowling piece at least, he was still a crack shot.

CHAPTER THIRTY-EIGHT

May 1797

New York City

"I was born a slave, but nature gave me the soul of a free man."
Toussaint Louverture, Liberator of Haiti, 1743–1803

"AREN'T THE DAFFODILS BEAUTIFUL?" ELIZA SAID as Ajax helped her onto the sidewalk in front of the Trinity Church graveyard. She nodded at the yellow flowers pushing up between the mossy headstones. "As if placed by God to comfort his children."

"Yes ma'am. They do look like that," Ajax said.

Eliza couldn't remember being happier. When Alexander moved the family back to New York, the controversy over Jay's Treaty made it seem that politics had followed them like a rabid dog. A man challenged Alexander to a duel, though he retracted the insult and the terrible event did not come to pass. Then Congress approved the treaty, the furor calmed, and John Adams succeeded George Washington as president. Philadelphia felt leagues away—though never far enough for Eliza.

Prominent businessmen now sought Alexander's legal advice. The family enjoyed a considerable income for the first time in a decade. Eliza bought whatever they needed. Family was close, too. Angelica and John Church had returned to America after fourteen years in England.

Eliza had just entered her seventh month of pregnancy and felt euphoric. The risk of miscarriage was over, labor far away. Work sometimes took Alexander on short trips, but they were safe expeditions from which he sent tender letters. *"I'm impatient to be restored to your bosom and the presence of my beloved children,"* he had just written from Albany.

Ajax Manly was part of Eliza's happiness, too. The entrepreneur was one of New York's busiest printers, yet he often showed up with the excuse that he was passing by and thought to inquire after their health. He sometimes met her older boys when they arrived at the ferry from boarding school on Staten Island. One time he hauled tempestuous fifteen-year-old Philip home from a tavern, where the boy had gotten into an argument over politics.

It appeared that Ajax had appointed himself unofficial guardian after Eliza's collapse during the Whiskey Rebellion. His visits increased in frequency when Alexander revealed his wife was expecting again.

Eliza had changed as well. She realized one day that she no longer saw Ajax's color. Instead, she noticed when he caught a cold or needed a haircut. She saw how he teased Alexander out of momentary irritations, and advised the son of the Marquis de Lafayette when the young refugee came to live with the Hamiltons. She saw a kind man who didn't help others because he was forced to, but because he chose to. Like Alexander, she even called him Ajax in private.

That very afternoon, when he heard she longed to inspect the new public waterworks over the spring at Mulberry and Baxter, he offered to escort her since Alexander was away. In bygone years, Ajax wouldn't have offered and she wouldn't have accepted. Eliza sometimes told herself it was selfish to accept so much and give so little, but the prosperous businessman wanted for nothing that she could see.

"How is the garden in front of the academy doing?" she said.

She knew he took great pride in the African Free School.

Ajax paused with a thoughtful look. He planted his elegant walking stick between his long legs. "Hmm. The neighbor's bulldog may have been digging in it. The new roof's on, though."

"That's important." Eliza made a mental note to ask Alexander if they could spare a donation for flowers.

"It certainly is. When it rained last month, the leak spoiled our best two—"

Loud hoofbeats and a woman's scream prevented Eliza from hearing the rest of his sentence. Ajax drew her back from the curb.

A phaeton was hurtling down Nassau. A man jumped out of the way and bumped into a vendor's table, overturning a basket of nails.

In the carriage, a horrified woman clutched a young child. She had somehow dropped the reins. If she didn't snatch them back, they would soon crash. The horse stopped and reared at a bystander who tried to stop it. The would-be savior grasped at the reins while the horse twisted and screamed in fright. Its sharp hooves stabbed the ground, then sprang to claw the sky.

The rescuer was a black woman. Dressed in the billowy muslin of the Caribbean, she tried again to stop the runaway animal. She staggered back, then leaped for the reins that flapped and danced about the animal's head.

All eyes were upon her. The horse's murderous hooves crashed down. Nails on the cobblestones scattered under the impact.

"Help her, Ajax!" Eliza cried.

The phaeton rocked backward with the horse's motion. The woman tried to hand her child to arms that reached from the crowd, but the movement upset her balance, and they fell back onto the precarious seat.

The screaming horse reared a third time.

"Get back!" Ajax yelled at the Caribbean woman as she reached once more for the reins. Her full skirt caught on her heel and she fell onto her hands under the hysterical beast. Eliza clutched her belly with fear.

Then Ajax had the reins.

The woman scuttled backward like a crab. She scrambled to her feet to stroke the neck of the horse, whose frightened eyes showed more white than black. "*Soyez tranquille, soyez tranquille, mon cher*." Her dress trailed in dung as she soothed the animal, which whinnied and snuffled, then dipped its large head.

The toddler broke into a wail. The mother was crying, too. She handed him down and someone helped her from the carriage. Ajax led the horse to the side of the road. Traffic resumed. Eliza looked in both directions and stepped off the curb into the street.

"Are you all right?" she said. The black woman, who had looped her torn hem over one arm, remained in the lane as if dazed.

She answered with a West Indian accent. "*Oui, madame*."

The woman's large, catlike eyes were calm, but her muddy hands shook convulsively. She had an exotic, fine-boned face, marred only by a long, pink-edged scar over one eyebrow. Her hair was wrapped in a plaid turban that matched the scarf on her shoulders, and earrings made from iridescent white shells swayed at her chin. She was tall, and her skin was smooth and dark.

Ajax took her elbow. "We'd best get out of the street, *mademoiselle*."

The woman appeared to notice him for the first time. She stood taller. The poised West Indian was beautiful, Eliza realized. She had a natural grace that eluded debutantes who spent hours tripping over New York's dancing masters.

"You saved my life, *monsieur*. *Merci beaucoup*."

"You saved *two* lives. You're very brave," Ajax said.

The nail vendor worked his way toward them with a broom, trying to salvage his merchandise. Ajax guided the woman to the sidewalk.

"You're trembling," Eliza said. "May we take you home? My coach is on the next block."

"This is not necessary. My mistress sent me to fetch a package."

Eliza looked at the woman's torn dress and dirty palms, one of which was badly scraped. "I insist. We shall take you."

Just then Eliza's belly grew hard. It bulged outward on the left, then on the right. Excitement wasn't good for the pregnancy. "Wait, the coachman will take me home first, then help you with your errand. Surely you don't wish to proceed on foot with a torn gown."

Eliza glanced at Ajax, who nodded with an absorbed air. He still held the woman's elbow though they were safely on the sidewalk. His face betrayed the self-consciousness of a schoolboy despite the flecks of gray in his curls.

"I'm Mrs. Alexander Hamilton," Eliza said with a smile.

The black woman curtsied deeply in reply and lowered her eyes. It was Eliza's first inkling that the West Indian wasn't free. The immigrant's command of the horse had led Eliza to assume she must be mistress of her fate, with a life that was hers to throw away.

How terrible. Alexander had told Eliza long ago that Ajax refused to court any woman not at liberty to give her heart. Yet here was a heroine and Ajax looked as if the horse had kicked him after all.

"*Bonjour, madame*. I am Genevieve."

"And your family name?"

Eliza would write the woman's owner to explain her torn dress, which might otherwise provoke a rebuke.

"I've no family, madame, other than *ma fille*, Claudette. But I'm called Genevieve Pearl. I belong to Monsieur and Madame Babineaux-de-Savigny. We come from Saint-Domingue."

Eliza recognized the name of a family of wealthy planters who had fled the violence on the sugar island when the local slave population—inspired by the American and French Revolutions—took to arms. Henri Babineaux-de-Savigny was a client of Aaron Burr. Alexander said Burr made an excellent attorney.

It was strange how their lives kept intersecting with the smooth-tongued Democrat who had just lost his Senate seat to the very man he defeated six years earlier, Philip Schuyler. Papa and Aaron Burr appeared destined to exchange blows far into the future.

Ajax removed his hat. "Allow me to introduce myself, *mademoiselle.*" Then, with an extravagance Eliza never expected—that made the beautiful spring day sweeter yet—he took Genevieve Pearl's hand in his and kissed it.

"*Je m'appelle Ajax Manly. Enchanté de vous rencontrer.*"

Enchanted to meet you. French was so much more romantic than English. Eliza was happy to discover Ajax knew some—and that he had made enough money to buy a woman out of slavery. If she was for sale.

CHAPTER THIRTY-NINE

July 1797

New York City

"After prayers, whilst the Speaker was in his chair . . . Mr. Griswold entered the House and observing Mr. Lyon he went up to him with a pretty strong walking stick in his hand with which he immediately began to beat him with great violence."

Annals of the US Congress, 1798

Day had broken but the nightmare continued.

James Callender, a hard-drinking Democratic mouthpiece, had published a pamphlet on the history of the United States that included the shopworn fable that Hamilton engaged in stock speculation while in office. But Callender produced new evidence as well: the letters Maria Reynolds had given James Monroe four years earlier. Someone had leaked them to the journalist, who printed them with the charge that Congress had failed to act on proof of corruption.

Alexander placed his hands on the tablecloth to steady them. A summer thunderstorm had cooled the city the night before, but rage and despair kept him awake until just before dawn. He was exhausted.

"May I please have more bread?" Jamie said. The round-cheeked boy looked at his mother, who had already sliced and buttered two pieces for him.

A Dutch frown passed across Eliza's face. "It's time to practice your violin."

Alexander knew his wife didn't want the chubby nine-year-old to have more bread. She should say so directly and not coddle the child. He would tell Jamie himself, but didn't trust his temper. Then Alexander reminded himself. Who was he to doubt Eliza was the better parent?

His wife refilled her cup with fresh tea when Jamie left the table. "Would you like some, my love?" she said.

Alexander set down the newspaper he was pretending to read.

Gray strands wandered through Eliza's dark tresses. Frowns and smiles had left their imprint, too. In the eighth month of pregnancy, Eliza looked her forty years. Yet she was still beautiful, and the face she turned on him shined as gloriously as the day he asked for her hand.

Many women had fluttered around the campfires of the revolution. General Schuyler's daughter offered respectability and a loving family, things he long dreamed of having. Nabbing her from Tench Tilghman heightened the adventure. But when Eliza yielded to him, and General Schuyler proved a man of compassion, Alexander's feelings deepened. He simply loved her. Now that his mistakes threatened to ruin everything, Alexander realized he cherished Eliza more than life itself. Honor alone had an older claim on his heart.

His wife set down the Limoges teapot. "Still upset? You know the scoundrels stop at nothing. They're like farmers. They plant a new crop of lies every spring." Eliza smiled. "There. A *bon mot* with breakfast. I declare I've become as adept as Angelica."

Was she just being brave? Could she really still suspect nothing, despite the revelations?

The hysterical correspondence of Alexander Hamilton's paramour littered tables across New York and Philadelphia. Over morning tea, friends and enemies were reading Maria Reynolds's references to Eliza, and James's threat to tell Alexander's wife "everything." Callender's pamphlet was undoubtedly on a sloop to Albany, where Alexander's in-laws would soon be forced to defend him to the entire Hudson River Valley.

He pushed his teacup toward his wife and came up with the best lie he could. "I just can't get these terrible slurs out of my mind."

Eliza lifted her chin. She filled his cup calmly. "Congress conducted its investigation years ago. They exonerated you completely."

Alexander couldn't look her in the face, so he walked around the table and rested his hands on her shoulders. If only Monroe, Muhlenberg, and Venable would quash the accusations. All they had to say was they entertained no doubts. Alexander had not swindled the American people. He could then ignore the newspaper story as one more ludicrous slander—which it was, except for the part about Maria Reynolds.

Alexander had written Monroe, Muhlenberg, and Venable with just that request. The latter two agreed that he had allayed their concerns long ago. Unsurprisingly, Monroe hadn't replied.

Jefferson and Monroe would destroy him if they could, Alexander believed, especially now that George Washington was retired and could offer no protection.

Alexander leaned forward and kissed Eliza's soft neck. The timing of Callender's ugly insinuations, on the eve of childbirth, was agonizing. "Don't worry, my angel. I'll take care of it. I'm meeting with Colonel Monroe later this morning. Our dear Church has agreed to accompany me."

Alexander knocked at the New York lodgings of James Monroe. Behind him stood John Barker Church. Angelica had long heaped praise on Eliza's husband for cutting a more dashing figure than her own, but on that warm summer morning, Alexander treasured his brother-in-law as a prince among men. If anyone would keep the secret, it was John.

A short Negro showed them into the parlor where James Monroe and David Gelston were waiting. Alexander wasn't surprised to see Gelston, a political insider associated with Aaron Burr. Monroe must want a witness. Alexander bowed to both gentlemen and introduced John Church. He accepted the offer of a chair, though he could hardly sit still.

"I presume we all understand the reason for today's gathering," he said.

Monroe nodded. His face was impassive.

"Colonel Monroe, along with Congressmen Muhlenberg and Venable, visited me in Philadelphia some years ago concerning a set of letters," Alexander started in. "James Reynolds's wife led them to believe I had paid her husband to purchase bank shares on my behalf. When I explained the circumstances, the gentlemen agreed there was no evidence whatsoever of official misconduct."

Monroe tapped his fingers on the armrest. "Surely you don't wish to rehash this, Colonel Hamilton. I attended that meeting."

Alexander ignored the provocation. Monroe knew that Washington had made him general, of course. It had been decades since they were both colonels.

"Indeed, sir," he said. "You took part in the meeting, and afterward kept the letters in question with the assurance they would remain confidential. Now they've been published."

"Upon my honor, sir, I had nothing whatsoever to do with the publication of that correspondence. I regret seeing it in print," Monroe said. "I gave those notes to a friend in Virginia for safekeeping. I have no idea how they came into print, and am truly sorry for your distress."

Jefferson.

Monroe must have given the letters to the sage of Monticello, who passed them to Callender. But why didn't his enemies stop at exposing his infidelity? Must they still pretend Alexander was a thief as well?

"If you feel as you say, Colonel Monroe, why did you not answer my letter of last week?" Alexander struggled to keep his volume under control. He heard his voice ricochet off the walls. "This matter touches grievously upon my character. It affects the reputation of my entire family and sullies the name of the Treasury Department. I expected immediate confirmation of my fiscal integrity at the least. Anyone would."

"If you would not be so intemperate, sir—if you'll be quiet a moment and stop your interminable arguing—I can explain," James Monroe said. "I intend to meet with Venable and Muhlenberg when I return to Philadelphia next week. Once we've consulted, we can pen a joint answer."

"You've no opinion right now? You must consult others before you can confirm what happened four years ago?"

"I assure you my memory is perfect, Colonel Hamilton. Would you like me to relate my understanding of what happened?"

"Yes, I would."

Alexander sat on his hands, fearing he would otherwise wipe the air of injured innocence off Monroe's face.

"When we met four years ago, you provided evidence that the funds you gave James Reynolds were for another purpose."

Monroe didn't say what everyone in the room knew. That Alexander had paid Reynolds to keep Eliza in the dark.

"After the meeting, our committee agreed to drop the investigation," he continued. "I commissioned copies of the letters on your behalf, and sent the originals to a colleague in Virginia, who I'm sure kept them sealed."

Did he really expect Alexander to believe that?

"The first half of that story is true enough, Colonel Monroe, but the second is totally false or the letters wouldn't be in every newspaper in New York."

James Monroe sprang to his feet. Alexander followed.

"If you're calling me a liar, Mr. Hamilton, then you, sir, are a scoundrel! A scoundrel and a monarchist."

"I'm prepared to meet you as a gentleman," Alexander said.

Monroe clenched his hands. His throat and face turned a mottled red. "Get your pistols. I'm ready!"

"So be it, sir. I'll duel you this very minute."

Gelston and Church both rose. Church placed his hand on Alexander's sleeve. "Please! Let's be moderate."

David Gelston stepped between the rivals and caught the colonel's elbow. "Valor isn't at issue."

James Monroe looked down at Alexander and repeated emphatically, "I have no idea whatsoever how Maria Reynolds's letters found their way into the press. I assure you, Mr. Hamilton, that I'm as surprised as you by the turn of events. That's the best I can say."

John Barker Church tightened his grasp on Alexander's forearm. The doughy financier was stronger than he looked.

"What's done is done, gentlemen," Church said. "Colonel Monroe will issue a statement with Misters Venable and Muhlenberg as soon as he returns to Philadelphia. They'll affirm they found no evidence of financial impropriety. General Hamilton was entirely innocent of defrauding the government."

David Gelston looked worriedly from Hamilton to Monroe. "Yes. Until then, please allow the matter to rest. We'll consider any intemperate expressions made this morning as forgotten."

Monroe looked at his accuser. There was a question in the Virginian's cold blue eyes. Was Hamilton calling him a liar, or not?

Alexander shrugged off his brother-in-law's grasp. James Monroe was an out-and-out scoundrel, but if Muhlenberg and Venable convinced the rat to tell the truth about the earlier investigation, honor would be satisfied. America's first Treasury Secretary had cheated his wife and family, not the country.

Alexander took a handkerchief from his pocket and blotted his brow. "I'll await confirmation."

A week later, the former Treasury Secretary gazed blindly out the window of the boardinghouse room in Philadelphia that he rented when in town on business. Pedestrians and carriages passed on the street below, but they were a blur. Purple storm clouds hung over the sooty city. He saw only the dark snake of the Schuylkill in the distance.

Two days earlier, he had followed James Monroe to the capital to gain satisfaction. Once again the slippery Virginian refused to fully exonerate Hamilton of financial impropriety. He simply had to let a little mud cling to his rival's reputation.

One had honor or one did not. There were no gradations. The thought of a stain on his public character infuriated Alexander. He must do something.

Alexander picked up the goose quill he had purchased that morning and took a stack of clean paper from his valise. He didn't know if he was doing the right thing, but could decide later. At present, he welcomed the familiar task of assembling documents, setting out facts, and arguing his case. He had prepared countless essays explaining thorny issues.

Alexander's hand steadied as he wrote. Even if he chose not to print the confession, simply writing it calmed him.

His first task was to explain how Maria had approached him five summers earlier, and the blackmail by Reynolds that ensued. "*My real crime is an amorous connection with his wife*," he scratched on the heavy vellum. "*This confession is not made without a blush.*"

Alexander wrote the first ten pages without stopping. The pamphlet would disprove James Callender's charges once and for all. He had never asked Reynolds to buy stocks. The attached correspondence between him and Maria would make that clear. Their letters were his best evidence that desire alone motivated the relationship.

A cramp finally overtook his hand. Alexander rested his pen on the paper. Friends had counseled him to ignore Callender's accusations. "The public is outraged at the depths to which he's sunk," Oliver Wolcott said.

"No one believes him," John Church agreed. Robert Troup counseled silence. "If you admit to anything, the Democrats will call it proof of everything."

Alexander couldn't ask the opinion of the person whose wisdom he valued above all others'. He would never cease condemning himself for what he had done to her. Eliza would understand best why he must answer the challenge to his honor, yet it would hurt her the most. What would she advise? Clear his reputation as treasury secretary or protect his name as her husband? Either carried a steep price.

"Will she ever forgive me?" Alexander said aloud. The reverberation in the empty chamber condemned him.

He picked up his quill, which had left a black blotch on the white paper, and reminded himself that he didn't have to publish the pamphlet. Society turned a blind, even amused eye to adultery, so long as those who snuck around kept their secrets. And what a person refused to admit couldn't be used against him.

Rumors of Thomas Jefferson's slave mistress had circulated for years, yet no one dared publish them, lacking hard evidence or the man's own admission. But political opponents hadn't connected Jefferson's extramarital affair with government corruption, either.

Alexander reread what he'd written. The prose flowed. The evidence was strong. Even at such a grim pass, he took satisfaction in his powers of persuasion. If he published the confession, Monroe and Callender wouldn't be able to make their damn mud stick, like it had to Mama.

CHAPTER FORTY

July 1797

New York City

"Had I been born to rank and condition . . .beyond the reach of any vile intriguer. . . I should have been above the greater part of that species of mankind who, for want of understanding, or honor . . . give themselves up to libertinism."

Samuel Richardson, *Pamela*, 1740

JULY MADE THE NINTH MONTH OF pregnancy particularly hot and miserable.

"Philip, darling, can you please lift the sash?"

Eliza pointed with her fan to the window that let in a breeze off the Hudson. She was glad to have her eldest home for the afternoon. Now that he was preparing to enter King's College, Philip was often out with friends. He'd sprouted past his father in the last year and his face had developed the square angles of a man. Eliza was conscious that soon he would be gone—though she tried not to think about that, as it gave her such a pang.

"Yes, Mother." Philip got up from the divan to open the window.

They had been listening to Angelica's tale about the prince of Wales, who promised to be more attentive when he learned that the Church family threatened to return to America.

Eliza's sister took a crystal pitcher from the tea trolley. She looked fresh and radiant in a white gown with gold embroidery at the wrists. "Betsey, please have more to drink," Angelica said as she refilled Eliza's water glass. "You must be perishing."

Eliza took a sip and fanned her face. "I hope you told His Majesty that neither love nor money could keep you in England a minute longer."

"He knew that already," Eliza's brother-in-law said. He patted his wife's hand. "The aristocracy look upon Angelica's republicanism as an eccentricity—and the English never try to talk a person out of his quirks. The prince accepted that she'd end up back in Bedlam one day."

Philip picked up a calico sleeping under the tall sash and sat down again. He had inherited his mother's fondness for animals.

"Is that how the Redcoats think of America, Uncle John? Bedlam?" Philip scratched behind the cat's ears.

Angelica's expression was merry. "They try not to think about America at all. We did our best not to remind them. Too frequently, that is."

"Your aunt was the only soul in London who could speak of George Washington without causing George III to burst a blood vessel," John said.

"She navigates between the New World and Old with the skill of Columbus," Eliza told her son.

"Columbus crossed the Atlantic four times," Philip said. "How many times have you, Aunt Angelica?"

"As many, I suspect. But I'm home to stay. How else can I take care of your dear mama?"

"I'll be fine, Ann, so long as I avoid reading rubbish," Eliza said. She picked up the shoddily bound publication she had meant to throw away but somehow hadn't. It contained the latest, most vile lies she'd seen, purporting that Alexander was a rake in addition to being a thief. She couldn't shield Philip from the vulgarity of politics any longer, but she would rather not expose the younger children. She didn't know why she hadn't gotten rid of it.

"I place no credence in a single thing written by our wicked opposition, but the bounders do make me grit my teeth." Eliza gave the pamphlet to John. "Here, dear brother. Please dispose of this. Surely you need something in which to wrap fish."

John Church took the journal without looking at it. "Absolutely. Cook can always put newsprint to use."

Eliza's brother-in-law glanced at his wife, who lowered her eyes and smoothed a metallic thread in her sleeve. John changed the subject to the problem of collecting money he had lent English aristocrats to cover their gambling debts.

"Wasn't the leader of the Whigs the worst?" Angelica said.

"No, Richard Sheridan was the worst," her husband said.

"The famous playwright?" Philip said. "You mean the author of *School for Scandal*?"

"Yes," Angelica said. "What a scamp. He bragged that repaying creditors only encouraged them."

John smiled weakly. "He certainly put me on notice not to expect my money anytime soon."

Philip pressed for details until it was time for the Churches to leave for a reception across town.

Angelica donned a gauzy mantle trimmed with seed pearls. "When does the Little Lion return from Philadelphia? I miss his ready wit and good company."

"This week, I hope," Eliza said.

"Is he seeing a new client?"

John placed a hand on his wife's arm. "Really, my dear. We must be going. Fashionably late is earlier in New York than London."

John spoke affably, but there was something about the quickness of his movements that set Eliza to wondering as her sister and brother-in-law took their leave.

"Do you need anything, Mother?" Philip asked soon thereafter. "Would you like me to keep you company or would it be all right if I met Herschel Price at the theater?"

Eliza assured him she was fine. When Philip had gone, she trudged to the scullery to arrange a bouquet of fresh flowers that Alexander had sent her, in what had become his weekly ritual. While she stripped the lilies' stems, Eliza allowed James Callender's accusations to enter her mind, normally double-bolted against disloyal thoughts. She lied when she said the man couldn't rattle her. Callender's first paragraphs turned her stomach. She stopped reading at the forged note a harlot supposedly sent Alexander.

When her husband had left for Philadelphia, he kissed her just as tenderly as ever. But his good cheer seemed strained. He mentioned that he intended to see James Monroe again, and she intuited that it had something to do with Callender, who had quoted Monroe more than once. Should she ask Alexander if any part of the awful story was true?

A cramp welled up painfully in Eliza's leg at that moment and she gripped the edge of the table while it passed. The fragrance of lilies filled the air, but their scent seemed heavy and sad, like flowers at a funeral.

Of course she wouldn't ask. Alexander would never betray her.

The clock in the upstairs parlor struck ten. Twilight crept slowly over the busy city during summer. Eliza found that by the time her youngest fell asleep, she often felt like turning in, too. That evening had been particularly long. She had spent more than an hour reading to her nephew, Philip Schuyler II, whom they had taken in when her younger brother John died some months earlier. The orphaned boy needed extra attention.

She was determined to stay awake this time. Alexander had sent word that he would be home after nightfall. She yearned for his arms. He had been gone nine days, an eternity at the end of a pregnancy.

Just when she felt she could keep her eyes open no longer, Eliza heard footsteps on the staircase—and he was in the parlor.

"My love!" Alexander rushed to the divan where she lay with a book. He kneeled next to her and placed a hand on her arm when she struggled to get up. "Don't stand. I'm home at last. How are you?"

Eliza lifted her face as he leaned to kiss her, eager to feel his beard on her cheek and forget the world.

"Elephantine, but alive. How are you?" She looked at his dusty boots and worn face. He must have traveled all day. She tugged on his hand, and he sat next to her, their fingers entwined.

"Much better now that we're together. The journey was interminable—and I was desperate to get home. I'm sure that mail carriage is a relic of Roman rule. It broke down twice. But, tell me. How are the children? Are you feeling well? I missed you terribly." He gave her hand two quick kisses, and then another.

"We missed you, too. The house isn't the same without you. I'm overrun with children and animals—yet all alone." A plaintive note she hadn't intended slipped out.

Alexander's brow furrowed. "Oh, darling girl, surely not all alone?"

"No. Not really. Philip has been watching over me, and Angelica and John visited a few days ago. Ajax dropped by this morning."

"Any word about his West Indian girl?"

"No. He's as close-lipped as a Long Island clam. I'm desperately curious, but don't dare ask."

Eliza had told her husband weeks earlier about the encounter with the beautiful slave. Alexander could hardly believe their friend would consider the woman, but Eliza assured him that Ajax's stupefaction meant only one thing.

"I'm glad he stopped by, even if he disappointed your matchmaker's curiosity," Alexander said. "It cuts me to the quick to think of your feeling lonely."

Alexander's expression was so sincere and sweet that tears started in Eliza's eyes. She simply had to ask. The ugly question of Maria Reynolds would not go away, no matter how many times she told herself that a lack of faith was akin to a lack of love.

She let go his hand and heaved herself straighter. "Alexander, I'm sorry. But there's something I need to ask you."

"Eliza, there's something I need to tell you first." He sighed deeply, which wasn't like him. He opened his mouth and closed it.

An awful sensation seized Eliza, as if the world as she understood it wasn't real. Her husband's expression was so foreign. She crossed her arms over her high belly.

Alexander squared his shoulders. "I'm sure you've read that James Callender accuses me of paying James Reynolds to speculate in stock on my behalf." His eyes darted to the corner of the parlor, then back. "It's not true."

The clock on the mantel chimed the half hour. The city outside was quiet.

Eliza hugged herself more tightly. "I didn't think so." Now he would refute the rest of the story.

"But I did give Reynolds money several years ago. I . . . I had an affair with his wife and he blackmailed me. I'm sorrier than I can ever, ever say, Eliza, but that part is true." Alexander spoke as evenly as a doctor delivering an unwelcome diagnosis.

There was a place in Eliza's soul she hadn't known until that moment, where blind fury dwelled. Her husband was calm and she hated him for it instantly. She felt on fire. Then anguish came, and the world fell out from underneath her.

Alexander looked down at his hands. His voice was now low. "I'm so ashamed, Betsey. Ashamed at what happened, mortified that it's now being dragged into the papers."

Eliza's anger increased. Which troubled him more, touching another woman or endangering his reputation?

Alexander seemed to know better than to take her hand again. "I didn't love her, Betsey." He shook his head. "I don't know what happened to my good sense. You're the only woman who means anything to me. I cherish you beyond words. Can you ever forgive me? Please?"

His words were hollow. The image of a fresh, slim, unblemished beauty—without the nicks and scars of motherhood—rose in Eliza's imagination to mock her. What did Alexander think when he saw the veins on his wife's legs, swollen from pregnancy? What had he felt when he held Maria Reynolds?

For sixteen years she had awakened every morning confident that she held the fortress of Alexander's heart, just as he held hers, only to learn that she was a nobody outside the castle walls. She mustn't have existed in those fevered moments when he turned his lips and naked skin to another woman.

Alexander leaned close and took Eliza's face in his hands. His Scottish complexion showed dark circles under the eyes, and lines made brackets in his cheeks. His auburn hair had gone rusty. He had aged. But the eyes that entreated her were still those of her own true love. The one she had lost.

"Speak to me, Betsey," he whispered.

Eliza flinched away. "It started when I took the children to Albany." She spoke flatly. There was no need to ask. The dates had been in the paper.

Then she remembered. All eyes had been upon him in Philadelphia that hellacious summer. He must have gone to great lengths to hide his sordid affair.

"Just answer me this. Did you take her into our home when I was gone? Your . . . your . . ."

Eliza's husband bit his lip. A tear spilled down one cheek. "Yes."

Eliza stared at the stranger she had loved all her life. Maria Reynolds was a trap door around which she had walked for years. How could she have been so naïve?

The thought of Alexander lying with another woman—under their blankets . . . she never wanted him to touch her again.

"Will you forgive me? Please?"

"I don't know if I can. What I do know is that I can't remain here now."

Eliza rose and went to their bedroom. Alexander could go to hell as far as she was concerned.

CHAPTER FORTY-ONE

August 1797

Albany

"Charity [and love]. . . beareth all things, believeth all things, hopeth all things, endureth all things."

St. Paul, King James Bible

ALEXANDER SAW HER TO THE ALBANY sloop the next day though he begged her to stay at least until the birth. He wore knee breeches and a coat suited for appearing in court, where he was representing the State of New York, but his was waistcoat was rumpled and he looked haggard. He had slept in his office.

"Please, Eliza," he said in a low voice. "Think of the risk."

"You didn't," she said.

Eliza couldn't bear to see her husband or anyone else they knew. She didn't even want to confront Angelica and John, whose familiarity with licentious England and France—where aristocratic rogues freely broke their sacred vows and wrote comic novels about such debaucheries—might lead them to excuse Alexander. She wanted to go home, her real home.

Her husband tried to kiss her cheek, but she turned her face and he leaned over to tighten the latch on her trunk. That morning he had revealed his abominable plan to wash their dirty linen in public.

"If I don't answer the charges fully, and admit my error, they'll never stop saying our reforms were simply a ruse to line my own pockets and those of bankers. Don't you see, Eliza? Our country is at stake."

"Our country? What about me? How will I hold up my head in public? How will our children? This doesn't affect just you and your government."

"I know, Betsey. But I'd be less of a man, less of a patriot, if I didn't face my mistakes honestly. Could you forgive that, too?"

Alexander's courage had attracted Eliza from the day they met. He said what no one else would, regardless of cost. Now it would cost her.

"Is this really patriotism?" She hardly recognized her own sardonic tone. "I doubt it."

She took Philip with her and left the other children behind. Their eldest seemed grave at the responsibility. He shook his father's hand at the dock, but Alexander pulled the boy close and hugged him as they boarded the sloop. Eliza turned her eyes upriver as soon as the crew cast off their lines. Her husband waved from the wharf until river mists obscured the Manhattan shoreline—or so Philip reported.

Alexander had paid for a special deck chair so she could take the air and avoid the sweltering cabin during daylight. Eliza rested as motionlessly as possible in the shade of an awning while the boat tacked upriver. The baby quieted as if copying her.

The Bible helped tamp down sorrow, anger, shame, and fear as the leafy shoreline slipped by. Just *read*, she thought, forcing herself to find meaning in characters that spilled like rice across the page. She prayed the entire desperate flight up the Hudson that she wouldn't go into labor. From the way Philip kept his eyes on her, she knew he prayed, too.

The boy refused to leave her side even at night, though she told him he ought to sleep on deck with the crew.

"Don't you want me here, Mother?" Philip sat on his heels on his partly unfurled bedroll. The minuscule cabin next to the captain's quarters barely accommodated a single bunk. A brass chest took up most the floor.

"You've nowhere to put your legs."

"This is fine. It's more comfortable than it looks." Philip pushed his bedroll into the tight corners. "I'm not leaving you," he muttered under his breath.

With God's blessing they made the Schuyler mansion in time, just two days before the birth of William Stephen Hamilton, her sixth child—a little boy with his mother's Indian eyes and Alexander's bow-shaped lips. She called him Willy.

Eliza looked out upon the unchanging Hudson from the corner room she once shared with Angelica, Peggy, and Cornelia, when their heads were filled with the adventures of childhood. What had happened to that optimistic girl who had more interest in animal husbandry than a human husband? Why had she ever left Albany, persuaded that the man she met by happenstance was different from all others?

Kitty Schuyler had placed Eliza's sickbed close to the window so she could enjoy every wisp of breeze off the river. Baby Willy slept in a bassinet at her side. The porridge a servant had brought cooled untouched. Eliza had as much appetite for it as for sawdust.

She thought again of the latest letter from Angelica, who reported that Alexander turned up on the Churches' doorstep as soon as she left. He spoke only of his wife. As usual, Angelica couldn't bear sadness in either of her favorites. She and Alexander had always been fond of one another—with their shared passion for politics and knack for bamboozling others. She had named her fourth son after her brother-in-law. "My dear brunettes," Alexander called Eliza and Angelica, as if they were celestial twins bringing the sun and moon to light his life.

Merit and talent always attracted enemies, Angelica wrote now. If Eliza hadn't married a man who flew so "near the sun," she would have spared herself grief, but foregone the exhilaration of seeing life through the eyes of an eagle. Alexander was an extraordinary husband.

Eliza surmised that Angelica knew the facts because she wrote, *"The dirty fellow who has caused us all some uneasiness and wounded your feelings, my dear love, is effectively silenced."*

Angelica meant cold-blooded James Callender. But the man who had injured Eliza was Alexander Hamilton. Her husband's bold ambition had always gotten him into trouble, and he had now compounded his other faults with a terrible moral lapse. Any other explanation was a flimsy excuse.

Six innocent children and two orphans bound Eliza hand and foot to a libertine who had dishonored them all before the world.

A knock sounded. Kitty Schuyler put her head around the door. "Are you resting comfortably, *mijn lief*? Did you finish your breakfast?"

When her mother saw Eliza's tears, she crossed the room and sat on the side of the bed, which sank under her matronly figure. "There, there." She wiped Eliza's face with her knobby hand. "Don't cry, my love. You mustn't lose faith. Marriage brings many trials."

"I thought Alexander was different, Mama."

Eliza knew that some husbands cheated on their wives. "Cuckold" was the term for a husband betrayed, but for a woman betrayed there was no word other than "wife." She always thought that Alexander's childhood had inoculated him against such low, hurtful behavior, but she was wrong. Perhaps it had had the opposite effect, corrupting him. Had it occurred to him that he might father a bastard? That he risked inflicting on another soul what had happened to him in Christiansted?

"Alexander *is* different from most," her mother said. "I've never met anyone possessed of such affection for family. But he's a man. These things happen."

"Not to you. Papa would never do such a thing."

Her mother hesitated. "War parted us many times when we were young. I never asked if he was tested. Sometimes it's better not to."

Eliza realized she hadn't ever asked Alexander either, despite many separations, though she knew he was as eager to make love regularly as dine on time. Couldn't a man simply be trusted?

Kitty Schuyler stroked her daughter's hand, which lay heavily on the coverlet. "Betsey. You must call on your strength and trust your judgment. With whom did you leave your children?" They both knew the question was rhetorical. "Alexander is an excellent father, and in most ways a fine husband. You owe it to the children to forgive him, or you'll never forgive yourself." Kitty Schuyler picked up the Bible on Eliza's bed table and handed it to her daughter. "If God accepts our sins, you can accept Alexander's."

Eliza doubted her capacity for mercy was equal to the Divine. Her feelings for Alexander would never be the same. But she took the book. It was something to hold on to when she felt like burning down the world.

CHAPTER FORTY-TWO

August 1797

Saratoga

"When you are in doubt, be still, and wait; when doubt no longer exists for you, then go forward with courage."

White Eagle, Ponca Chief, 1840–1914

PHILIP SCHUYLER LAID DOWN HIS QUILL pen and pushed his chair back. "Would you like me to go with you? I wouldn't mind stretching my legs a bit."

Eliza knew her father was only halfway through the stack of correspondence that had greeted him upon their arrival at Saratoga. "No thank you," she said. "Willy is sleeping. The nursemaid will watch him. I'm perfectly fine to go on my own."

Eliza didn't want company. When Papa had offered to take her to their country estate, she accepted immediately and left her eldest son behind in Albany to visit with his cousins. The farther away she got from other people, the better. Saratoga had always soothed her spirit. There she could hide.

"Are you sure you're strong enough?"

"Of course, Papa. I'm Kitty Schuyler's daughter. Ready to organize a sewing bee and lead a church picnic."

Eliza hoped he believed her. The body really had sprung back after a few weeks' rest, as it always did. Only her heart remained broken.

Papa nodded and smiled. "My Kitty," he said.

Eliza wrapped a light shawl around her shoulders to keep off the sun. She picked up her bonnet and tied it. "I'll be back in an hour or so."

She turned and went out the front door before her father changed his mind. The stairs were slippery from the afternoon thundershower that had dumped rain an hour before and she stepped carefully. Tears started down her cheeks. *My Kitty*. Her mother and father had a marriage she would never have. How strange, to envy one's parents. She wiped her face angrily.

The grass immediately soaked her slippers but Eliza didn't mind. The smell of wet earth was heady. Crickets made a cacophonous buzz, drowning out her thoughts. The humid summer air lay heavily on her skin. She walked quickly up the oyster-shell driveway to the dirt river road that ran from Albany to Saratoga. She turned north—away from civilization, away from the selfish husband who had betrayed her. A slave hoeing the vegetable garden looked up as she passed but Eliza stared straight ahead and walked rapidly.

When she got to the sugar orchard, safe from prying eyes, her strides widened. The forest ahead beckoned. The solid road under her thin slippers felt good. Soon she was running. Small pebbles bit into her soles. It was a country lane, not a city street. She ran faster. Her shawl slipped down her arms. She let it go. Her bonnet came untied. It fell behind her on the road. She reached for the ribbon in her hair and pulled it off, letting her hair spill. No one could see. Running, she felt like a girl of eight rather than a mother of eight.

A towering sycamore marked the path down to the creek that Eliza used to explore with her brother John when they were children. Weeds as high as her knees obscured the spot, yet to Eliza there was no mistaking it. She brushed past the wet vegetation that left splotches on her skirt and turned down the path. Trees and large boulders obscured the stream below, but she heard it gurgling over the rocks. Slowing on the slick mulch, she walked until she caught sight of the creek that fed into the fish weir, trapping speckled trout.

Eight years younger than Eliza, John had been her parent's oldest son. Mama and Papa brought four girls into the world, and a boy who didn't live, before they finally obtained the requisite male heir. John had been all they'd hoped for: hardworking, responsible, eager to take over the family's extensive farms. He married into the staid Rensselaer clan and threw himself into all facets of the Schuyler estate, relieving her father of many burdens. He had been a model son until two years earlier, when he died of a brief, violent illness at Saratoga.

Eliza hadn't been close to John. As a young child, he had gotten it into his head that he would be the lord of the manor one day—and lorded it over them. Angelica had laughed at his pretensions to authority, but Eliza resented them. She could still see the boy in the front pew at church, black hat on his lap, glancing over at his older sisters when the minister preached about dutiful daughters and obedient wives. Of her brothers, Eliza had favored Philip Jeremiah, the lovable pest.

Once John was grown, managing the Schuyler estates allowed him to provide luxuriously for his family until tragedy struck. When he died at age thirty, Eliza took in Philip Schuyler II, determined to love her nephew less reservedly than she had his poor father, gone before his time.

But there was one place where she and John had enjoyed each other's company. When he was very little, he'd been fascinated by the fish weir. They dropped oak leaves upstream, then raced down to the tall poles sticking out of the water to see whose leaf made it out of the trap first, bobbing toward the Hudson far below. Eliza told John how the Iroquois made weirs, too, and speared the caged trout instead of catching them with nets. He spent the better part of a week making a weapon and perching on his haunches. When John finally caught a small fish, he ran all the way to the house to show her. Eliza had been a good sister that afternoon—until he'd said that *all* the fish in Saratoga would one day be his.

Now John was gone. There was no point to the petty resentments she once harbored. Why was it so much easier to forgive the dead than the living? Eliza reminded herself, as she sat down on a rock next to the water, that some sins were venial, others mortal.

"Excuse me, miss."

Eliza jumped up, startled, and turned around.

A tall Iroquois in European clothes, with black hair to his shoulders, held out a muddy bonnet and shawl. Iroquois were impossible to hear coming. The man looked at her keenly, as if he was taken aback, too. "I think you may have dropped these."

Eliza stepped forward and took the bedraggled articles. "Thank you, sir. How did you find me?"

"I saw your trail. The grasses were bent, Onatah." He smiled. "One-of-us."

She stared. "How do you know my Iroquois name?"

"I was present when Chief Skenandoa gave it to you."

The man's sleeves were rolled above his forearms in the sultry heat. The image of hands clasping a wet rope, and a brown shoulder brushing hers, flashed through her mind. Surely this wasn't the same man. "Did we meet?"

He looked amused. "Of course. You saved my canoe."

The Mohawk spoke with only a slight accent. Eliza wondered how he had learned English. She pulled back her hair and retied the ribbon. "I'm surprised you recognize me."

"Recognize you, Onatah? That is simple. You are remarkable."

Eliza dropped her eyes, but found them drawn upward again. The man observed her silently. She turned and stepped closer to the bank. A blue jay chattered to its mate in the trees. The Iroquois came to stand beside her. They watched the waters hugging the boulders in the stream. She didn't know why she wasn't afraid of him, but she wasn't.

"You're dressed differently now," Eliza said.

"That was long ago. I went to the white man's college."

"Dartmouth?"

"To train for the ministry," he said.

"The ministry? That's not what I would have expected."

"It wasn't what I intended. But that is what Indians must study at Dartmouth."

He bent, picked up a flat stone, and skipped it over an eddy. It bounced three times before disappearing.

"What did you intend?" she said.

"I intended to become a lawyer. Which is what I am. I argue on behalf of my people."

Eliza smiled. "That's how I remember you. Arguing."

He laughed. "I usually was, back then."

"And now?"

"Now I argue with the white man. I was riding home from a meeting in Albany when I saw the bonnet on the road." The Indian's voice became softer. "Why did you drop it, Onatah? Are you well?"

Eliza looked back at the glassy stream rushing toward the Hudson, then Manhattan, far downriver.

"I'm sorry," she said. "I never learned your name. You have me at a disadvantage."

"I am called Otetiani."

"What does that mean?" Eliza said.

"He-who-is-prepared."

She bent and picked up a pebble, too. She aimed it at the stream, where it bounced twice before vanishing. Their conversation felt as if no time had passed since they pulled his canoe to shore.

"Does your name fit?" she said.

"Mostly. But I was not prepared to see you."

Eliza kept her gaze on the water. She knew he was staring. They didn't speak.

She turned. "General Schuyler is expecting me. I should go." Despite the words, she was reluctant to leave.

Otetiani pulled his sleeves down and buttoned the cuffs. "May I escort you, Miss Schuyler? The path is slippery."

Eliza took the arm he gallantly offered. As they started up the path, she noticed how much taller he was than her husband. When her slipper caught on a gnarled tree root and she stumbled, he placed a hand on the small of her back to guide her. She glanced up at him. He looked down and smiled. Eliza retrained her eyes on the tangled path, but didn't really see it.

When they reached the road, Eliza spotted a horse staked under the sycamore. Otetiani untied it. He offered her the reins. "Would you like to take my mount?"

She wondered, was he returning to the Mohawk castle?

Eliza felt a wild, strange, unexpected impulse to eat cakes of maize, splash in the river, lie on a rug next to a fire, and forget all her hurts. Alexander had embraced another woman. If Otetiani slipped his arm around her, would she resist?

A familiar tingle shot through her breasts—which meant Willy must be hungry. She needed to get back or her blouse would soon be wet.

"You're kind, but I need the walk," Eliza said. "Perhaps you'll stop by our home in Albany next time you come downriver."

"I'll make it a point. General Schuyler is an old friend of my people."

Eliza arched an eyebrow, smiled, and turned in the direction of the sugar orchard. A few moments later she heard a horse gallop upriver.

As Eliza walked back down the road toward her life, she swung the shawl and bonnet. She didn't put them on. They were a matron's garb and she felt like a young woman. She was still comely. At least one man thought so. She ought to have corrected

Otetiani when he'd addressed her as "Miss Schuyler," but it made her feel free, strong, and satisfyingly mutinous not to be called Mrs. Hamilton.

CHAPTER FORTY-THREE

September 1797

New York City

"I have seen a man who made the fortune of a nation laboring all night to support his family."

Talleyrand, 1754–1838, on Alexander Hamilton

AJAX MANLY AND A SMALL GIRL sat on either side of the tall woman in Alexander's Manhattan law office. The trio held hands in a pose that suggested they would never be separated willingly. With high cheekbones and almond-shaped eyes, Genevieve Pearl had a loveliness that was both regal and fierce. Ajax had found a beauty worth waiting for and she would drag him to his doom.

"I was given to Monsieur and Madame Babineaux-de-Savigny as a wedding present when I was twenty, just before I had Claudette."

Genevieve gave the child's hand a squeeze. Claudette looked up. Her smile revealed two missing teeth.

Alexander didn't ask about Claudette's father. From the child's light skin he was probably Genevieve's original owner. Some astute plantation mistress must have decided it was time to remove her rival. Alexander wished she hadn't. Ajax's happiness wouldn't be at risk.

"So you've been with Monsieur and Madame since then?" Alexander said.

"*Oui, monsieur*. I help with the children and run small errands for Madame, who has trouble with her nerves since we left the island. She thinks I'm at the milliner, collecting her hat."

"Will we get the hat, *Mère?*" the child said.

"Shhh. Not right now," Genevieve told her. "*Oui*."

"Do they have other servants, madam?"

"Monsieur and Madame had more than five hundred slaves on Saint-Domingue. They raised coffee. But when the revolution came, they fled and lost almost everything. That's when I was getting this." She pointed to the pink knife scar above her eyebrow. "I helped them escape."

Alexander wondered why Genevieve hadn't simply remained on the island when slavery was abolished.

"It was very dangerous for everyone, there was killing everywhere, and I had *ma fille*," Genevieve said, as if anticipating the natural question. "Ajax asks me why we didn't stay, but I tell him—'I was looking for you.'"

Alexander gazed over the spectacles he sometimes wore now. Ajax smiled beatifically. The man was a goner.

Alexander recalled when Ajax had fallen for another slave girl. As before, he wished he could talk his friend out of it. There was slim prospect of freeing Genevieve, and Ajax would be devastated again. The woman had been raised as a house slave, which increased her value and her owners' dependence. She had probably saved them from butchery. They would cling more tightly. The laws of slavery acted as if people were interchangeable beasts, but that was an illusion. In fact, the relationship between owners and their "chattel" was intensely human, even if inhumane. Some slaves were prized over others. It often worked to their disadvantage.

"I intend to buy Genevieve and Claudette from Monsieur Babineaux-de-Savigny," Ajax said. "Can you help us or not?"

Alexander ignored him. "How many other servants do your owners now possess?"

"There are four of us, though Monsieur speaks of purchasing another to help with the carriage," Genevieve said. "A *chauffeur*."

"Your master doesn't have a driver?"

"Etienne refused to come. He stayed on Saint-Domingue and Monsieur hasn't replaced him."

That was useful to know. The family must be smarting from its losses. Genevieve would be valuable on the open market with her language skills and striking beauty. Perhaps Ajax could tempt the family into selling her and the child, knowing that the proceeds would enable them to purchase two grown adults: a driver as well as another lady's maid. They might even have enough for an additional female to start rebuilding their stable. It was an ugly word, but there wasn't another.

"I suggest we petition Monsieur Babineaux-de-Savigny. I'll draft the offer when I return from a trip I must take to Connecticut. Mr. Manly can sign it then." He looked at his old friend.

"Thank you, General Hamilton," Ajax said.

"*Merci, mon général,*" Genevieve said with a tremulous smile. "I fear to hope, but you give me courage." This time she squeezed both Claudette's and Ajax's hands.

"Will we get the hat now, Mama?" the girl said.

"*Oui*, we will get the hat." Genevieve turned to Ajax. "You mustn't come. Madame would not be happy if she saw you."

Ajax drew Genevieve to her feet, and the child and her mother left.

He settled back onto the divan. "Why Connecticut? Eliza's just returned."

"I'm representing New York in the federal court at Hartford. It's a miserable case, but I have no choice."

Eliza wouldn't speak to him, but at least she was home. She had come back suddenly, when Philip contracted a bad fever in Albany and the country doctor was unable to help. Alexander wished he didn't have to go to Connecticut.

"I'll keep an eye on the family."

"I know," Alexander said, reminded of his debt to Ajax.

Gratitude required him to help Ajax obtain a wife of his own—and his foolish friend wanted Genevieve Pearl. Alexander must prevail come what may, though he didn't know how since Monsieur Babineaux-de-Savigny held every high card, including the trump.

"Eliza tells me you've had a letter from General Washington," Ajax said. "How is he?"

Alexander bristled at the second reference to Eliza, who was talking to Ajax even if she wouldn't speak to her own husband. He knew he wasn't being rational.

"The general is well. Enjoying retirement," he said. "If Napoleon doesn't sail for America once he's done with Europe, the old man can supervise Mount Vernon personally for the next ten years, down to the pigs and goobers. Though why they're scintillating is beyond me."

Both men laughed.

"Could America and France really come to blows? After all we've been through together?" Ajax said. Jay's Treaty had bought peace with Britain at the price of France's anger. French warships had seized more than three hundred American merchant vessels.

"If they don't stop attacking, we might. Adams has sent a delegation to Paris to sort through the mess, but I don't hold out much hope." Alexander walked to the sideboard and pulled out a pitcher of cider. He poured two glasses.

"Why is that?"

Alexander gave a glass to Ajax, who took a drink.

"I told Adams we should send people France will trust. That means Democratic-Republicans."

Ajax said, "Did you suggest anyone?"

"I did. James Madison."

Ajax set his glass down. "Madison? Surely you weren't serious."

"I was serious. Madison may hate me, but the Jacobins love him. If not Madison, then Jefferson. Avoiding war must be our top priority. Madison turned him down flat, though. He has a deathly fear of the Atlantic. Jefferson swears never to cross again, either. So the president sent the team his cabinet wanted anyway. All from our party."

"Eliza tells me General Washington sent you a gift. "

Eliza again. Each mention felt like Ajax had bumped against a broken rib.

"Yes. That's right. The general sent us a silver wine cooler with his and Mrs. Washington's compliments. Just as my pamphlet came out. It's magnificent. Holds four bottles. The first gift he's ever given me."

Ajax smiled. "That was mighty nice. He must've been following the situation."

"The whole world was. Down to the street sweepers and bottle washers."

Alexander felt shame wash over him yet again, but he gave Ajax a warm handshake when his friend stood to leave. He would still rather be condemned for crimes he did commit than ones he didn't. And he was relieved that Eliza finally knew.

If only she didn't despise him so greatly.

The muddy road to Connecticut was long. Alexander sent his wife a letter from the shoddy inn halfway to Hartford.

Philip's persistent fever troubled his conscience. He hoped it wasn't typhus, which sometimes resembled a bad cold. The boy was missing his first week at King's College. Alexander had engaged David Hosack, New York's most eminent physician, to treat the fifteen-year-old.

"*I pray heaven to restore him and in every event to support you,*" Alexander wrote, as if the painful chasm between them didn't exist. He recommended cold baths to bring down the fever. "*How much do I regret to be separated from you at such a juncture*."

When an express messenger ran into the Hartford courthouse with a letter a few days later, Alexander sprang to his feet from the bench with every nerve attuned to news he had been dreading. He pulled the note from the envelope. Dr. Hosack wrote that Alexander must return immediately to say good-bye. It was typhus. Hosack had sent Eliza from the sickroom so she wouldn't witness Philip's death.

Each second of the mad dash back to New York was agony. Every horse ran slowly, every carriage arrived late. He couldn't get home fast enough.

When Alexander finally reached Manhattan in the middle of the night, he flew over the dark threshold and up the stairs to the second floor.

A dim light shone under the door of the boys' bedroom. Alexander quietly pushed the door open, his heart pounding.

Eliza was asleep in the chair, holding their son's lifeless hand. He knew she would not let Philip face the end alone—no matter what the doctor said. Dear God, he was too late.

Alexander tiptoed to the body. Philip's dark eyelashes, as long as a girl's, brushed his cheeks. Their son's figure looked so small under the covers that it was as if he had run away and left a doll to fool his parents.

Dead. His boy was dead.

Alexander's hands shook uncontrollably. His folded them, and knelt beside the mattress. "Why didn't you take me?" he asked.

He felt a hand on his shoulder and turned his head to look up at Eliza.

His wife's face was drawn. "Alexander—" she began, and broke down crying.

He stood and took her in his arms.

Eliza clung to him until her sobs slowed. Then she drew back. "If it hadn't been for Dr. Hosack, we would have lost him. We came so close," she said. Her eyes filled again with tears.

Shocked, Alexander pulled away. He turned to the bed and laid two fingers against the boy's throat. There it was. The light beat that meant everything. Their son wasn't gone after all. God had spared him.

He had spared Alexander, too.

CHAPTER FORTY-FOUR

December 1797 & October 1798

New York City

"Have patience my Angel & love me always as you have done."
Alexander Hamilton to Elizabeth Hamilton, August 1798

ALEXANDER HOPED PHILIP'S ILLNESS MIGHT HEAL the breach, but Eliza knew it couldn't.

The look of horror on her husband's face that night softened her heart, and she now managed to be civil, but she couldn't forgive. Were it within her power, Eliza would set the clock back to when loving Alexander was like breathing. But life wasn't an hourglass to be turned over. She would never be the same.

Philip's terrifying brush with mortality had also banished thoughts of Otetiani. The Mohawk had awakened an impulse she didn't know she possessed—but Philip's illness shook her. She could never betray her children or her vows. Instead, she looked for new purpose, determined to set her face to the future in some other way. She found her answer when Isabella Graham came knocking three months later on a December day that threatened snow.

The housekeeper admitted a stout, white-haired Scotswoman. Angelica and Eliza were discussing names for Angelica's next child, expected in the spring, and Eliza was knitting a scarf for their nephew Philip. She wanted the orphan to have something she had made with her own hands.

"Mrs. Hamilton," the lady said, "I hope I'm not calling at an inopportune moment. My name is Isabella Graham."

Eliza invited Mrs. Graham to join them for tea. "How may I help you?" she asked when the lady had settled her bulk.

"I've heard so much about you, Mrs. Hamilton," she said.

Eliza stopped smiling. The last time she had braved a newspaper, when Philip was still struggling, she saw an article that she realized, too late, was about her. "*Art thou a wife? See him, whom thou hast chosen for the partner of this life, lolling in the lap of a harlot!*"

So the visitor had heard of her. For the thousandth time, Eliza asked herself how Alexander could expose her to such humiliation. It cut like a fresh razor each time.

Mrs. Graham was still speaking. ". . . your kindness to orphans and other unfortunates, including those poor French refugees. So many are widows with small children. They simply—"

"You need donations, Mrs. Graham," said Angelica. Her hands rested on her abdomen. She glanced at Eliza. "Perhaps my husband and I could help."

"Oh, no, Mrs. Church. Not that donations aren't welcome. But I was hoping Mrs. Hamilton might lend her good name to our cause, being the famous general's lady."

Eliza had missed the start of the story. "What cause is that?"

"Well, I myself was widowed when my husband died of yellow fever, poor soul, leaving me with three daughters to raise," Isabella Graham said. "I hardly know how we survived, but we did, and I opened a school for young ladies. It kept us from the almshouse. The good Lord knows I would have done almost anything to prevent that. My girls might have been bound out. Indentured. Who knows what they might have suffered in the homes of strangers."

Eliza nodded. "Few widows are so resourceful, Mrs. Graham."

"'Twould be wrong for me to take all the credit. I had the help of my clergymen from the Presbyterian Church on Wall Street. Such fine gentlemen. But now my youngest is married, and I don't need to work since her good husband, that's Mr. Bethune, has given me a very comfortable place in their household. So I have a new endeavor."

Eliza waited for the garrulous Scotswoman to make her point. The lady paused to take a deep breath—and a biscuit from the tea table. Eliza and Angelica exchanged amused glances.

"My daughter Johanna is a wonderful helpmeet," Mrs. Graham said, "and her new husband, Mr. Bethune, that is, has agreed to stake us in founding a charitable society. The Society for the Relief of Poor Widows with Small Children. There's nothing like it in New York. Perhaps the world! We're hoping you'll help us, Mrs. Hamilton."

Madame Le Grand and her boys came to mind. Eliza said, "What might that involve?"

"We're gathering a list of sponsors. We'd be grateful if you'd allow us to add your name."

Eliza considered. She didn't know Isabella Graham, but she knew the problem. Widows often found themselves destitute. Their children suffered terribly. Eliza had wished for a long while that some effort could be made. Alexander might not approve of her taking on a public cause—but what did she care, if the work was the right thing to do? It might also allow her to be something more than "the famous general's lady." A woman scorned.

Eliza sat up straighter. "I'd be happy to endorse your work, Mrs. Graham. I may even be able to give some of my time."

Isabella Graham pulled a ledger out of the bag at her feet. "If you sign right now, Mrs. Hamilton, you'll be one of our first subscribers. And we can certainly use your assistance. We take baskets of food to widows in need. Winter is nearly upon our poor lambs. We try to visit them once a week, but it's a long list and our families are scattered throughout the city."

Eliza suddenly felt less constricted. It would be good to get out of the house. She felt sturdier than she had in months as she wrote her name in the ledger. "When do we start?"

"As soon as you're able. We make up the parcels every day at my daughter's home. We hope to save at least a hundred widows from the poorhouse this winter."

"I can begin day after tomorrow," Eliza said.

Providence in the form of Isabella Graham had at last devised a practical approach to the misery of countless women. The work of the society seemed terribly important to Eliza—and it would take her mind off matters she'd rather not think about any longer.

The next year found Eliza delightfully busy. In addition to nursing Willy and delivering parcels, she had taken on fund-raising and purchasing for the society. With her wide social contacts, Eliza solicited money more easily than the organization's humble founder.

She found the exposure oddly freeing. Doyennes that Eliza would have previously avoided, she now courted. She no longer wondered what they knew about Maria Reynolds, only whether or not they would help widows and orphans. When ladies whispered in corners, she assumed they were plotting how to avoid requests for money rather than rehashing Eliza Hamilton's shame.

Home visits were the most rewarding part of her new work. The look of relief on the face of a lonely widow, the sight of hungry children eating bread, touched her heart every time. It reminded her there were things worse than infidelity.

Even her anger toward Alexander gradually changed. His cares remained complex and he often slept on the divan in his office. He still wrote affectionate letters whenever he traveled on business, as if his belief in their marriage never flagged. It relieved Eliza that he didn't press for intimacy. Her very physical husband seemed content with the platonic marriage they had developed since his infamous confession.

Political distractions also helped, Eliza reflected one night as she placed fourteen-month-old Willy in his bassinet. Her son's upper lip quivered as she drew the soft blanket to his chin, but he didn't wake.

Shortly after Eliza met Isabella Graham, Alexander had resumed his involvement in the New York Manumission Society. Instead of complaining about the work that took her from the hearth, he said she inspired him. "If you can give more, Betsey, I can, too," he told her, and took several new cases defending kidnapped freemen. He also pressed Ajax's suit with Henri Babineaux-de-Savigny, though his inquiries had failed to produce results.

Government service called again, too. President Adams's peace commission to Paris had faltered. The Jacobins demanded bribes before they would consider a peace treaty with America. Even the Jeffersonians were outraged. Then, when purple milkweed bloomed along the Hudson, a French privateer sailed right into New York harbor to apprehend American ships. Adams asked Congress to reappoint George Washington head of the army and the exhausted old trooper took up his heavy burden once more.

Washington told President Adams that he wanted Alexander at his side. Adams complained to anyone who would listen that Hamilton was a scheming foreigner and the bastard brat of a Scotch peddler—but finally yielded at Washington's insistence in the face of Bonaparte's threat.

The opposition exploded. But Eliza's work on behalf of the Society for Widows with Small Children gave her new strength, which she needed. The *Aurora* ridiculed President Adams for commissioning "*the same Hamilton who published a book to prove that he is AN ADULTERER!*"

Eliza was proud of herself. An article on carrier pigeons followed the one on her husband's latest attempt to reestablish a monarchy. She calmly finished the whole paper before burning it in the stove.

Ironically, Alexander was in his element, as he always was with a new challenge, resuscitating the army and writing a bill to build a military academy at West Point. He even brushed off his old Continental Army uniform.

One afternoon he made Eliza laugh until she wiped away tears as he tried it on while giving comical commentary about changes required to the mysteriously shrunken waistband and the odd need for a larger hat, perhaps to accommodate swelling.

Alexander's infectious *joie de vivre*, and the sight of him wearing the uniform in which they had been married, stirred surprising feelings in Eliza. After he left for his evening meeting at Federal Hall, she wondered if he missed holding her.

Eliza looked in the mirror as she brushed out her long braid that night, after the children had gone to sleep. Willy whimpered and she glanced down at the bassinet beside her, but he remained asleep and she returned to contemplating the slim, dark-eyed woman who stared back.

She had kept her figure despite the children, or perhaps from running after them. At forty-one, she felt as young and full of life as the first time Alexander touched her under the covers.

An unmistakable urge rose in her. She caught her breath at the memory of his nakedness in the old house at Albany. The golden freckles on his shoulders that she had discovered by candlelight, the sheen of sweat on his chest, the desire in his eyes.

Just then, Eliza heard the front door close. Alexander must be home. Willy pursed his lips and waved his pudgy hands at the noise, though his eyes remained shut. Eliza patted him softly, then slower and slower. She needed the baby to go back to sleep.

Even if she hated Maria Reynolds until the end of her life, even if she never forgave her flawed husband, Eliza found, unexpectedly, that she wanted him that night.

CHAPTER FORTY-FIVE

February 1801

New York City

"A little patience, and we shall see the reign of witches pass over, their spells dissolved."

Thomas Jefferson to John Taylor, 1798

ALEXANDER THOUGHT JEFFERSON WAS A LIAR, a coward, a fanatic, a hedonist, and a contemptible hypocrite. He had said so privately many times. As a result, it had been hard to convince the Federalist Congress they must elect the man president. But Jefferson wasn't a scoundrel and Aaron Burr was. Not that Alexander could say so publicly.

The sun had set early over the wintry city. He had almost finished dressing for the fete at Tontine Coffee House to welcome Oliver Wolcott to New York. Due to a newspaper campaign that included charges as ludicrous as setting fire to the State Department, poor Wolcott had finally gotten sick enough of politics to resign as America's second treasury secretary. Thank goodness the man had stayed on long enough to see the country through its problems with France. President Adams had spent considerable resources on a new navy. A treaty ending the conflict with Bonaparte had been signed only six months earlier.

Alexander hummed "Yankee Doodle Dandy" as he pawed through the stocking drawer for his best pair. He felt cheerful. It was amazing how ceasing to lie improved one's mood. Sitting down to draw the black silk over his foot, he broke into verse. "Stuck a feather in his cap—"

". . . and called it macaroni." Eliza sang the line as she entered the bedroom holding their newest child, a girl. She smiled as she sat in the rocking chair and put the baby to her breast. "Such a silly song."

Alexander was pleased to see his wife in good spirits. Some days she became angry over things she hadn't previously, or distant if he made innocent allusions to other women. But Eliza had never been one to relish resentments, and no woman on earth wore motherhood as well. His wife looked especially rosy as she nursed the baby that Alexander had insisted on naming Elizabeth—to honor the best woman he knew. He was so grateful she hadn't given up on him, though he deserved it.

"It is silly, but the British certainly rued their mockery after Saratoga. The Yankees never stopped singing it to those they took prisoner," he said.

"We never sang it to Burgoyne."

"You wouldn't, my love. The Schuylers have no notion of pettiness."

"Philip Jeremiah might have whistled it," Eliza said with a mischievous smile.

Alexander laughed. "Philip Jeremiah might. No one could have guessed he would become such a pillar of society."

"The church deacons of Rhinebeck don't know him as we do."

His wife adjusted the baby's position. Little Betsey was teething and Eliza approached nursing with caution.

"Have you decided upon your toast for tonight?" she said.

"No, not yet. I pray that tomorrow will be the last day of balloting. We can't afford to take victory for granted, though. I'd like to express my views if I can do so without getting my head shot off."

Alexander had spent weeks pleading with Federalist congressmen who might swing the decision. Everyone who had watched the election returns trickle in had known for months that John Adams was defeated, and Jefferson and Burr might get an identical number of votes.

It had to happen sometime. In the nation's first election, Alexander had persuaded a few electors to vote against Adams purely so Washington would win more votes than his running mate. Vice President Adams never forgave Alexander for what he considered mean-spirited trickery.

Yet the present situation had resulted precisely from ignoring such details. Aaron Burr told his fellow Democrats not to hold back. He conceded the party's intent to elect Jefferson president. But then, when both men received seventy-three electoral votes and the tiebreaker went to the House of Representatives, Burr supporters spread word that he was willing to "accept the office of president as the gift" of the Federalist-dominated Congress.

Aaron Burr was a clever lawyer and a droll dinner companion, but Alexander knew no man in politics with fewer scruples. He put nothing past Burr—a modern Catiline, the schemer who had tried to overthrow the Roman republic.

"Is tomorrow the sixth or seventh day of balloting?" Eliza said.

"It's the seventh, unless they resolve something today. Congress has voted at least two dozen times, last we heard, with the same result each time. Complete deadlock."

Arron Burr refused to admit that the country had elected Jefferson president over him.

Eliza put the baby against her shoulder and patted. "Why don't your Federalists see through Burr? Isn't it obvious he has no conscience?"

"They think Burr can be bought and that they're buying him. But there would be grave consequences, my dear. Burr's a menace. A rascal of the first rank."

A skeptical look crossed Eliza's face. "Is he really that bad? Might words be running away with you? It's happened before."

Alexander finished buckling his shoes and stood. His wife didn't used to question him. He took a favorite cravat from the bureau.

"What did you think when Burr challenged John Church to a duel last year? Tell me it didn't bother you that he pointed a pistol at Angelica's husband."

"You know I hate dueling. But what can any woman say? We're not even told until afterward. John shot a button off Burr's coat and Burr hit a tree. It hardly makes Aaron Burr a criminal or a rascal. More like a bad shot."

"John was rash in speaking his mind openly, but every accusation was true. Burr offered bribes and took them. And he defrauded all New York when he snuck his bank through the Assembly pretending it was a plan to give Manhattan clean water. Why don't we have enough water to put out fires, Betsey? Ask Aaron Burr. Surely you recall when he begged me for a loan so he wouldn't lose his house. And then took forever to pay us back? Remember when he said I ought to overthrow the Constitution since I headed the army—that, for a great man, *anything is moral*? No, Betsey. I don't exaggerate. Burr would be our ruin."

His wife didn't reply. At moments like this, Alexander wasn't sure if they were arguing about the matter at hand or his judgment and moral failings.

Eliza laid their daughter in the bassinet and glanced up when he joined her. They peered down at their sleeping baby. Alexander squeezed his wife's hand, then bent and kissed the infant on the forehead.

Eliza sat again in her rocker. "So what can you safely say tonight? Aaron Burr will despise you forever if he's not chosen president."

Her voice sharpened. "Don't you dare leave me with eight children to support."

Alexander looped the cravat around his neck and looked in the mirror to tie it, trying in vain to center the bow.

"I need to speak in code so I can't be accused of dishonoring Burr. But Jefferson must get the office. Congress should choose the lesser of the two evils."

Eliza looked amused. "I never thought I'd hear such high praise of Jefferson."

Alexander smiled. She had thawed again.

"I know. From me! I just don't think Jefferson would destroy the government. Think about Jemmy. Madison liked the idea of the Constitution. He just didn't cotton to being out of power. The Virginians might repaint the house we've built, but they won't burn it down."

"So what can you say without provoking a duel?"

"I think a reference to Condorcet might be appropriate."

Eliza stood up to retie his cravat. She smelled of milk and French perfume. "The mathematician?"

"Yes, mathematician and philosopher. Poor fellow. The refugees think the Jacobins poisoned him. Condorcet had a theory of voting that's relevant here. He's popularly interpreted as advocating the expedient candidate when it comes to matched pairs."

Eliza looked puzzled. "Meaning?"

"Let's just say that 'Condorcet' stands for Federalists who might cut off their noses to spite their faces—and foolishly elect Burr."

"How will you work that into your toast?"

Alexander examined his wife. She still praised her older sister extravagantly, as if Angelica was the most remarkable woman in America, but he knew he had picked the best Schuyler girl. Eliza had grown more radiant over time, unlike most human beings, whose poor habits and lowly deeds eventually caught up with them. And her accomplishments multiplied with each passing year. Eliza's success on behalf of the women's society had been remarkable. It was a challenge to be worthy of her.

"How's this, my darling?" He raised an imaginary wineglass. "May our government never fall prey to the temptations of a Condorcet, nor the vices of a Catiline!"

"Good advice. Temptation always beckons," Eliza said pointedly. Yet she raised her imaginary glass and smiled. "Huzzah! Huzzah!"

CHAPTER FORTY-SIX

July 1801

New York City

"Among other wise projects, lately brought forward in Congress, is the establishment of a national library at Washington . . . Books purchased [should include] . . . The Cuckold's Chronicle *for the use of General Hamilton."*

The Aurora, Philadelphia, 1800

Angelica and Eliza picked their way slowly to avoid soiling the hems of their dresses with tobacco spittle. Nassau Street was a mess from the July Fourth celebrations. Democrats had paraded to Brick Presbyterian Church the preceding day, where a thespian read the Declaration of Independence to a crowd besotted with liquor and jubilant at the recent inauguration of President Jefferson. Another speaker delighted them with a peroration against monarchical Alexander Hamilton—or so the newspaper reported.

Each of them carried a wicker basket. They intended to visit two widows nearby, one the mother of twins and another with seven girls to feed. Eliza was especially concerned about the latter. The poor soul must feel even Providence couldn't rescue her.

What if death came to the widow herself, who was but a flimsy lifeline for her children?

Eliza admired Isabella Graham, but she thought the good woman had neglected that question. Some children lost both parents. Alexander had.

"This street looks as if my maid had cleaned it," Angelica said.

Eliza's sister had been irritable all morning. Angelica had forgotten about their plan to set out early, before the humidity became unbearable, and was disagreeably surprised when Eliza arrived at nine o'clock. Eliza guessed that the Churches had attended a Fourth of July party that lasted into the wee hours. Habits acquired in London and Paris weren't easily shed.

"I thought you liked her," Eliza said.

"I do some of the time. But she's not as half as good as Sarah. I really ought to sack the girl for impertinence. Honestly, the democratical mood of the country infects every servant. Each is a Jacobin under the skin."

Eliza recalled when Angelica used to lecture her on the rights of colonists and duty of revolt. They had switched roles, perhaps as a result of Angelica marrying an Englishman. Eliza had an impulse to tease her sister about the reversal, but held her tongue. An innocent jest could easily sound like criticism. In fact, she did feel critical.

Just before the Churches sailed home from London, they had granted Alexander power of attorney to complete some transactions, including the lease of a palatial residence and the purchase of servants. As a solicitor, Alexander frequently carried out transactions for others that he wouldn't undertake for himself. "I'm a lawyer, not a judge," he told her.

Sarah was one of two slaves for whom Alexander had paid. Angelica had been delighted by the girl, and considered her particularly efficient, so she was dismayed when Sarah's name popped up at a meeting of the Manumission Society as a person illegally imported. Mortified at his complicity, Alexander persuaded the

Churches to give Sarah her freedom. Although Eliza loved John and her sister, their willingness to use slaves troubled her.

"Are servants in England any different?" Eliza said.

"Very different. Trained from birth. I admit it's abhorrent, but it's enormously convenient for running a household. In England, they don't raise their eyes above your chin. Here, I find myself called upon to explain to our cook why I prefer roast beef to mutton—and bargain over Sundays off."

Angelica stopped. She pressed a hand to her damp brow. "Might we stop for a cup of tea? I have a fierce headache."

"Of course. There's a tea garden right around the corner."

As they walked to the establishment, Eliza reflected that British servants sounded as docile as American slaves. Which reminded her of Genevieve Pearl, who was the bravest woman Eliza had ever met, yet curiously reluctant to stand up for herself.

Ajax was desperate to purchase Genevieve. Alexander said that their friend darkened his office door at least once a week to inquire about progress in the case. But Alexander's repeated bids had fallen on deaf ears. Monsieur Babineaux-de-Savigny considered himself generous because he allowed the pair to marry, an arrangement to which Ajax had finally relented. The printer now owned a home on the same block as the Babineaux-de-Savigny family, and his wife and stepdaughter went back to their owners each morning.

"I live in terror," he told Eliza one day at the African Free School, where she had gone with a basket of thread for student projects. The school had recently hired a woman, emancipated by a Quaker, to teach needlework to female students. Eliza and Ajax spoke in the entry hall of the one-room schoolhouse on Cliff Street. His voice was low but urgent. "I just don't know what I'll do if we have a child."

"Don't you want a son?"

"A son to whom I can leave my business? A son who can help me now? Of course, but not like this. I risked my life to free this country, yet any child I have will be born a slave. And this isn't Patrick Henry's poetry. It's literally true."

Two young boys pelted through the front door. Ajax placed a steadying hand on the shoulder of the taller one to slow him. The child looked up to see if he was in trouble, but Ajax just shook his head and the boys continued into the classroom. A small group of girls did needlepoint in the light of a window that faced onto the busy street.

"Hasn't the law changed?" Eliza said. She knew that New York had recently passed a bill guaranteeing gradual abolition. The Manumission Society had spent years getting it through.

Ajax pursed his mouth so tightly that he looked ready to spit. "Yes. They changed the law. If Genevieve remains the property of Monsieur, any child we have would go free at age twenty-eight. I could be dead by then." Ajax put a hand over his eyes, as if in unendurable pain. "I'm sorry, Eliza. This isn't your place."

It was the first time Ajax had ever referred to her color. She left the African Free School that morning feeling like an interloper. Later, she had asked Alexander about Henri Babineaux-de-Savigny.

Her husband explained that the West Indian planter wouldn't budge. Ajax's only choices were to accept the situation or run away and leave behind everything. Genevieve meanwhile remained loyal to the Babineaux-de-Savigny family, whom she foolishly trusted. Both she and Ajax expected Alexander to conjure a miracle. It didn't help matters that Vice President Aaron Burr, now ostracized since Congress had selected Jefferson, was the planter's attorney. Burr would never support a plan hatched by Hamilton. He must have counseled Babineaux-de-Savigny against the request.

"I'm sorry to upset you," Alexander told her with a tired air, "but I've done all I can. I can't change the world, Eliza. Not for everyone. Not all at once."

The tea garden at the corner of Wall and William Streets was frequented by ladies and gentlemen dressed in the height of fashion. Angelica looked around contentedly at its elegant décor. Their tea arrived promptly, accompanied by star-shaped biscuits flavored with mace that her sister insisted upon ordering but Eliza found herself unable to eat.

On the other side of the beautiful room, a patron berated a waiter for dropping a spoon. "Clumsy fool!" The man turned to his companion, a foppishly dressed younger blade. "I'm sorry, this establishment is normally above reproach."

Eliza stared at the vase of gorgeous peonies on their table. She didn't know why, but she felt less cheerful than when they had set out that morning. The more she reflected on the orphaned and enslaved, the angrier she became at the comfortable and powerful, including her husband.

Alexander and other founders had sacrificed slaves to get their Constitution—for that was the meaning of its three-fifths clause. In 1787, Southerners had been unwilling to endorse a government that didn't give them representation in proportion to their population, so everyone agreed to count Negroes as three-fifths of a human. Later, when the Treasury Department was at stake, Alexander sacrificed her peace of mind to save the government's reputation for integrity. It all seemed reasonable to her husband at the time.

But what about those who lived with the consequences? What about her? What about Ajax and the son he deserved?

Did Alexander really care about those closest to him? If so, why did they fare so poorly?

CHAPTER FORTY-SEVEN

November 1801

New York City

"Reputation, reputation, reputation! O, I have lost my reputation! I have lost the immortal part of myself, and what remains is bestial."

William Shakespeare, *Othello*, 1603

ALEXANDER'S BROTHER-IN-LAW STOOD IN THE DOORWAY of the law office. "May I come in?"

"Of course, John," Alexander said as he finished the letter to James McHenry.

He didn't have much time for conversation that Monday morning, and prayed the visit would be brief. Twilight came quickly as November blew to a close, and he needed to ride upriver that afternoon to inspect the house going up in the countryside. He and Eliza had decided to name their first real home the Grange in honor of the estate in Scotland from which his father had set forth half a century earlier. Alexander wanted to make sure the architect didn't skimp on the stables. His wife was partial to barns and he owed her a big one.

He set down his quill. "What's afoot?"

John Barker Church took one of the Chippendale chairs across from Alexander. He looked over his shoulder as if expecting someone to follow. A moment later Alexander's nineteen-year-old son appeared.

Philip Hamilton looked dashing in the blue suit his father and mother had purchased when he graduated with high honors from Columbia College the year before. It had been a grand day. They were so proud of him. Alexander was surprised to see his son wearing it on a drab Monday. The boy's uncle must have found him an appointment with a local magistrate or captain of finance. Like the new nation, at last safely beyond infant mortality, young Philip burst with promise.

The young man sat down. His cheeks were pale. "I have a confession, sir," he said.

Alexander folded his hands and looked sober. They had worried about this. Philip had shown a penchant for frivolity ever since college graduation. Eliza expressed fear more than once that their son's interest in theater and girls would get him into trouble.

Inside, Alexander was smiling. No wonder John Church had come along. He possessed considerable experience untangling the sticky consequences of the high life.

"What's occurred? Just tell me."

"Something happened on Saturday, Father. Herschel Price and I went to the Park Theatre."

"We talked about it. You saw *The West Indian*. Set in St. Croix, you said."

"I didn't tell you what else occurred. We saw George Eacker. Remember? The lawyer who made that speech about you last July Fourth."

Alexander didn't know Eacker but he did recall the speech that a Democratic newspaper triumphantly reprinted in full. The young New York attorney praised Jefferson for saving the Constitution and warned that Hamilton still plotted a crown. All the colorful old legends. Alexander recalled being relieved that the lawyer at least hadn't brought up Maria Reynolds.

He waited.

"Well, when we saw Eacker in his box, Price and I thought we should say something about that speech. The exchange became pretty heated. I suppose I was shouting. Eacker grabbed me and suggested we go outside. Eacker said . . . he said—"

Here Philip pulled a piece of notepaper from his waistcoat and read, "'*It's abominable to be publicly insulted by a set of rascals*.'" Philip looked up. The mask of maturity fell away and he appeared very young.

Alexander thought his heart had stopped. He reminded himself that political squabbles happened all the time. Insults often led to duels, but just as often did not.

"Did he say the same to Herschel Price? Did he call Price a rascal as well?"

John Church held up a hand. He looked grave.

"He did, Alexander. Herschel Price issued a challenge that same night. The boy and Eacker fought a duel yesterday."

"Was anyone hurt?"

"Fortunately not. They both got off two shots and called the matter settled. Neither was hit."

Alexander looked at Philip. "Did you issue a challenge, son?" To Alexander's own ears, the question sounded like a line in a play, recited on a stage dozens of rows away.

"Not at first. I wasn't sure I should."

"I advised him to do so yesterday," Church said. "I knew he must, what with Price having already defended his honor against Eacker. 'Rascal' is unpardonable. Philip will be ruined if he doesn't reply."

There had to be another way.

"It sounds as if you started the quarrel, Philip," Alexander said. "Have you considered making an apology?"

Hadn't they instilled this, he and Eliza?

"I tried, Papa. Uncle John suggested that very thing. We sent a letter to Eacker's second yesterday, asking if an apology would convince him to retract his accusation. The second wrote back that Captain Eacker considers me even more of a rascal than Herschel Price."

The clock struck the quarter hour. Alexander heard the seconds pass. He forced himself to focus.

Eacker and Price had already fought a duel. No one was hurt. Perhaps neither intended to hit the other. Perhaps this was the same. Or perhaps, given that Captain Eacker had rejected Philip's apology, he hoped to go down in history as the man who killed Alexander Hamilton's eldest son and put an end to hereditary monarchy.

Would his enemies never stop coming?

Alexander could see from the firm line of Church's mouth that he believed Philip must go through with the challenge. There was no other honorable choice. Most men would think so.

Church glanced at the mantel. "It's arranged for three o'clock, across the river in New Jersey. My carriage will take Philip to the boat. Perhaps you should alert Dr. Hosack in case either party requires assistance."

"You mustn't worry, Father." Philip said. "I'm a decent shot, after all."

"No," Alexander said. "*No.*"

His son flushed with indignation. "Price is no older than I. We drilled together at Columbia. I will defend my honor. I won't let it be said that I lack the courage of my friend."

Alexander's mind raced for a solution but all he could picture was Eliza with the baby boy whose long eyelashes they had admired in the cradle, whose life fickle Blind Justice held in her scales. *Oh, Eliza,* he thought.

"I mean, you mustn't shoot. If you refuse to aim for Captain Eacker—if you fire into the air—he will see and your honor will be satisfied," he said.

Alexander would have gotten onto his knees if it would have helped, but Philip needed him to be strong. "You know your mother's and my own feelings about dueling. One mustn't take a life if there's another choice. Not that I would encourage you to sacrifice your honor—not for anything in the world."

Alexander bit the inside of his lip to stay his nerves. This was his son's decision. He wished he could offer himself as a sacrifice, but he must let Philip be an adult and not rob him of that which was most precious.

"Don't forget, son, your Maker's judgment is more final than any man's. If Eacker sees that you refuse to fire, he might withhold his own shot. And if he does fire, you can discharge your gun in the air. You won't be guilty of taking a life without true cause. You won't have murdered a man."

Philip looked to John Church for confirmation.

"It's a version of the code duello," his uncle said. "Throwing away one's shot to prove mercy as well as courage. It's an honorable solution. But risky. He might aim for you anyhow."

Philip looked down at his fists, then at his father. "I'll think on it, Papa."

Eliza hadn't told anyone, but when Ajax revealed his news she decided she must try.

The brass door knocker was in the shape of an ornate lion with a ring through its nose. Eliza knocked twice.

"*Oui, madame?*" The liveried butler took a second look and glided easily into English. "May I help you?"

"Yes, *merci beaucoup*. I wish to see Madame Babineaux-de-Savigny. Is she receiving callers this afternoon?"

The servant bowed. "Yes, *madame*. Please come in."

The paneled parlor was decorated in French imperial fashion, with large gilt mirrors, paintings of shepherdesses tending their flocks, and marquetry furniture in the Rococo style of Louis Quinze. A plump woman in a satin morning dress rose to greet her.

"*Bonjour, madame*. I'm Mrs. General Hamilton," Eliza said. "Thank you for seeing me."

"*Bonjour, madame*," the lady said. "Thank you for coming. Won't you please sit?"

Madame Babineaux-de-Savigny was an attractive woman in her late thirties, but her voice was breathy and she blinked nervously, as if she might squeak at a spider.

Soliciting money from recalcitrant dowagers had taught Eliza boldness. She came straight to the point. "Madame, my husband served in the army many years ago, when France and America were allies. King Louis was our country's greatest friend. My husband and I were deeply saddened by the news of his death."

Madame looked surprised but pleased. "*Merci, madame*. We don't hear that often enough."

"One of the men who fought gallantly at my husband's side during the war happens to be a mutual acquaintance."

Madame smiled. "You must be speaking of *Monsieur* Burr. My husband's attorney. He is a famous war hero, no?"

"My husband knew the vice president in the war, but he knew Ajax Manly better. The husband of your servant, Genevieve Pearl."

Madame Babineaux-de-Savigny's smile disappeared.

"I've come as a mother to appeal to your kindness. I recently learned from Mr. Manly that his wife is expecting a baby. You must be pleased."

Next came the hard part. Eliza tried not to reveal—or experience—agitation. Dr. Hosack thought Eliza's own pregnancy might still be tenuous. Now that she had passed the third month, he allowed her short walks, but he would be horrified to know she was knocking down doors in the cause of manumission.

"I'm aware that Mr. Manly wishes to purchase his wife," she said. "Surely you understand his desire to assure his unborn child's future. Might you reconsider his offer? It would be a wonderful gesture of Franco-American friendship."

Eliza had thought for a week about how to phrase the request, and believed her solution diplomatic, but Madame Babineaux-de-Savigny looked far from pleased.

"Thank you for your good wishes, Mrs. Hamilton," Madame said after an uncomfortable pause. She had the flat, uncompromising tone of someone who had survived ugly reversals before. "My husband and I are indeed pleased to see our property increase. We lost much in the unrest on Saint-Domingue. Too much."

Eliza waited for the Frenchwoman to say more. She did.

"Good day, Mrs. Hamilton."

"I . . . thank you, madame. It's just, well, it's just that . . . I'm expecting a new baby, you see," she said, revealing a detail normally too personal to share. "Genevieve's plight touches my heart."

"Then congratulations are due you as well."

For a moment, Eliza thought she glimpsed compassion darting across Madame Babineaux-de-Savigny's stolid face, but then the lady rose and Eliza took her leave, terribly discouraged. She had had as little success as her husband.

There was a crowd outside Angelica and John's home when Eliza's carriage turned into their street half an hour later in the fall twilight. She wondered what the commotion was about and noticed that the front door had been thrown open despite November's chill.

Then she saw Dr. Hosack's carriage.

Eliza hoped no one had broken a bone or cracked a head. The youngest of Angelica's eight children loved to climb and was terribly accident-prone. The month before, three-year-old Richard had been strapped to a board for a week with a fractured collarbone. Angelica said she might keep him tied up until college.

The Church family butler opened the door of Eliza's carriage almost before it rolled to a stop. "Mrs. Hamilton. You're here at last," the white-haired man said with exceptional gentleness.

She wondered at his curious manner. "Yes, I am. Did Mrs. Church send for me? Is anyone hurt?"

The old man looked sorrier than anyone she had ever seen. "Yes, mum. She did, mum. This way, please, Mrs. Hamilton." He took her elbow and led her through the front door like an invalid. "The master and mistress are expecting you."

Eliza steeled herself. She had always been the strong one and still was. Angelica must need her. She quickened her pace and mounted the stairs with the butler holding her arm the whole way.

A knot of people stood outside a second floor bedroom. Eliza heard Dr. Hosack's voice. "We must wait until his mother arrives," he said as he came through the doorway into the wide hall.

Where was the child's mother? Where was Angelica?

The physician caught sight of Eliza at that moment. "Oh. Mrs. Hamilton."

What did he mean? Why did everyone keep saying *Mrs. Hamilton* as if there was something special in the name? This wasn't her son.

Then a familiar cry pierced the house. A familiar cry broke her heart.

Eliza's nostrils burned. She brushed away the smell. The ammonia stung again. She tried waving it away once more, then awoke.

She was in Angelica's arms. Tears streaked her sister's face like a Madonna in a painting. "My darling," she said, and broke down weeping anew. The Churches' butler stood to one side, holding a container of smelling salts.

"I'm all right. I'm all right," Eliza said. She placed a hand to her belly and struggled to sit up. Why was she on the floor?

Then she remembered the sound that had rent reality. She must find him.

"Where's Philip? What happened? Where's my son?"

Angelica helped Eliza to her feet. "He's in here," she said. "There was a duel. You must be calm. He needs calm."

A fire burned in the grate of the room and a single lamp illuminated Philip's wan face. An old man slumped in a chair at their son's side. Then she realized it was Alexander. Robert Troup, his college roommate, stood with his hand on her husband's shoulder. Everything else in the crowded room was vague to Eliza.

Except for the basin of bloody water next to the bed. That she saw with extraordinary clarity. Someone had wrung a cloth in it. The towel lay twisted in a knot on the table. It was pink with Philip's blood. That shouldn't be. It couldn't be.

"No, dear God," she said. "Please, no."

Her husband looked up. His face was hardly recognizable, his expression shattered. He struggled to stand, but his knees buckled. Troup buoyed his elbow. Dr. Hosack took Alexander's other arm and eased him back into the chair.

"General Hamilton," the doctor said. "Please sit. You're not well."

Alexander clasped Troup's arm. "No. Help me." He got to his feet and reached for her. "Eliza."

She approached the bed and took his hands. They gripped one another as if falling off a cliff.

"Let's kneel, my love. Let's pray," he said.

Eliza didn't speak. If she never spoke again, this thing wouldn't happen. Time would cease. Philip would lie in this bed, safe, and never go away.

"Betsey. Please. Pray with me."

Alexander helped her down onto her knees. His hands shook, but he held hers tightly. They were extensions of one another's flesh. He had always loved her as completely as she loved him, Eliza knew, and would until the end. They were linked. That thing he had done to her dwindled to a dot. Here on the bed was their child. That was all that mattered.

"Our Father . . ." he began.

The hours of that long night were unending but too short. Eliza and Alexander recited the words that had comforted and sustained and devastated generations of parents before them. Oblivious to all other sounds in the dark room, they knelt beside their precious son until life's last flicker.

CHAPTER FORTY-EIGHT

July 1804

New York City

"Human happiness and moral duty are inseparably connected."
George Washington, 1789

VICE PRESIDENT AARON BURR KEPT TO himself at the far end of the tavern table, where the dim lamps threw only enough light to make shadows of his deep-set eyes and cast dark lines of discontent around his mouth. The taciturn New Yorker ate methodically, as if stoking the furnace of his hate, and ignored the other revelers around him.

The celebration at Fraunces Tavern three years after Philip's death had brought together veterans whose former rivalries were now colorful anecdotes in their favorite war stories. Nicholas Fish had aged well, Alexander observed from his chair at the other end of the long table. With one arm draped over Robert Troup's shoulders, and a smile on his full lips, the prosperous New York attorney looked almost as he had in their King's College debating club or before the charge at Yorktown.

Fish gave Troup a playful shake. "Come, Robert. Admit it. Gates is a jackass."

"Speak ill of a great war hero and fellow member of the Society of the Cincinnati? I shall not." Troup glanced in Gates's direction. "Especially if he can hear me."

Gates sat at a table on the opposite side of Fraunces Tavern. The organizers had done a good job with their annual Fourth of July celebration. All the old adversaries, joined by their ancient devotion to the cause, were sprinkled among friends throughout the tavern to avoid rubbing against one another. The only mistake had been to seat Aaron Burr at Alexander's banquet table. But then, the committee couldn't know the men were secretly set to duel in barely a week.

"I think you're safe," Alexander said. "Gates looks fairly well occupied."

The former general had his arm around the waist of a plump matron pouring a sixth round of ale for the table and was talking animatedly to another old soldier seated next to him. Gates had just led his table in a rousing, off-key rendition of "The Drum."

When the Society of the Cincinnati first formed, men who hadn't served in the military—including Adams and Jefferson—criticized it as glorifying militarism and establishing an aristocracy since eldest sons inherited their fathers' membership. But the group was only what its organizers intended: a fraternal order for officers who had risked their necks together. One of the great joys of Alexander's life was being elected national president when George Washington died.

Nicholas Fish had commanded the local chapter for the past seven years, and appeared to be enjoying the fact that William Smith, John Adams's son-in-law, was relieving him. Fish took another glass of ale when a servant passed their table.

"You're just partial to Gates because you were with him at Saratoga," Fish said to Troup. His speech wasn't slurred yet but his eyes were glassy.

"That would be reason enough *not* to like Gates," said Troup, who had served under the difficult general and been present at

Burgoyne's surrender. "But when all is said and done, we did win at Saratoga."

Because of Benedict Arnold's quick thinking, Alexander thought, though he had learned enough tact not to express such heresy aloud. He despised General Arnold as much as anyone, but even the most objective praise of America's infamous traitor was easily misconstrued.

Reminded of his most recent slip, Alexander glanced down the table. Aaron Burr had joined the society the year before when courting the Federalist vote. He was now almost finished with his roast beef, but still did not speak to the man beside him. Burr had been so quiet that evening that Troup asked earlier if anyone knew what ailed the vice president.

"Being vice president?" said Fish.

Alexander didn't respond. He was determined to forget Aaron Burr for at least a night. A celebration with his oldest comrades was far too precious to waste, especially now.

Despite Alexander's best efforts to stave off the inevitable, the prospect of a duel had loomed for months, ever since his chance criticism of Burr at a private dinner had found its way into an Albany newspaper. Alexander didn't even remember the particular comment that the paper described as "despicable." All he recalled was table gossip to the effect that Burr couldn't be trusted and mustn't win his campaign to become New York's next governor. Nonetheless, everyone knew there had long been bad blood between him and the vice president. Burr rejected Alexander's apology as too little, too late. Perhaps it was. Alexander sometimes thought that only his death would satisfy Burr's resentment.

Had he really tried hard enough to avoid the awful encounter, or had he dithered because he'd known it was inevitable? It had always been his way to confront danger rather than shirk it. Some called that courage. Others called it foolishness. Or arrogance.

But what could he do? Comply with Burr's demand and publicly repudiate everything he had ever said about the man? That would mean calling the truth a lie. And what about the next time Burr ran for high office?

The tinkle of a knife on a goblet drew Alexander's attention. Others tapped their glasses as the new president of their state chapter rose to his feet.

Colonel Smith beamed at the room. "Fellow officers. We're gathered to celebrate our nation's birth and the gallant troops who made it possible." John Adams's son-in-law raised his cup high. "I give you the father of our country. To George Washington, my brave lads, the greatest soldier who ever lived!"

"To Washington! Huzzah, huzzah," a boisterous chorus echoed.

"More ale, girl," a white-haired man called after he had drunk his toast.

"More girls!" another veteran roared, though his gnarled hand rested on a cane.

Across the room, stout Richard Varick rose to his feet. Recently retired as city mayor, the esteemed Federalist had studied law at King's College before the war. New York was such a small world. Varick now faced Alexander's direction, holding his own cup aloft.

"When I served under General Philip Schuyler"—another chorus of huzzahs broke out in honor of the absentee Schuyler—"I had no idea that his beautiful daughter—obviously nearsighted, poor lass—would pick the shortest, chattiest, most penurious member of Washington's family as her husband. Had I, I would have spiked the man's punch and trundled him onto an India merchantman. But that would have been a terrible mistake. Gentlemen, I give you the national president of the Cincinnati. To Alexander Hamilton, brave soldier, firm friend. Without him, we would have no Constitution, no economy, no government."

"To Hamilton," other voices called. "Speech, speech!"

Robert Troup nudged Alexander. "Let's hear it. You know you've got one—or a dozen—inside."

Alexander glanced down the table. Flickering lamplight caught Aaron Burr's watchful eyes.

"General Hamilton," Varick said. "Come now. Speech, sir!"

Alexander stood. "Friends! Countrymen. Tonight we celebrate our triumph and our comrades. We remember the courage that brought us together and sustained us in every setback. We honor the ideas that moved mountains and inspired our country. A country devoted to liberty and justice for everyone."

He paused. "Yet not all of us are here tonight." He raised his glass. "Let us salute those gallant soldiers who are here in spirit but left their lives on the battlefields that forged our nation. Our most sacred responsibility is to guard it for their children, and their children's children. Gentlemen, I give you John Laurens, Nathan Hale, Tench Tilghman, Crispus Attucks, and all the thousands who died to make America free."

Many of the celebrants were now in tears and most on their feet. "Huzzah! Huzzah!"

Nicholas Fish rose, weaving slightly. "To our brave lads."

"A song, General Hamilton. Lead us in song, like you used to," someone called.

"On the table!" another yelled.

Troup put out his hand. "Up you go, Ham."

Alexander took Troup's hand, stood on the chair, and jumped to the tabletop—grateful he still had the agility. "*How stands the glass around*," he said, and voices broke out.

"How stands the glass around?
Let wine and mirth abound.
The trumpet sound,
The colors they do fly, my boys
To fight, kill, and wound
as you would be found,
Contented with hard fare, my boys
on the cold, hard ground!"

The light of the candles glowed on the joyous, upturned faces singing their hearts out. They were faces Alexander had known most of his life. Some were rivals, some were enemies, most were friends. They had slept on the cold, hard ground together for their country. He loved them so.

As the song came to an end, Alexander considered whether to jump straight to the floor without stepping onto the chair. It would be impressive, at age forty-seven. Although he had his back to Burr, Alexander felt the man's hostility and an unaccustomed vertigo seized him. The days were now rushing toward their duel—and the floor seemed far away. He had consumed his fair share of ale, after all.

Troup stood with his hand outstretched. "General Hamilton?"

Alexander smiled. Everything would be fine. He waved Troup away and leaped safely to the floor.

CHAPTER FORTY-NINE

July 1804

Weehawken, New Jersey

"To see a world in a grain of sand, And heaven in a wild flower, Hold infinity in the palms of your hand, And eternity in an hour."

William Blake, 1803

JUDGE NATHANIEL PENDLETON DREW ASIDE THE bush that hid the narrow path. The somber Virginian pulled his hat further down on his broad forehead and hitched up the mahogany box he carried under his arm. "This way, General Hamilton. Watch your step, sir."

Alexander had asked Pendleton to be his second in order to spare his best friends. He wanted as few people as possible to know about the duel in advance. Only the day before he had visited Robert Troup, sick in bed with dropsy, and advised a course of tea made from elder roots, without mentioning his own fateful appointment on the morrow. The last thing Alexander wanted was to alarm Troup unnecessarily. Judge Pendleton was a calm, sensible man. A former officer who understood why Alexander must meet the challenge or be stained forever.

"Thank you, judge," Alexander said. He turned up the narrow trail to the dueling ground on the broad ledge that jutted out above the Hudson. The Palisades' two-hundred-foot escarpment rose overhead.

David Hosack started to follow with his black physician's satchel but Pendleton raised a hand of warning. "I believe it best, sir, if you wait nearer the boat."

The doctor glanced at Alexander, who nodded agreement. It was wise to have as few witnesses as possible to an affair of honor.

"As you wish, sir," Hosack said. "I'll remain here." The doctor retreated a short way along the path and set his bag on a boulder under a chestnut tree.

Lower down, around a small bend, the oarsmen waited with their rowboat on the pebbly beach revealed at low tide. Fragrant summer vines and leafy hardwoods crowded the New Jersey shoreline, clinging to the narrow margin between the treacherous river and the Palisades' towering granite face.

The two men continued alone up the short, steep path. Alexander welcomed the exercise, which tempered his anxiety and steadied his legs. The hour-long row from Greenwich Village before sunrise had been cramped and he wanted to make sure his feet were sturdy under him.

The morning air was crisp. He drew in a deep breath as he reached the end of the forest trail, stepped into the clearing, and looked out upon the wide river and uninhabited shore opposite. Pink clouds streaked the crystalline sky. A cooling breeze had come up the night before, abating July's heat. Alexander heard songbirds calling to one another in a nearby tree and wondered what species they were. Eliza would know.

He mustn't think of her now. If he thought of her, he could never go through with it.

Yet he felt an absurd loss at not knowing the names of the cheerful birds. When would he learn them? New York's natural beauty had never seemed more poignant. Each sound that reached him was like music, each sight a painting, each breath a cool drink. He longed to wake up the next morning to experience it all again.

And he would. He had promised to meet in three hours with Dirck Ten Broeck, to whom he owed a legal opinion on a sticky property question. Alexander had had so much on his mind—Eliza, the children, the duel—that he had forgotten the matter. The Dutchman had been understanding when they crossed paths unexpectedly the night before. Alexander made the appointment for the following day as proof that his life would go on. Of course he would be happy to meet with Mr. Broeck after his rendezvous with Burr.

Two men in shirtsleeves and waistcoats looked over at the sound of their footsteps. The vice president and his second, William Van Ness, were just setting aside the cheap straw brooms they had brought to clear the ledge of small rocks that fell from the escarpment. The men had done a good job. The dueling ground was smooth. No one could stumble on a bit of granite.

Van Ness plucked his jacket off a bush and approached. Burr brushed dust from his hands, drew on his gloves, and donned a black silk coat that hung from a branch. Van Ness shook hands with Alexander and Judge Pendleton. "Good morning, gentlemen," he said.

Finished with his toilette, Vice President Burr joined them.

Burr shook his opponent's hand. "Good morning, Mr. Hamilton. I hope the day finds you well."

Burr's short dark hair was slicked back from the widow's peak that had become pronounced with age. Alexander recalled Burr at the Battle of Monmouth. Then he wore his hair long, tied with a ribbon, and his face was rosy and unlined. Now he had the sallow, crabbed look of someone perpetually dissatisfied—though an attorney's practiced smile briefly smoothed his sharp eyebrows.

"Good morning, Mr. Burr," Alexander said. "I'm feeling quite fit. Thank you for inquiring and for your labors this morning. I trust you are well?"

"I am, indeed, sir. Exceptionally well," Burr said.

Van Ness turned to Pendleton. "Would you assist me with marking the distance?"

The judge nodded, and the two men jointly measured off ten paces.

Pendleton took a leather pouch from the interior of his coat and proffered the bag to Van Ness, who drew a chit on behalf of Aaron Burr. Pendleton drew next and the men compared lots. Pendleton possessed the higher number.

He gestured to the wall of granite. "Since Mr. Hamilton and I win, I believe we shall take this side."

Alexander walked over to examine his ground. Judge Pendleton had positioned him facing New York and the Hudson, Burr facing New Jersey. The horizon was sharp in the morning light and Alexander made out the faraway city downriver. The rising sun created a glare on the water, but Alexander took it as a good omen that his position faced home.

"The pistols, Judge Pendleton?" Van Ness said.

Pendleton opened the mahogany box he had been carrying and withdrew the guns provided by Alexander's brother-in-law John Church. John had used them in his own duel against Burr in 1799, from which both men had emerged unscathed. A couple of years later, John had lent them to Alexander's son Philip, for the nineteen-year-old's fatal match with Captain George Eacker.

Pendleton now handed one pistol to Van Hess to prepare and kept the other. The seconds measured their powder, loaded the lead bullets, and cocked the weapons.

Alexander accepted his pistol from Judge Pendleton. He wondered if it was the same gun Eacker had used to take his son's life, or the weapon Philip himself had wielded. Alexander raised the pistol experimentally, gauging the weight. He aimed at the river, curling his fingers tightly around the walnut handle and looking down the brass barrel toward the sunrise over the city.

This was the closest he would ever come to holding his son's hand again.

Philip had pointed the gun at the ground that day, his arm slack at his side, Alexander learned later. Turned sideways to diminish their vulnerability, the two men gazed over their shoulders at one another a long minute. Captain Eacker finally lifted his pistol. After a beat, Philip copied him. The code duello proscribed that both opponents must raise their weapons or be judged cowardly.

Eacker fired. The slug entered just above Philip's right hip, ripped through his intestines, and lodged in his left arm. Philip's right hand jerked upward reflexively, discharging his shot in the air. Before fleeing the field ahead of the law, Eacker had praised the boy's dignity and courage.

When Alexander saw Philip laid out in Angelica Church's home, his son spoke only once before lapsing into unconsciousness. His voice was faint, yet clear. "I did it, Father. I withheld my fire. I defended us."

Us.

The word expressed all his son's love and loyalty, and struck Alexander like a bullet.

He turned now toward Aaron Burr. The light bouncing off the river had intensified. Ripples shimmered in waves of dazzling sunshine. The man's outline blurred. Alexander squinted.

"Are you ready, gentlemen?" Judge Pendleton said.

"I apologize. A moment, please. Would you take this, sir?" Alexander handed the pistol to Pendleton, fished spectacles from his breast pocket, and polished them thoroughly with a handkerchief. "In certain shades of the light, one requires glasses."

Alexander took the gun back at last. Testing the light and his vision, he pointed again at the river, then at the tree growing from the cliff on his right, then at Aaron Burr. He dropped his arm to his side.

"This will do. Thank you. I'm sorry for the delay. We may proceed."

"Are you quite ready, Mr. Hamilton?" Burr's jaw was flexed, his expression steely.

It was hard to tell if the vice president was angry or merely impatient. Did he have any mercy in his soul? Was he as cold as he looked? Was he thinking of his only child—married and living in the south—and how she would feel if he died?

"Yes. I'm ready."

In fact, Alexander had readied himself thoroughly. He'd drawn up a statement of debts and assets, composed a will, and left a letter for Eliza on his desk just in case. He had worked out a plan for the duel. He would not shoot at Burr—unless Burr missed the first time and insisted on a second opportunity to finish off his nemesis. Then even Eliza's God, more tenderhearted than Alexander's, would agree a man should defend his life.

Pendleton had begged him to reconsider. "At least practice," the frustrated judge said the day before. They met at Pendleton's office. The native Virginian pressed one of the pistols into Alexander's hand. "Please. You need to know how it works."

"I know how it works, my dear Pendleton," Alexander said. "It kills."

He raised the gun once, then placed it on the judge's desk. He hadn't fired a pistol since the war and didn't want to. It was one thing to aim a fowling piece at a duck on the wing, quite another to take an unmoving target in the sights of a handgun at close range.

Burr hated him, but he didn't lust for Burr's blood. Alexander must simply defend his honor—or he'd never be able to stand up as a man, do a single thing for the country, ever again. He would be written off.

Throughout the remainder of that long day, only twenty-four hours earlier, anxiety had pierced him more than once. How could he risk Eliza's well-being yet again, after all she had been required to forgive? He loved her so. And their children. Angelica, Alex, Jamie, John, Willy, Betsey, and now little Phil, named for his brother in Heaven. It was Eliza who had taught Alexander to believe in Heaven, since that's where Philip must be. It was Eliza who had convinced him that God forbade taking a life in cold blood. Any life.

Which meant he must let Burr live. Even if Burr meant to kill his rival, not merely test his courage. Alexander couldn't bear to think of it, but there it was . . . death staring him down. Refusing to defend himself would meet Eliza's high moral standards but might destroy her happiness.

His beautiful, darling wife, the kindest, strongest, best woman he had ever known.

Alexander looked at the vice president, who stared back. Not a muscle moved in the man's thin face. What if Alexander gave the gun to Pendleton and walked away? What could Burr do? What did it matter what people said?

"Present your arms," Pendleton said.

The judge turned his back, as did Van Ness, to avoid being called as witnesses if there was an arraignment.

Now was the moment, Alexander thought. He must raise his gun or lay it down forever. What had Philip—his boy—thought at this same instant? The son who died for his own honor and his father's sins?

Silhouetted by the sparkling river, Aaron Burr lifted his weapon.

Young men threw away their lives. Old men clung to them. But Alexander wasn't young or old. What had Nathan Hale said? "I regret that I have but one life to lose for my country?"

Alexander squinted, gripped his son's hand, and took aim. He mustn't miss. If luck was with him, he would survive. He had done so at Trenton, Brandywine, Monmouth, and Yorktown.

The gnarled cedar tree in his gun sights grew from the live rock at least four feet to Burr's left. The bullet's loud report bounced off the granite face of the cliff. The tree's topmost branch, swaying high above the vice president's head, snapped and bent with the shot. Satisfied at hitting his target, still hoping for mercy, Alexander lowered his gun.

Burr's shot pulled Alexander high on his toes. The horizon spun around as he twisted sideways and fell headlong to the earth. The vice president loomed over him in the next instant—or perhaps it was just Burr's shadow—and then he was gone.

Alexander's head whirled. The ground was hard, the dirt rough on his cheek. He was surprised to find himself lying down. Now he couldn't remember if he had fired at the tree. He ought to warn Pendleton the gun was still loaded. Or had it gone off?

The birds were silent now. A sweet river breeze caressed his face. He wondered why he could still feel it. He sensed his mother lying behind him on the bed.

"I'm a dead man," Alexander Hamilton said to no one in particular.

The light dimmed.

Eliza. He had failed her. And their children, dear God.

He must keep his eyes open. Must see her again.

CHAPTER FIFTY

August 1854

Washington, D.C.

"It appears to me impossible that I should cease to exist, or that this active, restless spirit, equally alive to joy and sorrow, should only be organized dust—ready to fly abroad the moment the spring snaps, or the spark goes out, which kept it together. Surely something resides in this heart that is not perishable—and life is more than a dream."

Mary Wollstonecraft, *Letters Written During a Short Residence*, 1796

THE GRAY-HAIRED WOMAN LOOKED UP FROM her crocheting, surprised at the doorbell. Unexpected guests normally dropped by after lunch, when it was more seemly to call on an elderly person who might not dodder out of bed until noon.

Not that Eliza had ever slept away the morning. Not once that she recalled, looking back on the forty years she directed the New York Orphan Asylum after 1806. A person couldn't snooze until noon and attend to the needs of more than a hundred children, all of whom required clothes and schoolbooks. The roof would fall in if one did that. Vines would grow through the windows and the legislature would neglect the gas bill.

The loud bell rang again.

Eliza didn't like the mechanical device, although she approved of most other modern inventions. She had taken the New York and Harlem Railway to work every day after it was built and sent telegraph messages to her youngest daughter, living in the District of Columbia, until her children insisted that Eliza move there when she turned ninety-one. She had agreed only after James promised he had seen it with his own eyes. Congress had shuttered the last slave auction house in the nation's capital.

"I'll be down in a moment, Mama," Betsey called down the stairs. "Don't you get up."

Even Betsey sometimes acted as if her mother was decrepit, though the child ought to know better. Eliza had climbed fences into her eighties to reach her son's home on the Hudson. James obstinately sent a carriage to fetch his mother from the train station even though Eliza always took the shortcut and the poor chauffeur had to talk to himself on the drive back. She refused to miss the stroll because of her son's kindly pigheadedness.

Even now, Eliza sometimes walked to the flower market, and she turned ninety-seven that very day.

"I'll get it," she called back.

Eliza used a cane whenever her knees felt stiff, and she employed one now. The front entry was far away. When she was very young, her parents' home seemed enormous. After she slowed down, her children's did.

The nineteen-year-old girl on the doorstep held a bouquet of fragrant yellow roses. A bright smile lit her dark face.

"Happy birthday, Mrs. Hamilton."

She smiled back. "Happy birthday, Julia."

Ajax's granddaughter had matured early, and ever since the girl turned twelve she had insisted it was her job to carry on family tradition since she and Mrs. Hamilton shared the same special day. Of all Ajax's children and grandchildren, Eliza concealed a partiality for Julia, who was as cheerful as a green grasshopper. One Manly or another had brought roses on her birthday for the past fifty years. *They're from Alexander*, Ajax told her that first August in 1804, when she was a new widow.

"Please come in," she said, and the girl whisked through the door with the uncanny sprightliness of youth.

"May I fetch a vase from the pantry, Mrs. Hamilton?"

"Of course, Julia. Make yourself at home."

The pretty girl returned in a moment with the flowers.

"Set those on the sideboard next to the pedestal, please. That way we can see them. And pour us some tea, if you can stay a bit."

The marble pedestal with her husband's bust occupied a place of honor next to the sideboard on which sat the silver wine cooler given them by President and Mrs. Washington so long ago. Visitors always wanted to see that. Eliza liked to look at it, too.

Julia poured two cups from the pot a maid had left on a trolley. "I was hoping for a visit. I've been working on our book day and night."

She generously called it *our* book, though Eliza had done little beyond carry the hope it would be written, like a candle in the dark. She was touched when the ambitious child said she wanted to write a biography of Eliza's husband. No one else had done so, and Eliza often worried that future generations would know Alexander only through the enemies who outlived him by decades and whose poison pens never stopped.

"There's something that's not quite clear in my mind." Julia handed her a cup. "I hope we might talk about it, Mrs. Hamilton. If it's no trouble."

Eliza didn't mind. She was used to people asking about the past.

President Fillmore had recently peppered her with questions at a White House gala. The First Lady gave her own seat to Eliza, who realized afterward that it meant she had to field the man's queries all night. James Polk, William Seward, General Winfield Scott, and other eminent men liked to drop by from time to time and ask what George Washington was really like, and how she had felt when Horatio Gates saved the cause at Saratoga, and if her husband's charge at Yorktown was as disappointingly bloodless as schoolbooks said.

The only famous man she ever turned away was the one whose name wasn't allowed in her home. The incident occurred when she traveled to Washington for a visit in the 1820s. Eliza supposed he came because he was feeling old. Old! He was the same age Alexander would have been had Aaron Burr not murdered him at Weehawken.

That day happened so fast. Like the one on which Philip died. One minute her husband was kissing her to leave for an early meeting, the next he was being rowed back across the dappled Hudson to die in her arms. He had said something to someone about Aaron Burr a couple of months prior, who repeated it to someone else, who printed it. Burr jumped at the opportunity.

The vice president had nursed an unyielding hatred toward her husband for thwarting his bid to unseat Jefferson, and then his bid for governor of New York. Alexander seemed to stand between Burr and all the fame and power he thought due him. Apparently, the vice president practiced shooting bull's-eyes at his New York estate in the weeks before the duel.

George Washington once told her that lesser men always resented greater ones. It was true.

But why had Alexander accepted Burr's challenge?

Eliza asked herself that haunting question countless times in the years she soldiered on without him. They had seven children to live for, the youngest only two. How could he abandon them? And why wasn't she alone enough? Alexander had left her with a mountain of debt, a well of resentment, and a decade-defying desire to see his face once more.

After the duel, Dr. Hosack carried Alexander from the rowboat to the mansion of a friend that fronted the Hudson River. The messenger that Hosack sent to fetch her from the Grange said her husband had been shot but there was still hope. When she saw Alexander's languid face on the pillow, his bloody clothes heaped on a chair, she knew the man lied. The French consul insisted on sending his navy's best surgeons from the frigates in the harbor, and they confirmed that nothing could save her beloved.

That day and the next, the bullet through Alexander's spine caused him agonizing pain that multiple doses of laudanum barely assuaged. He slid in and out of consciousness, though he was lucid when awake. "*Remember, my Eliza, you are a Christian*," he told her again and again, as if she might take a pistol to herself or someone else. Toward the end of his suffering, he asked to say good-bye to the children, but once all seven stood weeping around the bed—even the two-year-old in Fanny's arms—he had only the strength to look at them. Then he closed his eyes.

When her husband left his body at two o'clock on the afternoon of July 12, 1804, she wanted to go with him. If the children hadn't tethered her, she might have floated away. The years stretched away bleakly in prospect. First there was day one—twenty-four agonized hours—then day two. Eventually there were too many to count.

She met them like a man going to his work, as she could not be Alexander's woman anymore and didn't want to be anyone else's. She raised their children and others who were orphaned. Throughout, she asked herself *why*?

When anger and grief finally fell away like the leaves of autumn, she understood. How could Alexander refuse the task Philip had faced without feeling he would let down his son—their son—who had insulted someone, after all, in Alexander's defense? He could hardly be less of a man than their boy.

Her husband adored his family. She was the love of his life, and he hers. Alexander had accepted the penalty for telling the truth. Like Philip, he threw away his shot.

Afterward, to evade warrants for arrest in two states, Vice President Burr slipped into Washington, DC, that den of bullies and cardsharps where men who had no moral convictions preyed on those who did. Immune from prosecution on murder charges so long as he stayed in the District, Burr wielded the gavel of the US Senate with particular adroitness, it was said.

Eliza closed her eyes. They tired easily.

"I can come back another time, Mrs. Hamilton."

She opened her eyes and smiled at the youngster. "Oh, no, Julia. Fire away."

Julia set her teacup aside and took out the blank book she always carried in her reticule. Eliza had given the girl her first diary on another birthday they'd shared. "Grandpa said to ask you how Grandma got her freedom."

"Simple. Your grandfather paid Genevieve's owners. He freed her."

"Grandpa says you had a hand in it."

That was just like Ajax, she thought, and saw his dark face and white hair as vividly as if he had walked through the door, though he refused to leave New York anymore.

Eliza sometimes missed him fiercely. It was he who suggested she petition Congress for the veteran's pay her husband had renounced. The scoundrels were contrite for once and their guilt money supported her orphaned children. That, and the donations Gouverneur Morris and Robert Troup collected so she wouldn't lose the house.

"It happened right after my oldest son was killed. He was your age."

Julia sucked in her breath. "Oh, I'm sorry, Mrs. Hamilton. I didn't know."

Eliza thought the girl might not. Most people didn't. The infamy of her husband's death had overshadowed their son's.

"Your grandma's owners contacted my husband right after that and said they were ready to sell. I think they felt sorry. You see, I had pleaded with them to free your grandma, and they . . . they knew I had lost my own boy." Tears welled up. "I'm sorry, Julia." She dabbed at her eyes. "I didn't expect that."

"How did he die, ma'am?"

"He was killed in a duel like his father. With the same gun."

"By Mr. Burr?"

"No, by someone else but for the same reason."

"What was that?"

Eliza wasn't sure how to answer. Duels didn't happen much anymore. When news of Alexander's death hit the papers, New Yorkers had been stunned. His funeral procession took two hours to wind past the grief-stricken throngs that gathered on sidewalks, hung out windows, stared down from rooftops. Ships in the harbor flew their colors at half-mast, cannons fired from the Battery, church bells pealed across the city. Citizens wore black armbands for thirty days. The New York Supreme Court draped its bench in black crepe for months afterwards. A group of eminent men started the Anti-Dueling Association.

By the 1830s, it seemed almost no one was killed in an affair of honor anymore, at least north of Delaware. The South was another country—as more and more people were insisting, and which was just as well in Eliza's opinion, though her husband said on his deathbed, "*If they break this union, they'll break my heart.*"

Eliza recalled everything he said that last night. "*Guard our children for me, my darling, best of wives.*" In the hour of delirium, when his words no longer made sense, he fretted so persistently about a shoe he'd lost that she gave him one. It rested under his hand until it fell to the floor.

It would be hard for Julia to imagine why men once walked willingly to their deaths in defense of honor, a treasure that modern society valued very little.

"It was over politics—and Thomas Jefferson," she said.

"Did Northerners and Southerners hate each other even then?"

She shook her head a little too emphatically. "No. And they don't now, either, Julia. Americans fought over ideas, just like today. Everyone loved George Washington, and he was a Southerner."

Eliza privately admitted to a grudge against Virginians, but she didn't want the girl to carry that burden. When James Monroe knocked on her daughter's door in 1825 and asked to speak to Mrs. Hamilton, she had been dumbstruck. She'd done everything possible to avoid seeing the Virginian's face during his long presidency. He came to her.

Eliza was enjoying the sunshine of the garden with her grandson when a maid gave her Monroe's card, and she had trouble adjusting to the gloom when she went indoors. Against the light of the parlor windows, he looked like a silhouette cut by one of the portraitists on Pennsylvania Avenue. She knew she must welcome him to sit, but couldn't bring herself to do so.

"Good morning, Mrs. Hamilton," he said in that silky Tidewater accent. He must have sensed reticence because he continued without removing his tan riding gloves. He laid one hand atop the other on the head of his elegant cane.

"Good morning, sir." She couldn't say his name.

But she could be polite. She could hold her tongue, as Alexander had never learned to do well enough.

"I thought we ought to meet," Monroe continued. "Time softens memories. We're both nearing our graves and I'd like to think we could set aside our differences."

Differences? Was that what he called whipping the furies who hounded her son and husband to their deaths? Was that what he called cruelly exposing her marriage to public ridicule—an act so deeply damaging to her love that only Philip's death finally cauterized the wound? *Differences?*

The Virginian hesitated. "So much time has passed."

Eliza had to place her hands on a chair to control her trembling.

"Mr. Monroe. If you've come to tell me that you sincerely repent, that you are very, very sorry for the misrepresentations and slanders and stories you circulated against my husband—if you've come to say this, I accept your apology."

She lifted her chin. "But unless that's what you wish to say, unless you want forgiveness for what you did to us, no amount of time, no nearness to the grave, makes a whit of difference."

Alexander once told her that Monroe was very brave at the Battle of Monmouth Courthouse, but the man had become a coward. On that day in Washington, he dropped his eyes and left.

Eliza knew it was her Christian duty to forgive. *Forgive us our trespasses, as we forgive them that trespass against us*. If she didn't absolve the man who devastated her family, perhaps Heaven wouldn't ask her to sit, either. She could hardly expect God's mercy. But must one pardon those who never repented? Did the Lord?

In the end, she simply decided that since He had taken away so much, He must grant her this.

It comforted Eliza that Alexander had atoned for his own mistakes years before, even though it flayed her pride at the time. She knew she would find her husband in Heaven. His sacrifices and generosity—his mercy even toward Burr—far outweighed his sins.

Julia was speaking. "They were great men then, weren't they, Mrs. Hamilton?"

"Hmmm?" Eliza felt very tired. Perhaps she was getting decrepit.

Ajax's granddaughter had inherited Genevieve Pearl's natural grace. She quietly took Eliza's teacup, lifted a coverlet from a chair, and tucked the soft wool around her lap.

Eliza gazed up into alert brown eyes that shone with concern. She was a good child. Julia didn't want her to go, but Eliza had waited five decades to see to her husband and son. She knew it wouldn't be much longer.

"Thank you, dear. You mustn't worry. I just need my rest."

Morning sunlight glowed through the petals of the yellow roses next to Alexander's bust. Joy filled Eliza at their fragile beauty.

There it was. Life. Perfect and nearly complete.

The End

Author's Note

The Hamilton Affair IS AS FAITHFUL to history as fiction permits. Most persons are someone Alexander or Eliza knew. Many events actually happened.

Some are fabricated for the reason that historical fiction is like connecting the dots. We know that a character's lifeline passed through certain turning points, but must imagine the stretches in between. An Iroquois chief actually inducted thirteen-year-old Elizabeth Schuyler into his tribe, yet we don't know what she did to merit this or whom else she may have met. I have also modified language that might confuse today's readers, such as shortening the name of Thomas Jefferson's party, the Democratic-Republicans, to "Democrats," since the party assumed that name after 1830. Before this, Democratic-Republicans were more often called "Republicans," but they were not the predecessors of Abraham Lincoln or Dwight Eisenhower.

The one significant exception to the facts is Ajax Manly, who is wholly fictional, though conjured out of Hamilton's past to illuminate his lifelong opposition to slavery. When Alexander was a boy, his mother did own a child named Ajax that she assigned as a companion to her youngest son. The probate court sold this Ajax along with Rachel Lavien's other slaves. Alexander's half-brother Peter Lavien collected the proceeds. During the Revolution, Alexander fought alongside an unknown but considerable number of African American patriots in the Continental Army. He, John Laurens, and the Marquis de Lafayette defended their right to bear arms for liberty. After the war, Hamilton helped found the New York Manumission Society, which ran the African Free School, and he provided free legal services for men and women resisting enslavement. He knew many people of color. At any point in his life, he might have been intrigued had he met a freeman who shared the name of his childhood playmate and servant.

The tale of bitter partisanship recounted in these pages is true. Alexander Hamilton's political rivals, including Adams, Burr, Jefferson, Madison, and Monroe all outlived him by two or three decades. They set the tone for the popular impression of Hamilton as a manipulative elitist with monarchical leanings. Although a few contemporaries reassessed Hamilton soon after his death, the corrective wasn't revealed due to the same animosities that killed him. When Thomas Jefferson became president, he asked Treasury Secretary Albert Gallatin to investigate the "blunders and frauds" of his predecessor. The new secretary undertook the mission with "a very good appetite," he admitted, but later said, "I have found the most perfect system ever formed. Any change that should be made in it would injure it. Hamilton made no blunders, committed no frauds. He did nothing wrong."

Why the man on America's ten-dollar bill was so controversial will remain a matter of debate as long as there are those who care about the nation's history—and future. It is indisputable that, alone of the founders, he was what talent scouts today would call a triple threat: soldier, thinker, statesman. Elizabeth Schuyler Hamilton petitioned numerous individuals to compose a fair biography, but didn't live long enough to read one. Nonetheless, she and her husband were precisely as remarkable as this account endeavors to portray. Alexander was a self-made man of extraordinary vision, and Eliza was the only founding mother to establish and run a large institution that salvaged innocent lives, New York's first private orphanage.

There is one final matter that deserves mention: Hamilton's birth year. Hamilton reported it as 1757, and so reads the tombstone towering above Eliza's in Trinity Churchyard. Some historians think the year may actually have been 1755, and that Alexander lied in embarrassment at being older than his Trinity college classmates. Since the evidence is speculative, and Hamilton was so unreasonably mistrusted in his lifetime, I've decided to honor him by taking his word.

For their help and encouragement, I would like to thank my children, family, and friends, and colleagues at Texas A&M University, Stanford's Hoover Institution, and San Diego State University. I owe special debts to Catherine Clinton, Laurel Corona, Leon Nower, Michele Rubin, France de Sugny Bark, Sally Taylor, my agent Jim Donovan, editor Lilly Golden, publicist Gretchen Crary, and darling husband Jim Shelley.

My greatest obligation, however, is to those whose story I'm privileged to tell. I hope I've done them justice.